MEN
of the
OTHERWORLD

ALSO BY KELLEY ARMSTRONG

MEN
of the
OTHERWORLD

KELLEY ARMSTRONG

BANTAM BOOKS

MEN OF THE OTHERWORLD
A Bantam Spectra Book / February 2009

Published by Bantam Dell
A Division of Random House, Inc.
New York, New York

Book design by Sarah Smith

Bantam Books, the rooster colophon, Spectra, and the portrayal of a boxed "s" are
trademarks of Random House, Inc.

Library of Congress Cataloging-in-Publication Data

Armstrong, Kelley.
Men of the otherworld / Kelley Armstrong.
p. cm.
"A Bantam Spectra book."
ISBN 978-0-553-80709-7 (hardcover)
1. Werewolves—Fiction. I. Title.
PS3551.R4678M46 2009
813'.54—dc22
2008037372

Printed in the United States of America
Published simultaneously in Canada

www.bantamdell.com

10 9 8 7 6 5 4 3 2 1
BVG

For my readers, who asked for these stories,
which was just the excuse I needed to tell them.

INTRODUCTION

Years ago, when I first launched my Web site, I wanted to do something that would thank readers for their support. I decided to try my hand at e-serials—writing a novella and posting chapters as I went. I asked readers what they wanted, and they said "a story about the guys." The result was *Savage,* a prequel to *Bitten* covering the childhood of the male lead, Clayton Danvers.

The e-serials became an annual tradition. I'd poll readers, then write them a story. *Savage* was followed by a sequel, *Ascension.* Then that was followed by another prequel to *Bitten,* "Beginnings," which tells the story of how Clay met Elena. In 2005, I changed tracks and instead offered twelve short stories, again on topics or characters chosen by readers. The next year was my first "non-prequel" novella: *The Case of El Chupacabra,* an investigation by my spellcasters, Paige Winterbourne and Lucas Cortez.

As much as readers seemed to appreciate the online fiction, I was constantly being asked when they'd be in book form. I said that I'd only publish them if I could make it a charitable endeavor. I expected it would take years before I'd be in a position to do that, but in 2007, my publishers made me an offer.

This volume, *Men of the Otherworld,* is all about my werewolf Pack guys. It starts with one of the 2005 short stories, "Infusion," featuring the father of my current Alpha. Then it jumps forward in time to *Savage* and "Ascension." It then takes a giant leap to the present (well, 2007 at least), eight Otherworld novels later, for a brand-new story that readers have been asking for.

In 2010, you'll see volume two, *Tales of the Otherworld,* with "Beginnings," *The Case of El Chupacabra,* a couple of the 2005 short stories and at least one new tale. If you want a say in what that new story will be about, go to www.KelleyArmstrong.com/Tales.htm.

All of my proceeds from these volumes are going to World Literacy of Canada, a nonprofit volunteer organization dedicated to promoting international development and social justice (www.worldlit.ca). The stories were originally intended as a gift to readers and now they'll be "regifted" to a worthy cause. And there is still plenty of free fiction on my Web site and maybe more to come in the future!

MEN
of the
OTHERWORLD

Infusion
1946

"Antonio." Dominic walked to the table and plunked down a bottle of cheap champagne. "I've decided to name him Antonio."

Malcolm sipped his beer as a chorus of "good choice" rose up from the others. Wally and Raymond Santos glanced Malcolm's way, as if seeking permission to congratulate Dominic, but Malcolm just kept drinking and let them make up their own minds. After a moment, Wally joined in with a raised glass to the new father, while sixteen-year-old Raymond busied himself cleaning out a thumbnail.

Dominic paused behind the head chair. Billy Koenig scrambled out of it, making a quick joke about keeping it warm for him. Dominic thudded into the chair and dropped his burly arms onto the table so hard Malcolm's beer sloshed. Typical Dominic—always throwing his weight around, as if he was already Pack Alpha, not just heir apparent.

"A drink for Antonio," Dominic thundered, his voice reverberating through the dingy bar. He turned to the owner, across the room, counting bottles. "Vinnie! Glasses!"

Waiting tables certainly wasn't Vincent's job, but he hopped to it. As Vincent approached, Malcolm held up his empty mug.

Vincent paused, but only for a second, then took Malcolm's glass. Dominic allowed himself only a split-second scowl, but it was enough for Malcolm. It was easy to establish dominance when you were bigger than everyone else. Doing it without that advantage was the real accomplishment.

Once the glasses were filled and distributed, Dominic lifted his. "To fatherhood."

Everyone clinked glasses.

"Now, how about a wager?" Dominic boomed. "Take bets on who'll be the next new father. I'll pick Malcolm." A quick grin. "God knows, he's been trying hard enough."

Malcolm gritted his teeth as the others laughed and called out good-natured jabs. It was his own damned fault. Malcolm had meant to keep his hopes secret until he could show off the goods, but two years ago, sitting around this very table listening to Dominic brag about his sons, he'd announced a pending arrival of his own... only to discover a month later, when the child was born, that it wasn't his. Since then, everyone knew he'd been trying, and hadn't even sired a daughter. *That* was his father's fault—difficulty siring children was one family blight Malcolm couldn't overcome through sheer strength of will.

He had only to look at his father—sitting at the next table with the Alpha, Emilio—to see the second family blight, a cane resting beside his father's chair. He bristled, as he always did, at this physical proof of Edward's weakness. Not just weakness. Cowardice.

As a Danvers, Edward had been expected to fight for Alphahood, but when the opportunity arose, he'd somehow managed to cripple his leg. No one was quite sure how it had happened—the story changed with the teller—but whatever the cause, the injury permanently took him out of the line of succession. As a mediocre fighter, Edward had stood no chance of winning an Alpha match, so he'd intentionally taken himself out of the race. Everyone in the Pack knew it.

Malcolm had spent his life wiggling out from under the shadow of his father's cowardice. And he had. After Dominic, he was now the best fighter in the Pack, and among the mutts, his reputation for ruthlessness surpassed that of every other Pack werewolf. But when his father looked over, there was no pride in his face. Just a lifting of his chin, listening in on the younger men's conversation, making sure Malcolm wasn't saying anything to embarrass him.

As they drank the champagne, the cleaning girl stopped by to wipe off their table. She murmured something that was probably meant to be "excuse me," but her thick accent and whispered voice rendered the words unintelligible.

The girl didn't speak more than a dozen words of English. Malcolm figured the only reason Vincent had hired her was because he could pay her half what he'd pay anyone else, her being a Jap and all. Still, it had to be bad for business. How many ex-GIs came in here, saw her, and turned around and left? Malcolm wasn't sure whether the girl really was Japanese, but it didn't matter. People saw slanted eyes and they saw Pearl Harbor, and five years wasn't enough to make anyone forget.

The girl paused at Malcolm's side and lowered her head. Wally grinned and kicked him under the chair. Malcolm leaned back to let the girl wipe his place. Unlike the quick swipe she'd given the others, she made sure to get every spot, including a few that'd probably been there for weeks.

When the girl finished, she scurried off and intercepted Vincent with Malcolm's fresh beer. She took it and returned to the table. First she wiped a spot for the mug, then she wiped off the mug itself, and finally she laid it before him like a ceremonial chalice. As Malcolm grunted his thanks, snickers raced up and down the table.

The girl pointed to the nearly empty bowl of peanuts nearest him.

"Sure," he said. "Fill it up."

When she scampered off with the bowl, Wally hooted. "That girl has it bad, Mal. Gets worse every time we come here."

Malcolm only gulped his beer.

"Hey, come on, Mal. Think about it. She waits on you like that in public? Imagine what she'd do for you in private."

Another chorus of snickers.

"Not my type," Malcolm muttered.

Dominic leaned forward. "Because she's Japanese? Nothing wrong with that. From what I hear, they're damned eager to please, if you know what I mean."

Billy nodded. "Buddy of mine at work has one of them for a girlfriend, on the side, of course, and you wouldn't believe the stories he tells. Ever heard of geishas? All their girls learn some of that shit, and they'll do anything to make a guy happy. Nothing's too kinky—"

Dominic cut him short as the girl approached.

"What?" Billy hissed. "She doesn't understand English."

"Doesn't matter," Dominic murmured.

When she was gone, they started up again, regaling Malcolm with tales of Asian women.

"And," Dominic said as they finished, "unless my nose is wrong, there might be a bonus."

"Just what I need," Malcolm said. "A slant-eyed Jap brat."

His father looked over sharply, frowning his disapproval.

Billy snickered. "You're going to get a talking-to later, Mal."

Malcolm snorted and pretended it didn't matter. Edward

wouldn't give him a "talking-to." That implied anger, and Edward never showed that much emotion with his son. He'd calmly speak to him about stereotypes and prejudices, and counsel him to make better choices with his opinions and his language, all the while clearly doubtful that his words were having any impact. Malcolm was a fighter, not a thinker... to Edward's everlasting disappointment.

"You should give it a shot, Mal," Dominic said. "Don't worry about who the mother is. Look at Ross Werner. His momma was black and you can hardly tell. With us, it's the male blood that counts. Women..." He shrugged. "Just the vehicle. At most you might get a kid with dark hair and dark eyes, but yours are dark enough anyway. Wouldn't matter. And..." He leaned closer. "You never know. A little foreign matter in the mix might be just what your boys need to get the job done."

Malcolm gritted his teeth. Dominic always sounded so sincere, like a big brother who really wanted to help, but Malcolm knew he'd like nothing better than to see Malcolm humiliate himself by presenting a half-breed baby to the Pack.

As the night wore on, though, and Malcolm drank more beer, he couldn't stop thinking about what Dominic had said. Mixing up the bloodline *might* help. He'd never tried that. And Ross's case did suggest the foreign blood wouldn't show, which was all that mattered.

The girl was in the fertile stage of her cycle, and she obviously wanted him. An easy conquest. Plus, if Asian women were as submissive as the others said... Malcolm smiled. Submissive was good. Especially if it came from a girl who was in no position to complain if things got out of hand.

By the time the group settled the bill, Malcolm had made up his mind. He sent the others on without him, then cornered the girl as she came out of the back storage room. She started, see-ing him there, then dropped her gaze and made no move to get past him.

"Been a long night," he said. "Bet you could use a drink."

When she didn't answer, he pantomimed drinking, then pointed from her to himself. "Drink. You. Me."

"I—I work," she said. "Done soon."

"No, babe, you're done now. Let me handle Vinnie."

He reached for her apron and snapped it off. She gave a shy little smile, then nodded.

"Get drink," she said. "For you."

She took his hand. Hers was tiny, almost birdlike. He won-dered how hard he'd need to squeeze to hear those thin bones snap like twigs. Not very hard, he'd wager.

He turned to let her lead him into the bar, but she stopped at a locked door a few feet down and took out a key.

"Room," she said, gaze still lowered. "Upstairs. My room. Yes?"

He smiled down at the girl. "Sure, babe. Whatever you want."

Malcolm sat in a tiny room, empty except for his chair and a sleeping mat. A few candles cast a wavering, sickly light that lined the room with shadows. When the girl went to get his drink, he'd flicked the light switch, but nothing had happened.

That cheap bastard Vincent probably cut off the electricity when he let the girl take the room. Maybe, if the girl was as good as the others claimed she'd be, he'd see about "persuading" Vincent to spring for lights and heat up here. Wouldn't be any inconvenience to him, and the girl sure would be grateful. She'd leave the welcome mat out for anytime he felt like coming back.

The girl slipped from the back room. She'd changed out of her work clothes and into a white cotton robe with an embroidered belt. Her bare feet seemed to glide across the floor. Tiny feet, like the rest of her, slender and hesitant, as graceful and defense-less as a doe. Pretty as one, too. Now that he'd looked past his prejudice, he had to admit she *was* damned pretty, especially in that white robe, holding a tray like the offering of some virgin priestess. When she bowed before him, the liquid in the glass didn't so much as ripple. He peered at it. The drink was amber, like beer, but clear and … steaming.

"Tea?" he said, lip curling. "I don't drink—"

"No, no tea," she said quickly. "Special drink. For you. Make—" A meaningful look at the sleeping pad. "Make good."

"Make *me* good?" He started to rise. "I don't need any damned drink to make me good."

"No, no. Please." She backed away, gaze downcast. "Not you. *You* good. Drink make me good. For you. Make you…" She struggled for the word. "Feel better. Make it feel better. For you."

She babbled on some more, waving at the mat, but he got the gist of it. The drink was supposed to make the sex better. He'd heard of things like that, and as the others had said, these girls were supposed to know all there was to know about pleasing a man. This must be one of their tricks.

Malcolm took the drink and sniffed it. Herbs. His werewolf nose didn't detect any taint of anything noxious. He took a sip. Fire burned down his throat, like hundred-proof whiskey.

He closed his eyes and shook himself. The heat spread to his groin and he smiled. Not like he needed the help, but sure, why not. He took a bigger sip.

"Yes?" the girl said.

He looked up to see that she'd unfastened her belt. He could see a swath of pale skin running from her throat, down between her small breasts, over her flat stomach, to the dark thatch below. His cock jumped and he raised the glass in salute. Another sip and she let the robe fall off one shoulder. A third sip, and she dipped the other shoulder, and the robe slid down her body to pool at her feet. For a moment, she stood before him, naked and pale in the wavering candlelight. Then, without a word, she knelt and reached for his zipper.

Malcolm rolled over. A moment's sleep-fog of thinking *Why am I lying on the floor?* then he remembered and smiled. Whatever foreign hoodoo that girl had put into his drink, it was something else. He closed his eyes and sighed, the tip of his tongue sliding between his teeth as he stretched. Shit, he *hurt*, and it had nothing to do with sleeping on the floor.

After all those things he'd been thinking in the bar, about what he could do to a little slip of a girl like this, he hadn't even tried. Couldn't be bothered. He'd just laid back and let her work her magic. He'd roused himself for a bit of energetic thrusting, but that'd been the extent of his participation. She'd done all the work.

And work she had. Gave him three damned fine rides... maybe even four—he'd been getting hazy near the end. But three times was bragging rights enough. He rolled onto his back and grinned.

Whatever was in that drink was some powerful stuff... and so was the girl. Masterful, but never dominant, always letting him know he was in charge. After the second time—or was it the third?—he'd thought he was down, but she'd managed a revival, rubbing, licking, cajoling... begging. He felt a fresh surge and leaned back, savoring the memory until he was hard again. Then he rolled over for another go ... and found himself alone.

Malcolm grunted and lifted his head. The simple movement felt like tumbling headfirst out of a tree. He steadied himself.

When the world stopped whirling, he opened his eyes and peered around the dark room. Where was that girl? Helluva time to take a piss.

A voice wafted in from the adjacent room. A singsong voice. He chuckled. Singing while she sat on the john—guess she was still feeling pretty good, too. Maybe she was cleaning up for the next round. Better give her some time; there'd be a lot to clean up. As he lay down, a second voice joined the first. He blinked. A radio or record player? But if there was no electricity up here...

Malcolm pushed himself up again, so fast this time that he almost blacked out. He wobbled to his feet and had to rest a moment to get his bearings. His first step nearly sent his legs skidding out from under him like a newborn fawn's. He'd been hung over worse than this, though. Mind over matter, as with everything else in life. If you have the guts and the will, you can do anything.

He closed his eyes and ordered his muscles to obey. Still, it was slow going. His head pounded, and every fiber of his body urged him to lie back down and sleep it off.

Finally, he made it to the wall, then inched around to the door. When he reached it, he peered around the corner. The first thing he saw was the wallpaper. Strange white wallpaper with black geometric shapes. He blinked. No, not wallpaper. Someone had drawn on the walls. Drawn...symbols.

A smell wafted out. Something burning, giving off a sweetish odor so faint even his nose could barely detect it. The voices started up again. Singing, but with no tune. Chanting.

There, across the room, was the girl, sitting on a high stool, naked. But she looked...different. There were circles drawn around her breasts and stomach, but that wasn't what gave him a start. It was the way she sat, chin high, gaze steady, her poise exuding confidence, no sign of the shy girl he'd just bedded.

The girl's lips were still. She wasn't the one chanting. It was the two women in front of her, their backs to him, one white-haired, one dark. The white-haired one had her head bowed. The other swung a pendulum in front of the girl's stomach. The girl said something and the dark-haired woman snapped at her. The white-haired woman murmured a few words and the girl sighed, then said something that made both women laugh. The old woman patted the girl's bare knee and they started chanting again.

As Malcolm watched, his legs began to tremble, begging him to go lie back down. When he resisted, the room went hazy, and he seemed to float there, the chanting filling his head, lifting him up, symbols swirling around him . . .

A soft growl and he shook the sensation off. Goddamn that drink. First a killer hangover, now hallucinations. That's what this was—a dream or hallucination, caused by the drink. Had to be. His mind set, he stumbled back to the mat and crashed into sleep.

When he woke up the next morning, the girl was gone. He wandered down to the bar, but no one was there. He pushed back a stab of annoyance. Normally *he* was the one to vanish before breakfast. He told himself the girl hadn't taken off for good, just gone to get him something to eat, but he didn't stick around long enough to find out whether he was right.

That night, he returned to the bar alone, but the girl wasn't there. According to Vincent, she was scheduled to work, but hadn't shown up. Malcolm went upstairs to the girl's room, and found it exactly as he left it: a small room with a mat, a chair, and candles, now blackened stubs.

He glanced at the adjoining room, then hesitated before striding over and walking through the doorway. Inside was...nothing. Just another room, completely empty. No smell in the air, no symbols on the walls, not even the stool. Just as he'd figured—it'd been a dream, induced by whatever the girl had put in his drink.

One thing was for sure, though—the girl had cleared out, likely for good. And she might have taken something of his with her. The chance was slight, he knew, but they'd certainly been busy enough to start a baby and he sure as hell wasn't letting it go at that. Pack Law said that if he bedded a woman during her fertile period, he had to keep track of her. If there was a child, and it was a son, then it was a werewolf, and therefore had to come back to him. So whatever "pressure" he had to apply on Vincent to tell him where to find the girl...well, he was just obeying Pack Law.

By the time he finished with Vincent, he was certain that when the man said he didn't know where the girl had gone, he was telling the truth. He did, however, have an emergency contact for her, from when she first took the job.

Malcolm took the address—supposedly the girl's grandmother's—and arrived there just in time to find an old lady in the process of moving. He tracked the woman to her new apartment and saw the girl there. They'd moved only a few miles away, to a larger apartment. Obviously the girl had found a better job and invited Granny to move in. That explained why she'd been so eager to get him into her bed, having known it would be her last night at the bar, and her last chance with him.

Malcolm made a note of the new address and returned to the Sorrentinos' estate outside New York City. At the end of the weekend, he went home to his own family estate near Syracuse. The next month, when he visited his Pack brothers in NYC, he stopped by the girl's apartment. He saw her, but made no effort at contact. Finding out he'd tracked her there might give the girl a romantic thrill...or it might spook her.

Maybe he was being overly optimistic, but when he saw her, something seemed...different. Dominic always said he could smell it when he'd knocked up a girl, even before she started to show. Malcolm had always figured Dominic was full of shit, but now he wondered.

He stopped in again after the second and third month, just to make sure she hadn't shipped out. He was compiling a list of details in case she did—where she worked, where she shopped, places and people he could shake down for information if she moved again. But she didn't, and when he came by after the third month, he noticed she was wearing baggier clothing. Still too soon to hope—she might have only put on some weight—but hope he did. On his fourth visit, he was more convinced. By the fifth, he was certain. He was going to be a father.

When the eighth month came, he found excuses to stay at the Sorrentino estate, and went by the girl's apartment almost daily. There was no need for him to be there when the baby came—most Pack werewolves waited a month or so after the arrival before claiming their sons. But Malcolm couldn't be so nonchalant, not when so much could still go wrong. There could be birth complications. Or it might be a girl. Or it might not be his again. So he hovered close and waited, and in the middle of the third week, his vigilance paid off. He was there when his child entered the world.

Weeks ago he'd found a route up the fire escape and to a window that never quite closed. Normally, he'd just crouch on the fire escape, hidden in the darkness of night, where he could watch and listen. When he heard that first scream of labor, though, he wrenched open the window and squeezed through into the grandmother's bedroom.

The scream, and the voices that answered with soothing reassurances, came from down the hall. He slipped to the doorway and looked out. Risky, but if the baby was on the way, intruders would be the last thing on anyone's mind.

From the bedroom doorway, he could see into the living room, and the first thing he saw were the symbols covering the walls—the same black symbols from his "dream." He inhaled sharply. So that hadn't been a dream; big deal. They were foreigners. Who knew what religion they followed, what gods they worshipped? Painting stuff on the walls and on their bodies, chanting and waving pendulums around, it was all no stranger than a Catholic Mass. No reason for his heart to be thudding like a cornered stag's.

Another scream. Then the same two voices from his dream launching into the same chanting singsong. He moved into the hall and crept forward until he could see the living room. There was the girl, naked again, her torso covered with lines and circles. She wasn't lying on a bed, but crouched over a mat, as if she was trying to take a crap. The old woman—the grandmother—held the girl, giving her balance, while the black-haired woman lit a fire in a small dish. When whatever was in the dish began to smoke, she lifted it to the girl's nose.

The girl filled her lungs with the smoke, then went still. Her face relaxed. Then she lifted her face to the ceiling, raised her hands, and began to chant. Even when a contraction rocked her thin frame, her expression didn't change. The words only came louder, harsher, more determined.

Another contraction and she punched her fists into the air, her chant a near-howl. The lights flickered. Malcolm shook his head sharply, certain it was a trick of his vision, but then the lights flashed again, and again, dimming with each blink. The flames on the candles shifted, angling toward the girl as if she was sucking the energy from them. Malcolm's gut went cold and he knew then, as he'd known deep down from the start, that these women were another supernatural race—some kind of magic-makers.

There were others out there. Most werewolves admitted this. The Pack werewolves might keep to themselves, and feign ignorance of other supernatural races, but they knew. They knew.

As for what these women could be, Malcolm had no idea. He had only the vaguest idea what else was out there, but he knew there were people who used magic—spells and rituals and potions. That must be what they were.

An excited chirp from the old woman knocked Malcolm from his thoughts. Between the girl's legs, deep in her dark thatch, another dark thatch had appeared. The top of a baby's head. *His* baby's head. The girl slammed her hands down, her chant now a snarl, face tight and shiny with sweat. But she didn't cry out.

Malcolm held his breath as he waited for the first wail. Dominic, who always managed to witness the birth of his children, claimed that you could foretell a child's strength by his first cry. The loudest of his three had been Antonio, who'd already beaten his brothers' babyhood milestones, lifting his head sooner, sitting up sooner, crawling sooner, walking at not yet a year. So Malcolm braced for his child's first scream, and prayed it would surpass anything Dominic had heard from his.

After one final heave, the baby fell into the waiting hands of the attendant. And it made not a peep.

The child was dead. After all these months, all this hoping...

And yet he couldn't help feeling almost relieved. Having a half-breed baby was one thing, but this was an interracial mixing he wanted no part of. A werewolf who could cast magic? It was wrong. It reminded him too much of his father, always poring over his books, always living in his head, always thinking. A werewolf acted through physical power and strength. Cunning, yes. Magic spells...? That smacked of weakness. For all he knew, such a mix would mean this child couldn't even change forms. The humiliation of that would be too much to bear. Better to have no child at all.

His gut told him it was better this way, and Malcolm always trusted his gut, so he stepped back—

The baby kicked and made a noise, a little gurgle, almost a coo, as if to say "here I am" as quietly and politely as possible. The woman holding him laughed and said something to the baby's mother, who'd lain back on the mat to rest, unperturbed by her child's silence.

As Malcolm tensed, his gaze traveled down the child's blood-streaked torso. Then he let out a whoosh of breath. It was a girl. Good, he could leave and forget all—

The attendant lifted the child to show the mother. A tiny penis and scrotum fell from between its legs... and Malcolm's gut fell with it. There was still one last hope. Maybe the child wasn't his. As the woman wrapped the baby in a symbol-covered blanket, Malcolm closed his eyes and inhaled, and his stomach dropped to his shoes. His child. His son. And a werewolf.

The Law was clear. Father a son and you must claim him for the Pack. You couldn't allow a werewolf to grow up not knowing what he was. And yet that didn't apply here, did it? These magic-makers would know what the boy was when he came of age. They would take care of him, and there would be no risk of exposure to the Pack. Malcolm could leave and never think about this again.

So that's what he did.

When Malcolm returned to the Sorrentino estate, he went straight to Emilio, and asked whether there were any "tasks" the

Alpha needed done. It wasn't a surprising request. Malcolm was always ready to serve the Pack, if it meant boosting his reputation. This time, though, he had an ulterior motive—to wipe from his brain all thoughts of that strange, quiet child and those magic-makers. Emilio gave him a job—hunting down and terminating a troublesome mutt—and Malcolm was out the door before the Alpha could say good-bye.

Two weeks later, the mutt dead, Malcolm went home to Stonehaven. He barely got through the door before he heard the familiar thump-scrape of his father's footsteps. He tensed and ran through his mental list of things he'd done that grazed the boundaries of Pack Law. If his father was so quick to welcome him home, he wondered which of his infractions had been discovered.

Edward Danvers rounded the corner, his bad leg dragging behind. In public he used his cane, but in the house, he never bothered. He stopped at the end of the hall and straightened. He always stood straight in Malcolm's presence, those couple extra inches of height being the only physical advantage he had on his son.

Edward looked around the vestibule, his frown growing. Then a flash of sadness behind his dark eyes.

"It was a girl, then, was it?"

Malcolm froze. He'd told no one about the baby, certainly not his father. He opened his mouth to protest, but Edward cut him off.

"I know you well enough to know when you're up to something, Malcolm, and when you're excited about something. So, it was a girl, then?"

Malcolm considered saying yes, but knew even this lie was risky. A werewolf was supposed to take no interest in his daughters, which was logical because they were not werewolves and therefore could stay with their mothers. But his father was rarely logical, and more than once Malcolm had suspected that when a lump sum went missing from the bank account, the money—part of *his* inheritance—was going to Edward's other child, a daughter a few years younger than Malcolm. If Edward thought he had a granddaughter, it would be just like him to go looking for the girl, to make sure she and her mother were well cared for.

"Died," Malcolm said as he pulled off his other shoe. "In childbirth."

"Did he?"

Malcolm nodded.

Edward limped closer. "So it was a *he*? A son?"

Malcolm hesitated, then nodded and tossed his shoes onto the mat.

"Your firstborn son dies, and you aren't the least bit upset. How...odd."

Malcolm shrugged.

"Was it the Japanese girl Dominic mentioned? The timing would certainly be right. Let me guess, Malcolm. The babe didn't die. He just looked a little more...foreign than you'd like."

With another shrug, Malcolm turned away to hang his coat on the rack.

His father's voice hardened. "If you had a problem with a half-Japanese child, then you shouldn't have bedded the girl."

Malcolm grabbed his suitcase and tried to brush past his father, but Edward stepped into his path. One good shove, and the old man would topple. Hell, a *really* good shove into the wall, and he'd stay down forever. As much as Malcolm longed to do it, he couldn't. Edward had made sure of that once his son became strong enough to best him—rewriting his will so the estate would be held in trust by the Sorrentinos, meaning someday Malcolm would have had to go crawling to Dominic for money. That would be a fate worse than putting up with Edward.

"He's your child, Malcolm. Your son."

Edward's voice had softened. Malcolm's fists clenched. He hated that voice. He'd rather be screamed at, shouted at, swung at—anything that suggested Edward gave a damn. That gentle but firm voice carried no emotion. Edward was like a dog trainer with a none-too-bright puppy, convinced that he could correct the misbehavior simply by taking the right tone.

Edward continued, "There is nothing wrong with a mixed-race child."

Not this *mixed race,* Malcolm thought, but he said nothing, just let his father continue.

"I don't care if the babe is purple, Malcolm. He's your son, and my grandson, and probably the only one we'll ever see."

"There'll be more."

Edward shook his head. "I only had two children; you've shown no signs of faring any better, and certainly not for lack of trying. It's in our blood."

Malcolm met his father's gaze. "In *your* blood. Granddad had three sons and a whole passel of daughters. So the problem, *Father,* is clearly yours. Not that it surprises me."

He saw the barb strike home and smiled.

"Perhaps you don't want the child, Malcolm, but I do. Give me my grandson and I'll never trouble you with a moment of his care."

Malcolm hesitated, but knew his father would never give in so easily. As weak as Edward was, he could be relentless when it came to something he wanted, pursuing it as single-mindedly as Malcolm had pursued his reputation. Tell him no, and he'd go out and find the boy.

Malcolm couldn't allow that to happen. The thought of claiming that strange baby as his own made his skin creep, and made his gut roil with something almost like fear. No, not fear. Contempt. Contempt for those women and their petty magics and that peculiar child. He knew what had to be done, and that he should have done it when he'd first laid eyes on the boy. There was only one way to eliminate the problem—by *eliminating* the problem.

Malcolm shrugged. "You want him, fine. I'll go get him. Just don't bother me with the brat."

His father smiled. "I won't."

Malcolm's father insisted on accompanying him to New York. That he hadn't foreseen, but it turned out to be only a minor bump. Edward was quite content to stay at the hotel and wait for Malcolm to deliver his grandson. He never suggested helping Malcolm take the child. Didn't have the stomach for it, Malcolm figured.

He often wondered how his father got him away from his mother. Pack Law was clear on that. A son had to be taken, and all contact with the mother severed. Ideally, you'd convince the unwed mother that this was for the best—take the boy, and leave her free to marry without the burden of an illegitimate child. If that didn't work, kidnapping was the next option. The missing child of an unwed mother was a low priority for police. If she caused trouble, though . . . well, there was a final solution, though Malcolm had never known a Pack werewolf to resort to it. He didn't know why—it seemed the easiest route, and safe enough if you were careful. And he knew all about being careful. He'd had plenty of practice.

When he reached the apartment, only the grandmother was there. It was growing dark—night was always the best time for this sort of thing. He could have waited outside the building, taking care of the girl and the child without ever setting foot in that apartment, leaving the old woman alone, but that would be the soft way, the coward's way. His father's way. Strength meant doing what needed to be done with no half measures or short-cuts that could come back to haunt you.

He went in the window again and saw that he'd come not a day too soon. The room was piled with moving boxes. He could hear the old woman in the kitchen. It would be easy to slink down the hall, slip up behind her, and snap her neck. So easy...

He strode to the kitchen door, and shoved it open so hard it banged against the counter. The old woman spun around. Seeing him, her eyes went wide. He expected her to lunge for a knife, but she only stood there, wide-eyed.

"Where's my son?"

As he spoke, he advanced on the old woman, backing her into the corner. She went willingly, as if it never occurred to her to fight back.

"Where's my son?' he said, slower, enunciating the words.

"He—he is not here," she said, her voice heavily accented, but her English good. "We did not think—"

"That I'd be back? That I'd want him?"

She swallowed. "I know this...is your way. To take the sons. But this one—you do not want this one. He will be different. Better for us to take him." She managed a strained smile. "You will have more sons. Many more sons. Big strong boys like your-self." The smile grew and she tapped her temple. "This, I see."

He hesitated. "See?"

Her face relaxed and she nodded vigorously. "Yes, yes. I know this. I know many things." Her eyes grew crafty. "You have not heard of our race, have you?"

"But you've heard of mine."

"Who has not heard of the mighty werewolves? That is why we came here. We chose you. We are a rare race, a dying race. We needed a…" Her eyes rolled as if searching for a word. "An infusion. Stronger blood to mix with ours, and what is stronger than the werewolves? We chose your race, and then we chose you from your race, to strengthen our blood." Her gaze met his. "We honored you in this."

"You did, did you? Well, maybe it's not an honor I asked for, a freak of a son, a half-breed—"

"And no concern of yours." Her voice took on a tone at once soothing and authoritative. "This child need not be any concern of yours. We will take him."

She waved at the boxes on the counter. "We're already preparing to leave. We will go and never bother you again, and you will have more sons and grow to take your rightful place as Alpha, unencumbered by this child."

Caught in her gaze, he felt the urge to give in. Why not let her take the child? It would be easy. So easy…

He reached out and snapped her neck.

He'd barely finished stuffing the old woman under the sink when a sound came from the front hall. A panic-choked shout. The girl and the child. She called again, in English this time.

"Grandmama!"

A whimper cut through the silence. The child. Not screaming or wailing, just giving one soft whimper. Malcolm heard a torrent of foreign words as the girl tried to calm the child, then a bustle as she laid him down.

The girl shouted again. Light steps ran up the hall, racing for the old woman's bedroom.

Malcolm slipped from the kitchen and headed for the living

room. There was the child, in his bassinet by the sofa. His dark eyes were as wide and worried as the old woman's had been, and he writhed in his tightly wrapped blanket.

Malcolm stepped toward the child. The patter of light running footsteps sounded behind him. Then a shriek.

Malcolm turned. The girl stood in the doorway.

"Get away from my son," she said, her English perfect, barely accented.

"*Your* son? Oh, I beg to differ on that."

She stepped toward him. "Where is my grandmother?"

Malcolm only smiled. Her jaw worked and she spat an epithet he didn't understand.

"Get out," she said. "We've done you no harm."

"No harm? You hid my son—"

"*My* son. Your only part in his making is long over, and you were well compensated for that." Her lips twisted. "Not exactly a hardship for you."

"Nor for you, as I recall."

"You think I enjoyed—" She spat another foreign word, and pulled herself up straight. She barely reached his chest, but acted as if she stood on eye level with him. "You weren't even my choice. I wanted the big man, the one who'd proven he could sire sons. But they said no. Strength wasn't enough. It wasn't you who even made them decide your blood was right for our kind. They had their eye on another—wiser, with the right kind of strength for our kind. But he was too old, they said, so I had to settle for his son."

Malcolm swung at her, but she seemed to expect this, and nimbly dove to the side and raced for the child. He wheeled and shoulder-slammed her out of the way, but she kept coming, clawing, kicking, fighting to get to the child, stopping only when he reached into the bassinet and grabbed up the tiny body.

She went still. "Give me my son."

She held herself rigid, every muscle locked tight as if to keep from flying at him. Her eyes blazed and her lips were parted, teeth bared in a frozen snarl. She looked . . . magnificent, pulsing with fury and hate. A worthy mother for his son.

Looking at her, he realized how badly he wanted a child, how it ate at him, how he dreamed about it. There was a part of him that didn't care about the mixed blood—of either kind. He just wanted a son.

Malcolm ripped his gaze from hers. It was a trick, some magic, just like her grandmother had used on him, trying to bend him to her will, to break *his* will.

He looked down at the child in his arms. The boy gazed back at him, bright-eyed and calm. Malcolm forced his hands to the child's throat. He had to do this. His gut told him it was right, that if he didn't kill the child, he would always regret his weakness.

"Stop! He's your son!"

"I'll have more. Your grandmother said so."

"My grandmother—?"

"She foresaw it."

"Foresaw—?" The girl let out a bark of a laugh. "Is that what she told you? We have our gifts, but that is not one of them. No one can foresee the future, and that child you hold may well be the only one you'll ever see."

"Maybe I'm willing to take that chance."

He put his hand around the baby's throat. The girl flew at him. One brutal shove and she hit the wall hard enough that she should have stayed down. But she didn't. She pushed herself up, blood dribbling from her mouth, and came at him again. Her nails ripped furrows down his bare forearm. So he dropped the child. Just dropped him.

The girl screamed and dove for the baby. She almost caught it, breaking its fall before he kicked her with all he had, square in the gut. She sailed backward into the wall, arms still outstretched toward the child, who tumbled the last foot onto the floor, rolling, still silent. When she hit the floor this time, she lay there only a moment, then started dragging herself toward her son, whimpering now. Her nails scraped the floor. Malcolm reached down to scoop up the baby.

The front door swung open.

"Malcolm!"

He stopped, bent over the silent child, and looked over at his father. Edward's gaze was riveted to the girl.

"Oh, my God. What have you done?" Edward's cane clattered to the floor, and he limped to the girl, then dropped down at her side. His hands went to the side of her neck. "Malcolm! Call Emilio. Now!"

The girl's eyelids fluttered. She said a word and reached for the child. Edward gently laid her down and scrambled over to the baby. As he picked it up, the child kicked and swung his fists, but didn't make a sound. Edward hurried back to the girl and pressed the child to her.

"Help is coming," he said.

"Don't—" Her tongue flicked over her bloodied lips. "Don't let him..."

"He won't hurt the boy. Ever. You have my word on that."

"Take—" Her voice was ragged, eyes almost closed. "You. Take..."

Edward squeezed the girl's hand. "I will."

The words had barely left his lips when she went limp. Edward's head fell forward. Then the baby whimpered and he looked up sharply. He slipped the child from his mother's arms and gathered him up in his own. Then he pushed to his feet.

"Clean this up," he said, his voice tight.

Without a glance Malcolm's way, Edward limped to the door. Then he stopped, his back still to his son.

"Get a blanket. It's cold outside. He needs a blanket."

He watched his father, cradling the baby, murmuring to it. He could see a sliver of Edward's profile. His expression made something wither inside Malcolm, an icy rage seeping in to take its place. He saw the way his father looked at his grandson, and he knew this child wasn't *his* son, never would be. No more than he'd ever really been Edward's.

Malcolm looked at the blanket at his feet, the one that had fallen from the child. It was the one covered in those damnable symbols. He kicked the blanket under the sofa. If his son had to live, then no one could know about this "infusion" of magic-maker blood. He'd been used by these women, but that would be his secret, his shame—and his alone.

He grabbed a plain blanket from the bassinet, walked to the door, threw it at his father and strode past, leaving them behind as he walked on alone.

Savage
1967

Gift

It was a late summer night. Hot and sticky, like most summer nights in Baton Rouge. My family had retreated to an RV campsite on the city's edge, as they did every summer weekend. It was past midnight and I was wandering the woods alone. Nothing unusual about that. I suppose there should be something unusual about a young child roaming the forest at night, but my parents had a vague idea of my whereabouts, and didn't care about the specifics. As long as I stayed out of trouble and didn't bother them, I could do as I liked.

Saturday nights at the campground were always the same. My parents and their friends would gather at one of the sites, start a bonfire and drink and talk until morning. We kids were left to amuse ourselves. My older brothers were supposed to look after me but, as usual, they were with their friends, enjoying filched beer and cigarettes, and were quite happy to let me take off on my own, as long as I hightailed it back to the campsite when my parents finally whistled us in to bed.

I wandered the wooded paths for a while, but didn't expect to see anything. Not what I wanted to see, at least. I'd only seen it once, and when I had, I'd run and not stopped until I was safe with my brothers. I'd cursed my cowardice a million times since then. All my nights of exploring, and when I finally found something worth seeing, I'd bolted like a baby. Each Saturday night after that, I screwed up my courage and ventured into the woods... and saw nothing more wondrous than fireflies.

Time was running out. Just yesterday, my brothers had said there were only two weeks of summer left, which meant only two more weekends at the campground. Tonight, I decided I'd take the next step. I'd go to the string of cabins along the front road, see if he was in his, maybe catch him heading into the woods.

As soon as I neared the edge of the woods, I saw him. A gray-haired man, sitting alone behind his cabin, smoking and staring out into the night. I watched from the forest, heart hammering. Finally, the man stubbed out his cigarette, got to his feet and turned to head into the cabin.

In that moment, I made a decision—a decision only a child would even consider.

I stepped from the forest. The man stopped, but didn't turn around.

"Tired of hiding in the trees?" he said.

His voice was sharp, with an accent I'd never heard in these parts. He turned then. His gaze traveled over me, eyes hooded to bored slits.

"Well? What do you want, boy?"

"I saw what you did."

His expression didn't change. "How nice for you."

I'd expected him to deny it, or at least play dumb, so when he didn't, I was left standing there, arguments jammed in my throat.

"I—I saw you do it," I said finally. "I saw what you turned into. I know what you are."

"So you said." He yawned and rolled his shoulders. "How fast can you run, boy? Hope it's not too fast, because, truth is, I'm not really in the mood—"

"I want to do it."

He stopped stretching. "You want...?"

I stepped closer. "I want to do it myself. If you help me, I won't tell on you."

"Tell—?" He threw back his head and laughed, then looked down at me, lips still twitching in barely contained laughter. "And how do you think I'm supposed to help you? Wave my magic wand and poof, you're a—"

"You have to bite me." I pulled myself up as tall as I could. "I'm not stupid. I know how it works."

His gaze met mine and for a second he faltered. Then he shook his head sharply. "Well, boy, something tells me I'm going to wake up in that chair a few hours from now, and this will all be part of the strangest dream I've ever had, but sure, let's give it a whirl. If somehow I am awake, this is a hell of a lot easier than chasing you. Now, you just wait right here while I get ready, okay?"

I nodded.

"If you run away, I'll have to come after you. Neither of us wants that, right?"

I nodded.

"Good. Now, it'll sting some, but don't you worry. Before you know it, it'll all be over."

A final nod from me, and he disappeared into the forest.

Long minutes passed, and I began to worry that he'd cheated me. Then the brush rustled. From somewhere deep within me came the urge to bolt. I forced my feet to stay still, despising my weakness.

I turned slowly. I knew what to expect, but still didn't expect it. Before me stood a wolf as tall as me. His eyes met mine—eyes that were unmistakably human. Those eyes and his monstrous size were the only things left of the man. The rest was wolf.

The test had come. I felt my body betray me, arm hairs prickle, legs tremble, a heavy weight bearing down in my groin as if I was seconds away from pissing myself. I gritted my teeth and forced myself to meet his gaze. He had to bite me. I knew what a werewolf was, and how you became one. My older brothers delighted in scaring me with monster stories, never guessing that I wasn't scared at all, that I listened to their tales and thought only of how lucky the monsters were, that they never had to cower under a bed or hide in a closet, listening to drunken curses and punches, and knowing if they were found, they'd be next. Monsters didn't fear. They *were* fear. Now I had a chance to try that for myself. So I took a deep breath, held out my arm and waited.

Something flickered in the wolf's eyes—surprise, shock, maybe even the barest hint of uncertainty. He growled. I didn't budge. He snapped at my arm, teeth sinking in. Pain ripped through it. I stumbled back, tripping over my feet and falling as he let go. Warm blood trickled down my arm and hot urine soaked my jeans. I looked at my arm and saw blood flowing from twin gashes in the soft underside. I struggled to my feet. The wolf stared at me, as if confused. His tongue lolled out, blood-pink saliva dripping from its tip.

I met his eyes and grinned. I had done it. I'd been bitten. The gift was mine.

He lowered his head, his eyes never leaving mine. A low growl started in the pit of his stomach. He hunkered down. Then he sprang.

I should have died that moment. That was his plan, not to turn me into a werewolf, but to kill me, to put a quick and easy end to the minor inconvenience of my existence. So what happened?

Was I so brave and strong and smart that I outmaneuvered my fate? Hardly. I tripped.

I saw him spring. As I stumbled back, my foot caught on a root and I twisted sideways. Instead of landing on top of me, the wolf crashed down beside me, fur brushing my arm.

Somehow, I managed to keep enough balance to come out of the tumble running. Instinctively, I ran for the front of the cabin, for the main road heading past the campground.

Before I'd gone twenty feet, I heard a snort and knew the wolf had recovered from his fall. My throat dried up. My brain shut down. My legs seemed to move of their own accord, running so fast that slivers of pain shot through my calves and my lungs.

I raced for the road. I heard pounding, either the blood rushing in my ears or his paws on the hard-packed dirt—it didn't matter. I knew he was behind me.

I heard a scream. No, not a scream. The screech of tires and brakes. The flash of headlights. A car heading into the campground.

I tripped over the curb and sprawled onto the road. Someone shouted. I lifted my head to see two men jump from the car, arms waving. The wolf hesitated, then turned and ran for the forest.

"What the hell was that?" one man yelled. "It was huge!"

"Forget it," the other said. "Go call an ambulance. The kid's bleeding."

I wobbled to my feet.

"Whoa. Hold on there, little guy."

I looked up, saw them approaching, two large faceless shadows. I bolted for the opposite side of the road, heading for the highway across the embankment. Behind me, the men shouted. Instead of following on foot, though, they ran back to their car. By the time they got the car turned around, I was long gone.

I don't remember what happened next. I assume there was a search for me, maybe my picture made it onto a milk carton somewhere. If so, I knew nothing of it and, in later years, never checked back to see how big a fuss my disappearance had caused. As for my parents, I'm sure they played up the tragedy for all it was worth, but stopped searching the moment everyone else stopped caring. If there was a search, I escaped simply by avoiding people—an aversion that became second nature after I was bitten.

Of those first few weeks, all I remember is the pain. Pain and hunger. My mind retreated to some dark hole in my psyche, emerging now and then to spout ribbons of gibberish, then muttering away into silence. The world turned to permanent shadows, even while the Louisiana sun parboiled my skin. Ordinary shapes contorted into funhouse mirror reflections. Alley cats grew to the size of ponies, with gaping mouths and fangs that threatened to swallow me whole. Children's laughter twisted into the taunting laughs of the old werewolf. I had only to hear a human voice and I'd run scuttling to the shadows. And still the hunger grew.

Survival

As a human child, I'd already begun learning to fend for myself. With my transformation came the boost I needed to survive. A young child can't live on his own, but a half-grown wolf already has the tools and the instincts he needs. Instinct made me avoid humans and other potential predators. Common sense told me to take shelter from the elements. My sense of smell sharpened and tuned to the scent of food, leading me to trash bins and Dumpsters and roadkill.

I never went home. Never tried to. I could say that I'd forgotten where home was or that I was afraid of how my family would react, but that's a lie. I chose not to return.

I don't remember the first time I changed into a wolf. One night, I passed out and awoke to find my body covered in yellow fur. My brain was beyond reacting. It took this in stride, as it had everything else in my new life. I got to my feet and went in search of food.

As a wolf, I learned to hunt…or at least to scavenge. If I managed to kill the odd mouse or sparrow, it was more dumb luck than skill. Even that added food wasn't enough to feed the fire in my gut.

* * *

One day, as the hunger threatened to gnaw through my stomach, I realized I had to find something larger than a mouse or half-eaten hamburger. I left my bed of matted newspapers and went hunting.

The city was in the midst of a midautumn heat wave. The sun shoved through the buildings and trees, and broiled the pavement into a stinking stream of asphalt. Every living thing with a brain had taken shelter, leaving me hunting for food in a scorched wasteland.

Fortune let me stumble onto a cat napping beneath a bush. The cat jerked awake and stared at me in heat-stupid confusion. I flung myself forward . . . and leapt clear over the cat, which quickly regained its senses and ran away. I got to my feet and went in search of new prey, but it was no use. Fortune, thoroughly disgusted with my ineptitude, left to find a worthier recipient.

I wandered through the alleyways, eating from the open trash cans and drooling at the ones sealed tight. In this weather, most people covered their cans, so easy pickings were rare. Finally, after what seemed like hours of searching, a smell hit me, the stink of dirt and decay, but underlaid with something that cut short my retreat. The smell of death. Of fresh meat.

I followed the stench, rounded a corner and came upon a pile of rags shoved under a concrete step. The smell overpowered my senses, making my eyes water, and prodding me to turn tail and run for cleaner air. But the lingering scent of meat kept my paws riveted to the pavement. Buried somewhere under those rags was food, and I damned well wasn't leaving until I found it.

I eased forward until I was under the step. Then I grabbed the first layer of cloth between my teeth and tugged. A filth-crusted blanket pulled away from the heap beneath, and the heap became a man. A dead man. A derelict. I don't know what had killed him. Maybe the heat. It wasn't important. All that mattered was that he was dead, and I was starving.

*   *   *

With the added strength of a full belly, I was able to roam farther in search of food. After a couple of days I came to the bayou, and soon made it my home. My den was probably a cubbyhole in some hillock or outcropping of rock. I remember it only as someplace warm, dry and safe. I was comfortable there, away from people. I quickly learned to hunt rats and birds. While they didn't always fill my stomach, they kept me from starving, and that was enough.

One evening, I found myself back in the city. I don't remember how or why. Maybe somehow I knew that on that day I had to be in Baton Rouge, at that hour I had to be in that particular park, at that moment I had to be beside that pathway, waiting. My life pivoted on this point as much as it had the day I'd confronted the old werewolf.

I was in wolf form. This wasn't intentional—it was no longer a matter of intention, if it ever had been. I vacillated between forms endlessly, falling asleep human, waking a wolf, hunting as wolf, eating as human. I'd stopped noticing the difference. The agony of the Change became part of my life, like the ache in my gut.

That evening, I lay hidden in a stand of flowering bushes, watching the passersby. When the scent first wafted past, my hazy brain recognized it as familiar, bringing to mind an image of the old werewolf who'd bitten me.

A growl escaped before I could choke it back. The sound was soft, barely louder than the rustle of dry leaves. Nobody noticed except one dark-haired man, maybe as old as my father, and about the same size, average height and broad-shouldered. He was strolling through the park gardens with a young woman. When I growled, he turned and scanned the area.

I pushed back into the bush. He caught the movement. His eyes narrowed and his nostrils flared. He said something to the woman, the sound reaching me only as garbled noise. Leaving her behind, he started toward the bush, his long strides devouring the ground between us.

As he approached from upwind, I caught a whiff of scent. It was the smell that had reminded me of the old werewolf. But this obviously wasn't the same man. My muddled brain struggled to make sense of it. Finally, some deeper instinct solved the riddle, and I realized that what I'd recognized was the common scent of a werewolf.

As my brain hit the answer, it freed my legs. I tore back out of the bush and didn't stop running until I reached my den in the bayou.

The next morning I crept from my den in human form, groggy, shivering and eager to find a warm place in the sun, so I could go back to sleep. The mornings and evenings had grown too chilly for human form. I didn't wear clothing. The impulse to cover myself had died long ago under the sheer impracticality of finding my clothes each time I Changed.

I stumbled out, still half asleep, heading for a trail that would take me to a warm clearing. Like any wolf, I had my favorite trails—paths through the swamp that I'd walked along so many times that they reeked of my scent. It was a matter of habit and safety, sticking to what I knew. All the trails led, in some convoluted way, back to my den.

I'd walked about five feet when something grabbed me around the neck and hoisted me into the air. The panic came slowly, formless, my sleepy brain still trying to decide whether this was another of my nightmares. When I realized it wasn't, I twisted and kicked, but my feet struck only air.

A man laughed. The grip on my neck tightened. I struggled harder, twisting and flailing. My leg struck the man in the chest, and he cuffed my ear so hard my vision clouded. The trees swayed. When the spinning stopped, I resisted the impulse to fight. Resistance only makes them hit harder. A lesson long learned, though often challenged.

As I went limp, I caught a whiff of scent. Werewolf scent. It was the one from the park. He'd used my trails to track me to my den. Instinctively I started struggling. Again he struck me, and the world toppled into momentary darkness.

He said something—a volley of words that made as little sense as the chirping of the birds overhead. I'd long since lost the ability to understand human speech. When I didn't respond, he shook me and repeated himself. His words sounded clipped, impatient. Still dangling me by the neck, he swung me around to face him, then lifted one brow and said something. I still didn't react. He tossed me to the ground.

I hit the dirt hard, my head striking a half-buried rock. When I opened my eyes, he was crouched with his head inside my den. I tried to growl, but the sound came out strangled and ridiculous. He swiveled on his heels, looked at me and laughed. He said something, then went back to investigating my den. After a few minutes, he got to his feet, grimaced and wiped his hands on his pants. Then, without so much as a glance in my direction, he left.

I lay on the grass, listening as the thud of his footsteps retreated through the trees. When the sound stopped, I lifted my head, then gritted my teeth and tried to stand. The pain forced me back down. I lay there, panting and trying to focus. I had to get up, get away. He might come back. My heart hammered so hard it drowned out the birds in the trees. I stretched my legs and rolled onto my stomach. Waves of agony pulsed through my skull. I closed my eyes and concentrated, got to my knees, then passed out.

*   *   *

When I came to, I'd changed into a wolf. I couldn't remember what happened or why I was lying outside my den. The sunlight jabbed needles through my eyes. It hurt to blink, to turn my head, to move. As I stumbled forward, my legs tangled and I fell headfirst to the ground, muzzle bulldozing through the dirt, nostrils filling. For a second, I couldn't breathe. Mindless panic sent me flying to my feet. Excruciating pain forced me back to the ground.

Lifting my head, I saw my den. It wavered, miragelike, just feet from my nose. I crawled forward, belly to the ground. Time crawled even slower. Only the promise of my den kept me moving. Finally, I was there. Forcing myself to my feet, I made that last step. Then, just as I was about to lurch onto my bed of leaves and rags, the scent hit me. His scent.

I backed away, my legs shaking. Old emotions—human emotions—surfaced. Frustration. Humiliation. Rage. Hate. Impotent, overwhelming hate. I threw back my head and howled my anguish to the rising moon.

I spent days lying outside my den. My brain prodded me to find shelter, but my throbbing head wouldn't let me move. The den was soiled for me now. Cold nights, bitter rain, the fear of predators, nothing would make me take that final step inside. Sleep brought no relief from the pain or the cold. I was too terrified to close my eyes, certain he'd come back. A few times, the hunger and exhaustion became too much and I passed out. More than once, I thought he'd returned. I saw him there, looming over me, but just as my teeth were about to graze his throat, he'd vanish into mocking laughter.

One day I awoke and found the strength to stand. I stumbled to the swamp and drank the fetid water, coughing half of it back up again. Next, my nose led me to the decaying carcass of a nutria and I ate. And life continued.

Days, maybe weeks later, I was sunning myself on a rock by the bayou, enjoying one of the last rare bouts of early winter heat. A cloud kidnapped my sunlight, and I shifted my position. As I moved, I caught sight of something. It was him—the werewolf who'd beaten me—standing downwind less than twenty feet away. My heart jammed in my throat.

He leaned against a tree, arms crossed. When I moved, his arms fell to his sides and his lips curved in a crooked, almost hesitant half-smile, nothing like the arrogant grin of my nightmares. Also, I remembered him as shorter, more muscular. Older, too. This man looked barely out of his teens. But the dark hair and something in his face matched my memories exactly.

I began to wonder if I'd fallen asleep and was dreaming. I rubbed my eyes and looked around. Everything was as it should be. Everything except the intruder. I shaded my eyes from the sun to get a better look.

Yes, this man definitely resembled the werewolf who'd invaded my den. Therefore it must be him. So why was I sitting here? Was I eager for another beating? My gaze slid from side to side, evaluating my escape options. The man was still watching me, making no move to approach.

Maybe he didn't see me. I focused on his eyes. They were black and slightly slanted over high cheekbones. When I saw them, I knew this wasn't the man who'd violated my den. I had looked into the other man's eyes and I would never forget them.

The stranger said something. The inflection reminded me of the other man, but the timbre was different, deep and low. He tilted his head and smiled, even more hesitant this time. He spoke again. I barely heard him. My attention was focused on his body, waiting for the first twitch of movement. I was in human form, vulnerable.

After a short silence, the man resumed talking, his voice low and soothing, the sentences stretching into a monologue. Then his left leg moved ever so slightly. I tensed. He stepped forward, moving slowly, still talking. I inched backward. My toes brushed water and I froze. I looked from side to side. The bayou surrounded me, blocking off all escape.

The man continued his approach. I began to shake. He stopped, now only five feet away, then dropped to one knee. I watched his hands. He lifted them and turned them, palms toward me. Bending down more, he tried to make eye contact. His shoe slipped in the mud. At the sudden movement, I panicked. I leapt at him. He yanked back, fast, but not fast enough. My long nails raked down his forearm, three rivulets of blood springing up.

He inhaled sharply. I fell back, shielding my head, waiting for the retaliatory blow. Everything in my early life had conditioned me to recognize this simple cause and effect. I cowered, head under my arm, eyes clenched tight.

Nothing happened. My heart thudded. I knew this trick. He was waiting. The second I exposed myself, the blow would come, a cuff across the head or shoulders that I'd feel for days.

I opened one eye, keeping my arm over my head. He crouched on his heels, tying a handkerchief around the wound with one hand. When he noticed me watching, he managed a pained half-smile. Then, still crouching, he eased backward and stood.

I closed my eyes, tensed and waited. When I peeked again, he was gone.

Domestication

Only a few hours passed before he returned. The day was darkening and I'd begun to hunt. I'd changed to a wolf, possibly in a subconscious reaction to the fear.

I was chasing a mouse when I heard a noise behind me and turned to see the man step into the clearing. He smiled. I wheeled and ran.

I ran full out until I was certain he wasn't following. Then I turned around and went back to find him.

I crept through the undergrowth, ears perked. As I approached the clearing, I slowed, crawling along the ground, ready to bolt at the first sign that he saw me. I slunk into a thicket bordering the clearing. Then I closed my eyes and inhaled. He was there.

I heard nothing. I crouched, sniffing and listening, every muscle poised for flight. After a few minutes, I worked up the nerve to peer through the weeds. He sat on the grass, leaning against a tree, legs outstretched, arms crossed and eyes shut, as if dozing. I stopped, confused. I'd seen people do a lot of strange things, but settling down for a nap in the middle of the bayou was not one of them.

I pushed my muzzle out farther to sniff again. Not a leaf rustled, but somehow he seemed to hear the movement. His eyes snapped open. I jerked back into the thicket. He laughed. No, not a laugh really—a deep chuckle that rippled through the night air.

I heard a rustle and peeked out to see him rooting around in a paper bag. He pulled something out and threw it. Although I was over thirty feet away, it sailed through the thicket and landed squarely at my feet.

I bent to sniff it. A piece of cooked meat. I gulped it before I could have second thoughts. A second piece flew into the thicket with equally perfect aim. I ate that one, and the next, and the next. He threw each to my feet, not trying to entice me out of my hiding spot.

At last, the meat stopped coming. I waited patiently. Nothing happened. I poked my head out of the thicket and looked at him. He said something, turned the bag upside down and shook it.

My nose twitched, catching the lingering hints of meat in the air. My stomach growled. He got to his feet. I darted back into the thicket.

Minutes passed. When I peeked out again, he was still by the tree, standing now, hands in pockets. He murmured something under his breath, turned and vanished into the forest.

Once he was gone, I crept to the crumpled bag and tore it apart, frustrated by the scent of meat permeating the paper. I licked the scraps, but only got enough of a taste to make my stomach start growling again. Reluctantly, I left the bag in tatters and went to hunt.

I barely had time to pick up another mouse trail when a sharp crack of undergrowth startled me. I spun to see a form emerge from the trees. Though it was in the shadows, I could see the outline of a large dog.

I was about to bolt when it stepped into the moonlight. It was a wolf—a tall, rangy black wolf. My leg muscles seized, riveting me to the ground. Instead of walking toward me, though, the wolf loped to the east, circling me while coming closer. There was something in his mouth, but he was too far away for me to see it.

A light breeze blew through the trees and his scent fluttered down to me. With a start, I recognized it as the man from the clearing. I don't know why it surprised me to realize he was a werewolf, but it did.

Staying upwind, he moved a few steps closer. Then he drew back his head and threw whatever was in his mouth. His aim and distance weren't nearly as good as when he'd been a man and it landed about five feet northwest of me.

I stayed still, watching. He backed up, then lay down, putting his muzzle on his paws. Now a second smell shifted to me in the wind. Freshly killed rabbit.

My stomach overrode my fear and I raced forward, finding the rabbit where he'd thrown it. It was larger than anything I could ever catch. The throat had been ripped open, but he hadn't fed. I lowered my head and ate.

When I finished eating, my brain reminded me that I should escape, but the warning was buried under the weight of the food in my belly. With the black wolf still lying less than ten feet away, I stretched out and fell asleep.

The next morning he was gone. He reappeared around noon, in human form, again bearing food. I ate it, then crept back into the woods. He didn't follow. That night, he returned with more food.

With that, a pattern was established. Each day, he brought food, and he talked to me, sometimes changed form and hunted for me, but always kept his distance, never following when I grew nervous or bored and wandered away.

Gradually his patience wore down my fear. Although I still didn't trust him, I learned to tolerate his presence—especially since it was always paired with generous helpings of food.

About ten days later, after lunch, while he dozed against a tree, I screwed up the courage to approach him. I was in wolf form and he wasn't, which fortified my nerve. I circled around behind the tree, then crept forward, ears perked and straining for any change in his breathing.

Finally, I was behind the tree. I craned my neck and sniffed the back of his shoulder. He didn't move. Inching forward, I sniffed his arm and shirt sleeve, then his side and hip.

He had a rich natural smell mingled with human smells— soap, fabric, car exhaust, processed food and scores more. I sniffed him thoroughly and was about to retreat when I noticed a bag at his side. He'd already fed me and the empty food bag was lying in the middle of the clearing.

I eyed the new bag. Something bulged within it. More food? Was he holding out on me? Gingerly, I snagged the corner of the paper bag with my teeth, then dragged it to a safer spot behind the tree. It didn't smell like food. But it had to be. What else was a bag for?

Grabbing one corner, I jerked my head up and dumped the bag. A shower of fabric fell to the ground. I tossed the bag aside and pounced on a piece before it could escape. I snuffled through the pile.

As the fabric spread out, it revealed its true nature. Clothing. A small pair of jeans, a shirt and sneakers. I tore through the clothing looking for the hidden food. It wasn't there.

Behind me, the bag tumbled away in the breeze. I raced after it and caught it just as a gust of wind was lifting it into the air. Tipping it onto its side, I thrust my head inside, hoping to find the missing food. There was nothing there, not even the tempting scent of meat soaked into the paper.

I pulled back. The bag stuck behind my ears. I shook myself. It stayed on. I tried backing away from it and tripped, tumbling head over ass to the ground. It was then that I heard it. Laughter. Not a dry chuckle or a quiet laugh, but a tremendous whoop of choking laughter.

I caught the bag under my paw and yanked my head out. He stood there, arms crossed over his chest, trying to stop himself from laughing and failing miserably. I glared at him, salvaged my last shreds of dignity and stalked off into the woods.

The next day he brought extra food, so I decided, after much contemplation, to forgive him.

Each day following, the clothes reappeared in a fresh bag. I ignored them. On the third day, I was in human form when he brought my lunch. He fed me just enough to stop the gnawing in my gut, then produced the bag of clothing.

Lifting each piece, he pointed at the corresponding article of clothing on his own body, then pantomimed putting it on. I fixed him with a cool stare and curled my lip. I knew perfectly well what clothing was and what was supposed to be done with it. I wasn't an idiot. And I certainly wasn't stupid enough to put them on, which seemed to be the end goal of this little demonstration.

I laid down in my patch of sunlight and closed my eyes. Then I heard the crinkle of paper and a smell I knew all too well. Food. I opened an eye.

The man held out both hands, a cooked hamburger patty in

one and the shirt in the other. He arched one eyebrow. I closed my eyes.

The scent of the meat wafted over. My mouth watered. I peeked again. The hamburger was still there. So was the shirt.

With an annoyed growl, I got to my feet, marched over, grabbed the shirt and tugged it on, first trying to pull the arm-hole over my head, but eventually remembering the proper sequence. Then I held out my hand. He gave me the meat patty. I ate it, yanked off the shirt and threw it back. Unperturbed, he reached down for the jeans and a second meat patty and we started again.

By the third day of playing this game, I surrendered. It was an uneven match. His patience seemed endless. Mine wore out in five seconds. Besides, I was curious to see what this clothing business portended.

I put on the whole outfit, then followed him out of the bayou. On the edge of the woods was a parking lot for weekend fisher-men. He walked over to the only car in the lot, opened the passenger door and turned to say something to me. The tail end of his words floated into the night as I plunged back into the forest.

The next day, he brought fresh clothes. He also brought extra food, so once again, I forgave him. To show that I didn't bear a grudge, I even played the clothing game again. This time, once I was dressed, he led me not to the parking lot, but on a longer walk, right to the outskirts of the city.

Backing onto the bayou was a run-down motel. He walked to the door closest to the woods and opened it. I tensed, ready to bolt. Instead of calling to me, though, he just walked inside, leaving the door open.

I hovered on the forest's edge for at least thirty minutes. When he didn't reappear, I crept forward. A car roared into the parking lot. I dove for cover behind a bush. Two people stumbled from the car, voices too loud, laughter too harsh. Drunk. I knew what that sounded like.

I watched them go into a room farther down, then slunk out from the bush and started toward the open door again. When I got close, I circled wide, keeping my distance.

A blast of hot air billowed from the room. I paused, letting it chase some of the night chill from my bones. Then I scooted around to the far side and peered through the open doorway. The man was inside, lying on a bed, ankles crossed, reading a newspaper. He glanced around the edge at me, nodded and kept reading.

I inched toward the door, testing how close I'd need to get to feel that glorious warmth again. I was just close enough to feel the tugging tendrils of heat when the newspaper crackled. My nerve snapped and I bolted for the safety of the woods.

I didn't go back to my den though. It was getting late and morning would be coming. Morning meant breakfast. I dimly remembered breakfast. Maybe if I stuck around, I'd get more than the two meals a day he'd been providing so far. So I crawled under a bush and fell asleep.

Late that night, I woke up shivering. Louisiana was suffering through a cold snap that winter and even the clothing the man had provided didn't help much. I remembered that burst of heat from the motel room.

For a long time, I lay there, shivering, fear warring with discomfort. Finally, I leapt up and dashed for the motel. The door was still open. Inside, the man was asleep on the bed. I curled up in the doorway and went to sleep.

And so I let myself be domesticated. In the end, like any stray, I was conquered by the promise of continued food and shelter. Trust would take longer.

For at least a week I slept in the doorway, not letting him close the door no matter how cold the night got. One day, another man came by. While I hid in the bushes outside, the other man yelled at my man, motioning at the door. Money changed hands and the other man left. That was the first of many such exchanges I'd see in my life—cash buying tolerance for my idiosyncrasies.

After a few days, with the right amount of food for coaxing, the man convinced me to come inside the room. He left the door open, so this seemed safe.

By the bed was a huge mirror with a web of tiny cracks down one side. I glanced into it by accident and startled myself so badly I dove under the bed, provoking a spate of laughter from the man.

Pretending that I'd simply fallen under the bed, I pulled myself back up and looked into the mirror. Staring back at me was a puny runt of a kid. Disgust filled me. If I'd seen myself somewhere else, my first reaction would have been "easy pickings." Definitely not the dangerous predator I liked to imagine myself.

I was skinny and filthy, from my ragged mop of yellow curls to my bare feet with gnarled toenails. Scabs and bruises covered my face and bare arms. The clothing—my third set so far—was already torn and dirty. I glared at my reflection, sniffed and stalked from the room.

When I came back that night, the man had covered the mirror with a sheet. The next day, he introduced me to soap, shampoo, scissors and nail clippers, along with a huge bowl of steaming jambalaya. I deigned to let him do what he wanted with the soap and scissors while I ate.

When he finished, he smiled and made a move to pull the sheet from the mirror. My growl stopped him. As long as I was in the room, that sheet was staying up. No amount of personal grooming was going to make me anything but a scrawny little kid, and I preferred to keep my illusions unshattered.

During this time at the motel, I was also reintroduced to language. Since it was more a matter of remembering than learning, it didn't take long for me to pick up the basics. Soon I knew enough nouns and verbs to understand the gist of simple sentences. Saying the words was harder.

After two years of being asked to do nothing more than growl and yip, my voice box complained at the strain of speech. I preferred to listen and spoke only grudgingly. During one of our first lessons, I volunteered to speak just once and only because I recognized the information was too important to withhold.

We were sitting on the floor near the door, before the time when I'd come farther into the room. The man was pointing to furniture and naming it. When I refused to repeat the words, he changed tactics and would instead say a word and I'd point to the appropriate object.

After exhausting every item in sight, he started opening drawers, looking for more things. I pointed at him. He paused and lifted his eyebrows. I jabbed my finger toward him, rolling my eyes when he didn't catch on immediately.

After a second, he pointed at himself and said "Jeremy" hesitantly, as if unsure this was what I wanted. I recognized the word as a name and nodded. He smiled. Then he pointed at me.

I opened my mouth and nothing came out. A surge of panic raced through me. I couldn't remember the answer. Quickly, he turned and started naming the items in the room, trying to change the subject. It didn't help. My brain spun frantically. I had to know this. I had to. Finally, the answer bubbled up from my subconscious and came out before I even realized I was speaking.

"Clayton," I said. I jabbed my chest. "Clayton."

He stopped. A slow smile spread across his face, lighting up his eyes. He reached out, as if to touch me, then caught himself and pulled back.

"Clayton," he said.

I nodded. He smiled again, hesitated, then resumed checking the drawers for more items to name.

While the motel room seemed like a perfectly good shelter to me, it eventually became apparent that it wasn't Jeremy's home. His home was far away, and he planned to take me there.

Figuring this out was a long, involved process. While I knew perfectly well what a house was, the concept of home was too abstract. For me, home meant shelter and shelter could mean a house, den, bush or any convenient place. Since this motel was as convenient as any, I couldn't understand why Jeremy wanted us to go somewhere else. On the other hand, since I felt no particular tie to this motel room or this city or this bayou, I had no compunction about leaving. I'd follow the supplier of food and provider of shelter wherever he wished to take me.

However, there was one problem to be overcome. Wherever Jeremy wanted to take me wasn't accessible by foot and as long as I refused to be shut into a room, much less a car, we couldn't go. So, Jeremy continued working with me, building up trust.

To pass the time, he also coached me on other things that I

deemed a complete waste of brain space—useless skills like table manners and rules of public behavior. Stand up straight. Speak clearly. Don't eat with your hands. Don't growl at people. Don't piss on the furniture. And above all, don't sniff *anything.*

Jeremy didn't work miracles with me. In the end, I think he decided that if he waited until I was fit to be seen in public, we might celebrate the coming of the next millennium in that motel room. So one day he decided I was good enough for my first foray into the human world.

Identity

Before we left the motel, Jeremy had spent a lot of time making phone calls. Not that I understood what he was doing. For whatever reason, I had holes in my memory such that I'd know perfectly well what a car or money was for, but objects like telephones and toilets were unfathomable mysteries.

At the time, it seemed to me that Jeremy was spending a lot of time with a piece of plastic pressed against his ear, talking to himself. Which was fine by me. We all have our eccentricities. Jeremy liked talking to plastic; I liked hunting and eating the rats that ventured into the motel room. Or, at least I *did* like hunting and eating the rats, until Jeremy caught me and promptly kiboshed that hobby. Some of us are less tolerant of eccentricities than others.

After much plastic-talking one morning, Jeremy announced our first mutual voyage into the human world. The only part I understood was "car" and "out," but I got the idea. I was okay with the going-out part. It was the complex preritual that I objected to—the new clothes, the dressing, the hand washing, the face scrubbing and the hair combing. As I endured this torture, I decided there wouldn't be many more of these "goings-out" in the future if I had any say in the matter.

The car ride itself was uneventful. I clung to the door handle, closed my eyes, screamed now and then, but only sent Jeremy swerving into opposing traffic once.

Past the busy downtown district, Jeremy turned onto a side road, then slowed. After consulting a piece of paper, he turned down a wide alley, navigated trash bins and parked outside a battered metal door.

Before we could walk to the door, a thickset man opened it. The man said something. Jeremy replied. The man laughed and motioned us through the door. As we passed him, I edged closer to Jeremy so I wouldn't risk brushing against the stranger.

We walked into a windowless room. Across the room, under a blinking lightbulb, was a massive desk. Along the far wall, a row of machinery whirred and chirped and emitted waves of some noxious stink. Behind us, the metal door clanged shut. I jumped, grabbed a fistful of Jeremy's trousers, sticking so close he nearly tripped over me. He steered us toward the desk.

The machinery gave a *thunk* and went silent. A second man stepped out from the bowels of the beast and shouted something at Jeremy. Despite his raised voice, he was smiling. He walked toward us, smiling and shouting.

This was my first real lesson in human interaction. Although Jeremy had tried to teach me how to act in public, I'd absorbed the rules without understanding the logic behind them, like a child learning complex algebraic formulae. Now, watching him, I began to pick up tips, though not necessarily the ones he meant to impart.

He smiled when the other men smiled and laughed when they laughed, but no hint of humor warmed his eyes. He shook their hands and accepted a backslap from the first man, but initiated no physical contact and, whenever possible, kept his distance.

He clearly didn't want to be here. So why was he? Because

these men had something Jeremy wanted. Papers. A small stack of papers, different sizes, different shades of white and cream, each covered with squiggles that smelled faintly of the black liquid that coated the machinery.

As Jeremy examined the papers, I clung to his leg. At a sound from behind us, I turned to see three boys in the corner, hidden in the shadows, their smell swallowed by the stink of the machines.

All three were laughing at me, not with the good-humored chuckles of the two men, but with the acid laughter of derision, the kind that seeps under your skin and burns holes in your dignity. The largest caught my eye and stuck his thumb in his mouth, making a show of crying. The other two howled with silent laughter. I turned away.

Jeremy reached into his back pocket and pulled out a wad of money. He counted off most of the wad and handed it to the machinery man. I glanced at the boys. The leader stared at Jeremy's back with narrowed eyes. I followed his gaze and saw half a bill sticking out of Jeremy's rear pocket.

The boy sauntered out into the open. He walked past and retrieved a soda bottle from the desk. On the return trip, he ambled to the right, bringing him closer to us. I tensed. As the boy passed, his hand darted toward Jeremy. My reaction was purely instinctive, devoid of forethought or reasoning. I saw what I perceived as an attack on my master and reacted.

I launched myself at the boy, hitting him full in the chest and sending us both soaring across the room. We crashed through a stack of boxes. I closed my eyes, but kept my hold on him, fists clenching his shirtfront.

We slammed onto the floor. I landed on his chest and righted myself, pinning him down. The boy started to scream—not a yell of pain, but a high-pitched shriek of panic that reminded me of a rabbit's death throes, which reminded me that I was hungry.

Jeremy grabbed me by the shoulders and ripped me off my prey. The door-opener man scooped up the boy by the scruff of his neck, shouting at him. The boy's screams died to whimpers. The man let him go and the boy slunk back into the shadows.

Jeremy said something. The door-opener man laughed and shook his head. Keeping a tight grip on me, Jeremy went back to the desk and picked up his papers. A few more words were exchanged, but Jeremy's pleasantries had turned brittle. He put a quick end to the conversation and escorted me out, not releasing his grip until I was safely locked in the car.

As the car navigated the city streets, the only sound was the rumble of the engine. Jeremy kept his eyes on the road. His face was impassive. He started heading down the road toward the motel. Suddenly the car skidded to a halt.

Without a word, Jeremy swung around in a tight U-turn, ignoring a cacophony of horn blasts. At the next light, he veered north, heading out of the city. I gripped the sides of my seat, scarcely daring to breathe. I knew what was coming. Not a beating—Jeremy had never so much as raised a threatening hand to me. Worse than a beating. He was taking me back to the bayou.

The meeting with the men had been a test. I'd failed. No more regular meals. No more warm place to sleep. He was sending me back.

I sank into my seat and slowed my breathing, as if by being small and silent I might convince Jeremy that I'd be no trouble if he kept me. The car continued to zoom away from the city. I closed my eyes. I felt the car turn again. Then again. Any second now it would screech to a stop, the door would open and I'd be flung out to fend for myself.

The car turned again and slowed. I clenched my teeth and scrunched my eyelids shut even tighter. Something roared above the car. I crammed my hands against my ears. The car stopped. The door opened. Smells wafted in. Strange smells, mechanical smells. Not the bayou? Then where? Someplace worse? At least I knew the bayou.

"Clayton?"

I took my hands from my ears, but kept my eyes squeezed shut. The vinyl seat squeaked as Jeremy moved closer. His hand went to my shoulder, his touch tentative.

"Clayton?"

I didn't budge. He sighed. I opened one eye. He was twisted around in the driver's seat, facing me, fingers still resting on my shoulder.

He didn't look angry. It was hard to tell with Jeremy. Anger was the slightest tightening of the lips. Happiness was the faintest ghost of a crooked smile. Worry was the barest gathering of the eyebrows. That's what it looked like now. Worry, not anger.

I opened the other eye and looked around. Airplanes. That was the first thing I saw. Three airplanes behind a fence about a quarter-mile away. Following my gaze, Jeremy smiled.

"Yes?" he said. "Go?" He pointed to an airplane taking off. "Home?"

It was a spur-of-the-moment, now-or-never, bite-the-bullet decision. Rather than return to the motel, even to get his things, he'd decided to take me straight home. It could have been an act of incredible bravery and determination. Or it could have been sheer desperation, fear that if he didn't act now, things might never get any better. The truth probably lies between the two.

*   *   *

Once we were inside, we had to wait in a line of people. I clung to Jeremy's pant leg, shuddering each time some stranger brushed past me.

Finally, we approached the counter. Jeremy talked to a young woman, bestowing a generous portion of smiles on her. She bent down and said something to me. I only stared at her. Jeremy said something and she tsk-tsked sympathetically.

Jeremy handed her some papers from his pocket, then the papers he'd bought from the man. The woman leafed through the papers, smiling and nodding. Then she handed them back to Jeremy along with some more papers and we left the line.

Jeremy bought some candy bars, drinks and other unidentifiable things at a small shop in the airport. Then he took me to a phone booth. While he talked to the plastic thing, I downed two candy bars and a carton of milk. When he finished his phone call, he led me into another area and we sat down.

I finished a third candy bar, then noticed the papers still in Jeremy's hand. I pointed at them. He lifted an eyebrow. I reached for the papers and grunted. Another raised brow. I grumbled, but gave in.

"See," I said. "Want see."

He nodded, cleaned the chocolate off my fingers, then handed me the top paper. I saw only several lines of typed text. I couldn't understand the squiggles, but if I could, I would have read in them my future. My name: Clayton Danvers. My date of birth: January 15, 1962, making the day Jeremy found me my seventh birthday. And, if I'd been able to read the other papers he had bought for me, I would have learned that I was orphaned and under the guardianship of my cousin, Jeremy Malcolm Edward Danvers. And my home? A house in the state of New York, near the town of Bear Valley—13876 Wilton Grove Lane or, as Jeremy's great-great-grandfather had named it, Stonehaven.

Stonehaven

I don't remember much of the airplane ride. I slept through it, which probably had something to do with the chalky taste in the second milk carton Jeremy gave me on the plane.

We arrived in Syracuse later that day. Outside the airport, a string of cars idled by the sidewalk. Jeremy led me to one, opened the back door and nudged me inside. Then he crawled in beside me. Just as I was wondering how he planned to drive from the rear seat, I noticed a man sitting up front. Jeremy said something to him. The man nodded, and the car broke ranks with its brethren.

As we drove, Jeremy pointed out sites of interest, which didn't really interest me. I pretended to be paying attention, partly because it seemed to be what he wanted and partly because it helped me forget we were sitting very close to a stranger, but mostly because I just liked listening to Jeremy talk. When we pulled away from the city, Jeremy's travelogue slowed, until finally he turned to stare out the window and seemed to forget I was there at all.

I leaned over to see what held his attention beyond the window. When I didn't notice anything, I looked up at Jeremy and followed his gaze. But he wasn't really staring at anything. His eyes were unfocused, black mirrors that reflected nothing.

Tension vibrated from his body. More than tension. Unease. Worry. Fear. The last startled me. Fear? What did Jeremy have to fear? He was an adult, a werewolf, my protector. He took away fear; he wasn't supposed to feel it.

Jeremy's anxiety fed my own subconscious worries, and I reacted with the only defense mechanism I had. I started to Change. I felt the tingling in my fingers, then the throbbing in my skull, and finally the first licks of white-hot pain. Yet I didn't make a sound. I accepted it. If you grow up with pain, it becomes a fact of your existence.

As my heart rate accelerated, my breathing kept pace. Jeremy turned. His eyes were still blank. Then they focused, looked at my hands. He let out an oath and grabbed the driver's shoulder. The car veered. The driver snapped something. Jeremy's reply was apologetic. He said something else, forced calm.

The driver pulled the car to the side of the road. Jeremy swung open my door, grabbed me around the chest and bent my head down toward the gravel, as if I were vomiting. I barely noticed. The Change had spread to my arms and legs. My clothing began to rip. Jeremy coughed, barely fast enough to cover the sound, then hoisted me from the car, jogged down the ditch and laid me at the bottom.

"Stay," he said. "Yes?"

I could barely understand him, much less reply. Jeremy bent over me. He stroked my head, whispered something, then scrambled up the embankment to the car.

Seconds later, Jeremy returned. The Change was almost done. I lay on my side, panting. He crouched beside me and gently removed the clothing tangled around my arms and legs. Once I'd caught my breath, I clambered to my feet and started investigating my surroundings.

A trickle of icy water ran along the bottom of the ditch. I lapped a mouthful, then looked back at Jeremy. He was still in human form. I ran over to him and whimpered. He patted my head, brushed his bangs back with a sigh, then got to his feet.

Lifting me in both arms, he carried me to the other side of the ditch, then set me down away from the road. The car and driver were long gone. Jeremy stood there a moment, then started walking in the direction the car had been traveling.

I sat on my haunches and watched. He went a few steps, then turned and waved me forward. I didn't understand. He called my name. I yipped back. He whistled. I howled. Apparently, still not the right response, as he threw up his hands and walked away. I watched him until he was nearly out of sight, then ran to catch up.

It must have been a long walk, but I didn't notice. I had fun bounding through the frost-covered tall grass, hearing it crackle as I trampled it. Once I found a hole in a fence and sent a herd of sheep stampeding for cover. Great fun. Jeremy didn't agree and hoisted me back over the fence by the scruff of my neck. It was a glorious day, sunny and bright and cold. My breath snorted out in billows of smoke, like the man at the warehouse, except my smoke smelled of nothing but crisp, clean air. For a while, I amused myself by running ahead, hiding in the brush, then leaping out and snapping at Jeremy's hands as he passed. Great fun. Jeremy even seemed to agree this time. At least he did until I got carried away and took a chunk out of his finger.

The road was quiet. When the rare car did drive by, Jeremy didn't seem concerned. We were on the opposite side of the ditch, and anyone passing would only see a man out walking a boisterous dog. Of course, I didn't look like any dog. I looked like a young, yellow-haired wolf. But no one expects to see a man walking a wolf, so no one sees it.

Finally, Jeremy stopped. He picked me up and carried me over the ditch, across the road and down a long driveway. I burrowed my cold nose against his neck and licked him. He chuckled, the vibration coursing through me. The fear was gone. His strides lengthened and he picked up his pace, as if eager to reach our destination. When we were far enough from the road, he put me back on the ground. I yawned and trotted after him.

We'd barely gone twenty paces when the Change started again. This time, Jeremy noticed it immediately, seeming to sense it. He led me behind a massive pine tree, waited until I'd finished, then draped his jacket over me as I rested a few minutes to recuperate.

Instead of going back to the driveway, Jeremy led me across the treed front lawn. We wove through another row of evergreens. Suddenly, the house appeared before us, as if a magician had yanked off the covering sheet and shouted "Ta-da!" A two-and-a-half-story stone wall spread as far as I could see. If it wasn't for the windows and gardens and front porch, I'd have mistaken it for some other kind of building. I'd never seen a house this big.

When I stopped gawking, I noticed Jeremy watching me. He was smiling, not the forced smile he used with humans, but the crooked smile that crept up to his eyes.

"We're home," he said. "Welcome to Stonehaven."

As Jeremy pushed open the front door, his manner changed again. Tense now. Careful. He stepped into the hall, gaze darting from side to side. His nostrils flared, testing the air. I saw a flicker of movement from the shadowy hall. Jeremy saw it, too. He backpedaled out the door. A figure raced down the hall and barreled into Jeremy, plowing him backward and toppling them both off the porch and onto the grass.

I saw only a blur of motion. Again, I didn't think. I launched myself onto the attacker's back and sank my teeth into his shoulder. The man yowled, reared up and reached back. One large hand grabbed me, lifted me into the air and swung me overhead. As I inhaled, I smelled what I'd come to recognize as the underlying scent of a werewolf.

When I came down, I found myself looking into large brown eyes. I twisted, but couldn't get free. One glance at the man told me I wasn't getting free until he decided to set me free. He was almost a head shorter than Jeremy but twice as wide, and all the extra weight was in muscle.

Despite his size, I couldn't resist one last-ditch effort. I pulled back my foot and kicked him in the chest, hard enough to send shock waves of pain through my foot. The man grunted, then started to laugh.

"Big balls for such a little scrap," he said.

"Serves you right."

That was Jeremy. Twisting my head, I saw him sitting on the grass, retying one shoe. He didn't seem the least bit perturbed about my predicament. The man set me down. I growled at him, then lunged to hide behind Jeremy.

"Bully," Jeremy said, tucking in his shirt tails.

"That's the boy?" the man asked.

"I should hope so. I'd hate to think there was more than one." Jeremy got to his feet and pulled me up by my hand. He pushed me forward. "This is Clayton. Clayton, meet Antonio."

The man grinned, flashing white teeth. He extended his hand. I backed up.

"He doesn't do physical contact," Jeremy said.

"I see." Antonio flashed another grin and looked me over. "Wild-looking little thing, isn't he? Clothing might help. I trust he was wearing some on the plane?"

"Don't ask. We'd better get inside before he freezes." Jeremy prodded me toward the door, then stopped. "He's not back yet, is he?"

"House was locked tight when I got here. I was waiting for your call. You should have phoned from the airport."

"No need."

Jeremy led me into the house. The hall floor was cold stone, marble actually, though I wouldn't know that. I hightailed it through an adjoining door to a carpeted room. A long wooden table gleamed beneath a glass candelabrum. What caught my attention, though, were the plates and silverware set out at each place. Jeremy stood in the doorway. I reached over and tugged at his shirt.

"Yes?"

I pointed at the place settings and grunted.

"Can he talk?" Antonio asked.

"Can, but won't. Tell me what you want, Clayton."

I growled, stamped my foot and gestured at the dining room table. Antonio laughed.

"Don't encourage him," Jeremy said. "Talk, Clayton. Say what you want."

I growled again, but gave in. "Food. Want food."

"Ah, yes. Of course." To Antonio, "He likes food."

Antonio grinned. "A boy after my own heart. Come on then, scrap. Let's raid the pantry."

Sometime later we were in another room, still eating. I'd refused to go with Antonio alone, so the three of us had gone to the kitchen, where I'd discovered heaven in the form of a massive re-frigerator, deep freezer and two fully stocked closets of food.

Antonio had fixed the meal, piling mounds of cold cuts, breads and cheeses onto a platter so big I could have curled up on it and gone to sleep. To this, he'd added a second platter of salads, fruits and desserts. I decided this was someone I could allow myself to tolerate.

Instead of returning to the dining room, Jeremy got clothing for me, then led me into a room with several large padded chairs and a couch. A stone fireplace filled one wall. Jeremy had lit the fire earlier and I was lying beside it now, basking in the heat and stuffing myself with food. Paradise.

Jeremy and Antonio sat in the chairs. At first, I'd stuck close to Jeremy. But Antonio kept hogging the food, inching the platters over to his side of the coffee table. I'd followed the food and ended up lying on the rug by the fireplace. I was wearing a shirt of Jeremy's, which came down to my knees, and a thick pair of woolen socks. I'd just as soon have gone naked, but Jeremy had a thing about clothes, so I humored him.

The two men were talking. I wasn't paying much attention. Occasionally I caught words like *boy* or *child,* so I knew they were talking about me. To understand them, I'd have to concentrate and at that moment, all my concentration was required for the arduous task of filling my belly. Once that Herculean chore was accomplished, I stretched out and listened to them talk. I wasn't always sure what they were saying or what they meant, but I listened anyway.

"Are his Changes lunar?" Antonio asked.

Jeremy shook his head. "Emotion-based sometimes. Other times...I don't know. They're frequent. Too frequent. Usually two, three times a day."

"Ouch. Poor kid. He's so small. How old do you figure?"

"I guessed seven for his birth certificate. He's probably closer to eight, like Nicky, but with the developmental delays, it seemed safer to go with seven."

"How long ago do you think he was bitten?"

"I don't want to think about it." Jeremy sipped his drink. "He's worse than I expected. I'm not sure...I wasn't really prepared for this."

"Second thoughts?"

Jeremy put his glass down. "No. Of course not. I'm just questioning my own..." He stopped. Shrugged. "Ah, well. He's stuck with me now."

"It'll be fine. He seems bright enough. He'll learn fast. And he's a handsome boy. Those big blue eyes. Those blond curls. People see that, they'll expect a little angel. That'll help."

"You think so?" Jeremy looked up, hopeful.

"Sure. Don't worry about it. In a few months, he'll be a normal boy."

"You think so?"

"I'm sure of it."

Temper

Over the next few weeks, my language recognition skills went into overdrive. I learned best the way most children learn: eavesdropping. Antonio left the day after we'd arrived, but he returned the next weekend, and the weekend after that.

Days of listening to Jeremy and Antonio helped me far more than Jeremy's lessons could. That's not to say that my verbal skills kept pace. I talked when I had to, but I didn't really see the point. My needs were simple, so there wasn't much I had to communicate. Gesturing and grunting seemed far more efficient than speech. Jeremy disagreed.

By the end of the second week at Stonehaven, he wasn't even content with mere words anymore. He wanted sentences. *Whole* sentences. And, in forcing me to speak when I didn't want to, we both learned one more thing about me. I had a bit of a temper.

"Out."

Jeremy glanced over his newspaper and lifted one eyebrow. I was learning to hate that particular facial gesture.

"Out."

Antonio lay on the floor, surrounded by papers, writing in a ledger book. He looked up. "I think he wants to go outside. Why don't we—?"

"I know perfectly well what he wants. And he knows how to ask for it."

"Want out." I planted myself in front of Jeremy and pushed down his newspaper.

Jeremy shook the newspaper from my hand. "Ask for it properly, Clayton. A full sentence. *I want to go out.* 'Please' would be nice."

I growled and stamped my foot. Jeremy turned the page.

"Want—"

"No, Clayton."

I grabbed the newspaper and ripped it from his hands.

"I want to go out! Now!"

Jeremy plucked the torn paper from my hands, folded it and laid it aside. "You don't speak to me that way, Clayton. Go upstairs, please. You can come down for dinner."

My request had seemed simple enough. All Jeremy had to do was give me permission. I could open the door and let myself out. I knew the boundaries: the broken statue, the bronze urn, the kitchen window and the back door.

For weeks, he'd given me what I wanted when I wanted it. Now, all of a sudden, these simple wishes were granted only when I complied to outrageous demands like having to speak in full sentences. The unfairness of it raged through me.

I grabbed the newspaper and ripped it in half. Jeremy ignored me and reached for his coffee mug. I knocked it from his hand as it touched his lips. It smashed into the wall, shards flying in all directions.

"Clayton!" Antonio leapt to his feet.

Jeremy put out a hand to stop him. His face stayed impassive, which infuriated me more. I flung myself in his face.

"Out!" I screamed, spraying spittle flying. "Want out nowwwwww!"

I snatched up the nearest thing to me, which happened to be an end table, and flung it against the brick fireplace. It smashed into sticks and splinters. I swung back to face Jeremy. He arched one eyebrow.

"Done?"

I stormed to the back door, grabbed the handle, then stopped.

I couldn't do it. My fingers refused to turn the door handle. I could not disobey Jeremy. It was like a subconscious override that shut down my synapses.

With a snarl, I spun from the door and stomped up the stairs, making as much noise as a forty-pound body can make.

I ran into the first room on the right, an empty guest room, and threw myself onto the bed. Burying my head under the pillow, I gulped stale air. The rage dissipated. On its heels came horror.

Somewhere deep in the recesses of my damaged memory, I knew that you never lashed out at an adult. You did not argue. You did not shout. And you absolutely did not break things. To do so was dangerous...painful. It was an old lesson, etched in my brain, yet one I'd never been able to follow. Now, I had a reason to follow it. I had a home. Shelter and food. Someone to protect me. Yet I seemed hell-bent on screwing it up.

I pulled the pillow around my ears and sobbed, dry heaving sobs that racked my body until I was too exhausted to move. Then I lay there, feeling sorry for myself.

After a while, I heard footsteps on the stairs. I lifted the pillow a bit and listened. The footfalls sounded too heavy for Jeremy, but I still peered out hopefully. When Antonio rounded the doorway, I yanked the pillow down over my head and flipped over, turning my back to him.

"Good, you picked the old room," he said. "Nothing valuable to break."

"Go away."

"What's that? A complete sentence? Short, but grammatically complete. Very good." He thudded onto the foot of the bed. "That's a wicked temper you've got there. Great pitching arm, though. When you grow up, Jeremy can send you down to try out for the Yankees."

I lifted the corner of the pillow. "Send me away?"

"No, no." Antonio shook his head and pulled the pillow away. "I was joking. Teasing." He studied my face for some sign that I understood him. "Jeremy's not sending you anywhere."

I relaxed. "He come? Up?"

"'Fraid not, scrap. That's why I'm here. I figured you might need some help."

"Not come up?"

"No. He'll call you for dinner, like he said, but he won't come up after you. Here's what I'd suggest. You go downstairs and apologize. Understand?"

I shook my head.

"Go downstairs. To Jeremy. Tell him you're sorry. Say 'I'm sorry, Jeremy.' A complete sentence. Understand?"

I nodded. It sounded too easy. I should have known there was a catch.

I followed Antonio downstairs, found Jeremy in the study, walked up to him and said, "I'm sorry, Jeremy." He nodded and let me help him wash the coffee off the wall. And so I was forgiven. As easy as that. No lecture. No icy silence. No grudges held. Yet there was something in his eyes that stung worse than all the beatings in the world. Disappointment. No apologies, however heartfelt, could erase that.

The next day, I was in the kitchen with Antonio. He'd shanghaied me on a "special mission." He was baking a cake and swore he needed me. I suspected Jeremy needed a break more than Antonio needed the help.

"Now, you can't tell Jeremy about the cake," Antonio said, bending down and pulling a bowl from the cupboard.

"Why?"

"Because it's a surprise. It's for his birthday."

My blank look made him gasp in mock horror.

"You don't know what a birthday is? It means our Jeremy's getting older. Tomorrow he will be a very ancient twenty-two. Do you know how old you are?"

I shook my head.

"Seven." He lifted seven fingers.

I pointed at him.

"Me? I'm twenty-four. One foot in the grave. Not enough fingers for that." He grinned and poured white powder into the bowl. "Next year, when you turn eight, we'll throw you a party. My boy just turned eight a few months ago. Bet you didn't know that, did you? I've got a son just about your age."

I frowned and looked around. "Where?"

He laughed. "At home, scrap. With his grandfather, where he belongs. I'm a bad influence. Someday soon you'll meet him. He'd like that. I'm sure you will, too."

Personally I doubted it, but I didn't say anything. He handed me an egg and showed me how to crack it into the bowl. I got more shell than egg in the bowl, but Antonio only laughed and handed me another one. This time, I got most of the egg in the bowl and only one sliver of shell.

"Well done, scrap. At least someone in this house will be able to cook."

Antonio continued to chatter. I didn't understand most of what he said. I didn't care. Nothing seemed to faze him. When I knocked over the milk bottle, he laughed and threw down some dish towels. When I snuck a fingerful of batter, he laughed and gave me a spoonful. There was no mistake that couldn't be wiped away with a laugh and a wink. And best of all, he didn't make me speak in full sentences.

When the cake was done, Antonio pronounced it perfect. It looked a little lopsided, but I didn't argue. We hid the cake in the toaster oven. Antonio swore it'd be safe there. He doubted Jeremy knew what a toaster oven was for, much less how to operate it. Most of our meals came straight from the cupboards and refrigerator, cold cuts and fruit, breads and cheese, steaks and vegetables, whatever could be served with a minimum of preparation. Dinners appeared miraculously on our doorstep every day, in a cooler, with instructions for reheating.

After dinner that night, Jeremy said he was going out back to "practice." I was welcome to come out, but forbidden to sneak up on him. Intrigued, I started to follow. Antonio caught me and pulled me aside.

"I'm going out, scrap. Jeremy's birthday present is ready. Want to come?"

"Where?"

"Town. Go. In car. You and me. Yes?"

I shook my head. "Go Jeremy."

"Are you sure? He won't be much fun. He's busy."

"Stay Jeremy."

"All right then. I'll see you when I get back. He's outside. Go through the patio doors. Make sure he hears you coming. Our Jeremy gets pretty wrapped up in his practicing and he might not notice you. Be careful. Understand?"

I nodded.

"Can I get you something from town? Bring something home for you?"

"Food."

Antonio laughed and rumpled my hair. "You're easy to please, scrap. Go see Jeremy then."

I found Jeremy outside shooting pointed sticks. This I accepted as a perfectly fine hobby, much the same as I had the plastic-talking. Jeremy was my god. Whatever he did was good and right.

I'd later learn that this hobby had a name. Archery. Not the sort of thing I saw people doing every day back in Baton Rouge. Not the sort of thing you'd expect a werewolf to do either. Why learn to use a hunting weapon when you came with your own built-in set?

For Jeremy, though, archery had nothing to do with hunting. It was all about control, developing and improving the mental and physical control needed to put an arrow through a target. Of course, I wouldn't know that for years. Right then, it looked like he was shooting sticks at a tiny dot out in the field. Strange, but if it made him happy, then I was happy.

When he saw me watching, he offered to show me how to use the bow. Didn't look like much fun, really, but if it meant spending time with him then, sure, I was game.

Jeremy was repositioning my hands on the bow for the

umpteenth time when a sound came from the house. We both stopped and listened. Somewhere inside, a door closed. Jeremy straightened.

"Antonio's ba—"

He stopped in midword. He turned toward the house. His eyes took on that strangely intense blank look I'd come to recognize, searching but not really looking—or not looking at anything the rest of us could see. Jeremy sensed things and saw things no one else could. At the time, I didn't understand and knew only that he seemed to be all-seeing, coming running whenever I was in danger, which was, after all, only proper behavior for a god.

Whatever he sensed, it made him go rigid, his shoulders squaring, anxiety coming off him in sharp spurts. He took a step backward toward me, as if to shield me. The patio door squawked as it swung open.

"I thought you weren't coming home until next month," Jeremy said.

"That's a fine welcome."

Jeremy's back blocked my view. All I saw of the newcomer was a pair of loafers below tan slacks. The voice definitely wasn't Antonio's, though. A stranger? Coming into our house? Invading our territory? Outrage shot through me and my hackles went up. I sniffed the air, but the newcomer was downwind.

"Welcome back," Jeremy said. His voice was stiff. He stepped back again, keeping me shielded behind him.

"My, my, now I *do* feel welcome," the man said cheerfully. "Of course, an even better welcome would be to return to find you've moved out. Or perhaps had an unfortunate run-in with a local hunter. But that would be too much to hope for, wouldn't it?"

Jeremy said nothing.

"Did I see Tonio's suitcase upstairs?" the man asked.

"Yes."

"He's here? My timing isn't so bad, then. Where is he?"

"Out."

Keeping his back to me, Jeremy picked up the bow and adjusted the string. It was a subtle dismissal, but the man seemed in no hurry to leave.

"Still playing with your toys, I see," the man said.

Jeremy said nothing.

"What exactly is the point?" the man continued. "You don't hunt. You're afraid of everything that moves. But I suppose that bull's-eye is a safe target. You don't have to worry about it attacking you, not like one of those vicious little bunny rabbits. Of course, it could give you a nasty sliver."

Jeremy plucked at the bow string.

"Well, come on then. Let's see you take a shot," the man said.

Jeremy didn't move. The man snorted. I saw his legs move as he turned to leave. Jeremy's back relaxed ever so slightly. Then, in midturn, the man stopped.

"What is that?" he asked.

"What's what?" Jeremy said.

"Behind you."

"Oh. That." Jeremy reached back for my shoulder and pulled me out a few inches, still shielding me. "This is Clayton."

He propelled me out a bit farther, keeping his hand on my shoulder. I looked up, my gaze moving from the man's trousers, to his shirt and finally to his face.

"Clayton, this is Malcolm. My father."

It was the werewolf who'd beaten me in Baton Rouge.

Malcolm

If I'd seen this man again in Baton Rouge, I would have turned tail and run. But things had changed. I was no longer a frightened castaway defending a speck of territory. I had a protector and I had a home. The outrage that had surged a few minutes ago flared, fueled by something stronger than anger. I looked at this man and felt hate.

I snarled and charged. Jeremy snatched me from behind and yanked me back. I howled, lashing out with all my limbs. In midswing, I realized who I was swinging at and stopped short.

"Don't," Jeremy whispered. "It won't help."

"I see you're teaching him cowardice already."

Malcolm hadn't budged, even as I'd been flying at him. As I met his eyes, I knew why. I was no danger to him. And, if I attacked him, he was fully justified in hitting back. If anything, he was disappointed to have lost the opportunity.

Malcolm turned to Jeremy. "What is he doing here?"

"I brought him here."

"You?" Malcolm laughed. "Not goddamned likely. You're afraid to leave the house. You certainly wouldn't cross the country chasing some brat. This is another scheme you dragged Tonio into, isn't it? I told you about the boy and you got all misty-eyed, and Tonio offered to fetch him for you. A pet for poor Jeremy."

While Malcolm was speaking, Jeremy crouched down in front of me, his back to his father. My heart was still hammering. Jeremy rubbed my shoulder.

"Let's go inside," Jeremy said.

"I'm talking to you," Malcolm said.

"You've upset him. I'm taking him inside."

"You're not taking him anywhere. He's not staying."

"I'm sorry you don't approve."

Jeremy started steering me toward the door. Malcolm stepped in front of us.

"Did you hear me? This is not open for negotiation, boy. You are not keeping that mutt in my house."

"It's not your house."

Jeremy propelled me past him and through the patio door. Just inside, Antonio was leaning against the wall, almost collapsing with silent laughter. He thumped Jeremy on the back.

"I never thought I'd hear you say that," he said. "Congratulations. Now, the next step is to boot him out and change the locks. Need some help?"

Jeremy gave a small shake of his head and kept walking, pushing me in front of him. When we got to the stairs, a sigh rippled the surface of his composure. He turned to Antonio.

"I should have warned Clayton. I kept putting it off and—" He stopped and turned to me. "I'm sorry, Clayton. I can't imagine what you must be thinking."

Antonio rumpled my hair. "Oh, you're fine, aren't you, scrap?"

I'd just discovered that my new sanctuary was the home of the werewolf who had destroyed my last place of refuge. So, no, I shouldn't have been fine. I should have been frightened, even angry. I should have felt betrayed. But I didn't. I was confused, maybe a little apprehensive, but I knew Jeremy would do nothing to hurt me. Whatever was going on here, I was still safe, and that was all that mattered.

Taking my cue from Antonio's tone, I nodded, and threw in a "yes" for good measure. Jeremy didn't look convinced. Antonio grabbed me around the waist and swung me over his shoulder.

"Come on, scrap. I have something in the kitchen that should take your mind off the big bad wolf. Go wait in the study, Jer. We'll be there in a minute."

Without waiting for an answer, Antonio carried me to the kitchen, then put me down on the tabletop and closed the door.

"I suppose that was a bit of a shock. Jeremy wanted to tell you, but we didn't expect Malcolm back for a few weeks." He paused. "Do you understand me?"

I nodded. He opened the oven and took out the birthday cake.

"Malcolm is Jeremy's father. He does live here, but he's hardly ever around. Probably just stopped in for money. God forbid the bastard should earn his own keep. Expects Jeremy to hand over—" Antonio stopped, shook his head and reached for a stack of plates. "With any luck, he'll clear out in a couple of days."

Antonio pulled mugs from the cupboard, then handed me the cake plates.

"Can you manage those?"

I nodded.

He smiled and thumped me on the back. "Good. Don't worry about Malcolm, scrap. Just stay out of his way. He'll curse and threaten but as long as you stick close to Jeremy, he won't hurt you. He doesn't dare. Remember that."

I nodded again and he waved me toward the door.

* * *

Jeremy was in the study. When I entered, he had his back to me and was stirring the fireplace embers. The poker circled slowly, sending up fountains of sparks. He stopped, shoulders tightening as I walked in. He inhaled sharply. Then he relaxed, turned and smiled.

"Happy birthday," I said.

Jeremy's crooked smile widened. "Thank you."

He glanced up and I heard Antonio behind me. As I turned, Antonio kicked the half-closed door open with one foot. The overburdened tray in his hands started to tip. Jeremy lunged to grab it, but Antonio righted it at the last second and waved him back.

"Sit down and relax," Antonio said.

Antonio poured the coffee, adding a half cup of milk to mine and an equal portion of brandy to the other two. I passed out the filled cups and plates, leaving only a small trail of coffee droplets. Before Antonio sat down, he took two brightly colored boxes from the mantel and handed the larger one to Jeremy.

Jeremy took the gift, but made no move to open it. His eyes were unfocused, his mind still elsewhere. Antonio nudged him, then leaned over and whispered something in his ear. Jeremy's gaze flicked to me and he forced a quarter-smile.

"Open," I said.

"Hmmm?"

"He's eager to get to the cake part," Antonio said. "I told him he has to wait until the gifts are opened."

"Ah. I'll get to it then."

Jeremy lifted the box and peeled off the colored paper. Underneath was a hinged wooden box. He undid the tiny latch and lifted the top. His eyes widened. Smiling, he lifted a strangely shaped piece of molded metal and carved wood from the box. Although I didn't recognize it at the time, it was an antique revolver, one of a pair.

"Beautiful," Jeremy murmured, turning it in his hands so the light glinted off the barrel.

"You said you wanted to try handguns," Antonio said.

"I wasn't imagining something quite so fancy. It's only for target practice."

"Do I ever do anything by halves? Besides, I'm hoping you might use it for something more productive." Antonio tossed the smaller box to Jeremy. "See if this gives you any ideas."

Jeremy unwrapped a velvet jeweler's box. When he opened it, he threw his head back and laughed, the sound echoing through the room. I scrambled up and over onto his lap to see what caused such an uncharacteristic outburst. All I saw in the box was a polished metal chunk with scratches on the side.

Behind us, the door opened and a voice said, "Well, I'm glad to see everyone is having such a good time. If I'd known my return would have made you this happy, I'd have stayed away."

"Fuck off, Malcolm," Antonio said. "This is a private party."

Malcolm walked in and closed the door. "And what might we be celebrating?"

"Your son's birthday, which you've obviously forgotten."

"Hardly. I remember every second of the day that slant-eyed bitch whelped him. Much the way one might remember the day one is diagnosed with a terminal illness. Had I known how he would turn out, I'd have put him in a sack and dropped him off the nearest bridge. I should have guessed the outcome, really, right from the moment he was born. Any normal child would come out into the world bawling his lungs out. My brat? He didn't make a peep. Even as a baby he didn't have the balls to complain."

"Cake?" Jeremy said, holding out a piece.

Malcolm ignored him and dropped onto the sofa. Jeremy shrugged and gave me the piece. Antonio rolled his eyes and mouthed something to Jeremy. The corners of Jeremy's mouth flicked in the faintest of smiles, but he kept the rest of his face impassive.

"Did you bring Jeremy a gift?" Antonio asked.

Malcolm snorted and reached for the brandy snifter.

"Want to see what I got him?"

Antonio grabbed the tiny jeweler's box from the table and tossed it to Malcolm. A spark of worry passed behind Jeremy's eyes, but when Malcolm saw what was in the box, he laughed nearly as loudly as his son.

"A silver bullet with my name on it," he said. "One can never accuse you of subtlety, Tonio."

"Regular bullets may work just as well," Antonio said, "but I thought this one might find a special place in your heart."

Malcolm laughed again. "Only if you fired the gun, my boy. That one would never do it. He doesn't have the nerve. You're too good to him. You inherited your father's soft spot for weaklings. Your intentions are admirable, but you should pick more worthy friends."

"Like you? Sorry, Malcolm, but I already have a father. And you already have a son."

Jeremy closed his eyes, the barest wince, fingers tightening around his cake plate as if bracing himself.

"Son?" Malcolm snarled. "That's not a son. It's a punishment. An embarrassment I would have rid myself of twenty-two years ago if my father hadn't—"

"But he did," Jeremy said softly. "And you were stuck with me, as you've reminded me every day since." He got to his feet. "I think someone is getting tired."

He looked at me, but it must have been a mistake, because I was wide awake and absorbing every word.

"Does he have a kennel out back?" Malcolm asked. "Or is he housebroken already?"

"Off you go," Jeremy said, putting one hand behind my back and propelling me to the door.

Antonio closed the door behind us and followed us up the stairs.

Jeremy's bedroom was at the far end of the hall. I'd been sleeping there since I came to Stonehaven. Jeremy had tried setting me up in a room of my own, but I was having none of that. Now that Malcolm was here, it would be a while before he started encouraging me to take a separate room again, which was the only obvious advantage to his father's return.

Jeremy's room was furnished as a place to sleep and nothing more, just a bed, a nightstand and a dresser. The floor was bare wood, no carpet. The walls were unadorned except for a cluster of small framed sketches by the window. All the sketches were portraits, Antonio being the only one I recognized. It would be years before I realized Jeremy was the artist.

I did know that Jeremy drew. He painted, too, though this was rarer. Usually, he just sketched, sometimes not even pictures, just symbols. He'd be working and he'd get this faraway look in his eyes and when I looked at the page, I'd see weird symbols drawn in the margins. When I asked what they were, he'd mumble something about doodling, tear off the page and get back to work. The drawings he let me see, especially the ones of me in wolf form. I liked those.

With the portraits in his room, though, I didn't make the connection to his drawings. When I'd asked about them, he'd only named the people pictured and explained their relationships to one another. It would have never occurred to him to say he'd drawn them.

Antonio walked in behind us and threw himself onto the bed. "Paradise lost. The serpent has returned."

"Get ready for bed, Clayton. Just push Tonio out of the way."

Antonio propped his head up on his arms. "I could help you regain that paradise, Jer. Just say the word and he's—"

"That's enough," Jeremy said, jerking his chin at me. "He doesn't know you're joking."

"Am I? The Pack Laws don't always apply to the beloved youngest son of the Alpha."

I'd spent the last few exchanges standing there with my shirt pulled up around my neck, listening. Jeremy tugged my shirt off and lifted me onto the bed. He shoved Antonio to the side, folded back the covers and motioned me inside.

"All right," Antonio sighed. "Forget the permanent solution. How about just kicking him out? After all, it is your house." He grinned. "I still can't believe you actually said that to him."

Jeremy sat on the edge of the bed and pulled off his socks.

"You shouldn't let him forget that," Antonio continued. "There's a reason Edward passed over Malcolm and left it all to you. Because he knew his son was a psychotic son-of-a-bitch and he hoped you'd toss him out on his ass the moment the will was read."

"I don't think that was quite what my grandfather had in mind."

Jeremy folded our clothing and laid it on the dresser. Then he turned out the light and crawled into bed beside me. Antonio ignored the hint. He stripped off his shirt and pants and thudded back on the bed.

"This bed isn't that big," Jeremy said.

"I wasn't done talking."

"Are you ever?"

"Watch it or I'll take back those revolvers. Now shove over, scrap."

Antonio wriggled under the covers and knocked me with his hip. I held my ground. I'd been here first.

"If you kicked him out, my father would support you."

"Hmmm."

Antonio flipped onto his side. "Don't think you can fool me, Jer. You're not afraid to kick him out; you're just too damned stubborn. It's like the ultimate challenge of willpower. If you can survive Malcolm, you can survive anything."

Jeremy said nothing.

"Don't pretend you've fallen asleep either."

"I'm not pretending anything. You were pontificating so nicely, I hated to interrupt."

"Ha."

Silence fell, punctuated only by heartbeats and slow breathing. I curled up between them. Waves of heat and scent ebbed out from either side of me. As I closed my eyes, the anxiety of the last few hours washed away. After a while, the bed creaked and I sensed Jeremy looking down at me.

"He's asleep," Antonio said.

"Hmmm."

"What's wrong?"

"I was just thinking." A pause. "Perhaps I haven't done the best thing for him. Bringing him here. Into this."

"You know, I was thinking the same thing myself—what a monster Jeremy is, snatching this poor kid from that swamp, hauling him across the country and forcing him to endure some semblance of a normal life. I mean, the boy is absolutely miserable here. Anyone could see that."

"You don't need to be sarcastic."

"And you don't need to be stupid. If you didn't rescue Clayton, he'd have been dead within the year, and I don't mean by natural causes. The whole Pack heard Malcolm's story. How long do you think it'd be before someone decided it was too risky, having a child werewolf running around Louisiana? No one else would think of rescuing him. Not even me. You're different."

"So I've been told," Jeremy murmured.

"You did the right thing, Jer. End of discussion."

Silence. I was starting to drift off when Antonio started up again.

"You don't need to worry about him, you know."

"End of discussion?"

"End of your discussion, not mine. Malcolm has too much to risk by hurting him. He knows you wouldn't stand for it, and he wouldn't find sympathy anywhere else. My father won't put up with that shit. He keeps Malcolm around because he's useful, but he's not useful enough to earn his keep."

Jeremy paused, then spoke, his voice barely audible. "If ever I wanted to throw him out, it would be now. But I can't risk retaliation."

"I know. He'd go after the boy. I'll shut up about it."

"Careful. I wouldn't want you hurting yourself."

Something shot over my head. I peeked to see a pillow sail clear over the bed and land with a soft *whump* on the floor.

"You need to work on your aim."

"It was just a warning shot."

"Ah."

Jeremy rolled over. I waited until I was certain I wouldn't be missing anything, then let myself fall asleep.

It would be years before I figured out the terms of Edward Danvers's will. The simple version is that Jeremy's grandfather left everything to him. I've heard that before Jeremy's birth, Edward had bequeathed his property to the Sorrentinos. One could say that he was only taking care of his son—knowing he'd burn through the money and mortgage the property, and instead ensuring he'd have a slow but steady income throughout his life. More likely, it was life insurance. Will everything to Malcolm and Edward would be signing his death warrant.

When he changed the beneficiary to Jeremy, he protected his grandson with a similar clause—on Jeremy's death, if he was under thirty-five and had no children, the estate would be auctioned off to charity . . . and a letter would go to the current Alpha, listing details of murders Malcolm had committed that he couldn't defend under Pack Law.

The understanding, as with the original will, was that Malcolm could continue to use the house and receive a stipend. Maybe Edward was only thinking of protecting his grandson and his legacy. Maybe he even hoped that rather than be indebted to Jeremy for his living, Malcolm would actually get a job. If so, he hadn't understood his son very well.

As much as Malcolm complained about needing to go to Jeremy for money, I think he took a perverse pleasure in it. While he was off traveling the world, Jeremy was stuck home managing the estate. While Malcolm was at Stonehaven laying about the house, reading magazines and watching television, Jeremy was working long hours and agonizing over accounts, trying to keep the creditors at bay.

Jeremy could have kicked Malcolm out. There was no stipulation in the will forbidding it. But to do so meant relinquishing the only control he had over his father's behavior. Rid himself of the monster, and he'd only unleash him on the world. That was something Jeremy would never do.

The next day, the three of us were in the backyard, and had been for most of the afternoon, namely because Malcolm was indoors.

Antonio and Jeremy were wrestling. At first, Antonio thought it would be fun to teach me a few moves, but after a flip sent me skidding to the ground with a bloody nose, I was relegated to spectator status.

Personally, I would have continued playing, but when Jeremy hoisted me off the ground and set me on the stone wall, I knew I'd better stay there. Watching wasn't so bad. It was an interesting study of maneuvers and strategies, possibly transferable to more important things, like hunting.

Antonio had the clear advantage of weight and muscle, but he pinned Jeremy less than half the time. He'd thunder and charge, and Jeremy would just dart out of the way, often slipping around behind him and taking advantage of the momentum of Antonio's charge to knock him face first to the ground. Soon Antonio had a bloody nose to match mine, but no one suggested *he* stop playing.

Jeremy didn't always get out of the way in time. Once, when he was a split second too slow and Antonio had him flat on his back, the phone started to ring. Now, the phone was over a hundred feet away and inside the house, but all three of us heard it. Even in human form, we share a wolf's keener senses of smell and hearing.

"Will he answer it?" Antonio asked, taking his knee off Jeremy's chest.

"Only if he's expecting a call."

"Are you?"

"No." The phone continued to ring. "It's probably for you."

Antonio grunted, grabbed his shirt from a nearby bush and wiped the streaming sweat from his face. He looked toward the house, hesitated, then headed for the back door. Jeremy sat up in the grass and rotated his shoulders, wincing as something cracked.

"Hop down, Clayton, and I'll show you some moves."

We played for a few minutes before Antonio came back, walking out of the house even slower than he'd walked in.

"Trouble at home?" Jeremy said.

Antonio muttered something and dropped onto the grass. "A meeting in Chicago. My father can't make it. Something's happened at the factory and he's stuck in New York."

"When do you leave?"

"Tonight. Damn. I hate responsibility."

Jeremy smiled. "You're good at it. Better than anyone expected."

Antonio snorted and broke an icy twig off a tree. He pretended to study it. "My father thinks you should stay in New York with him for a while. You and Clayton."

"No."

"Don't be—"

"I appreciate the concern, but Clayton's not ready for that yet, the new surroundings, the new people. We'll be fine here."

Antonio threw down the stick. "You have to introduce him to the Pack eventually. Why not now?"

"I don't want to rush him."

"You're stubborn."

"No, I'm realistic."

"Stubborn."

"Up you get, Clayton," Jeremy said, lifting me under the armpits. "It's getting cold and I imagine you're hungry."

Antonio muttered something under his breath, but followed us into the house in silence, probably afraid Jeremy would withhold the food if he continued arguing.

Campaign

That night, after Antonio left, Jeremy and I were in the study, where we spent most of our evenings. I lay on the carpet before the fire, eyes half closed, content to doze and daydream. Jeremy was poring over some ragged book that stank of time and poor storage. On top of the book he kept a notepad, and wrote in it as he read, his eyes never leaving the page.

I know now that Jeremy was working, though at the time I just thought he spent a lot of time reading. To be honest, I wasn't even clear on the reading part, not remembering having seen anyone in my family partake of that pastime. Now I realize that much of that reading time was actually work. Jeremy made his living translating, mainly for academics. It wasn't going to make him rich anytime soon, but it kept the bills paid, and it was something he could do from home, which suited him better than any office job.

We'd been in the study for about an hour when the door swung open. I smelled Malcolm and kept my eyes shut, hoping he'd see we were both very busy and go away.

"Christ," Malcolm said, footsteps thudding into the room. "He's like a goddamned puppy, curled up at his master's feet."

I lifted one eyelid just in time to see Malcolm take a swipe at me with his foot. His aim went wide, coming nowhere near me, but I growled to let him know I'd seen.

"Don't growl at me, you little—"

"Then don't antagonize him," Jeremy said, still reading. "Leave him alone, and he'll leave you alone."

"He'd damned well better leave me—"

"What did you want?"

"I need money."

Jeremy's expression didn't change. Nor did he glance up from his book. "I've had some unexpected expenses with Clayton. I can spare a few hundred now, but if you'll be gone for a while, I can wire you more when I get paid."

"I'm not going anywhere."

At that, Jeremy stopped reading. The barest reaction flitted across his face, but vanished before Malcolm could seize on it.

"I see," Jeremy said slowly, laying his book on the side table. "What happened this time?"

"Don't take that tone with me."

"I wasn't taking any tone. If there's another . . . problem, I need to know about it, don't I?"

Malcolm thumped onto the couch, sprawling across it, a clear invasion of our territory. I squelched a growl, and settled for inching closer to Jeremy.

"Just a dispute with a mutt," Malcolm said. "A disagreement over a lady. Not that I'd expect you to know anything about that. You'd have to leave the house to get—"

"You do more than enough for the two of us."

Jeremy pulled out his wallet, took some bills and handed them to Malcolm.

"Eighty bucks?" Malcolm said. "How the hell am I supposed to live—?"

"That's all I have. If you're staying, then you don't need more.

Things are tight this month. I'll be lucky if I can pay the electric bill."

"The trials and tribulations of home ownership."

Malcolm slid a crocodile grin Jeremy's way, then stuffed the money into his pocket and left.

So we were stuck with Malcolm.

Long before I'd arrived at Stonehaven, Malcolm and Jeremy had perfected the art of living together without actually living together. Despite what I'd thought on my first day, Stonehaven was no mansion, but it was a roomy five-bedroom house, just big enough that two people could pass their days without spending more than a minute or two in the same room.

Most times, Malcolm ignored us. Several times a day, though, he'd corner Jeremy with some petty complaint or slam him with a sarcastic put-down. With Malcolm there, Jeremy was always wary, stiffening at the sound of a footstep, lowering his voice, scuttling me off to another room when Malcolm approached.

The cure for Jeremy's discomfort seemed obvious enough. We had to get rid of Malcolm. Foolishly simple ... or so it appeared to me. As Antonio had said, the house belonged to Jeremy. I understood little of what went on between Malcolm and Jeremy, but the concept of territory was hardwired in my wolf's brain. This was Jeremy's territory, and if Malcolm made Jeremy miserable, then he had to go. Foolishly simple.

By getting rid of him, I don't mean killing him. However dangerous I liked to imagine myself, I knew I stood no chance against Malcolm. For now, I'd have to settle for getting him out of the house. To do that, I needed to understand him. The wolf in me knew this, and told me how to do it. To understand your adversary, you watched him. You studied him. You stalked him.

*   *   *

My first opportunity came a few days after Antonio left. Jeremy was out back practicing with his new revolvers. Usually, I was content—if not downright happy—to sit and watch whatever he was doing. Today, though, I had a more important mission, so I left Jeremy in the courtyard and slipped into the house to find Malcolm.

Malcolm was watching television in the back nook, a room Jeremy and I rarely entered. Though I vaguely recalled the delights of cartoons, sitting in front of a television no longer held any appeal for me, probably because it held no appeal for Jeremy, and he was the yardstick by which I now measured the attractiveness of any activity.

For nearly an hour, I peered around the doorway and watched Malcolm watch TV. Finally the show ended. Malcolm turned off the TV. I darted into the hall closet and waited until he started down the hall, then slid out and followed. Several times he paused and seemed ready to turn, but only shook his head and kept walking.

On to the kitchen. When he wasn't looking, I ducked inside and crouched beside the counter. Malcolm fixed himself a sandwich. Though I failed to see the importance of his selection of cold cuts, my brain told me it was critical information. Finally, he finished making his sandwich, poured a glass of milk and headed for the dining room. I scurried after him, then watched from the doorway.

Malcolm sat down. He took two bites. Then he turned fast and caught me watching. I raced for the back door.

"Jeremy!" Malcolm shouted.

*   *   *

"He's following me," Malcolm said before Jeremy got through the back door.

Jeremy unzipped his jacket and wiped a line of sweat from his forehead.

"Who?" he asked.

"Who? How many people live in this house?"

"Clayton? Where——?" Jeremy looked around and frowned, then saw me hovering behind him. His gaze swiveled to Malcolm. "What did you do to him?"

"Do? I didn't do anything. He's been following me around for the last hour, watching me."

"Of course. He's a child. He's curious."

"Curious, my ass. He's stalking me."

"Stalking?" Jeremy's lips twitched. He coughed and rubbed a hand over his mouth, erasing all signs of a smile. "He's a little boy, Malcolm, not an animal. He's playing a game with you. Spying. All children do it. If you ignore him, he'll tire of it soon enough."

Before Jeremy could lead me away, I snuck one last glance at Malcolm. He returned a glare. In that glare, I saw my victory. My stalking had unsettled him. Jeremy hadn't forbidden it, which meant I was free to do it as often as I liked.

This was going to be easier than I thought.

In stalking Malcolm, my only goal had been to gather information, but I quickly learned that the very act drove him crazy. Within days, all I had to do was slip past a room and he'd be on his feet, storming into the hall to glower at me. And all he did was glower. Never said a word, never raised a hand, never again complained to Jeremy.

Once I learned how much he hated being stalked, I stopped

making any attempt to hide my efforts. If he was watching TV, I'd walk right into the room, sit down and stare at him. He'd scowl at me and try to sit it out, but I outlasted him every time.

In Malcolm's refusal to challenge me, I read cowardice. Yes, he'd terrorized me in the bayou, but this was Jeremy's territory, and here, Malcolm didn't dare touch me, which made me decide that in our little pack, Malcolm's status was no higher than my own. If anything, it was lower because I enjoyed Jeremy's personal protection.

I wondered, then, if Malcolm was so powerless, why hadn't Jeremy kicked him out years ago? But the very thought felt like betrayal, so I swept it from my mind. Had I been older, I would have realized there must be more to it. Yet at the time, I was too pleased with my success to question it.

After two weeks of being stalked, Malcolm showed the first sign of cracking. One day, when Malcolm retreated to the back nook to read, I followed, perched on the chair across from his and stared at him. Just stared. After ten minutes, Malcolm threw down the magazine, shot a single scowl my way and stormed from the room. He gathered his jacket, wallet and keys, then shouted to Jeremy not to lock up, and stalked out the door.

I had him on the run.

Now all I needed to do was give him a reason to keep running... and not come back.

Again, my wolf's instincts blessed me with a centuries-old plan for handling this next step of the fight. To keep an enemy running, one had to give him a reason to believe that staying would be bad for his health.

I knew I stood no chance in a fight against any grown werewolf. In a fair fight, that is. But what about an unfair fight?

Strategy, that was the key. The world of the wolf is heavily de-
pendent on might and muscle, but there's plenty of wiggle room
for a beast with brains.

I didn't need to hurt Malcolm. I only had to make him think I
could. And the only way a pup could take on a seasoned fighter
many times his age was to catch him off guard. Attack when he is
most vulnerable.

When are we most vulnerable? When we're asleep.

Two nights after I first scared Malcolm out of the house, I decided to act. I had a plan in mind. I'm not sure how I came upon
it, but most likely had dredged it up from a half-remembered
movie or television show. Whatever the plan's origin, I was certain it would work.

I didn't sleep that night. I kept myself awake by fantasizing
about life post-Malcolm. About how happy Jeremy would be,
and how happy that would make me.

When Jeremy came to bed, I feigned sleep. Then I waited and
listened for Malcolm's return. Finally his footfalls thumped
down the hall. His door slammed. Jeremy started awake, mumbled something and fell back onto the pillow. I listened to his
breathing. It took awhile for him to return to sleep. It always did.

By the time Jeremy fell asleep, Malcolm's distant snoring signaled that he'd done the same. I reached between the mattress
and bedspring and removed the prize I'd secreted there earlier in
the day. Then I slid from the bed.

It took a long time for me to get out of the bedroom, moving
as slowly as I could, so I wouldn't wake Jeremy. I scampered
barefoot down the hall to Malcolm's room, eased open his door
and peered through the crack. Malcolm was on the bed, his back
to me. I pushed open the door and looked around.

Unlike Jeremy's room, Malcolm's had stuff. Lots of stuff, all in a jumble that smacked of carelessness more than untidiness. Clothing hung on the chair back and piled on the seat. Dual dressers, both covered in toiletries, cuff links, watches, paperback novels. Where Jeremy's only decorations were pictures of his friends, Malcolm didn't have so much as a photograph on his nightstand. Everything was his: his acquisitions, his hobbies, his life.

I dropped to all fours, crawled forward and peeked over the bedside. Malcolm still faced the other way. I considered my options. Over the bed or around it? Having grown accustomed to Jeremy's fitful sleep habits, I knew the danger of crawling onto the mattress. Better to take the longer route around the bed.

When I was on the other side, I lowered myself to my belly and inched along the hardwood floor. A board sighed. I froze. Malcolm's snoring continued, undisturbed. I crept to the front legs of the bed. My fingers tightened around my prize. A steak knife. I'd considered one of the carving knives, but decided it would be too awkward to carry, and too easily missed.

I eased my head over the mattress edge. A warm puff of Malcolm's breath tickled my face. I watched his eyelids, tensed for any sign of movement. Then I lifted the knife and laid it on the pillow, so it would be the first thing he saw when he awoke.

Message delivered. Time to retreat.

I waited all the next morning for Malcolm to wake. A bloodcurdling scream would be nice, but I'd settle for a good shout of surprise.

Shortly before lunch, Malcolm came downstairs. He passed the open study door without so much as a glare in my direction and headed to the kitchen. He fixed himself breakfast and took it into the dining room.

Had the knife fallen off the bed? In rising, Malcolm could have shifted the pillow, causing the knife to slide to the floor undetected. How else to explain this complete lack of shock and terror?

After lunch, Jeremy retreated to the study again. Once he was enrapt in his work, I sneaked out and followed the sound of the television to the back nook. The door was open. I peered through. The TV was on and the recliner was turned toward it, facing away from the door. I slipped inside.

I tiptoed toward the chair. When I'd made it halfway across the room, the door clicked shut behind me. I whirled to see Malcolm standing in front of the closed door. I backpedaled, eyes darting about for a second exit.

"Relax, brat," Malcolm said. "I'm not going to touch you. I'm just playing a game." He smiled and tossed the steak knife onto the side table. "You like games, don't you?"

I backed up until I hit the wall. Malcolm stayed in front of the door.

"I bet I can guess the name of your favorite game," he said. "Let's see ... Is it: 'Get Rid of Jeremy's Old Man'?"

I said nothing, just stayed pressed against the wall, watching his body language for signs of impending attack.

"Lots of fun, I bet," Malcolm said. "It's pretty close to a new game of my own. Do you know what mine's called?"

I didn't move.

"'Get Rid of Jeremy's Little Beast.' It's still in the planning stages, but I'm quite looking forward to playing."

He sauntered to the recliner. I lunged toward the door, but he was in my path before I got halfway there. In the distance I heard a clatter, as if Jeremy's sixth sense had told him something wrong, and he'd leapt up, his work falling to the floor.

"Want go," I said, then cleared my throat and pulled myself to my full height. "I want to go."

"Oh, don't worry. You will. In . . ." Malcolm glanced at his watch. "Today's Monday . . . so let's say by Wednesday night, you'll have your wish. You'll be gone." He grinned. "Unless you can get rid of me first. But it'll take more than a steak knife to do that."

He picked up the knife. My gaze flew to it. Jeremy's footsteps thundered down the hall.

"Oh, don't worry, brat," Malcolm whispered. "I won't hurt you. Won't lay a finger on you. That would suck all the challenge out of it. No, I know a better way. Rid myself of a growing inconvenience and get a little payback in the bargain. Teach my son a lesson about the danger of picking up strays."

Malcolm tucked the knife into his pocket and sauntered out, as Jeremy raced in.

I didn't tell Jeremy anything. He knew something had happened, but seemed only able to sense a general danger, with no specifics. He pressed, but when I insisted I was okay, he took me back into the study and told me to stay with him.

As he worked, I took my spot on the rug and set about working on a revised plan of attack. I considered Malcolm's threat, and dismissed it. He hadn't even dared box my ears for the knife incident. I understood enough of his babble to know he wanted me out of the house, but I wasn't concerned. He admitted he couldn't touch me. So how could he hurt me?

What I forgot, though, was that it wasn't me Malcolm wanted to hurt. I was nothing to him. Nothing but a new tool in a campaign he'd been waging for years.

Territorial

Though our days at Stonehaven may have seemed unstructured, there was a schedule at work. Jeremy liked order; therefore, Jeremy liked schedules. Mornings he devoted to me—teaching, playing or more often, a combination of the two. After lunch, he squeezed in a couple of hours of work while I napped, then came a walk, snack time and the dreaded daily speech lesson. Once my lesson was done, he took an hour of much-needed personal time, reading or doing target practice or sketching. Next came dinner, followed by a walk or a game, another snack, then back to work while I dozed by the fire.

On Tuesday and Friday nights, Jeremy went for a run. Although he often Changed when I did, he spent that time playing with me rather than running or hunting. Adult werewolves need more. A Pack wolf knows that he must Change at least once a week and run off that excess energy, adrenaline and aggression. Otherwise, he risks a spontaneous Change, likely at a very inconvenient moment.

So the day after my knife-scheme failure, Jeremy went for his run, as he did every Tuesday. Leaving me alone was relatively safe. I was in more danger of emptying the refrigerator than sticking something in an electrical socket. As for Malcolm, he always left around dinnertime, and never returned until near morning, so Jeremy assumed I faced no danger from that quarter. Yet, as it turned out, I wasn't the only one who paid attention to Jeremy's schedule.

That night, Jeremy left me with a plate of cold cuts and a *National Geographic*. The pictures in the magazine fascinated me—not the photos of humans, but the ones of wilderness and wildlife. I was studying a spread on lions hunting gazelle when the side door to the garage opened. Knowing it had to be Malcolm, I growled and got up to close the study door. Then I smelled something that made me stop. There was a human in the house.

No werewolf likes having strangers in his house. It's a territorial thing. They learn to tolerate the occasional repair or delivery person, but most will go out of their way to avoid having a stranger step through their front door—like Jeremy having our groceries and dinners left in a cooler on the doorstep, claiming convenience for the deliverer.

Yet, while it only made them uncomfortable, it drove me crazy—synapses deep in my brain went wild when they scented a stranger on our property. We'd discovered this last week, when a woman selling cosmetics had rung our bell and Malcolm let her in, which had more to do with her youth and attractiveness than a sudden interest in lipstick.

What happened next was as much her fault as his. Jeremy and I happened to be at the other end of the hall when Malcolm invited her inside. When she stepped in, I snarled. When she screamed, I pounced. If she hadn't screamed, I would have backed down and retreated to a safer part of the house. But a scream shows fear, and fear shows weakness, and weakness showed that I had the upper hand. So, recognizing my advantage, I acted accordingly. Luckily, Jeremy was right behind me, and managed to grab me in midsprint and hustle me upstairs.

This time, when I smelled the stranger in the house, I jumped to the obvious conclusion. Someone had broken in. With Jeremy gone, it was up to me to defend our territory. I swung into the hall, prepared to do battle. Then I heard familiar clomping footsteps.

"Whoops," a female voice giggled. "Is there a light switch?"

"To your left, my dear."

Malcolm. I stepped back into the study and closed the door, not so much locking him out as barricading myself in. After the Avon-lady fiasco, Jeremy had explained the concept of "invited guest," and my brain understood it even if my body didn't. Although I had little control over my instincts, I was learning to thwart them in small ways.

As far as I was concerned, Malcolm had no right to invite anyone into Jeremy's house, and doing so was a serious insult, but I'd cause Jeremy trouble if I interfered. Better to stay locked in this room until Jeremy returned to deal with the matter.

"The estate has been in the family since the eighteenth century," Malcolm was saying. "The current house was built in 1894."

"Wow, that's old. That's back in pioneer days, isn't it?"

Malcolm chuckled. "Close enough."

The footsteps drew closer. I rapped my knuckles against my thighs, eyes clenched, willing them to move on.

"That is the formal dining room," Malcolm said. "The parlor is beyond that."

"Parlor? Like in England?"

"That's right. Now, over here..."

The footsteps paused outside the study door. I watched the doorknob twist one way, then the other. I jammed my foot against the door base and put all my weight against it.

"Appears to be jammed," Malcolm murmured.

"That's okay. Show me—"

"One moment, my dear. I'll get this."

He knew I was there. He couldn't help but smell me. He knew how I'd react to confronting a stranger in the house. And he forced open the door.

I tried to dart past him, but he grabbed my shoulder, fingers digging to the bone. With his other hand, he tugged the woman into the room. I don't remember what she looked like; I never looked. She was human and she was a stranger, and that was all I needed to know.

"Oh!" she said as she saw me. She waggled her finger at Malcolm. "Did you forget to tell me something?"

"He's not mine. He's visiting. A very short visit."

Malcolm propelled me forward, pushing me within inches of the woman. I dug my heels into the Oriental carpet and closed my eyes.

"Say hello, boy."

I kept my eyes screwed shut, concentrating on inhaling and exhaling without smelling the intruder. Mentally, I screamed for Jeremy, but outwardly made not a sound, not daring to provoke Malcolm.

"Say hello, boy." Malcolm's fingers dug deeper into my shoulder.

"Oh, leave the poor kid alone."

She leaned down, bringing her face so close I could smell the beer on her breath. I opened my eyes and tried to step backward, but I hit the solid wall of Malcolm's legs.

"What a little cutie," she said. "Are you shy, hon?"

She reached out and touched my cheek. I growled and

knocked her hand away. She stumbled back, catching herself on the bookcase. Malcolm laughed.

"That's not funny," she said, straightening up and brushing off her miniskirt as if I'd soiled it. "You should have warned me he was a retard."

"Oh, but he isn't. Quite intelligent, actually . . . in a feral way. I suppose you could call him simple, though. A very uncomplicated set of values with clearly defined likes and dislikes. You happen to be one of those dislikes."

The woman blinked, then made another show of smacking imaginary dust from her skirt.

"You can take me home now," she said without looking up.

"May I? You're too kind. But I brought you here to teach the boy a lesson and we've barely begun."

She sniffed. "You can teach the brat manners after I'm gone."

"Hardly possible, my dear. You are the lesson. A hunting lesson." His index finger stroked my shoulder, grip still tight. "You see, the boy likes to stalk. To hunt. A born predator. Given his size, he hasn't had much experience with the killing part yet, but I hate to limit such intriguing potential."

"I—I don't think that's funny. I'm going to hitch a ride home."

She tried to walk past us to the door, but Malcolm grabbed her arm with his free hand. She gasped and her eyes widened.

"Does that hurt? I'm barely squeezing."

His biceps twitched, werewolf strength kicking in. The woman yelped and yanked back. Malcolm released her arm, letting her crash to the floor. Then he pulled me forward.

"Go ahead, boy. Kill her."

I closed my eyes and willed my feet into lead weights.

"Come now. None of that. She won't hurt you. She's a woman, and a weak one at that. You're already stronger than she is. I won't let her escape. It's an easy kill."

"Not hungry."

Malcolm threw his head back and laughed. "Did you hear that, my dear? He's not hungry. No troubling moral barriers there."

"Th—this isn't funny."

Fear seeped into the woman's voice, draining any confidence from the words. Holding the chair, she slowly rose to her feet, eyes locked on Malcolm. He waited until she was up, then shot out his leg and hooked hers. She crashed to the floor.

"See how easy that is, boy?"

The woman started to crawl toward the door. Malcolm pushed me toward her.

"Yes, I know you're not hungry, but this is a lesson, for when you *are* hungry. Now—"

"No," I said.

The woman was at the door. Malcolm reached down, grabbed her by the hair and threw her across the room. She lay still, then her shoulders convulsed in a sob. She curled up on the rug and made mewling noises.

"Want to go," I said, straining against Malcolm's grip.

"You're not afraid, are you? If you need help—"

"No kill humans. Jeremy say no."

It was the wrong answer. Malcolm flung me into the center of the room. I caught myself before I fell and lifted my arms to ward him off. When I turned toward him, though, he was leaning against the door.

"Jeremy's not here, is he?" His voice was calm, the fake camaraderie back in place. "Even if he was, he'd have to agree. The girl must die. We can hardly let her go. She's seen you. She knows about you. A shame, really, but—" He shrugged. "—what must be done, must be done. If you'd prefer, we could wait for him to get back. Of course, I'd have to tell him what you did."

"Did nothing."

"You let her see what you are."

"I—I didn't see anything," the woman snuffled from the corner.

Malcolm smiled. "Of course you did. A shame, but one easily remedied."

The woman pulled herself to her elbows. "No, it's true. I didn't see anything. If you let me go—"

"If I let you go, you'll tell what you saw. That the boy is a were-wolf." He paused, smiling at her reaction. "Oh, you didn't know? My mistake. But, now that you do—"

He started advancing on her. She lifted her arms and inched backward.

"I don't know anything. I don't believe you anyway. You're crazy. Just let me go and I'll—"

He grabbed her outstretched arms and snapped the hands back. Two sharp cracks and a piercing screech. The woman fell back, chest heaving, lips moving soundlessly. Malcolm lifted one of her broken wrists. Bone pierced the skin. He filled his hand with blood, then let the woman fall.

"Can you smell this, boy?"

He lifted his hand, letting the blood drip.

"Can you feel this?" His eyes gleamed. He stepped forward and turned the bloody palm toward me. "Can you feel it? Close your eyes and smell it."

I could smell it, the hot coppery scent filling the room. But I felt nothing. Why would I? To me, blood only smelled like food, and I wasn't hungry.

Malcolm closed his fist, then opened it and wiped the blood on my face.

"Do you feel it?"

His voice was hoarse, his eyes glowing. He leaned down to

look into my eyes, gaze searching mine. Then his eyes dimmed with something like disappointment. He strode across the room, grabbed the woman by the back of the neck and swung her toward me. Her lips still moved soundlessly.

I looked in her eyes and I saw the fear of a trapped animal. Malcolm's free hand went around the woman's throat. He started to squeeze. Her eyes went wild and she kicked at him.

I turned and ran to the door. As I touched the handle, I heard the distant sound of running footsteps. I pulled open the door. The woman yelped. There was a crack, louder than the sound of her wrists snapping, then a thud. I walked into the hall.

Jeremy skidded around the corner. His shirt was off, pants undone and feet bare. His eyes were black with dread. As always, he'd known there was trouble. This time, he'd just been too far away—and probably in the wrong form—to help in time.

When he saw me, he stopped. I raced over to him. He put out one hand, as if to pull me closer, but pushed me behind him instead, and held me there, shielding me.

When I peeked around Jeremy, I saw Malcolm standing outside the study door. Malcolm blinked once, a second's worth of confusion passing over his face.

"How did you—?" Malcolm started, then shook off the question. He knew Jeremy sensed things; that's why he'd made sure to do this when Jeremy was on a run. But he never liked to question his son's powers, didn't want specifics. "You're too late. He's already done it. Killed a woman. I brought—"

"No!" I screamed and lunged forward.

Jeremy caught my arm. "I know," he said softly. "I know who did it."

He motioned for me to stay, then walked forward, pushed past his father and stepped into the study. When he came out, there was a look in his eyes I'll never forget, a look that made me swear never to kill a human, if only so I would never be the cause of such a look.

He stood there, caught in the doorway. I thought he was looking at me, then saw the blankness in his eyes. If he was seeing anything at all, it was nothing out here, but something inside his head.

His lips twitched once and he swallowed. Then he snapped back. Ignoring his father, he strode down the hall, gently herding me ahead of him. We walked to the parlor. He motioned for me to sit on the sofa and headed for the telephone.

Cleanup

"What are you doing?" Malcolm hurried into the room, then slowed and tried to saunter.

Jeremy picked up the receiver. Malcolm grabbed it from his hand. Jeremy steered me into the front hall and took our coats from the hall stand.

"Where are you going?" Malcolm said.

"To finish my phone call."

"Who are you calling?"

"You know very well who. Dominic."

"For what?"

"Stock tips," Jeremy spat, then inhaled and met his father's gaze. "You know why. To tell him what you've done."

"To tattle."

"Yes, to tattle."

Jeremy helped me zip up my coat. His fingers were trembling. He shifted sideways to block them from Malcolm's view.

"I've never told Dominic anything you've done," Jeremy said. "He's asked. He suspects you've killed humans, but he needs proof to banish you. I've always refused to give him that proof. It seemed . . . safer."

"Avoid confrontation at all costs. That's my boy. A coward to the very—"

"I told myself I could handle it." Jeremy's voice was as calm and emotionless as if he was reading from a book. "Better for you to be in the Pack, subject to its laws, than living outside it, with nothing to stop you from killing whenever the whim strikes."

Malcolm stepped in front of Jeremy. "I have never killed any human who wasn't a threat to the Pack. That's the Law. If a human threatens us, we can kill him. We're supposed to. I was only following the Law."

"That poor girl in there was no threat until you brought her into this house. You broke the Law even by bringing her here. That's proof enough." He stopped fidgeting with his jacket, pulled himself up to his full height and looked down at Malcolm. "I told myself I could handle it. But it's not just me anymore. I have other responsibilities. Other considerations."

"You mean this stray—"

"Do you think I've forgotten?" Jeremy roared, making me stumble back, shocked. He advanced on his father. "Do you think I forget what you did? Do you think I forget the last time you killed in this house? I was nine years old. You told me it was my fault. Well, it wasn't my fault, and this wasn't his fault, and I swear you are never going to do anything like this again. It ends here."

He took hold of my shoulder and turned us toward the front door. As his fingers grazed the handle, Malcolm's voice cut through the silence.

"I'll leave," he said.

Jeremy paused, then turned slowly.

"You want to protect the brat from me?" Malcolm said. "Fine. I'm not the one he needs protecting from, but have it your way. I'll leave for a few weeks—"

"Ten months."

"I can't—"

"Until the end of the year. I'll give you enough to live on, but I don't want to see you again before Christmas."

"And how's that going to look? Me taking off for nearly a year? The Pack will know something's up if I don't go to the Meets."

"Then they'll know something's up. As for the Meets, come up with an excuse and I'll go along with it."

With that, Jeremy led me upstairs. No parting shot. No final threat. No "be gone before I come down." He had what he wanted. Malcolm was leaving.

Jeremy took me into his room and set me on the bed, then crouched in front of me. For several minutes, he studied my face.

"Are you okay?" he asked finally.

Was I? I wasn't sure. The death of the woman meant little to me. I'd say it meant nothing, but I feel I should leave some opening for interpretation on the matter. To admit that I, as a child, felt nothing at seeing someone die shifts me into the realm of unfeeling monster. So I'll say I felt little.

I knew, even then, that I *should* feel something. I saw it in Jeremy's expression, the expectation that I should be at the very least shaken. But the woman was nothing to me, so how could I mourn her passing? Her death was wrong. Unjust. That I understood. The law of the wild is clear on such matters. You kill to survive—for defense and for food. There's no excuse for anything else. But to feel more for a stranger? It was, and still is, beyond me.

Footsteps sounded in the hall. Jeremy stopped, tensed and swiveled his head to track them. Along the hall. Down the stairs. Slam. Jeremy rocked back on his heels and nodded.

"He's gone." He swiped his bangs back from his face, then met my eyes. "There's something I need to do now. I'm sorry, but it must be done right away. I'll make sure he's gone and I'll be close enough to hear him if he comes back. Can you wait here?"

"Go?" I tried again. "Go with you?"

He went very still, then squeezed my hand. "No, Clayton. I'm sorry. I don't want to leave you right now, but—"

"I am okay."

He blinked, as if startled, then he hugged me, a spontaneous two-second hug, broken off quickly and hidden under the guise of an awkward back pat.

"You're a good boy, Clayton," he whispered as he drew back. "I'm sorry ... I'll be back as quick as I can and we'll talk. All right?"

"I am okay."

A twist of a smile, and he was gone.

Just enough time passed for me to wonder whether I should go after Jeremy, make sure Malcolm hadn't come back and hurt him. Then I heard the bathroom taps running full tilt, water thundering into the basin and down the ancient pipes.

I crept to the hall bathroom and inhaled. Jeremy. Good. I turned the doorknob. With the sink water running, I knew Jeremy wasn't doing anything private but, the truth is, I would have opened the door anyway. In the transformation from human to werewolf, some learned behaviors slid free from my brain. Some, like the proper use of a telephone, I recovered. Others, like the concept of privacy, never returned. Undressing, bathing, urinating, defecating, it was all a normal part of life. You weren't doing anything wrong, so why did you need to hide to do it?

I pushed open the door. Jeremy was hunched over the sink, his back to me. At first, I thought he was throwing up, having had some experience with this myself only a week ago, after I mistook a carton of cream for milk. I inhaled, but didn't detect the sour taint of vomit.

Jeremy's shirt lay in a heap on the floor. I stared at it, scrunched up in a ball, nowhere near the laundry basket.

"Jeremy?"

The rush of water drowned me out. Jeremy leaned down until his face was nearly in the bowl. When he shifted, the light caught the sweat on his back, the rivulets cutting through a fine dusting of dirt. He splashed water on his face. Then he turned off the taps and braced his forehead against the mirror.

Even now, I have to remind myself how young Jeremy was when he found me. He never acted young, never did the sorts of things you'd expect a young man to do. He couldn't. Long before I'd arrived, he'd had to take on adult responsibility, getting a job, running a household, looking after his father. Looking back on that moment in the bathroom, I can see how young he was. Young and tired and confused, not yet confident enough to be sure he was doing the right thing, but trying so hard to do it.

I wish I could have done something, said something, to make him feel better. But when I looked at him then, I saw only my savior, my protector. An adult, with no needs or fears of his own. Standing in that bathroom doorway, staring down at that discarded shirt, I saw only a sign that the world was off-balance, and wanted only to right it again, to get *my* Jeremy back.

"I am sorry," I said.

He turned, saw me and rubbed his hands over his face, finger-combing his hair in the same motion. Then he dropped to one knee before me, took hold of my shoulders and looked into my eyes.

"You didn't do anything wrong, Clayton. Absolutely nothing."

"Get rid—" I stopped and restarted. "I try get rid of him. Scare him. He not like. Say he get rid of me. Want me kill her. Make you mad."

Jeremy took a moment to assimilate this, then sighed, dropping his head forward. "So that was his plan. I thought—" He shook his head. "It doesn't matter. You had absolutely nothing to do with what happened tonight. It wasn't your fault. Do you understand that?"

I nodded.

"What he did, Clayton, was wrong. Killing that woman was wrong. You understand that, too, don't you?"

"No kill humans. You say that. I remember."

"Good. That's a good boy. I'm sorry you had to ... to see that. It was wrong. Very, very wrong. I should have been there. I shouldn't have left you alone. I should have known he'd—" Another shake of the head. "I should have made sure from the start that he never got that chance. He's gone now, Clayton. Do you understand that?"

I nodded.

"Gone for a long time," Jeremy said, pushing himself to his feet.

"Will come back."

"That's for me to worry about, not you. It'll be a long time before he comes back and, when he does, I'll work something out. You don't need to worry about him. I'll make sure of that."

I looked up into Jeremy's eyes, and I knew, if I hadn't before, that what happened tonight had nothing to do with me, and everything to do with him, with hurting him. As he vowed that I wouldn't need to worry about Malcolm, I made a vow of my own. Someday, *he'd* never need to worry about Malcolm again. I'd make sure of it.

Dominance

Spring deepened into summer and Malcolm stayed away. Weeks passed like a leaf floating downstream, unconcerned with progress or destination. I gave in to the equally gentle but unrelenting force of Jeremy's will, and learned to speak properly and behave with passable normality in public.

I didn't need to worry about public behavior very often. Jeremy rarely went out. Everything we needed was here—food and shelter, companionship, land to run on and endless diversions of our own devising. Food was delivered. Banking and legal affairs were conducted by telephone and mail. Jeremy's work also came and went by the mail. Antonio drove up from New York City every few weeks to visit. We had no reason to leave.

Over that spring, Jeremy taught me more than just language and manners. I learned to shoot an arrow within ten feet of the target, to swim in the back pond, to read the Sunday comics (even if I didn't understand the humor) and to sneak up on a rabbit (even if I couldn't catch it). An idyllic spring, which gave way to an equally idyllic summer. Then I went and screwed it up.

*　　*　　*

Jeremy and I were in the backyard replacing a section of stone wall that had crumbled over the winter. Actually, Jeremy wasn't so much fixing it *with* me as in spite of me. I'd already knocked two stones out of the fresh mortar, one of which had landed on Jeremy's foot. But I wanted to help, and enthusiasm always overruled ability with Jeremy. He wouldn't discourage me even if it meant wasting half the day and breaking a few toes.

"Pull it back," Jeremy said as I put a stone in place. "Not so much. A bit more. Now toward me. Perfect."

It wasn't perfect, but I knew that once I turned my head, it would miraculously find its way to the right spot. I bent to lift the next stone.

"Hello?" a voice shouted from the back of the house.

I dropped the stone. Jeremy yanked his foot out of the way, then straightened and brushed his bangs back from his face, mortar streaking his black hair with gray.

"There you are." Antonio strode around the back wall. He skirted Jeremy and rumpled my hair. "You aren't getting any bigger, scrap. Isn't Jeremy feeding you enough? It's past noon and I didn't see anything on the table."

"We weren't expecting you," Jeremy said.

"So you don't eat when you're not expecting company?" Antonio grinned, but avoided Jeremy's eyes. "Are you hungry, scrap?"

I looked up at Jeremy. He was watching Antonio, his eyes narrowed ever so slightly. I recognized the look. It was the same one I got when he caught me sneaking back to my new bedroom late at night, smelling faintly of cold roast beef.

"So, you just happened to be in the neighborhood, thought you'd pop by for lunch?"

"What? I can't make a surprise visit?"

Jeremy didn't answer. He scraped the trowel off in the bucket, then laid it on the wall. "I suppose we should go in for lunch."

"Before we do, I—"

The creaking of the distant back door cut Antonio off. I tensed, inhaled and caught the scent of a stranger. The hairs on the back of my neck rose.

"Dad?" a voice called.

"Just a sec, Nicky," Antonio called back.

"I thought we agreed to wait."

Jeremy's voice was low, his tone even and calm. I shivered in spite of the warm sun. I recognized this, too—the voice I got when Jeremy went downstairs the next morning to discover that not only was the roast gone, but the fridge had been left open and the milk was spoiled.

"It's been four months, Jer," Antonio said. "Stop fretting about it."

He clapped Jeremy on the back. When Jeremy stiffened, Antonio pulled his hand away and shoved it into his pocket.

"He's not ready," Jeremy said in that same measured tone. "I asked you to wait."

There was more to the discussion, but I didn't hear it. I'd tuned out, concentrating instead on listening for sounds from the house. A child. A boy. In my house.

Tension strummed through me. I strained toward the house like a bird dog on point, waiting for the word of release. Every second seemed interminable. A boy in my house. Strange adults were one thing; I was learning to deal with that indignity. But children? Sneaky, sneering boys like the ones at the print shop? In my house? That was beyond tolerating.

"Clayton?" Jeremy said, laying a hand on my shoulder. "I'd like to speak to you. Come around to the garden and—"

The back door swung open, then slammed shut. Jeremy's hand tightened on my shoulder. A boy bounded around the corner and stopped short on seeing us.

"Hello, Nicky," Jeremy said.

Jeremy said more and the boy responded, but I ignored them as I sized up the boy. So this was Antonio's son. He had his father's dark wavy hair and dark eyes, but was built slender and tall, already outstripping me by at least a foot. He had a good twenty pounds on me, too.

The first prickling of fear zinged through me. Then I noticed my advantage. He was unprepared. As he talked to Jeremy, his eyes darted over to me, but they held nothing but curiosity.

"Clayton," Jeremy said. "This is Nicholas. Antonio's son."

The boy extended a hand and a wide grin. I knew it was a grin, but the bared teeth still made my hackles rise.

"He's like you," Antonio said quickly, stepping forward. "A werewolf. Or, he will be, when he gets older."

The boy said something. Ignoring his words, I stared into his eyes and saw nothing but open trust. I sniffed the air and caught only the barest undercurrents of werewolf scent, heavily over-laid with the stink of a human child. Like me? This boy? Not likely. At least I had the sense to be wary of a stranger.

I sniffed and turned my face away, not quite willing to turn my back.

Out of the corner of my eye, I saw the boy step toward me. I turned, slowly, and met his gaze. He smiled at me with that affa-ble smile that made me curse him doubly a fool. I bared my teeth. He seemed to think I was returning his smile and grinned broader.

"Man, I thought I was never going to get to meet you," the boy said. "Dad's been talking about you all the time and then he said maybe you guys were coming to the Meet last month, but then you didn't and I kept bugging Dad and ..."

He kept talking. I stopped listening.

As he spoke he moved closer. His shadow fell over me, making me feel suddenly very small. I clenched my fists at my sides and pulled myself up straighter. I still only came up to his chin.

I inhaled. The werewolf scent was stronger now. So this was a werewolf child, was it? Well, if so, something had to be done and quickly. You only get one chance to establish dominance.

I lunged without warning. I hit him in the stomach, knocking him back to the ground. As I held him down, he didn't struggle, but just stared at me, eyes wide. The acrid scent of something vaguely familiar floated up. I felt a dampness seep through the knee of my pants and looked down to see a dark patch creeping outwards from the crotch of his trousers. As I wrinkled my nose and pulled back, Jeremy hauled me into the air.

The next few minutes blurred past in a series of images. Jeremy's face, shuttered and hard, not looking at me. The stink of urine. Antonio bending to help his son up. The boy jabbering something. As I was being carried into the house, I caught the boy's eyes. I saw no anger there, no lingering fear, just complete bewilderment. Any struggle for dominance had existed only in my head. Then I felt something I'd never felt before. Guilt, regret and more than an inkling of shame.

After a few hours of being left in my bedroom, Jeremy brought up my belated lunch. He explained, calmly, that as Antonio's son, Nicholas must be treated with the same respect I would accord Antonio. Although Nick wasn't a full-fledged werewolf, he would be when he grew up.

There were no others like me, no child werewolves. There never had been. There were other children of the Pack, like Nick, who would grow into werewolves, but not until they became adults. These would be my Pack brothers. No matter how I felt about them, I would have to learn to get along with them.

I offered to apologize, but Antonio and Nick had already left Stonehaven. I'd blown my first chance at fitting into the Pack. Although Jeremy never said this, I understood it.

Deep down, I sensed his other fear, too. That I'd never fit in. I was determined to prove him wrong. Of course, I'd also been determined never to raid the fridge again, never to attack strangers again, never to . . .

As summer passed, Jeremy began steering me into situations where I'd be with other children. After the fiasco with Nick, I was eager to please him, so I did my best to tolerate the little monsters.

Twice a week, for an entire month, he took me to a playground in Bear Valley, the nearest town. I behaved perfectly. I sat motionlessly on a swing, watched the children and gritted my teeth until the ordeal finally ended. Whenever a child ventured too close, a covert growl always sent him or her scrambling to find another piece of playground equipment.

I was so busy congratulating myself on my model behavior that I failed to realize the obvious—that these excursions were leading up to something. Had I known, I would have kicked and screamed and thrown my finest temper tantrum each time I so much as saw a swing set. Instead, I behaved so well that at the end of the summer, Jeremy pronounced me, with no small amount of trepidation, ready for the next major phase of my integration into human society, a torture worse than anything I would have thought him capable of devising. I was to go to school.

Schooldays

The school secretary escorted us into a small room that looked as if it had been carved inside a tree. Everything was wood, from the floor to the baseboards to the desk to the chairs. Two lights shone overhead, but even their combined power was not enough to win the battle against the all-encompassing darkness. All the lights seemed to do was illuminate the oily, lemon-stinking sheen on the wood. Jeremy sat down amid the cluster of chairs. I touched the seat beside him. It felt as greasy as it looked. I looked at him and curled my lip.

"Sit," he said.

I sat.

A door opened on the other side of the room and in walked a sour-looking middle-aged woman who smelled like fruit left on the tree to rot. Jeremy stood, tugging me to my feet, and extended his hand. She ignored it and skewered me with a snarl masquerading as a smile.

"So this is Clayton," the woman said. "Welcome to Harding Academy, Clayton."

"Thank you, ma'am," I said, remembering the response Jeremy had taught me.

"Your cousin here has already taken care of all the enrollment arrangements, and I don't believe in protracted good-byes, so let's take you straight to Miss Fishton's kindergarten class."

"Kindergarten?" Jeremy said. "Oh, there's been a mistake. I know he looks small for his age, but he's seven—eight in January."

"With no formal education, am I right?"

"Yes, but he's been homeschooled—"

"By whom?" She snatched a paper and pen from the desk. "You should have provided the reference when you enrolled him. The instructor's name, please."

"I've tutored him myself."

"Ah," she said, lips twitching. "And your credentials, *Mister* Danvers?"

She said the formal salutation with a mocking lilt that made my muscles tense. Jeremy's hand gripped my shoulder, restraint disguised as an affectionate squeeze.

"I don't have any formal qualifications," he said. "However, I can assure you that Clayton is well beyond kindergarten level. He's an extremely bright boy—"

"I'm sure you think he is."

The hand on my shoulder tightened, then relaxed. "Perhaps you could test him. He knows basic addition and subtraction, and he reads at a third-grade level."

"I believe you mentioned socialization problems?"

"Problems? No, I didn't say problems." A slight hitch in his voice here, undetectable to anyone who didn't know him. "I said he lacked socialization experience. There was some early trauma, before he came to live with me. I have, however, been taking steps to correct this and he's been making progress."

"I'm sure he has. However, given the combination of no formal schooling and socialization 'issues,' I'm standing by my decision.

He will go to kindergarten and if he proves himself ready, he will progress to the appropriate level. Clayton? Come with me."

"May we have a moment?" Jeremy said.

"As I've said, I don't believe in protracted good-byes. Children can't have their parents hovering over them—"

"I would like a moment," Jeremy said, meeting the head-mistress's gaze. "And I will escort him to his classroom myself."

They locked gazes. The headmistress broke first. She muttered directions to the kindergarten room, then shooed us out of her office.

"We only have a moment, Clayton," he whispered as we walked. "Now, remember what I told you? Where will I be?"

"On the other side of the playground. In the forest."

"Right. So when you go outside for recess, you'll be able to smell me, but don't come over or I'll have to leave. Just remember that I'm there for you. If you can't handle it, absolutely can't, you come to me. But try, Clayton. Please try. It's very important that you go to school."

I nodded and he led me down the hall.

"Oh, this must be Clayton!"

A young woman with bright red lips and a high-pitched cheep of a voice flew at me. I ducked. Jeremy's hand tightened on my arm, pulling me up straight and propelling me into the class-room.

I squinted against the brightness, not only of the sun streaming through the windows, but of the screamingly vivid colors that assaulted me from every direction. The classroom walls were painted in bright primary colors, the tones so overwhelming they made me cringe. When Jeremy had decorated my bedroom last month, he'd asked what color I'd wanted, and I'd picked two:

black and white. That's what I liked best. I didn't mind colors, as long as they weren't too... colorful.

"I'm Miss Fishton, Clayton," the woman chirped, then turned and fluttered her hands at the gaggle of children behind her. "Class, this is our new student. Can we say hello to Clayton?"

"Hello, Clayton," a dozen voices chimed in monotone.

"You're just in time, Clayton," she said. "We were just getting ready to sing 'Old MacDonald.' Do you know 'Old MacDonald'?"

I looked up at Jeremy.

"I don't believe he does," Jeremy said.

"Oh, that's okay. We'll teach you, won't we, class?"

"Yes, Miss Fishton," the class intoned.

"And then, after we sing, we'll do some finger painting. I bet you love finger painting. Now just come on in, Clayton, and we'll join hands and sing 'Old MacDonald.' You can be the pig. Do you know what a pig says, Clayton?"

I looked up at Jeremy. He rubbed his hand across his chin, then bent and whispered, "I'm sorry." A quick pat on the back, one last apologetic glance, and he hurried from the room.

By the end of that week, I hated school as I'd never hated anything in my life... except Malcolm. I knew I was here to learn, but learn what? How to sing songs about farmers? How to distinguish red squares from green circles? How to build towers of blocks? After a month, we'd only begun the alphabet, and I could already read every book in the teacher's story library. Yet nobody seemed the least bit interested in moving me to a higher grade.

So Jeremy continued my academic lessons at home and instead stressed the importance of other lessons I could learn at school, namely how to fit in. This I understood. I needed to know how to pass for human. Unfair, to be sure, but necessary. Jeremy could do it, and he was very good at it; I resolved that I would learn to be just as accomplished an actor. So I studied my classmates. I watched them. I stalked them. I learned how to imitate them.

The watching and stalking portions of these lessons prompted many parent-teacher interviews in those first two months, but Miss Fishton could never quite pinpoint exactly what I was doing wrong, just vague concerns about me "making the other children uncomfortable," which Jeremy dismissed as an obvious consequence of putting a seven-year-old with five-year-olds. Developmentally, I was light-years ahead. Yet another reason, he argued, to bump me up a grade or two. Still they refused.

At home, Jeremy decided to distract me from my boredom at school with lessons that I deemed long overdue. Though I'd hunted with Jeremy for months, he preferred to do the killing. He insisted that this was because I needed more practice with the prekilling parts of the hunt—stalking and chasing—but I suspected it had more to do with my killing method, which basically consisted of chomping on my prey until it stopped moving.

Once I did manage to catch a rabbit while out running by myself and, after I Changed back, I proudly showed my accomplishment to Jeremy. He took one look at the unrecognizable mangle of fur and bone and declared he would handle all kills for a while.

In late October, he finally deemed me ready. To my surprise, these new lessons were conducted not in the woods, but in the kitchen. For the next two weeks, Jeremy produced dead specimens of every small wild animal found at Stonehaven—rabbits, opossums, raccoons, squirrels, even a skunk. He then dissected them and showed me where the vital organs were located. For the skunk and raccoon, he pointed out their defense systems, how to avoid getting sprayed or clawed. For the prey animals, he showed me how to kill them quickly and what parts were edible.

At school, our classroom had a small rodent zoo consisting of two rabbits, three hamsters, a litter of baby gerbils and a guinea pig. At first, I'd thought the teacher was raising snack food, which impressed me, being the first sign of intelligence she'd shown. Soon, though, I'd figured out the animals' true purpose and left them alone, though I would never understand the appeal of petting and coddling perfectly good food.

Once Jeremy began my killing lessons, I began to see the classroom pets in a new light. Maybe I couldn't kill them, but I could study them, just as I studied the children. I began to spend my free time sitting near the rodents and watching them, studying how they moved, their weaknesses and blind spots, and how they could be most easily killed.

My fascination with the classroom pets was a great relief to Miss Fishton, who had probably given up hope of interesting me in anything. The next time Jeremy stopped in after school to discuss my behavior, her report was near glowing.

"He just loves the animals," she said. "He could sit and stare at them for hours." She beamed at me. "I think we might have a little zoologist on our hands."

Jeremy glanced down at me. I adjusted the clasp on my lunch box and pretended not to notice the look he gave me.

Miss Fishton continued. "He's absolutely enthralled by them. It's just so cute. Have you considered getting him a pet? I have a friend whose cat just had kittens."

I stopped playing with the lunch-box clasp.

"Would you like a kitten, Clayton?" Miss Fishton asked.

"Yes." I looked up at Jeremy. "I would like a kitten."

"I'm sure you would," Jeremy said. "But you know we can't have pets in the house." He turned to Miss Fishton. "Allergies."

"Oh, that's too bad. But it's good to see him taking such a keen interest."

"Yes, it is."

After we left the classroom, Jeremy bustled me out to the car without so much as a "how was your day?" Once he'd pulled from the near-empty lot, he looked over at me.

"I know you must get hungry at school, Clayton. It's not easy getting through the day without as much food as you're accustomed to. Perhaps I can slip in another half-sandwich into your lunch box. Would that help?"

"I would like another *whole* sandwich," I said. "Or two."

Jeremy sighed. "Yes, I know, and I wish I could give it to you, but you can't eat so much more than the other children. Are you getting enough to eat at breakfast?"

I shook my head.

"Then I'll start making you more."

I smiled.

"Now, about these animals," he said. "I know they're a temptation but—"

"I am not allowed to eat them," I said. "I know."

"Good."

He leaned over, popped open the glove compartment and handed me a candy bar.

"Two?" I said. "I am very hungry."

He gave me two.

"So we're clear on this?" he said. "No eating the pets in your classroom." He paused, then added. "Or any other classroom." Another pause. "Or any pets anywhere at all." Still another pause. "No killing them either."

I nodded. "No killing and no eating any pets. I understand."

"Good."

As Jeremy continued his dissection lessons at home, I continued my live-animal studies at school. The rodent that interested me the most was the guinea pig. I'd never seen one in the wild, but it looked like the ideal prey, much fatter than a mouse and much slower than a rabbit. This one was even slower than most of its kind. It was dying. I could tell by the smell, and the fact that the teacher seemed oblivious to this only proved her intelligence was about as high as that of the birds she resembled.

The more I studied the guinea pig, the more I became convinced that I'd found the ideal food source for a young wolf. There was, however, one problem. I didn't know where its vital organs were. I could guess, based on the similarities between the guinea pig's anatomy and those of the other rodents, yet this was, at best, an imprecise science and Jeremy had taught me that precision begets accuracy. For a swift kill, you needed to know exactly where to strike.

The answer, of course, was very simple. Jeremy had forbidden me to kill the guinea pig, but I didn't need to. It was already dying. All I had to do was wait.

One day in mid-November, the guinea pig climbed into its house and died. I could tell by the smell that it was dead, but Miss Fishton paid no attention, knowing the creature wasn't the most active of the classroom pets.

When recess came, I went out with the rest of the children, then slipped back in and went to my lunch box, where I'd been secretly transporting a knife in preparation for this moment. I took the knife, opened the guinea pig's cage, dumped its body out of its house and set to work.

By the time the first-grade teacher snuck in to swipe some chalk, I was so engrossed in my work that I didn't hear her, even as she walked up behind me. I did, however, hear her scream... as did everyone else in the building.

"You weren't ready," Jeremy said as he drove me home, his hands gripping the steering wheel. "I was too eager. I wanted to get you in right at the start of the school year and I should have waited until you were ready. There's no rush. No rush at all." He exhaled and glanced over at me. "I think we'll stick with home-schooling for a while."

So our lives settled back into the old comfortable pattern, and I was glad of it. There was nothing a school could teach me that Jeremy couldn't. As for socializing, the only people I needed to socialize with were those in the Pack, and I'd be doing that soon enough. With the end of November came a quarterly Pack meet. After the school fiasco, I think Jeremy would have preferred not to rush me into yet another new experience, but the Alpha, Dominic, insisted. All Jeremy could do was prepare me and hope for the best.

Freak

The Sorrentinos lived on an estate north of New York City. All three generations of the family lived together, as was Pack custom. The family was headed by Dominic, who had three sons, Gregory, Benedict and Antonio. Benedict had left the Pack several years earlier and moved to Europe with his two sons. Gregory had also fathered two sons, but the eldest had been killed in a dispute with a mutt five years ago.

Dying young wasn't uncommon for werewolves. Under Dominic's rule, fifty percent of Pack werewolves didn't live to see their fortieth birthday, and most of those deaths were at the hands—or jaws—of another werewolf, usually a mutt, but sometimes a Pack brother.

This was an improvement over previous Alphas, who'd often seen at least two-thirds of their Pack dead by forty. Dominic himself was close to seventy and had been Alpha for nearly two decades, an almost unheard-of longevity, in both age and length of rule.

I learned none of this from Jeremy, of course. On the drive to the Sorrentino estate, he talked about the Pack, but not its problems. Instead, he relayed facts. Most important, he told me who

would be there, how they were related and their place in the social structure. Hierarchy is very important for werewolves, as it
is for wolves. Jeremy didn't attach meanings like beta wolf or
omega wolf or outline a rigid structure of who topped whom. He
simply told me whom I had to respect, and whom I had to obey,
and from that my wolf's brain assessed status.

Jeremy expected most of the Pack members to show up at the
Meet. Those would include Dominic, Gregory, Antonio, Nick
and Gregory's remaining son, eighteen-year-old Jorge. The
Santos family would also be there, the elder generation, brothers
Wally and Raymond, and Raymond's three sons, sixteen-year-
old Stephen, thirteen-year-old Andrew and seven-year-old
Daniel. The Danverses, the Sorrentinos and the Santoses comprised the three main families, their ancestors having been
members since the American Pack began. Of the peripheral
members, Ross Werner, Cliff Ward, Peter Myers and Dennis
Stillwell were to attend, plus Dennis's son, twelve-year-old Joey.

The Meet was scheduled to run from Friday to Sunday.
Jeremy and I arrived at noon on Saturday, not because we'd had
more pressing business, but because Jeremy hoped that by re-
ducing the length of my first visit, he could reduce the possibility of disaster.

For the last hour of our trip Jeremy ran through the do's and
don't's. Most of them were don't's. The simple act of dining now
came with even more rules than Miss Fishton had for the
kindergarten sandbox. I couldn't raid the refrigerator. I couldn't
ask anyone except Jeremy for snacks. I had to eat with utensils. I
had to chew with my mouth shut. I had to sit with the other Pack
youth. I couldn't touch any food before everyone older than I
had taken their share. I couldn't take seconds until everyone
older than I had taken seconds. I couldn't eat other people's

scraps. I couldn't eat food I found on the floor. I began to hope it would be a short weekend.

Finally, we arrived. The Sorrentinos' house was a sprawling Italianate manor set amid acres of forest. The house was probably three times as large as Stonehaven, but the grounds were less than half the size of our property, which convinced me that we had the better deal. Better to have more room to roam than more rooms to vacuum. The minute we stepped from the car, though, I discovered that it was unlikely Nicholas Sorrentino ever had to do vacuuming duty. The place stank of human.

When I asked Jeremy about the smell, he told me that the family employed a part-time housekeeper. We wouldn't see her, since she came only during the week, while the Sorrentinos were out of the house, at work and school. Still, given the choice between letting a human in the house or vacuuming a few carpets, I'd stick with my hated household chores.

We walked from behind a row of cars and along a walkway through the gardens. At the front door, Jeremy didn't knock, he just opened it and walked in. That was normal Pack etiquette. Knocking or ringing the bell would imply you didn't think you were welcome, which would insult your host. Instead, you walked in and shouted a greeting. Jeremy has never shouted a greeting in all the years I've known him. He does what he did now, stepped inside, closed the door and paused to see whether anyone heard him enter. When no one came to greet us, he followed the scent of his host toward an open door, then paused again and called a hello.

There was a scuffle of movement from within the room. Then a large man with graying dark hair wheeled around the corner, grinned and embraced Jeremy.

"Finally!" the man boomed. "I was about to send Tonio upstate to drag you here." He shouted toward the front of the house. "Gregory! Jorge! Come!" He turned back to Jeremy. "Now where is this troublemaking pup of yours? The one who attacked my Nicky?"

I looked over my shoulder, measuring the distance to the door.

"Is that him? Hiding behind you? That little runt?" The man's laugh boomed so loudly it hurt my ears. "Come here, boy. Let me get a better look at you."

I tried to take another step backward, but Jeremy put his hand between my shoulder blades and propelled me forward.

"Clayton, this is Dominic."

I hadn't needed the introduction to know this was the Pack Alpha. Dominic Sorrentino was one of the biggest men I'd ever seen, as tall as Jeremy, yet as stocky and muscular as Antonio. Of course he was the Alpha.

Dominic looked me in the eye, his gaze so fierce I could barely hold eye contact. At least two excruciatingly long minutes passed. Then I had to drop my gaze. Dominic's laugh roared through the hallway and he clapped one huge hand against my back.

"Did you see that?" he said to Jeremy. "Did you see how long it took him to look away? Tonio's right. The boy has balls. He'll make a good playmate for Nicky." With his hand still at my back, Dominic steered me past him. "Head down that hall, turn left, go downstairs and you'll find the other boys in the basement. Nicky will do the introductions."

"Perhaps later," Jeremy said. "He's quite shy—"

"All the more reason for him to go. You and I need to catch up, and I'm sure Clayton will be happier playing with the other boys."

"Yes, but perhaps I should make the introductions. He's not entirely comfortable with other children—"

"You worry too much, Jeremy. Clayton? Off you go now. Find the others."

I looked at Jeremy.

He hesitated, then forced a smile. "Go on, Clayton. Just...be good and I'll see you soon."

I stood there as Dominic prodded Jeremy into the room, then closed the door behind them. I hesitated, torn between wanting to obey Jeremy and wanting to just sit on the floor and wait for him. From the front hall I heard footsteps coming down the stairs and remembered Dominic had called his son and grandson down. Better not to be caught challenging the Alpha's authority quite so early in my visit. I turned and hurried down the hall to seek out Nick and the other boys.

I'd forgotten the directions Dominic had given for reaching the basement, having been too disturbed by the prospect of being separated from Jeremy to pay attention. I still remembered Nick's scent, though, and although it permeated the house, I was able to find and follow the most recent trail to the basement steps.

At the bottom of the stairs, I stopped and inhaled. I could pick out five separate scents—the five Pack sons Jeremy had told me to expect: the three Santos boys, Nick and Joey Stillwell. These five comprised the Pack youth—all the sons who had yet to undergo their first Change. Jorge Sorrentino had made his first Change the year before, so he was now considered an adult, and would be upstairs with the men.

Of the five boys I smelled, one was taking on the distinctive odor of a werewolf. This would be the oldest Santos boy, Stephen. Although werewolves don't make their first Change until their late teens, it's only the end of the lengthy process of maturation. With puberty, a werewolf begins developing his secondary traits, primarily the sharpened senses and increased strength necessary for life as a wolf. Right now, Stephen Santos was the only one of the Pack youth who had begun this process.

The basement was a series of rooms branching off a central corridor. Most of the doors were closed. Of those propped open, only one near the end led into a room that wasn't dark. I started down the hall. Halfway to the end I heard Nick's voice.

"Can I have my radio back, Steve?"

"What's the magic word?" an older voice said.

"Come on, Steve," another voice said. "Don't be a prick."

"You calling me a prick, Joey?"

I peeked around the doorway. Inside, a tall teen with long red hair was approaching a slowly backpedaling acne-pocked boy. Nick stood beside the threatened boy, hovering there, as if wanting to stand with him, but not sure he dared.

Across the room two other red-haired youths looked on, wearing twin toothy grins. The youngest wasn't much bigger than me.

I'd drilled Jeremy's litany of names into my head, understanding the importance of knowing who was who in this new world, so now I could look across the faces and identify all the players. The boy backing away was Joey Stillwell. The boy bearing down on him was Stephen Santos, and the two on the sofa were Stephen's younger brothers, Andrew and Daniel.

"You think I should give this back?" Stephen waved a light-blue transistor radio over his head. "Come on and take it then."

Stephen held out the radio. Joey didn't move.

"Can I have my radio, Steve?" Nick said. "Please."

"Why? You don't need it. Your daddy can buy you fifty of them." He turned to his youngest brother. "I think Danny would like a radio. You want a radio, Danny-boy?"

Daniel jumped from the sofa. "Sure."

"Then here's what we'll do. Danny gets the radio, and Nick tells his daddy he gave it to him, as a gift." He turned to Nick. "Got that?"

"No."

Stephen's eyes narrowed. "What did you say?"

"N-no. It's m-mine."

Stephen started to advance on Nick. I felt an urge then that surprised me, the urge to protect Nick. I recognized the unfairness of this assault, perhaps more than a human would. Stephen was double the young boy's size and quadruple his strength. Though I couldn't imagine why anyone would fight over a radio, it *did* belong to Nick. It was his property. I could even see his name etched on it, like Jeremy did with all my clothes, though there wasn't room for a name on the tags, so he drew a little symbol that he said would help me know it was mine if I left it somewhere.

But the radio was clearly Nick's. So, in this dispute, he was, by every reckoning, the wronged party. Jeremy had told me to be nice to Nick. Getting his radio back would be nice, wouldn't it? On the other hand, Jeremy had told me not to attack anyone. I was allowed to defend myself with reasonable force—Jeremy had always been clear on that. Which was more important: that I be nice to Nick or that I not start a fight?

"You want your radio?" Stephen said, holding it up out of Nick's reach.

"Yes." Nick paused. "Yes, please."

Stephen turned and whipped the radio at the brick fireplace beside the doorway. It shattered, pieces scattering across the orange shag carpet. No one seemed to notice the broken radio, though. They were all staring at me.

I stepped inside the rec room, reached down and scooped up the biggest pieces of the radio, then walked over to Nick.

"Yours," I said.

Nick smiled and took the pieces. "Thanks." He turned to the others. "Guys, this is Clayton, the boy who's living with Jeremy."

"The werewolf," Joey said, smiling at me.

"Of course, he's a werewolf," Andrew said, getting up from the sofa. "We're all werewolves, stupid."

"I mean he's a full werewolf. My dad says he can Change already." Joey looked at me. "That's so cool."

"It's not cool," Stephen said. "It's freaky."

"So that makes him a freak," Daniel piped up. "Right?"

"He's not a freak," Nick said. "He's just different."

Daniel met my eyes. "Freak."

Stephen tousled his little brother's hair. "That's right, Danny." Then he turned to me. "He's worse than a freak. He's a mutt." His eyes gleamed and I knew he'd lobbed what he considered the worst possible insult. When I didn't react, disappointment darted through his eyes.

"He's not a mutt," Nick said. "He's Pack. Poppa says Jeremy can keep him, so he's Pack."

"Maybe, but he *was* a mutt," Andrew said. "Once a mutt, always a mutt. That's the rule."

"Doesn't count," Joey said. "He's a kid. A kid can't be a mutt."

"So does that mean he's bitten?" Daniel said, lips curling back.

"That's right, Danny," Stephen said, rumpling his brother's hair again. "He's not even hereditary. A total freak."

"Stop that," Nick said.

"Ignore them," Joey said, turning to me. "They're being stupid."

"*We* aren't the stupid ones," Stephen said. "Look at him. He doesn't even know what we're talking about. Call him a mutt and he doesn't even flinch. Our dad was right. He's a retard."

"He's not a retard," Nick said. "He just doesn't talk much."

Stephen lowered his face to mine. "Retard."

I stared him in the eyes and said nothing.

"See?" Stephen said, straightening. "He's a retard like Gregory and a freak like Jeremy."

My head whipped up, gaze going to Stephen's.

Stephen laughed. "Oh, ho. He didn't like that. Freaks stick together, boy. Everybody knows that. The minute my dad heard Jeremy brought some wolf-cub home, he said 'at last, that idiot's done something so stupid Dominic will finally kick him out.'"

"Jeremy's not an idiot," Nick said.

"No, he's just... different, right?" Andrew said from across the room. "If he wasn't your dad's friend, he'd have been banished after his first Change."

"No, not banished," Stephen said. "Executed. Put down like a dog, before he embarrassed the Pack."

I clenched my fists, every ounce of willpower going into keeping them still. Jeremy had warned me about this. He'd said I might hear things about him. I hadn't known what he'd meant, and he hadn't elaborated, just forbade me to start a fight over it.

"Jeremy's fine," Joey said. "My dad says he has some interesting ideas—"

"His own father's ashamed of him, can't stand to be around him." He turned to me. "You think Jeremy's special? Ask him how many mutts he's killed. Not a single one. Only time he ever fights them is when he's cornered. He won't even go on a hunt—"

"He hunts," Nick said. "He hunts with my dad all the time."

"For what? Rabbits? I meant the real hunts. Jeremy never goes on the mutt hunts."

"That's because he doesn't believe in them," Joey said. "Jeremy thinks we shouldn't kill mutts unless they do something wrong, and my dad says that's okay, everyone's entitled to their opinion, and if Jeremy doesn't want to fight mutts—"

"Don't give me that 'opinion' crap," Stephen said. "Everyone knows the truth. Jeremy doesn't fight mutts because he's afraid of them. A freak and a coward. A yellow-bellied coward who hides behind the Pack for protection—"

I launched myself at Stephen, knocking him off balance. We hit the floor. All the defense lessons Jeremy and Antonio had taught me flew from my head, and I acted solely on impulse, kicking, punching, clawing, and getting kicked, punched and clawed in return.

Dimly I heard the shouts of the other boys, Stephen's brothers egging him on and Joey yelling at Stephen to leave me alone. Though I got in a few good hits at the onset, when I caught Stephen off guard, soon I was receiving more than I was giving. A seven-year-old werewolf versus a sixteen-year-old werewolf is as uneven a match as the human equivalents, and all the rage-fueled energy in the world wasn't going to even the odds.

Just as my initial fury cooled, and I began to realize that Stephen wasn't going to let me off without a good thrashing, a hand reached down, grabbed me by the back of my shirt and hauled me into the air. I twisted to see Dominic holding me. Nick stood beside him, panting from running to get help. Jeremy rounded the corner. I couldn't see his expression, and was pretty sure I didn't want to.

"Looks like you bit off more than you could chew, pup," Dominic said with a laugh. "You need to put on a few more pounds before you try that again." He glanced over his shoulder, voice hardening. "Raymond, I expect you to have a talk with your son about this."

"But he started it," Stephen whined, wiping blood from his nose. "He attacked me. I was just standing there and he jumped me—"

"You weren't just standing there," Nick said. "He attacked you because you were making fun of—"

"Of him," Joey cut in. "He kept making fun of Clayton, and he wouldn't stop."

I looked at Jeremy and I could see in his eyes that he knew the truth, that I wouldn't have attacked Stephen if I'd been the one he insulted. I tensed, waiting for that dreaded look of disappointment, but it didn't come. Instead, Jeremy took me from Dominic, stood me up and checked me over, his expression neutral, neither approving nor disapproving of what I'd done. When he didn't find any major injuries, he patted me on the back, murmured a soft "Let's get you cleaned up," and steered me from the room.

Hierarchy

Nick came with us to the bathroom. While Jeremy cleaned my bloodied nose, Nick told him about the broken radio, making it sound as if the incident was another reason for my scrap with Stephen. Jeremy said little, but I could tell by his expression that he considered defending Nick a more acceptable excuse than defending *him*. So here was the answer to my earlier question. Fighting to help a weaker party was an acceptable use of force.

Afterward, as further proof that my actions hadn't been too objectionable, Jeremy left me alone with Nick. He told us that lunch would be ready soon and we should wash up and head for the dining room.

"Man, it's about time we get to eat," Nick said, swiping his hands under the running water then wiping them on his jeans. "We were supposed to hours ago, but then Poppa said we had to wait for you guys to get here and you've been here for what, an hour already and we still haven't had lunch."

I finished drying my hands and we headed into the hall.

"Do you get to eat at the grown-ups' table?" Nick continued. "I bet you do, because that's where you eat after your first Change and you've had lots of Changes, so I think you get to eat with the grown-ups."

I shook my head. "Jeremy said I eat at the kids' table."

"Whoa, bummer. So how do they know when you're ready to join the grown-ups' table? Do you think they'll pick an age? Like sixteen? That's kinda young, but Poppa had his first Change when he was sixteen, so I hope I do, too. Maybe they'll let you join the grown-up table when I do. Then if I Changed at sixteen, you'd be fifteen—"

"Hey, Nicky?" Stephen said, walking up behind us. "Does that mouth of yours come with an off button?"

"I wasn't talking to you." Nick glanced at me. "Do you think I talk too much?"

I shook my head. Nick flipped his middle finger at Stephen, who shouldered past us, knocking Nick against the wall.

"Asshole," Nick muttered. "I can't wait until *he's* at the grown-up table, away from us. When we sit down, you sit with me, away from him. If you're beside him, he'll swipe your food."

"No one swipes my food."

Nick grinned. "Hey, maybe we *should* sit next to him, then. See what happens. You almost took him downstairs. Just a few more minutes and I'm sure—"

A laugh sounded behind us. Before we could turn, Antonio scooped us up, each under one arm.

"What's this I hear? Poor Clayton's only been here an hour. You've already led him into one fight and now you're tempting him into another? Shame on you, Nicky."

Antonio's laugh belied his words and he twisted us around in midair, then thumped us down on our feet.

"When did you get back?" Nick asked.

"Just this very minute."

"And you're done working now? You don't have to go back to the plant after lunch?"

"I fixed the problem and I'm home until Monday." Antonio glanced down at me. "So where's Jeremy, scrap? Don't tell me you left him at home."

"I'm right here," Jeremy said, stepping through the next door. "Just waiting for Clayton so I can introduce him to the others."

"Is everyone here now?" Antonio asked.

"Everyone except Peter."

Antonio winced, then caught Jeremy's look of concern and thumped him on the back. "Don't worry. I'm sure he's just busy with school. Once he graduates, he'll start coming to Meets again. Now let's get some lunch before we all starve."

Everyone except Dominic was already in the dining room, milling about, talking, as they waited to uncover the cold food platters. Jeremy introduced me to the adult members of the Pack.

Although it almost certainly wasn't intentional, Jeremy performed the introductions in order of rank. First came the remaining two members of the Alpha's family: eldest son Gregory and his son Jorge.

Jorge was a quiet, solemn young man who took after his grandfather and uncle Antonio in appearance only. Jorge stayed close to his father, always hovering, ready to get whatever Gregory needed. At the time, I mistook this closeness for a lack of self-confidence, the boy preferring to stay under his father's protective shadow. I'd eventually realize the situation was reversed. It was Gregory who needed his son nearby.

On the drive to the Meet, Jeremy had explained that Gregory had been brain-damaged in a fight with a mutt six years earlier—the fight that had led to his eldest son's death when that son had gone seeking revenge. When Jeremy introduced me to Gregory that day, I saw nothing wrong with him…just a slightly unfocused look in his eyes, as if he wasn't quite paying attention.

That's how I remember Gregory best, a vague man who never seemed to be fully present. Though I've never been clear on the full extent of his injuries, I believe they affected random areas of short- and long-term memory. He could debate politics, discuss global economics, predict stock market trends, and yet, if Jorge wasn't there to help him, he'd forget where to find the bathroom.

The next Pack members Jeremy introduced me to were Wally and Raymond Santos—the Santos boys' uncle and father—two red-haired men who barely let him finish the introduction before Raymond cut in.

"Where's Malcolm?" he asked.

"In Tampa," Jeremy said. "He's been chasing a mutt who showed up at Stonehaven last year."

"In other words, he's doing your job," Wally said. "If a mutt shows up on your territory, *you're* supposed to take care of it."

"Jeremy does—" Antonio began, but Jeremy silenced him with a look.

Wally continued, not noticing the interruption. "Malcolm has enough to do, hunting mutts for Dominic. He doesn't need to clean up after you, too, Jeremy."

I looked from Jeremy to Antonio, waiting for one of them to correct Wally, to tell him the real reason Malcolm wasn't at the Meet, that he'd been banished by Jeremy. From the look on Antonio's face, he was biting his tongue. Another warning look from Jeremy, and he stomped off, muttering about stubborn sons-of-bitches.

"Tell Malcolm if he needs any help with that mutt, he can give us a shout," Wally said. "Anything we can do for him, we will. He knows that."

"I'm sure he does," Jeremy murmured.

Jeremy steered me over to Joey's father, Dennis Stillwell, a small man who greeted me with a warm smile. Then Ross Werner, who was at least Dominic's age. Ross clapped me on the back, proclaimed me a "good-looking young man" and commended Jeremy for doing "a fine job" with me. Finally Jeremy introduced me to Cliff Ward, a young man no older than Jeremy, with an insincere smile and eyes that always darted on contact.

Cliff also asked after Malcolm, proving that Jeremy's father had a higher standing here than I'd anticipated. Yet I hadn't heard Dominic or any of the other Sorrentinos ask after him. It was Jeremy they'd wanted to see. That had to count for something.

"Where's Poppa?" Nick asked the moment Jeremy finished the introductions.

"He had to take a call from the office," Jeremy said.

"Working?" Nick fell into a chair with a groan. "Everyone's always working. When I grow up, I'm never going to work."

"No?" Antonio said. "Then I guess your poppa and I will have to work harder, so you won't have to. Come on and take Clayton to the kids' table. Poppa will be down any moment."

"He'd better," Nick said. "I'm starving. I hate these rules. Why do we have to wait for him before we eat?"

"Because he's the Alpha," Antonio said. "If you want to eat first, then *you* need to become Alpha."

"And do all that extra work?" Nick said. "No way."

Dominic walked in then, and the chatter died down as everyone swung into their places at the table and started uncovering the food. Nick led me to the children's table, which was in the corner. Nick watched to see where Stephen sat, then picked seats for us on the opposite side of the table.

"See how far away we are from the grown-ups?" Nick

whispered. "They do that so we can't hear what they're talking about."

"I can," I said.

He hesitated, taking a moment to figure this out, then grinned. "That's right. You've got the superhearing already. Cool."

As we settled in, I looked at the main table. As I expected, it was arranged by Pack hierarchy, with Dominic at the top, his sons on either side of him, then radiating down the table to Ross Werner and Cliff Ward at the end. Jeremy sat beside Antonio. I must have looked pretty satisfied with this arrangement because Stephen followed my gaze and sneered.

"You think that means he's something special?" Stephen said, voice lowered to a whisper. "Jeremy only gets to sit there because he's Antonio's best friend. It's bullshit. Look who sits at the old man's right hand. Gregory. A fucking retard."

Ross and Cliff, sitting at the end of the adult table and therefore closest to us, both turned and I knew they'd overheard. Ross glowered and shook a finger at Stephen, but when the older man turned away, Cliff shot Stephen a grin.

"Now, boys," Dominic boomed from the head of the table. "I think we may have a problem down there."

"S-sir, I—I didn't—" Stephen began.

Dominic continued. "Ross put out the food, but I don't think he knows how much Clayton eats. From what Tonio tells me, those dishes on your table are just barely enough to feed Clayton alone." He looked at me. "Is that right, boy? Can you eat that much?"

I looked at the uncovered plates and nodded.

Dominic threw back his head and laughed. "You think so, do you? Well, then, maybe we should do something about that. We don't want you boys scrapping over the food. Grab your chair

and come on up here, Clayton. You can eat with me today. We'll
see which of us eats more."

From the other boys, I caught a wave of disgruntled looks,
ranging from Joey's mild envy to Stephen's outright fury.

"Lucky," Nick mouthed and shot me a grin.

I searched his expression for any trace of envy, but saw none.
He was simply happy for me. Had the situation been reversed, I
knew I couldn't have been so unselfish. I took my chair, carried it
to Dominic's side and asked him a question.

He laughed. "You don't want to sit up here alone with the old
men? I don't blame you." He craned his neck to see the children's
table. "Nicky?"

"Yes, Poppa?"

"Bring your chair on up here. You're keeping Clayton company."

Nick's smile lit up his face. He grabbed his chair and scrambled to the head of the table.

Dominic out-ate me by a half-sandwich and a banana.

"He would have beaten you," Antonio said. "But he knows a
good Pack member always lets the Alpha win. He's a smart boy."

"So I hear," Dominic said. "Tonio tells me you're reading already." He looked out across the table. "Can you believe that?
Less than a year ago, this boy was living in the swamp. He
couldn't talk. He couldn't control his Changes. He could barely
even walk upright. And now he's going to school. School! Can
you believe it?"

I waited to see whether Jeremy would correct Dominic. He
didn't. I decided Dominic's statement was close enough to the
truth to be an acceptable facsimile. I *had* been in school...for

a while. And I'd be returning to school...eventually. In the meantime, Jeremy was giving me daily lessons so, technically, I was still being schooled.

Dominic continued. "When Jeremy told me he brought this boy home, most of you know how I felt. I was against it. I thought the boy would be dangerous. I thought he'd have to be locked up in a cage and if he ever escaped, he'd put us all at risk of exposure. I thought we should—" He glanced at me and stopped short. "Well, you know what I thought should be done. But I trusted Jeremy. I told him he had one year to show me that the boy could be controlled." Dominic laughed. "Controlled? Look at him. This boy could walk around New York City and he'd be no more an exposure risk than you or me. I have a lot of faith in Jeremy, but I'm still amazed by the job he's done."

Jeremy murmured a thank-you as the rest of the Pack pitched in with congratulations of varying degrees of sincerity.

Dominic continued. "Jeremy, I know there's still two months to go on that year's probation, but I've made my decision. The boy is yours, and he's a member of the Pack."

"Thank you," Jeremy said.

From Jeremy's other side, Raymond Santos cleared his throat. "Shouldn't we...give the kid some kind of test. I agree Jeremy *appears* to have done a good job—"

"Appears?" Dominic said, skewering Raymond with a glare. "Clayton, come up here. Jorge? Grab me today's paper."

Dominic pushed back his chair and lifted me onto his lap. The boys at the children's table took advantage of the break to pull their chairs close enough to hear. When Jorge brought in the newspaper, Dominic laid it in front of us.

"Can you read the headlines, Clayton?"

I nodded.

"Well, you go ahead and read me what you can, then."

I selected the first article, a piece on the Vietnam War. I stumbled over a few of the place names, but managed to get through the whole article. When I finished, the room was silent.

Dominic looked at Raymond. "How about you ask Daniel to read the same piece?"

From the end of the table, Cliff said, "Hey, Jeremy? Think while you're teaching him to read you can teach him to *speak*? Kid sounds like a goddamned hillbilly."

A few chuckles greeted this. This was the first time anyone had mentioned my accent—I talked so little that it usually wasn't apparent. I suppose it makes sense that when I regained my language skills, I'd speak as I always had. Jeremy had certainly never commented on it.

"He sounds just fine," Dominic said, patting me on the back. "Nothing wrong with being different. As for the reading, I'll be the first to say school smarts aren't everything. No one in my family ever went past high school and we do just fine. My point is that the boy can learn, and learn quickly. I have no concerns about Clayton's future with this Pack."

"Nor do I," said Antonio.

Gregory and Jorge added their agreement, quieter but equally firm. Dennis Stillwell and Ross Werner chimed in with their support. The Santos brothers and Cliff Ward said nothing. That was fine; they were permitted to disagree. Only the Alpha's decision mattered.

"Now," Dominic continued. "Speaking of the Pack and the future, I've been considering something for a while, and seeing how well Jeremy has done with Clayton has only confirmed my feelings on the matter. As you know, when Jorge came of age, I allowed Jeremy to mentor him, guide him through his early Changes. That was Jeremy's idea and, although I'll admit I didn't see the need for it, Jorge thought he'd like to try it. The transition from a boy to a full werewolf is never easy, but Jeremy made it smoother. Jorge learned control much faster and his Changes come easier."

Jorge nodded. "I remember what Peter went through, and I had a far easier time of it."

"Everyone's transition is different," Wally said. "Peter's was tough. Mine wasn't. There are a million factors. You can't take one example—"

"Of course you can't," Dominic said. "And that's why I'm thoroughly testing this theory of Jeremy's by having him try the same with the other boys as they come of age."

"What?" Stephen squawked, but his father shushed him.

"Furthermore," Dominic said, "last year Jeremy asked for permission to tutor the adolescent boys, so they're better prepared for their first Change. I'm granting him permission to do so, starting today. After lunch, Joey, Andrew and Stephen will go with Jeremy for a few hours. They'll do the same at each Meet until they reach their first Change."

"Cool," Joey said.

Stephen and Andrew shot Joey looks that said he'd pay for his enthusiasm later.

Raymond cleared his throat.

"Yes, Ray," Dominic said, his voice heavy with warning.

"I, uh, don't entirely disagree with the *idea* of someone prepping my boys for their first Change. But Jeremy...?"

"And what is wrong with Jeremy?" Dominic asked, infusing the words with a near-growl.

Raymond glanced at Wally for support.

"Jeremy's very young," Wally said. "Not only to be taking on a position of this responsibility but, don't forget, he only went through his own Change a few years ago—"

"Which is exactly why he's the right person for the job. He still remembers what it was like. I've made my decision. End of discussion."

Dominic picked me up off his lap and plunked me on the floor. "You've done well, Clayton. Now go play with Nicky and Daniel. Jeremy, take the rest of the boys into the living room. Antonio, you can help Jeremy if you like. Everyone else, amuse yourselves until dinner. I'll be in my office."

Before anyone could say another word, Dominic walked out. Antonio murmured something to Jeremy, then rounded up the three older boys and shepherded them from the room. Jeremy followed.

"What do you want to do?" Nick asked me.

"Can we go outside?" I asked.

"Sure. Let's go."

As we headed for the door, I glanced over my shoulder to see Daniel trailing along behind us.

"Don't worry," Nick whispered. "We'll ditch him as soon as we're out of the house."

And with that we left.

Snitch

We pulled on our shoes and coats, and went out the back door. Daniel followed.

"Once we get to the path, run," Nick whispered. "Keep running until he gives up."

As plans went, this sounded somewhat primitive, but Nick had the experience in this matter, so I went along with it.

The path led into the forest behind the house. It started behind a wooden shed, which meant that by the time we reached it, we were out of view of the house, so no one would see us abandon Daniel.

When we reached the path, Nick took a quick look around, then whispered, "Run!"

I quickly discovered one drawback to the plan. A werewolf's special skills are intended to improve our chances of survival. Yet Mother Nature is selective with her gifts, apportioning no more than necessary. She gave us additional strength for fighting off our enemies, so that was what we were designed to do when faced with danger: fight, not run. In wolf form we run as fast as a wolf and in human form we run as fast as a human. So Nick, who had a tall, long-legged build, was a whole lot faster than Daniel . . . and a whole lot faster than me.

After a quarter-mile of enduring Daniel panting at my heels and Nick's impatient waves for me to catch up, I stopped and turned to face Daniel.

"Go away," I said.

He looked past me to Nick who was jogging back to us. "Your grandpa said you're supposed to play with me."

"I didn't hear that," Nick said. "You hear that, Clayton?"

This didn't seem like a good time to become talkative, so I kept my mouth shut.

"Your grandpa said—"

"He said Clayton was supposed to play with you and me. But I'm not playing with you, so Clayton can't play with us both, can he? He has to pick." Nick stepped up beside me. "Who do you pick, Clayton? Me or him?"

One could point out that this was a pivotal moment, and had I refused to choose one boy over the other or suggested that we all play together, I would have saved myself a whole lot of pain twenty-five years later, might have even saved the lives of two people I cared about. Call it denial, but I don't see it that way. I honestly believe that had I acted differently, things would have turned out the same, that there were too many other factors that built up over those twenty-five years to blame it on something as simplistic as this.

The truth is that I was incapable of making any other decision. Even to call it a decision implied a choice between two options. For me, there was only one answer. Nick had been nice to me; Daniel had not. I have zero capacity for political insight—I cannot look at a situation like this, mentally play out both sides and make a conscious choice based on what might be the politic thing to do, what might earn the best long-term results.

"I want to play with Nick," I said.

Another boy might have flaunted his victory by grinning at his opponent or sticking out his tongue. Nick just nodded, waved for me to follow him and raced down the path. I tore off after him. As for Daniel, I don't know what he did. It never occurred to me to look back.

Nick led me to the middle of the forest, where Antonio had built him a tree fort. It was no more than eight feet off the ground— high enough to be fun, but not high enough to be dangerous. We climbed up and Nick took two bottles of soda and a bag of beef jerky from his secret stash.

"I know I shouldn't be mean to Danny," he said as we opened our bottles. "Pack brothers and all that but, man, he is such a sneaky little shit. Sometimes I play with him, because I'm supposed to and there's no one else my age, right? And I'm nice to him, share my stuff and everything, and he pretends to be really nice back, so I think, okay, he's not so bad. But then, later, when his brothers get going, making fun of me, saying I'm stupid and spoiled and stuff, Danny's right there with them, laughing at their jokes, calling me names." Nick champed off a piece of beef jerky. "You know any kids like that?"

I shook my head.

"Well, you're lucky, then. You know what else about Danny? He's a sneak. A sneak and a snitch. Nothing worse than that, is there?"

I had no idea what Nick was talking about, but I nodded because it seemed like what I was supposed to do.

"You like school?" Nick asked, passing me another strip of jerky.

I shook my head.

He grinned. "Good. I hate it. Especially math. Do you guys have to do multiplication yet?"

I shook my head.

"Lucky. What grade are you in anyway? Oh, wait, you're a year younger than me, so you'd be in second grade, right?"

I considered this, but felt compelled to honesty. "Kindergarten. They made me go in kindergarten."

Nick scrunched up his face. "Why?"

"Because I didn't go to school before," I said.

"Oh, right. Yeah, I guess that makes sense. But kindergarten? With the babies? Bummer. They'll move you up soon, though. 'Cause you're smart and all. You read better than me, so they have to move you up. Maybe they'll do it after the Christmas break. That's when they change stuff at my school, after the Christmas break and after the spring break. I can't wait for Christmas break. We get almost a whole month off, because some of the kids live in other countries and stuff. How long do you guys get?"

Again, I felt compelled to set the record straight. Nick had called Daniel "a sneak and a snitch." I wasn't exactly sure what those terms referred to in the lexicon of preadolescent boys, but I suspected some form of dishonesty was involved, and I was determined not to follow in Daniel's footsteps.

"I'm not in school now," I said. "I got kicked out."

Nick's eyes went wide. "Kicked out? Wow. That's so cool." He paused, seeing my expression. "Hey, don't worry, I won't tell anyone. I'm real good at keeping secrets. What did you do?" Another pause. "You don't have to tell me if you don't want to."

I could tell by his expression that if I didn't tell him, he wouldn't hold it against me, but he would be disappointed. So far I'd seen nothing to indicate he was anything less than trustworthy. I was also, I'll admit, somewhat eager to explain what had happened, to get another child's opinion on why something as innocent as a scientific experiment had warranted screams of horror and swift expulsion.

So I told him about dissecting the guinea pig. He listened with rapt attention. The last words had barely left my mouth before the bushes near the base of the tree erupted, and Daniel flew out from his hiding spot and raced for the house.

"He's going to tell!" Nick said, jumping up so fast he bumped his head on the low ceiling. "Come on! We have to catch him!"

As he climbed down and started to run, I hesitated, wondering what Daniel was going to tell, and to whom. Then I figured it out, leapt up, spilling soda onto my jeans, and vaulted out of the tree house. That was a mistake: jumping down instead of climbing. It was an easy leap for a werewolf, and I landed on my feet, but it shocked Nick enough to race back, thinking I'd fallen. By the time he started running again, Daniel had too much of a head start. We tore from the woods just in time to see the back door to the house closing behind him.

As we ran across the lawn, I told myself the situation wasn't as bad as it might be. When we'd left the house, Jeremy and Antonio had been teaching the older boys and Dominic had been in his office. Daniel would undoubtedly blurt his news to his father and the others first, leaving me time to find Jeremy and warn him. Then Jeremy could tell Dominic about my school mishap before Daniel did . . . and put a less damning slant on the story.

Nick pulled open the back door. Down the hall I saw Daniel dart into the living room, and heard his father call out a greeting.

Nick sprinted down the hall. I slowed to sniff the air, searching for Jeremy. Then I heard Dominic's voice . . . coming from the living room. He asked Daniel where Nick and I were.

Everyone was in the living room.

"No!" I shouted, nearly tripping as I stumbled forward.

"Clayton got kicked out of school," Daniel announced, his

voice ringing down the hall. "He killed the class guinea pig and cut it up."

I lunged past Nick, nearly knocking him flying as I swung around through the living room doorway.

"He's lying!" I said. "It was already dead!"

Apparently, the state of the guinea pig before the dissection was not the issue. Getting kicked out of school was. And I suspect they were a little concerned about the dissection part, too. Killing the animal they would have understood; cutting it up after it was dead just seemed . . . strange.

Although Jeremy hadn't asked me to lie about still being in school, he'd really hoped Dominic wouldn't learn the truth, and for good reason. At lunch, Dominic had said he'd given Jeremy a one-year probation period with me. It would be several years before I fully understood what that meant.

When Dominic learned that Jeremy had brought me home, he'd evaluated the situation, based on what Malcolm had said about me from that first encounter in Baton Rouge and what Antonio reported from his first visit, taking into account that Malcolm had exaggerated my wildness to embellish his story and Antonio had downplayed it to help Jeremy's cause. With these quasi-facts in mind, Dominic made a decision. Jeremy could keep me for one year. If at the end of that year, I was civilized enough to walk down the streets of New York without raising eyebrows, Jeremy could keep me. And if Jeremy failed? Then I had to die.

That explained why Jeremy had been so eager to get me off to school, sending me as soon as I had my Changes under control. Socially, I'd been far from ready for daily interaction with other children, but Jeremy had been desperate, seeing the end of the year only months away and me still growling at children in the town playground.

He had been determined to give me a permanent place in the Pack by proving that I could be a normal child. What better way to do that than to have me successfully enrolled in school, like every other normal child?

So when Dominic found out otherwise, what did he do? Laughed it off.

As Dominic pointed out, my early interest in anatomy might put some question marks in the psychological fitness section of my school records, but it wasn't as if I'd been caught tearing the animal apart with my nails and gulping bloodied chunks. No one was going to read that report and think "oh my god, the kid's a werewolf!" And, really, that was all Dominic cared about.

I walked upright. I could speak enough to be understood. I rarely growled at people. I was no more likely to piss on a tree than any other seven-year-old boy. I could pass for human, and that was all that mattered.

If I couldn't pass for human, would Dominic have really ordered my death? Yes. I'm sure of it. That never bothered me, never altered my opinion of him. Nothing in my life had ever given me reason to think that I had a God-given right to live. Werewolves don't have the luxury of sentimentality. Like a wolf Alpha male, every decision a Pack Alpha makes comes down to one question: how does it affect the safety of the Pack? A feral child whose Changes are uncontrollable is a clear exposure risk for all werewolves.

Where Dominic failed, though, is where Jeremy's wider vision succeeded. When Dominic learned of my existence, he'd left me out there in the bayou where any human could have found me. He wasn't able to see the larger picture. Had I been on Pack territory, he would have handled the situation. As it was, I was on the other side of the country, having no connection to the Pack, so he didn't see the threat. Jeremy did.

Jeremy knew that if I was found, the effects of that discovery would ripple back to the Pack. It was not, however, in Jeremy's nature to eliminate the threat by killing me. To the other Pack members, I was a mutt—vermin werewolf. To Jeremy, I was a child werewolf, as entitled to protection and to a normal life as any Pack son.

As for mutts, if the Pack's view of them seems harsh, one must remember that integral question: how does this affect the safety of the Pack? Mutts are a threat. They are always a threat. No matter what kind of lives they lead, whether they kill humans or not, their existence threatens the Pack because they are beyond the control of the Pack and they are beyond the safety net that the Pack brotherhood supplies.

Dominic's approach to handling mutts was the same as that of every Alpha who came before him. He imposed rules of engagement that every Pack wolf was supposed to obey. If a mutt steps onto your territory, kill him. If you encounter a mutt off Pack territory, kill him. And if you're feeling restless, have some excess aggression to spend, then go find a mutt and kill him.

As a plan for dealing with the mutt problem, this was about as sophisticated as Nick's method for getting rid of Daniel and, not surprisingly, Jeremy saw the flaws in it. He hadn't yet come up with a solution—or not one that anyone would listen to. In the meantime, he bowed out of Pack-organized mutt hunts and, since he rarely left Pack territory, he didn't need to worry about killing any he bumped into while traveling. This did, however, leave one problem. If a mutt came near Stonehaven, Jeremy was supposed to kill him. So far, in my year with him, this hadn't happened. Jeremy's luck, though, couldn't hold forever, and the next spring I had my first encounter with a trespassing mutt.

Duel

Winter came and went, and spring returned. It was later this year, but by early May snow was a memory and the ground had hardened enough that Jeremy no longer handed me a mop and pail each time I raced into the house without removing my shoes.

Little had changed at Stonehaven. Malcolm came back in late December, but his week-long stay was uneventful. He paid no attention to us, we paid no attention to him and, before we knew it, he was gone again, having scarcely sent a ripple through the calm of our day-to-day life.

With spring came fresh litters of baby rabbits under the old-est, biggest pine tree in the front yard. A group of rabbits had made their warren here years ago, and lived under the shadow of werewolves in relative safety. Jeremy had decreed the warren off-limits. Having it there was like having a food factory on our front lawn. Jeremy didn't use those exact words, but I got the picture. Adult rabbits bore baby rabbits—lots of them—and the warren was small, so those baby rabbits had to find a new place to live. Most moved into the woods of Stonehaven. Once there, they were fair game.

One day in May, as late afternoon stretched into evening, the baby rabbits ventured out to explore their new world, and I was using the opportunity to practice my hunting skills. I was in human form, which added challenge. The game was to see how close I could get, both upwind and downwind, before the mother rabbits noticed me and herded their babies back into the warren.

After they went into hiding, I'd back off until they returned, then start over. Being skittish animals, they often waited a half-hour or more before venturing forth again. I didn't mind the wait. It was a warm spring evening, my lessons were done, Jeremy was sketching on the front step and I had all the time in the world.

As the light faded, Jeremy crept over near my hiding spot, being careful not to disturb the rabbits, and motioned that he was going to take his sketch pad inside, then join me in my game. I grinned and nodded, and he slipped off to the house.

Almost as soon as the door closed behind Jeremy, I heard the rumble of a car slowing near the house. From where I sat, I couldn't see it. The Danverses built the existing house to suit their needs in every way. The house itself was over two hundred feet from the road, with a winding driveway and a front lawn strategically dotted with evergreens. From the road, you could barely glimpse our roof. The world couldn't see us, and we couldn't see them.

The car engine died. A door opened, then shut. From the distance of the noise, the driver had stopped at the end of the drive. I tensed and listened. Footsteps crunched along the gravel. Heavy steps. A man. A salesman? Stonehaven didn't see many door-to-door salespeople, and I'd recently overheard Jeremy joking to Antonio that the one upside of my incident with the Avon lady was that he hadn't seen an encyclopedia or vacuum salesperson in months.

Of course, Jeremy hadn't known I'd been listening or he'd never have said that, putting a positive spin on negative behavior. When I overheard things like this, though, it only confirmed my suspicion that when it came to such matters, what Jeremy told me was not always what he'd like to tell me. He might say it was okay for salespeople to come to the door, but the truth was that he didn't like trespassers any more than I did. That meant I had all the more reason to scare them away. I just had to be sneakier about doing it.

So now, with a stranger on the property and Jeremy in the house, I knew what I had to do—get rid of the interloper before Jeremy knew he was there. I pinpointed the man's location and looped around the tree.

I kept downwind. With humans, this was unnecessary, but it was second nature to me.

As I crept around behind the man, I spotted him. He was short and stocky, maybe ten years older than Jeremy, with a light brown brush cut. Before I could take another step, I caught a whiff of the man's scent.

He was a werewolf.

I stopped short and tried to get a better look, see whether he resembled any of the sketches in Jeremy's room. Maybe he was this "Peter" that Jeremy was concerned about. Yet the man had his back to me and in the waning light I could see no more than his build and hair color.

I decided to scoot back into the shadows, zip around him and get Jeremy. I'd just turned when I heard the swish of Jeremy's loafers in the grass. I looked to see him a few yards from the stoop. He stood hidden by the shadow of a pine. He was upwind of the other werewolf, which meant the newcomer should have scented him, but he didn't notice Jeremy until he was less than a few feet away.

Jeremy opened his mouth, then blinked, catching the other man's scent. He hesitated only a split-second, then said, "May I help you?"

"Sure," the other man said, his voice grating with a strange accent. "You can get your daddy for me, boy. Tell him Carl Pritchard wants to talk to him."

"My father isn't home," Jeremy said. "And not likely to return anytime soon."

For several minutes, neither man spoke, but just stood there, watching one another.

"That's a shame," Pritchard said at last. "Course, it'd be even more of a shame if I came all this way for nothing. I'm thinking maybe I could have that talk with you instead."

"If it's my father you wanted, I'm a poor substitute."

Pritchard rocked on his heels. "Maybe, maybe not. Your daddy does have a damned fine reputation, but a rare opponent is just about as good as a famous one. Can't say I've ever met anyone who fought the elusive Danvers Junior."

"That doesn't mean no one ever has. It just means no one ever returned to tell the tale."

Pritchard barked a laugh. "Nice try, boy, but from what I hear, the real reason is you've never stuck around long enough to let anyone throw a punch."

Jeremy tensed, but quickly hid it with a shrug. "If that's true, it won't gain you anything to bother with me, will it? So I would suggest that you return when my father is home and take up your quarrel with him."

The man laughed again. "Another nice try, but you aren't going to weasel out of it that easily. I'm throwing down the towel."

"You're giving up? Can't say I blame you."

Pritchard scowled. "I'm challenging you."

"Ah. Well, in that case, for future reference, the correct phrase is 'throwing down the *gauntlet*.' And, you know, that's a fine idea, so why don't you just go out, find yourself a gauntlet, bring it back, throw it down and we'll talk … or fight, though I must warn you, I'm a much better talker."

For the next couple of minutes, Pritchard said nothing. I think it took him that long to process Jeremy's words, and even then, when he did speak, there was an air of hesitancy.

"I'm challenging you to a duel."

"Right then. A duel. At dawn? Does that work for you? Pistols or rapiers? My swordsmanship is a bit rusty, but I could probably make do."

Again, Pritchard hesitated, dull brain whirring. "I don't think you're taking this seriously."

"No? Really? Perhaps that's because the situation itself is so ludicrous I find it impossible to take seriously." Jeremy stepped forward. "You're here because you want to challenge my father. At worst, you could die. But even at best, if you kill him, what have you have gained? A better reputation as a fighter. What will that get you? More challenges. More challenges equals more chances that you aren't going to live to see forty."

"Yeah. So?"

"It's *stupid*," Jeremy said, meeting Pritchard's eyes. "Is that obvious to no one but me?"

"This is the way it works. The way it's always worked. I come here. I'm on your territory. You have to kill me."

"No, I don't have to. That may be the practice, but it's not the Law."

"Damn," Pritchard said with a laugh. "You're as yellow as they say."

Jeremy's cheek twitched and Pritchard tensed, obviously expecting that would goad Jeremy into a fight. Instead, Jeremy turned his back and began to walk away.

"You think about what I said," Jeremy said. "I'll give you one hour to get off my territory. Then I'm coming after you."

"Whoo-hoo. I'm scared now."

Jeremy just kept walking. Pritchard waited another minute, then snorted in disgust, turned on his heel and stormed back down the drive. At the front door, Jeremy turned and peered into the night. Seeing Pritchard gone, he hurried over to where I hid in the trees.

"Come on, Clayton," he said. "Into the garage. We need to follow him."

Jeremy followed Pritchard's car, keeping his lights off.

"I know you might not understand what you heard," Jeremy said after a few minutes. "I'm not sure even I can explain it, not in any way that makes sense to me."

"He's a mutt, isn't he?"

"Yes, and they aren't supposed to come on our territory, but they do. We say they can't, but the Pack doesn't always mean it. It's...complicated. The point is that mutts think if they hurt a Pack wolf, it'll make them important, and the best way to get a chance to do that is to come on our territory."

"Because you're supposed to fight them."

"Yes. But I didn't, and I'm sure you're wondering about that."

"It's like you said about him. If you win, more mutts will come. They'll want to fight you, too."

Jeremy blinked, as if surprised that I'd picked up on this. Then his lips curved in a quarter-smile. "Smart boy. Amazing how that can make sense to you, yet no one else seems to see it."

"What if he doesn't leave? Will you fight him?"

"I said I would. I have to follow through."

"But at the Meet, Wally said..." I let the sentence trail off.

Jeremy glanced over at me. "He said I don't fight mutts. That I let Malcolm do it for me. That's what he believes—what most of them believe—and I see no reason to enlighten them. If they know I fight trespassing mutts, they'll expect me to fight more, perhaps even challenge me."

"This mutt . . . will you kill him?"

"Not if I can help it. Usually a fight is enough."

"But if you killed him, then he couldn't come back. And he couldn't tell other mutts he fought you, so they wouldn't come either."

"If only it was that easy. Before mutts come here, they tell other mutts what they're going to do, who they're going to challenge. That's part of the game. If Carl Pritchard's friends never see him again, they'll know he lost the fight. They'd probably think Malcolm killed him, and that's fine with me, but it doesn't solve the problem. The higher my father's reputation is, the more mutts will come looking for him. And more often than not, they'll find me instead."

"You need to stop them from coming."

"If I knew how to do that, Clayton, believe me, I would." Another small smile. "Maybe someday you can figure it out for me."

For ninety minutes we crouched in the woods behind the Big Bear Motor Lodge, watching Pritchard's motel window, hoping to see the light turn out and hear the roar of his car engine as he beat a hasty retreat from Bear Valley. It never happened.

Finally, Jeremy sighed and shook his head. "Looks like I need to finish this, Clayton. I want you to go back to the car and wait." He handed me the car keys. "Do you remember where we parked?"

I pointed into the woods. "On the other side. Behind the warehouse."

"Good boy. Now, you need to stay in there and be quiet. Don't let anyone see you." He reached into his pocket, took out something, then undid his watch band. "Here's two dimes and my watch. Listen carefully, okay?"

I nodded.

"It's just past ten thirty. When it's eleven o'clock, if I haven't come back yet, then you leave the car and run to the gas station across the road. It's closed. Go to the phone booth and put in a dime. Call Antonio collect. Do you remember the number?"

Jeremy had drilled me on this months ago, teaching me Antonio's phone number even before our own.

"Call him and tell him what happened. He'll—" Jeremy faltered. "He'll look after everything. Okay?"

When I nodded, he had me repeat back the instructions, then sent me off.

I walked back to the car, got inside, waited just long enough to ensure that Jeremy would think I'd obeyed him. Then I headed back to the motel.

This was not a simple matter. Even opening the door handle was a monumental struggle. There was nothing wrong with the door; the problem lay within me.

My wolf's brain was wired to obey my leader without question. Dominic may have been Pack Alpha, but Jeremy was *my* alpha, and I don't think he realized how much sway his words had over me.

Yet as much as I was hardwired to obey, there was now another equally strong instinct conflicting with that one: the need to protect Jeremy. When obedience runs counter to protection, the protective instinct always wins.

So I made my way back to Jeremy. I never reached the motel,

though. By that time, Jeremy and Pritchard had moved into the middle of the patch of woods between the car and the motel. I stopped short as their words reached me.

"How do I know you're not going to attack me while I Change?" Pritchard asked.

"Easy," Jeremy replied. "We're not going to Change."

They kept their voices low, so no one outside the woods would hear them. I left the path, got downwind of the pair and crept through the brush until I could see them.

"But we have to Change," Pritchard said. "That's the rule."

"Are you a better fighter as a wolf?"

"Well, no, but..."

"Then I'm not taking advantage of you, am I? Since you've mentioned the possibility of me attacking you while you Change, I can't help but suspect you've considered doing the same thing."

"Hey! I know the rules—"

"Then you know that Changing form first isn't one of them. We're barely a hundred feet from humans. Either you fight me like this, or you don't fight me at all."

"Oh-ho, so that's what you're hoping, is it, boy?"

Jeremy's right hook flew out so fast that all I saw was Pritchard stumble backward. Then I saw Jeremy's arm retract from the blow.

"Does that answer your question?" Jeremy said.

With a roar, Pritchard charged. Jeremy feinted out of the way, swung around behind Pritchard and slammed a fist into the side of his head. Pritchard reeled.

"Anytime you want to stop, you say so," Jeremy said.

Another roar. Another charge. Again Jeremy feinted, but didn't have time to land a blow before Pritchard wheeled, fists swinging. Jeremy backpedaled fast, catching only a glancing blow in the side. He landed another strike on Pritchard, but couldn't avoid a hook to the jaw. As Jeremy recovered, he spat blood. Pritchard barreled toward him, but Jeremy recovered in time to feint and strike from behind.

And so the fight went. Jeremy avoided roughly two-thirds of Pritchard's attacks. Of those he couldn't dodge, at least half resulted in glancing blows that didn't even throw him off balance. In contrast, Pritchard felt the full impact of most of Jeremy's hits.

I'd seen enough of Jeremy and Antonio's wrestling matches to recognize exactly where Pritchard went wrong. Jeremy's fighting style was largely defensive. Antonio knew how Jeremy fought and he adapted accordingly, changing tack as soon as he picked up on Jeremy's pattern. Then Jeremy would change his pattern, and Antonio would adapt to that, and so on.

Both men had very different styles, but neither was significantly better—one just suited each better than the other. What Jeremy and Antonio both excelled in, though, was adaptability. I didn't realize this until I saw Pritchard losing to Jeremy. He may have been stronger, and he may have been more experienced, but he couldn't adapt. No matter how many times Jeremy dodged a charge, wheeled and landed a blow, Pritchard never stopped charging.

Finally, after one of Jeremy's lightning-fast blows to his head, Pritchard went down and stayed down.

"Enough?" Jeremy wheezed, wiping blood from his mouth.

Pritchard nodded.

Jeremy straightened and turned away. He'd gone no more than a yard when Pritchard pulled himself up, moving slowly enough not to make any noise. His narrowed eyes were on Jeremy and I knew what he was going to do. I opened my mouth to shout a warning, but before I could, Jeremy slowed. His head turned just slightly. Then his mouth tightened, and I knew he'd somehow sensed Pritchard moving. He didn't turn around, though. He kept walking.

Pritchard pushed himself to his feet, then charged. Jeremy swung around and dodged easily, but this time wheeled at the very moment Pritchard passed, and threw himself onto his back. Both men went down.

From my vantage point, I couldn't see what happened next. The men hit the ground. There was a sharp crack. And everything went still. A long moment of silence passed, then Jeremy stood. Pritchard stayed on the ground, his head to the side, dead eyes fixed in a look of disbelief.

"Goddamn you," Jeremy said, his voice infused with cold fury. "Goddamn you."

He stood there a moment, staring down at Pritchard's lifeless body. Then he turned and strode back toward the motel. I scampered to the car.

About ten minutes after I got into the car, the trunk clicked open. The car dipped as Jeremy lowered Pritchard's body in. He would have to be buried at Stonehaven. That was Pack Law, that mutts killed on our territory be buried on the victor's land, not as a trophy, but as a safety precaution, so they wouldn't be dug up by plows or bulldozers or hunting dogs. Every member of the Pack knew how to dispose of a body. It was part of the lessons young werewolves received as they approached their first Change.

The trunk snapped shut. Then the driver's door opened and Jeremy slid in. I looked over at him.

"It's over," he said softly. "There's nothing to worry about."

But I knew there was. That night, I had my first glimpse into a problem that had plagued Jeremy from the moment he'd become a full-fledged werewolf, and one that would continue to plague him for the next decade. As long as mutts continued to treat Pack territory as a gladiatorial arena, our home would never be a true sanctuary. Someone needed to stop the mutts from coming.

Jeremy had half-jokingly invited me to come up with a solution. It would take nearly a decade before I did, but I never forgot that it was a problem that required solving.

Dare

For most children, fall means school. For me, it only meant cooler weather, which I always welcomed after two months of sweltering heat. Compared to Louisiana, New York might not get that hot, but when you're racing around the woods in a fur coat, anything over seventy is hot.

As for school, Jeremy and Dominic had decided to keep me out until high school. Shortly after my expulsion, Jeremy had started me on a formal home-schooling program, which satisfied the state. I was happy at home, Jeremy was an excellent teacher and I was well ahead of my public school peers, so there was no need to hurry me back to institutionalized learning.

Being home schooled, though, did mean that I missed out on a convenient form of peer socialization. To compensate, Jeremy enrolled me in extracurricular programs in Syracuse. Bear Valley did offer some recreational programs for children, but the Pack has always counseled its members to limit their participation in the local social scene. People in Bear Valley knew us enough to say hello, but little more than that. So Jeremy drove me in to Syracuse for my weekly programs.

Choosing activities for me proved a test of Jeremy's intuitive abilities. First, he tried soccer. I put my foot through the ball. Then he tried model building. After two weeks gluing plastic bits onto a model of the *Titanic,* I decided to stage a historical re-creation—using the classroom wall as my iceberg.

By this point I'm sure Jeremy gave up trying to pick a program to suit me, closed his eyes and randomly pointed at one in the recreation guide. The result? Drama. And, to Jeremy's surprise, I liked it. Not that I enjoyed performing—I loathed that part, and managed to contract an inexplicable case of laryngitis every time family performance day rolled around. What I liked, though, was the opportunity to learn how to play a role. For me, that was a far more useful skill than knowing how to kick a ball or build a ship.

So Jeremy kept me in drama classes one season a year, and for the other three we tried different things. He quickly learned what worked and what didn't. Team sports, like baseball, didn't. Individual sports, like swimming, did. Purely artistic endeavors, like music, didn't. Functional skill-building classes, like cooking, did. Yes, I enjoyed home ec, even if I was the only boy there and the girls fell into fits of giggling every time I walked in. Cooking was a useful skill. And, living with Jeremy, who couldn't heat canned soup without scorching it, I knew that cooking was an *essential* skill.

With these classes, I learned life skills and basic socialization. I also learned that children could rival Malcolm for sheer malicious cruelty. Despite Jeremy's hopes, I never made a friend in those classes. I was different, and other kids sensed that like a Pack wolf can sense a mutt.

Not understanding what made me different, the children seized on the differences they could see. They mocked my accent. They made fun of my height, being still a head shorter than most boys my age. They ridiculed my interest in cooking and drama, which the other boys considered "girlie" classes. On a slow day, they'd even make fun of my hair, which was either worn too short or too long, depending on their mood.

I knew there was nothing I could do or say to win their favor—and I had no desire to, which didn't help matters. When Jeremy was around, I gritted my teeth and made nice with the other kids. The rest of the time I ignored them and did my own thing.

As for friends, I had my Pack brothers. While I never did befriend Daniel, Joey and I got along fine. As for Nick, after that first Pack meeting, when we were together, we were inseparable.

The October after Jeremy killed the mutt Pritchard, Antonio and Nick came down for a weekend, as they did at least once a month. Saturday morning, Nick and I were out back, having some trouble deciding how best to use our time together.

"No way," Nick said, slumping cross-legged onto the ground. "You're not hunting me again."

"But I need more practice."

"Yeah, well I don't need you giving me another black eye."

"I didn't give you a black eye. You tripped."

"And you pounced and slammed me face-first into a rock."

I leaned against a tree trunk. "That's because *you* need more practice."

"At what? Getting the crap beaten out of me?"

"At escaping. If you let me hunt you, then I can teach you how to do that."

"How about you teach me how to hunt? *You* play the helpless victim and I'll chase you—"

"You're not a werewolf yet, so you don't need to know how to hunt. You need to know how to run away." When he didn't answer, I sighed. "Okay, how about wrestling then? Jeremy taught me this new move—"

"Which you can't wait to try out on me. Uh-uh. No hunting. No wrestling. No games where Nicky gets the shit beat out of him, okay? Think up something else."

I thought about it. And thought about it some more. While I continued to think, Nick stood and stretched his legs. He wandered to a nearby oak and peered up into its nearly bare branches.

"Bet you can't jump from that branch," he said, pointing up to one about twenty feet from the ground.

Nick loved testing the limits of my werewolf abilities. Not a pastime that lacked challenge, though it ran a distant second to hunting-and-stalking games.

"If I can, will you let me try my new wrestling move?"

"Only if it doesn't make me bleed."

"It's not my fault you bleed easily."

"If I bleed, I'm not sneaking you any extra food tonight."

"Fine, you won't bleed." I grabbed the lowest tree limb and swung up onto it. "Come on."

We climbed to the branch. Nick tried to stop halfway, but I egged him on until we were sitting side-by-side on the branch he'd chosen for his dare.

"You really think you can do it?" Nick asked, looking down. "Seems pretty high." He slid a smile my way. "I wouldn't blame you if you chickened out."

I flexed my legs and measured the distance to the ground. It *was* too high. Not that I'd ever chicken out, but I had to be careful how I landed. The last time we played this game, I'd miscalculated my leap and twisted my ankle, then had to tough it out for three days so Jeremy wouldn't know what I'd done.

I was visualizing my jump when a car pulled into the driveway.

I cocked my head, listening. The engine died. A car door slammed. Neither noise sounded as if it came from any car I knew. I jumped from the tree, hitting the ground hard enough to send pain stabbing through my calves.

"Whoa," Nick called down. "That was—"

I dashed off toward the house.

"Clay?" A moment's pause. "Clayton! Don't leave me here!"

I kept running. I'd return for Nick later. He could wait; this intruder couldn't.

I tore from the woods and around the side of the house, scrambling over the low fence and heading for the front yard. I was certain I'd be too late, that the trespasser would already have made it to the door and disturbed Jeremy, but as I rounded the house, I saw a figure still standing by a car. It was a young man, maybe a year or two younger than Jeremy, with red hair past his shoulders. He stared up at the house, chewing on his lower lip.

One whiff and I knew he was a werewolf. My first thought was *mutt*, but then I saw his face and recognized him from a sketch in Jeremy's room. This was the elusive Peter, the only Pack member I hadn't met.

When I slipped from the hedge, his nostrils flared and, scenting me, he turned. He blinked, then offered a tentative smile.

"Hey, you must be Clayton. Hello."

I returned the greeting with a nod and took a few cautious steps closer. Yes, this was a Pack wolf, but I didn't know the man, so I wasn't going to rush out and hug him. Okay, even if I did know him, I wouldn't rush out and hug him, but the point is, I had reason to be wary. All I knew about this guy was that whenever Jeremy mentioned his name, there was a note of concern in his voice. I moved closer to the front door, putting myself between it and him.

"Is Jeremy here?" Peter asked, enunciating each word slowly, as if speaking to someone of limited mental capacity.

I nodded.

"Is Mal—is Jeremy . . . alone?"

I shook my head.

"Oh, okay, then." Peter turned back to his car. "Well, maybe I'll come back later."

"Malcolm's not here," I said. "Just Antonio and Nick."

Peter blinked, as if surprised that I could speak. "Oh, ummm, well, maybe I should still come back. He's probably busy with Antonio—"

"He's not." I pulled open the front door. "Jeremy!"

Peter winced at my shout, then gave one last longing look at his car, and pocketed his keys. Jeremy appeared at the front door. Seeing Peter, his lips curved in a smile.

"Peter," he said. "This is a surprise. Good to see you. Come on in."

As he ushered Peter inside, his gaze went to me. Then behind me. His brows arched in a look I knew only too well.

"I'll go get Nick," I said.

"Good idea."

Nick had managed to make it down from the tree easily enough. The trouble was finding his way out of the forest. You'd think that anyone who had been visiting Stonehaven since he was old enough to toddle would know his way around the woods there, particularly when that someone had werewolf blood, but Nick often had trouble finding his way out of the forest at his own house.

He obviously needed more practice, but no matter how often I abandoned him out there, his sense of direction never seemed to improve. That, of course, only increased my resolve to keep leaving him there. What were friends for, if not to help you over-come your weaknesses?

Antonio met us as we exited the forest.

"I was just coming to find you boys," he said. "Jeremy's going to be busy with Peter for a while, and they don't need us bugging them, so how about we take a ride into town? Pick up dinner, maybe grab an ice cream cone?"

I glanced at the house. As tempted as I was by Antonio's offer, I had a responsibility here that outweighed any duty I owed to my stomach.

If Antonio went into town, Jeremy would be alone in the house with another werewolf. A Pack wolf, to be sure, but my ex-perience so far hadn't led me to decide that Pack membership meant a werewolf could be trusted. Until I knew more about this Peter, I wasn't leaving him with Jeremy.

"I'll stay," I said.

I expected Antonio to tease me about turning down food, but he just gave me a long, hard look that led me to suspect he knew exactly why I was staying. His gaze traveled to the house, then back to me, and his mouth opened, as if to say something. Instead he only patted me on the back.

"Just stay outside, okay, scrap? They need to talk. Nicky? You coming?"

Nick shook his head.

"All right, but behave yourselves and don't bother Jeremy and Peter. I'll be back soon."

We did as we were told, staying outdoors and not bothering Jeremy and Peter. Yet that could be done while sitting outside the study window, where we could listen to the conversation within. Kids who don't eavesdrop on adult conversations are doomed to a childhood of ignorance.

Of what I heard that afternoon, I understood only one key point: that Peter was leaving the Pack. Why he was leaving, what that meant for his life, how difficult that decision was for him to make, all that I wouldn't fully understand for years to come. From the tone of the conversation, though, I knew that this decision marked the end of a long personal struggle with the issue of Pack-hood. I knew too that this was a decision Jeremy had both known and feared was coming.

Roughly half of all Pack youth left the group in their early twenties. It was like membership in any regimented segment of human society—children stay with the group because they have to, then when they hit adulthood, they realize that they have a choice. Some, like Antonio, chafe at the rules, but not enough to consider leaving. Some, like Jeremy, disagree with many of the principles, but believe in the institution itself enough to stay and try to effect change from within. Others look around and say, "I don't belong here," and this was the case with Peter.

In the tight-knit Pack, family is all-important—not just the figurative brotherhood of the group, but the literal bloodlines. The Sorrentinos, the Santoses and the Danverses were the founding families of the American Pack. Being part of one of those families automatically elevated your status.

Peter's father had brought them to the Pack when Peter was little more than a baby, the new responsibility of fatherhood having made him decide that he wanted a more secure life for his son. Yet he'd never really been accepted, and Peter had grown up seeing and feeling that ostracism. With his father having died five years ago, there was nothing to tie Peter to the Pack.

Now, halfway through a college degree in audiovisual technology, he'd been offered a job on the road crew of a band.

When Peter had told Dominic of the job offer, the Alpha's answer had been clear. A twenty-year-old werewolf, barely old enough to control his Changes, could not leave the safety net of the Pack and go off roaming the country with a rock band. If Peter took this job, he would be banished from the Pack. That was just the excuse Peter needed.

Jeremy argued with him, offered to intercede on his behalf with Dominic and negotiate a compromise, but I could tell by the tone of Jeremy's voice that he knew his offer would be refused. Peter hadn't come to discuss the matter. He came to Stonehaven to see the only Pack member who cared whether he stayed or left.

Finally, his arguments at an end, Jeremy walked Peter to his car. Nick and I slipped around the house to watch and listen.

"Say good-bye to Antonio for me," Peter said as he climbed into his car.

Jeremy nodded.

"You're doing a great job with the boy. Really great."

Jeremy nodded.

Peter started his car and leaned out the window. "I'll call you when I'm settled." A weak smile. "Send you cool postcards from the road, show you what you're missing out there."

Jeremy nodded, but I could tell by the look in his eyes that he didn't expect to ever get that call or see those postcards.

"If you ever need anything," Jeremy said. "Anything at all…"

"I know where to find you," Peter said. "Don't worry about me, Jer. I'll be fine."

Jeremy nodded, then watched the car back down the long drive.

*　　*　　*

The next day Antonio decided Nick and I needed new winter boots. Jeremy bought almost all our clothing by catalogue, which was fine by me because I knew of few tortures worse than spending an afternoon crammed into a dressing room while some middle-aged woman tried to persuade Jeremy that a blue shirt would bring out my eyes so much better than the plain white one I'd chosen.

When it came to footwear, though, it was safer to make the trip ·to the store and find a pair that fit properly. With winter coming, Antonio saw the perfect opportunity to get Jeremy out for the day, with a combined boot-buying, lunch-eating and movie-watching excursion.

Our first stop was lunch. Then off to the shoe store. I found a pair of boots within minutes. Nick took longer, insisting on a brand that "all the other kids had." To me, that would have been the very reason *not* to buy that brand, but Nick was already growing particular about such things, and Antonio always went the extra mile—or block—to get Nick what he wanted. So it was off to the department store down the road, a five-story monstrosity that sold everything from washing machines to hammers to children's boots.

Once Nick had his boots, Jeremy wanted to take a look in the appliances section. We needed a new toaster. I'd broken ours by stuffing two pieces in each slot at once, trying to speed up the process. Since the toaster was one of the few cooking tools Jeremy could reliably operate, we needed a new one—fast.

Few departments hold less interest for young boys than the small appliances section, so Nick asked whether he and I could check out the sporting goods. When Jeremy hesitated, Antonio pulled the "you worry too much" routine, which usually worked; Jeremy hated sounding like a worrywart. He told us we could go, as long as we waited there for them and I didn't touch anything.

Jeremy pointed us in the direction of the store map, and we took off.

According to the map, the sporting goods department was on the first floor. We were on the fifth. That left us with a decision: elevator or escalator. For me, there was no choice. I'd pick zooming down motorized stairs over waiting for a crowded elevator car any day. As we raced past the elevator, though, we saw that we didn't have a choice after all. The elevator was out of order. We ran past the sign, then Nick stopped and walked backward for a better look.

"Cool," he said. "Clay, come here. Check this out."

He disappeared around a rack of girl's dresses. I backtracked and found him stepping over a cord that roped off the elevator area.

The elevator door was open. There were tools scattered around the opening, as if someone had been working on it, but the serviceman was nowhere to be seen. I walked up beside Nick and we looked down the elevator shaft.

"Whoa," Nick said. "Where's the elevator?"

I looked around, then pointed up. It was just above our heads.

"How far down you think that is?" Nick said, peering into the inky black of the shaft. "Twenty feet?"

"Maybe thirty," I said, though I could barely see the floor through the darkness.

"Bet you couldn't jump down that."

"Bet I could."

"Bet you couldn't."

"Could."

"Couldn't."

I looked up at him, meeting his eyes. "How much?"

"All the movie popcorn. You do it, you can have mine. You chicken out, I get yours."

"You're on."

At a low murmur of women's voices, I tensed and motioned for silence. We waited. No one appeared.

"You stand watch," I said.

Nick nodded and walked back to the dress rack. As he went, I squinted into the darkness. Thirty feet? That didn't seem right. If it was five floors, and each floor was at least— I stopped calculating. It didn't matter. I'd taken the dare.

I stepped up to the edge, bent my knees, counted to three... and jumped.

Broken

The first thirty feet of the drop went fine. It was those last twenty that did me in.

By the time I reached the second floor, I'd picked up so much speed that when my elbow glanced off the side of the shaft, my arm whipped up over my head, wrenching my shoulder, and whacked against something protruding from the wall. I heard a crack, but didn't have time to register pain before my feet struck bottom.

I hit hard and, had I not positioned myself exactly right, I'm sure I would have broken my legs...or worse. As it was, I slammed onto the floor of the shaft with my knees bent, absorbing the shock, but the force of the sudden stop pitched me forward. My head hit the wall and I blacked out as pain ripped through my right arm.

I don't know what happened next. Being unconscious does that. Nick might have gone to get Jeremy and Antonio, but knowing Jeremy, he was probably already coming, knowing I was in danger—his usual sixth sense when it came to my safety.

They'd have wanted to get me out of there without alerting anyone, but I'm sure the moment Jeremy had realized I was lying at the bottom of a five-story elevator shaft, unconscious, he'd decided this wasn't a time to worry about calling attention to ourselves. When I regained consciousness, I was lying on the floor, being examined by paramedics, and surrounded by what looked like every customer in the store.

The paramedics declared that I had miraculously escaped serious injury, which they chalked up to a child's resilience. My arm was the worst. When I came to, the first thing I felt was pain. Though the paramedics instructed me to lie still, I managed to twist around and get a look at my arm before they could cover it up.

My forearm was bent above the wrist in a way I knew wasn't natural. Just above the elbow was a gash at least two inches wide and an inch deep. My first thought was *hmmm, that can't be good.* I suppose the sight of my own insides should have been more disturbing, but living in the world I did, where I saw flesh and blood every time I caught a rabbit, it didn't bother me. The pain *did* bother me. I won't say I sucked it up and toughed it out. I was eight years old. I'm sure I cried.

The paramedics wanted to take me to the hospital. An obvious step when a boy fell down an elevator shaft. Not such an obvious step, though, when that boy was a werewolf. Pack werewolves didn't go to hospitals. Mutts had been known to die from infection rather than risk a hospital trip. Fortunately, the Pack had devised a better system.

The Pack has always relied on the power of greed when it comes to finding services it doesn't dare accept from regular sources. If you're willing to pay a premium, you can find a doctor—even a good one—who's willing to set broken limbs and perform minor surgery, no questions asked.

Dominic had found such a doctor in New York, a well-respected physician who ran a side business offering medical services to the Mafia. Dominic insisted we go to him and paid all our bills. And if the doctor ever wondered why he saw a lot of ripped flesh and very few bullet holes, he never said a word, just took our money and stitched us up.

The problem was that our doctor was over four hours away, and I had a gaping wound on my arm plus a good blow to my head. Jeremy and Antonio talked it over—out of earshot of the paramedics, but close enough for me to hear.

Antonio wanted me to go to the Syracuse hospital. Pack wolves are allowed to do this in emergencies, using the ruse of religious beliefs to prevent the staff from analyzing our blood or doing anything else that might lead them to suspect we weren't quite human.

When Jeremy hesitated, Antonio pulled the "you worry too much" routine again, but it wasn't necessary. Had Jeremy himself been lying on the stretcher, he'd have let Antonio drive him to New York, and if he'd suffered as a result of the delay in treatment, so be it.

But this was me. If I needed immediate medical attention, I would get it immediately. We went to the hospital.

The paramedics gave me something for the pain, so most of the ambulance ride was a blur. Next thing I knew I was in a white room being examined by a white-haired man in a white lab coat. After a few seconds of drowsy confusion, during which I feared the fall had affected my ability to see colors, I recognized the setting from a movie and knew I was in a hospital.

"So," the doctor said, holding open one of my eyelids and peering through a silver instrument. "Why aren't you boys in Vietnam?"

I was about to answer when my fuzzy brain cleared enough to realize that it was unlikely he was directing the question at me.

"Haven't been called up yet," Antonio's voice said from somewhere to my left.

I tried to glance at Antonio, but the doctor wrenched my head back so I was facing straight. At Jeremy's touch on my shoulder, I swallowed a growl and kept still. Both Jeremy and Antonio moved behind the doctor so I could see them.

"The recruitment offices closed shop?" the doctor said, shooting a glare Antonio's way.

He shot back a rueful frown. "I wish I could. I really wanted to sign up, but now that my brothers are gone, I'm the only one left to work on the farm. After the heart attack last year... well, my dad's just not the same. And, of course, Jeremy has the boy to look after. But when they call us up, we'll go. Gotta fight for your country. Can't argue with that."

Jeremy made a noise of assent and the doctor seemed placated. Neither Jeremy nor Antonio would be called for the draft. No one in the Pack would. It wasn't a question of patriotism; that much prolonged contact with humans wasn't safe. Like I said, the Pack had long since learned how to take advantage of human greed, and they'd had two World Wars with which to perfect their system of buying draft passes for their members, and those that wished to contribute found other ways to do it.

"You giving these guys a hard time, Doc?" said a young dark-haired nurse as she walked around Jeremy and handed the doctor a chart. She flashed a too-friendly smile at Jeremy and Antonio, then winked. "You want my opinion, I think they should stay out of that hellhole as long as they can."

"When I want your opinion, I'll ask for it," the doctor said, snatching the chart.

While he read it over, the nurse mouthed "grumpy old bugger" at Antonio and Jeremy, and rolled her eyes.

The doctor thrust the chart at her. "Take him down for X rays."

"Sir?" Jeremy said as the doctor turned to walk away. "Do you think he'll need surgery?"

The doctor seemed ready to snap something back, but noticed the concern in Jeremy's eyes and softened his response. "We can probably do this without operating, but let me see the X rays first."

"Thank you."

We picked up another nurse on the way to the X ray room. I didn't think my situation required a second one, but when we passed a young blonde in the halls, our nurse motioned to her, she saw Jeremy and Antonio, and seemed to decide our case was more important than whatever she was currently working on.

Although there was nothing wrong with my legs, the nurse insisted I be transported on a rolling bed. That meant as I was being wheeled down the hall by Jeremy, everyone else could talk literally behind my back. Everyone except Nick, that is, who walked beside me, looking miserable.

Jeremy had told Nick the accident wasn't his fault. I'd told him it wasn't his fault. Even Antonio, after a brief talk about "peer pressure" had, seeing how upset he was, agreed it wasn't entirely his fault. But he was still miserable. So he walked beside me, gaze on the floor, and said nothing.

The nurses said plenty, most of it seeming to have very little to do with my medical condition. They seemed very impressed by Jeremy taking guardianship of his "poor orphaned cousin," and almost equally impressed by Antonio treating his nephew to a day in the city.

Antonio always introduced Nick as his nephew. That was always easier than having people calculate how old—or how young—Antonio had been when his son was born, and giving their opinion on the subject of teen parenthood.

For werewolves, it's common to tangle the limbs of the family tree when dealing with humans. Not only is it an added layer of protective falsehoods, but it solves one problem with our delayed aging.

Werewolves age slowly. Whether this means we can live longer than humans is debatable, since few werewolves live long enough to test the theory. It does mean, though, that we stay physically young longer. Like most of our special abilities, this is all about survival—the longer we stay healthy, the longer we can fight off attacks.

When dealing with the human world, though, it can be tricky. Although it's not impossible for a fifty-year-old man to look thirty-five, it does call attention to him, and no smart werewolf wants that. So we fudge our ages, and lie about our family relationships.

The slow aging doesn't kick in until one becomes a werewolf, so at Antonio's age, the difference was still unnoticeable. No one would look at him and say, "Twenty-six? My god, he doesn't look a day over twenty-four!" Yet in twenty years, they'd have a hard time passing themselves off as father and son. To make things easy, they'd played uncle and nephew right from the start.

The next few hours were unpleasant. Fortunately, the doctor had taken advantage of my drugged state earlier to put in my IV and stitch up the gash on my arm, so I didn't need to suffer through that. Next they x-rayed the break, which they called a dinner-fork fracture, one that could be treated with or without surgery.

elbow. Under the cotton ball was a single blood-crusted pinprick. His eyes shot to mine. "Did someone draw blood from you?"

"I don't think so."

"When I left for dinner did anyone—no, you were asleep, you wouldn't know. Did they move the IV? I would have noticed—"

"Someone came in when you were gone," I cut in. "I was pretty sleepy. I felt something, but I thought they were fixing that other thing."

"Okay," Jeremy said, standing and inhaling deeply. "It's okay. It's only been a couple of hours. They won't have touched it yet. I can call the hospital, tell them they drew blood against my wishes and demand—" He paused and shook his head sharply. "I have a better idea. Just wait—No, let me get you into bed—No, lie down and rest and I'll be right back."

I tried to answer that I wasn't tired, but he was too caught up in his own thoughts to hear me...just as he was too distracted to notice that I followed him downstairs.

I watched from the study doorway as Jeremy rooted around for a phone book. He called the hospital and asked for the phone number of their laboratory, then hung up. For a few minutes, he stood there, as if thinking, then he made a second call.

"This is Dr. Lawson," he said, using the name of the doctor who'd attended to us. His voice took on a clipped, authoritative tone. "I've just been informed that someone took a blood sample from one of my patients—a patient who was not supposed to have any blood work done."

Pause.

"Clayton Danvers."

A longer pause.

"Yes, of course I know his family requested no blood work be done. That's the problem, isn't it? Someone drew his blood against his family's wishes, and if his family finds out, we could face a lawsuit."

Pause.

"Yes, that's the correct room, but the boy was in bed B, not D."

Pause.

"I don't want to know how it happened. My only concern is making it *un*-happen. Take that sample and dispose of it immediately, then shred any accompanying paperwork. Can you do that?"

Pause. Then Jeremy's hand tightened around the receiver.

"I don't care if you've already started analyzing it—"

Pause.

"I don't care what the tests showed, his family was very clear—"

Pause. A line of sweat trickled down Jeremy's forehead.

"This is a matter of religious freedom, do you understand that? If his family doesn't want blood work done, we can't do it, even if we find something alarming—"

A pause. A very long pause, during which Jeremy went pale. He argued with the person for a few minutes, but it became obvious that whatever that lab tech had found, he was determined to report it.

"Yes, well, perhaps you're right," Jeremy said at last, the words coming slow. "Let me contact the hospital administration and they can have our legal experts look into it. In the meantime, this stays between us. Have you told anyone else?"

Pause.

"You're the only one on tonight?" Jeremy said, his eyes closed. "I see. That's good. And your shift ends at . . . ?"

Pause.

"Why don't I meet you there then, and we can discuss your

findings, so I know exactly what I'm taking to the hospital board."

They arranged to meet in just over an hour, and Jeremy hung up. When he turned, he didn't seem surprised to see me there.

"We need to go back to the hospital," he said, his voice barely above a whisper.

I nodded and went to find my shoes.

I don't know what Jeremy did to the tech. Well, yes, I do know. He killed him. It's the "how" that I can't answer. This time when he told me to stay in the car, I did. After all, he was just going to speak to a human lab technician. That didn't require my protective eye.

It would be years before I figured out that he'd had to kill the man and destroy the test results. All I knew at the time was that I fell asleep in the car, and when I awoke, he was driving us home. I asked him how it went and he only nodded, eyes fixed on the road.

Jeremy didn't sleep for three days after that. Knowing he never slept well, I'd grown accustomed to waking and checking on him. For three days after my hospital visit, each time I went to his room at night I found it empty.

On the fourth day he made a phone call. That night, he slept for a couple of hours, and the same for the few nights following. Then, just over a week after the lab tech incident, a package arrived. It was a box of medical texts. That night Jeremy stayed up from dusk to dawn reading. Then, each night after that, he read for a few hours and slept for a few more.

By the end of the month, he was satisfied enough with his progress to sleep an entire six hours. Though he could never fix an arm that was fractured as badly as mine had been, he now had enough knowledge of emergency medicine that he could have evaluated the break and my head injury, stitched the gash on my arm and given me the first aid I needed to make the trip to our doctor in New York. And that was what he needed to let himself sleep—the knowledge that he'd taken every possible step to ensure that what he had done that night, he would never need to do again.

And yet, although he'd solved the immediate problem, there was a larger underlying one that could never be solved. Humans would always pose a danger to us. Pack Law said we could kill them if they did. Jeremy had always thought that could be avoided. That night, when he'd killed the lab tech, he realized he'd been wrong.

That changed Jeremy. You can talk about disillusionment, about loss of innocence, about the tragedy of broken ideals. Bullshit. I have no idea what private hell Jeremy went through in those days after he broke his own rule and killed a human. But I know it was necessary—the first step along the road he was destined to travel.

Ascension
1972

Initiative

I raced over the snow, head down, eyes slitted against the flurries thrown up by Jeremy's paws. Although Jeremy was cutting the path for me, I could still barely keep up, and with each bound, I fell farther behind. For once, he didn't slow to let me catch up. He couldn't. Just ahead of him ran a doe. Antonio kept pace on the deer's other side, reining her in and keeping her running straight.

At a soft growl from Jeremy, I glanced up. Still running, Antonio ducked his head to peer at Jeremy under the doe. Jeremy growled again, and they both checked their speed, letting the deer pull ahead. They fell a foot behind, then a yard, and the doe found her last reserves of strength and shot forward, all attention fixed on the field just ahead.

She made it another couple of yards. Then Jeremy's father, Malcolm, sailed from the bushes on her left. The deer skidded and wheeled on him, hooves flying.

As Malcolm danced out of her way, Dominic flew from the bushes on the other side. He vaulted onto the doe's back. Her thin legs buckled and she went down. Malcolm lunged at her belly, teeth bared, but Dominic snapped at him and Malcolm veered out of the way, leaving the final blow for the Alpha.

As the deer's blood seeped into the snow, Dominic fed. Everyone else had to wait, which they did with varying degrees of patience, from Malcolm and the Santoses, who paced icy ruts in the snow, to Antonio and Dennis Stillwell, who stood poised like setters on point, to Jeremy, who found himself a clear patch of snow and laid down, head on his paws.

After Dominic took a few gulps, he glanced my way and snorted, jerking his muzzle toward the deer. When it came to eating, I wasn't expected to follow the rules of Pack hierarchy. I might have been the only child werewolf they'd ever known, but in this, like most things, they instinctively followed the rules of a real wolf pack. The feeding of pups was too important to be left to chance. So I was permitted to eat with the Alpha.

For the first few years, I'd accepted the privilege but at ten, I no longer considered myself a pup needing handouts. I declined Dominic's invitation with a grunt, and walked over to lie down beside Jeremy.

After Dominic ate his fill, it was the next highest ranking wolf's turn. As for who held that position ... well, that was open to interpretation. Since Dominic's older son, Gregory, didn't hunt, his youngest, Antonio, usually ate second. But today Malcolm—who usually grumbled that deer hunts bored him to tears—had decided to join us.

When Dominic backed off, both Antonio and Malcolm stepped forward, approaching the deer from opposite sides. They looked across the deer at one another. Malcolm flattened his ears against his head and raised his hackles. Antonio lowered his head between his shoulder blades and growled. There was plenty of meat—and room—for both to feed, but that didn't matter.

As the two faced off over the deer, Jeremy pushed to his feet. When I glanced at him, his mouth opened, tongue lolling out in a wolf-grin. As Antonio and Malcolm growled and snarled at one another, Jeremy slipped up behind Antonio, stopping just behind his field of vision. No one else noticed, all too intent on the fight brewing.

Jeremy crouched, wiggled his hindquarters as he tested his grip in the snow, then vaulted forward, darting in right under Antonio's nose. He grabbed the deer's fore-haunch, ripped it free and backpedaled out of the way.

With a roar, Malcolm flew over the deer at his son, but Antonio knocked Jeremy out of the way, then fell on him, snapping and snarling. To an outsider, Antonio's thrashing would look real enough, but a wolf would notice that none of his snaps did more than graze Jeremy's skin. A playful drubbing for a good-natured trick.

As Antonio and Jeremy rolled together tussling, Malcolm stood back, hackles still raised, waiting for them to stop so he could let his son know what *he* thought of his trick. But they kept at it, tumbling out of the clearing, the deer forgotten. Malcolm snorted, then grabbed the haunch Jeremy had ripped off and dragged it away to feed.

Once Malcolm was preoccupied with the leg, Jeremy and Antonio raced back into the clearing, before the others could decide they'd forfeited their share. They ate together, side by side, bickering over the choice bits with mock snaps and snarls.

By the time Jorge and the Santos brothers moved in, it was apparent that there wouldn't be much left for me. I'd wind up with scraps, and I'd need to battle Stephen even for those. Time to find my own meal.

*   *   *

I had to cross the forest before I stood any chance of finding a rabbit. A Pack hunt is pure sport. Keeping quiet isn't a priority— if they miss their target and scare off every animal within a half- mile radius, it's hardly a matter of life and death. They can just head for the house and raid the refrigerator instead.

The first rabbit I found, I lost just as quickly. No big surprise. I could count on one hand the number of times I'd caught my first target. There were grown werewolves in the Pack who couldn't catch a rabbit if it ran under their nose, so I didn't feel so bad.

It took me a while to find rabbit number two, but when I did, I nabbed it on the first pounce. It'd been worth the wait. The first had been a scrawny winter-starved yearling; this one was a fat hare—more than a meal even for my appetite.

As I tore it open, another scent pierced the smell of fresh blood. As I lifted my head, I caught a glimpse of dark fur. Jeremy probably. Maybe Antonio. But when my muzzle rose above the rabbit, I got a better whiff and my hackles rose.

Stephen Santos slid out from the trees. He met my gaze, and his lips curled back in a grimace more sneer than snarl. I grabbed my rabbit and backed into the brush. Stephen advanced on me, nose twitching from the smell of fresh meat. Drops of saliva dribbled into the snow.

I growled, telling him to get his own meal. He bared his teeth and continued forward, ears going back, fur rising...as if he needed to make himself larger. The young werewolf was not only double my age, but nearly triple my weight, and filling out with more muscle each time I saw him.

I backed up another few feet and hit a solid wall of tree trunk. I looked from side to side, but the brush here was too thick. There was no chance of a breakway—not with a rabbit in my mouth, and I sure as hell wasn't leaving that behind.

I crouched. Stephen's mouth fell open in a grin, interpreting my posture as a sign of submission. When I dropped my gaze, he snorted a chuckle and loped toward me. I watched his forepaws, waiting until they were close enough for me to see his claws. Then I threw myself forward, snarling and snapping.

Stephen fell back. Before he could recover, I wheeled, snatched my rabbit and tore past him. He jumped at me, but slid in the snow, yelping as he crashed into the thick brush. I kept running—and almost plowed headlong into a tall pair of dark legs. As I skidded to a halt, I caught a whiff of scent and my gut twisted. Still holding my rabbit, I looked up and met Malcolm's eyes.

Malcolm looked down at me, then over at Stephen, who was still disentangling himself from the bushes. He shook his head and shot a disgusted glare Stephen's way. Stephen rose to his feet, gaze fixing on mine, eyes blazing hate and humiliation. I looked from him to Malcolm. I was trapped.

I laid the rabbit down. Malcolm's muzzle dipped, nodding, as if this was what he expected from me. I released the rabbit and stepped away. As Stephen lunged for it, I grabbed the rabbit by the rear legs and ran the other way.

I got about twenty feet before Malcolm leapt into my path. From behind me came the pound of Stephen's running feet, growing closer each second. Malcolm jerked his muzzle to the side, telling me to toss down the rabbit. I planted my feet and pulled myself up as tall as I could, my head barely reaching his chest, rabbit still in my mouth. His eyes met mine. He tilted his head and, for a moment, just looked at me. Then he stepped aside.

I got to keep my dinner that night. I might not be able to outfight or outrun Stephen, but I could outsmart him, which I did by picking a path through brush too thick for a full-grown wolf to pass. By the time I finished eating, I heard Raymond Santos whistling for his son, and I knew the others had Changed back. I did the same, then ran to catch up.

I found Jeremy with Dominic and Jorge, about a quarter-mile from the house. As I ran to Jeremy, Antonio ambushed me from behind a tree, scooping me up in the air.

"Hey there, scrap," Antonio said. "Where'd you run off to?" He held me out at arm's length and made a show of sniffing. "Is that rabbit I smell? I hope you caught enough for all of us."

"If he can catch one for himself, he's doing just fine," Dominic said.

"But he can always use more practice. I say, next Meet, we let Clay catch our dinner. A bunny buffet." He grinned down at me. "Or guinea pig. He knows how to carve up a guinea pig."

"No, I don't," I said. "They never let me finish."

Everyone laughed. Antonio swung me down to the ground. At a shout from the yard, I looked to see Nick running toward us.

"Good hunt?" he called.

Antonio shot his son a thumbs-up. Nick raced up beside me.

"Did you get to help?" he asked.

"Course he did," Antonio said. "And he caught his own rabbit."

"Oh, man," Nick said. "You are so lucky. Was it a big one? Where'd you find it? How'd you catch it?"

While I answered his endless questions, the rest of the Pack caught up with us. Only Ross Werner and Dennis Stillwell joined our group—the Santoses and Cliff Ward hung back with Malcolm.

"Is someone here?" Ross asked, pointing at the driveway.

He was off to our right, the only one who could see around the rows of cedars lining the drive. A few more steps, and we all saw what he meant—a black pickup truck in the lane, new paint glinting in the winter sun.

"Oh, right," Nick said. "That's what I came out about. Some guy dropped it off about an hour ago. Didn't come to the house or anything. Just left it there. Joey said you guys must have forgotten to tell me we were getting a new truck."

"Truck?" I said, wrinkling my nose. I glanced over my shoulder at Antonio. "You bought a truck?"

Dominic mock-scowled at me. "And what is wrong with a truck, Clayton?"

Antonio put his arm around my shoulder, his other going around Nick. "They aren't fast, are they, boys? And we like 'em fast."

Jeremy rolled his eyes.

"So whose truck is it?" Nick asked. "Jorge? Poppa?"

Jorge shook his head. Dominic looked around, pretending not to hear.

"Hey," Antonio said. "I think we're missing a car in that driveway. Not that I'm surprised. Damn thing was on its last legs. Probably crumpled into a pile of rust."

I scanned the driveway, then looked over at Jeremy, who was doing the same, his brows knitting.

"Where's our car?" I asked.

"The junk heap," Antonio said. "Where it belongs."

Jeremy turned to Dominic. "Please don't tell me you—"

Antonio grinned. "It was a mercy killing."

I watched Jeremy, seeing him struggle to keep his face impassive.

"I appreciate the gesture, Dominic," he said slowly. "But I don't need—"

"I know you don't," Dominic said. "But *I* do. Last month, when

Nick had a fever, it took you eight hours to get here in that snowstorm. We can't have that."

"Hell, no," a voice muttered behind us. "Kid might have died. A fever. Imagine that."

Dominic turned sharply, lip curling. Stephen, Wally and Raymond Santos all stood behind us. Dominic's gaze slid from one to the other, but he couldn't tell who'd made the comment.

"Dominic has a point," Jeremy said softly. "My car wasn't suited to winter driving, and if I'm going to provide emergency medical care, I need something that is. So I will buy myself a truck—"

"What?" Antonio said. "Some old beater that doesn't run any better than that car?"

Jeremy stiffened.

Antonio slapped his back. "Come on, Jer. Stop being so damned stubborn—"

"An old truck won't do," Dominic said. "This isn't a gift, Jeremy. You're taking on this new responsibility, and saving me a bundle on doctor's bills. I know you won't accept anything more than gas money—"

"I don't need payment."

"Of course you don't. You're doing it for the Pack. And, in return, the Pack will make sure that you have everything you need to do the job properly—including reliable transportation."

"I—"

"Enough," Dominic said.

He shot Jeremy a scowl that said he meant it. Jeremy hesitated, then nodded.

Wally strode up beside us. "So, let me get this straight. Jeremy plays doctor and he gets a brand-new truck for it? Hell, if I'd known that I'd—"

"You'd what?" Dominic said, turning on him. "You'd have

thought of it first? You've had years to think of it, Wally. And you didn't. No one did."

"That's—"

"It's called showing initiative," Dominic said. "Something we could always use more of around here. Now, Jeremy, go check out that truck of yours. Make sure it's the way you want it. If not, you and Antonio can pick out something else. Before dinner, though, I want you to have a look at Cliff's shoulder. It's been acting up again."

Cliff shook his head. "It's nothing. I don't need—"

"You were favoring your right foreleg. First mutt that catches you doing that will fix your shoulder for you—permanently. Did you see Clayton out there today? You'd never know he broke his arm. All those special exercises paid off. That's what I want Jeremy to do for you." He shot a look at Cliff. "And you're going to let him."

"Come on," Nick whispered to me. "Let's go see the truck."

As we started to run, I caught a glimpse of Malcolm. He was watching Jeremy with a strange, unreadable look in his eyes. I stopped and circled back, sliding between Jeremy and his father. Malcolm shook his head, glanced over at the truck, shook his head again and strode off toward the house.

Vision

Late that spring, when Jeremy was called in to deal with Gregory's sprained ankle, Dominic found excuses to extend our stay for nearly a week. Why? Because Malcolm was at Stonehaven, and had been for a month. Not only that, but Malcolm had invited Wally, Raymond, Stephen and Cliff up to Stonehaven, which turned an uncomfortable visit into sheer torment. Dominic knew we could use a break.

When we returned to Stonehaven, Malcolm was still there. Most times he only stopped by long enough to get money, but occasionally he stayed longer. I had no idea what his excuse was this time. Like Jeremy, I'd stopped caring *why* he was there, only gritting my teeth and toughing it out until he left. Asking him when he was leaving only invited trouble. I'd done that last year, and he'd extended a planned two-day visit to two weeks.

By the time we got home from New York, only Malcolm remained. He pounced before we could so much as pull off our boots.

"All done playing doctor?" he said.

"Yes," Jeremy said. "Gregory is fine."

"No, Gregory is not fine and hasn't been for years. If you

really wanted to do us a favor, you'd give the idiot strychnine instead of aspirin. But I'm sure that wouldn't help your cause, would it?"

Jeremy only gave a half-shrug and took off his boots, then turned to me. "Go into the kitchen and we'll fix dinner." He glanced at his father. "We're having sandwiches. Can I make you one?"

"Don't pretend you don't know what I'm talking about."

Jeremy tugged off his coat, hung it on the rack and steered me toward the kitchen.

"How's that new truck working out for you?" Malcolm said, sticking at our heels.

"It does the job," Jeremy murmured.

"Dominic must be pretty pleased with you these days. Taming stray pups. Training the boys. Learning emergency medicine. What'd he call it? Initiative. That's right. Showing initiative. The question is: what do you hope to initiate?"

When Jeremy didn't answer, Malcolm swung in front of him and brought his face to Jeremy's.

"You get in my way, boy, and I'll squash you."

"I never doubted it," Jeremy said, and sidestepped into the kitchen.

Malcolm's next extended stay came in early December, a month away from my eleventh birthday.

That weekend, Antonio and Nick were coming up to take me Christmas shopping for Jeremy. Although the Pack didn't really celebrate the holiday the way humans did, we would have a Pack Meet and exchange gifts. The original shopping plan had been for me to go to New York and stay with the Sorrentinos, but then Malcolm showed up, and seemed prepared to hang around until the holidays, so Antonio decided they'd come to us, minimizing the time Jeremy would need to spend alone with his father.

On Wednesday night Jeremy woke up from a nightmare. When I heard a muffled cry from his room, I bolted upright and nearly fell out of bed in my haste to get up. As I scurried into the hall, I heard the click of his door handle, and backed into my room.

I listened, heart thumping, almost certain it was just a nightmare, but unable to shake the fear that someone had attacked him in his bed. When I heard his soft footfalls in the corridor I knew it had just been another bad dream. Staying behind my door, I waited until he passed, then slid out after him.

Normally after a nightmare, Jeremy would fix himself a sandwich, or pour a glass of brandy, depending on how bad it had been. This time, though, he walked into the study, passed the brandy decanter and headed for the desk.

He stopped in front of the phone and stared down at it, as if expecting it to ring. For at least five minutes, he stood there. Then he sighed, picked it up, moved it to the table beside his chair and sat down.

He picked up his sketch pad and tried to draw something, but his attention kept wandering, and he'd start to draw those strange symbols he did sometimes. When he noticed, he'd rip off the page and try again. And again, his gaze would go distant, pencil moving across the page, drawing symbols instead of pictures.

Finally he tossed the sketch pad down and took up a paperback mystery novel he'd left by his chair, but after ten minutes of staring at the same page, he put it aside and eased back in his chair. A few minutes later, he started to nod off. His eyes were only half closed when he jerked up, mouth forming a silent *O*.

From my post outside the door, I swear I could hear his heart pounding triple-time. His gaze shot to the door and I pulled back farther out of sight. He tensed, listening, as if afraid he'd cried out and alerted Malcolm. He listened to the silence for a minute, then looked back at the phone, swore under his breath and rolled his shoulders.

"Call, damn it," he whispered. "I can't help if you don't call."

The phone didn't ring. After glaring at it for a few minutes, he sank back into his seat.

Twice more, he began to drift off and twice more a vision startled him awake. It *was* a vision, not a nightmare. At the time I didn't understand that, but I do now, looking back.

Jeremy saw things. I don't know how to explain it any better than that. I *can't* explain it any better than that. I've never understood much about this side of Jeremy's life, because I don't ask.

Wolves like conformity. In the wild, a pack will drive out a member who doesn't fit the accepted standard of wolf behavior; most animals do. While the Pack wasn't so heartless, even those less attuned to their wolf side were uncomfortable with change, and with those who were "different."

I knew Jeremy didn't like to fight, and I knew that wasn't normal werewolf behavior. Yet I could accept that, because I knew he *could* fight. As a wolf, what was important to me was the ability, not the desire.

Not every member of the Pack felt that way. Take Malcolm. To him, a werewolf was a fighter, and a werewolf's value was directly related to his martial skills. For Malcolm, having his only son show no interest in fighting was a humiliation beyond bearing.

If Jeremy's refusal to fight lowered him in the opinion of some Pack members, knowing that he had visions would have only made it worse. Such a thing went beyond the realm of individual difference. Unlike the rest of the Pack, though, I knew that Jeremy sensed—and sometimes saw—threats facing his Pack brothers.

After nearly two hours, Jeremy fell into a semidoze, disturbed only by the twitches and moans of a fitful sleep. When I was sure he wasn't going to wake up again, I crept into the room and fell asleep on the sofa.

The next day, Jeremy stayed close to the phone. Malcolm noticed. Malcolm always noticed Jeremy's moods. He hated the thought that something might be bothering his son and he couldn't claim the credit for it.

The phone rang twice that day. Both times Jeremy bolted for it, which didn't escape Malcolm's notice either. The first time it was Pearl, the woman who cooked our dinners, confirming our menu for the next week. The second time it was one of Jeremy's translation business clients asking whether he'd received a delivery.

Late that afternoon, Malcolm went out. Jeremy tried to curb his restlessness by painting, one hobby he never dared practice in front of his father. At least marksmanship was a sport. Painting would open him up to a whole new arena of mockery. So when Malcolm was home, the sketch pads and canvases stayed in a basement storage box.

Today, though, even art couldn't distract Jeremy from whatever bothered him. Instead, he threw himself into physical activity, playing two hours of touch football with me before dinner. While we played, he kept the study window open, despite the bitter December cold. Every now and then he'd stop in midplay, motion for me to wait as he looked toward the window, as though he'd heard the phone ring. When no sound came, he'd shake it off and resume the game.

After dinner I reminded Jeremy that it was our hunt night. We had one joint Change night per week. As well, Jeremy encouraged me to run by myself once a week, and he did the same.

One advantage to Changing so often was that if anything interrupted our schedule, we could miss a run with no ill effects. Given Jeremy's mood, I figured he planned to skip our hunt, but I wasn't going to let that happen without a fight.

When I reminded him, I braced for battle, but Jeremy told me to grab our coats and boots. Like playing touch football, a hunt was action; it was something to do.

If someone phoned, he'd miss the call, but I think in some ways Jeremy was even less comfortable with his psychic abilities than I was. At that age, he hadn't yet learned to trust them and, when the phone hadn't rung all day, he'd decided it wasn't going to ring at all.

We caught a fawn that night. Normally young deer aren't on our menu, but it was a fall fawn, born out of season and abandoned by its mother. Better to kill it quickly and let its death serve some purpose, rather than leave it to starve.

We were still feeding when the phone rang. Jeremy had left the study window open again, so the distant ring cut through the stillness of the forest. Jeremy tore off to Change.

The phone rang only three times, then stopped. Jeremy was fast with his Changes, but he wasn't that fast.

By the time I finished my Change, Jeremy was already in the house. I ran inside to find him striding down the hall, peering into each room. One sniff and I knew what he was looking for. We found Malcolm in the kitchen, pouring a beer.

"Did you—?" Jeremy started, then stopped and made his voice casual. "I thought I heard the phone. Was it for you?"

"No idea. Strangest thing. I picked it up, said hello and no one answered." He fixed Jeremy with a look. "Very strange, don't you think?"

I didn't think it was strange at all that someone wouldn't want to speak to Malcolm, but he wasn't asking me, so I kept my mouth shut.

Jeremy shrugged. "Probably a wrong number."

"I'm sure it was."

Jeremy poured me a glass of milk, then grabbed a bag of cookies and led me to the study. Malcolm followed. He walked to the sofa and dropped onto it, beer sloshing to the floor. I looked at the frothy puddle and bit back a snarl. Of course he ignored it. *He* wasn't the one responsible for cleaning the floors. I wasn't wiping it up with him looking on, though. I'd let it dry and scrub the spot off tomorrow.

Jeremy stood in the doorway, looking at Malcolm and struggling to hide his dismay. "I have work to do," he said finally.

"That's fine. You do it. I'll just sit here and keep quiet." Malcolm's gaze traveled to the phone—the only one in the house.

Jeremy poured himself a brandy, took a sheaf of his work papers and sat down. I grabbed my book and plopped onto the throw rug to read.

Twenty minutes later, the phone rang. After a furtive glance toward his father, Jeremy answered it.

"Hello?"

Relief flooded Jeremy's eyes as I heard a man's voice reply. Malcolm put down his newspaper and perked up. Jeremy gripped the receiver tighter to his ear, muffling the voice on the other end.

"Slow down...no, slow— Wait. Stop. You can tell me when I get there. Let me grab a pen."

He took a pen and paper from the desk. Malcolm sauntered over and leaned around Jeremy, trying to see the paper. Jeremy covered his notes, then ripped the page from the pad and stuffed it into his pocket.

"I'll be there as soon as I can."

When he hung up, he turned to Malcolm and tensed. But Malcolm just yawned as if the whole affair had proved disappointingly dull, and strolled to the door. He took one step into the hall, then leaned back inside.

"Oh, if you need someone to look after the boy while you're gone, just ask." He looked at me with a teeth-baring grin. "I'll take good care of him."

When Malcolm was gone, Jeremy glanced at me.

"I'm going with you," I said.

"No, Clay, not this time."

He picked up the phone and dialed.

"Jorge? It's Jeremy. How are you?" A short pause. "Is Antonio there?" A longer pause, then Jeremy winced. "That's right. And he's flying straight here Saturday afterward, isn't he? Can't believe I forgot that." Pause. "No, no. It's not important. I was just calling to discuss our plans for the weekend."

Jeremy chatted for another minute with Jorge, then hung up. After a moment's pause, he sighed, shook his head and looked at me.

"I'm going with you," I said.

"Yes, I suppose you are."

Lesson

We caught a plane to Los Angeles and arrived there later that day. Once in the city, Jeremy rented a car, bought a map and found the address he'd been given. When he reached the motel, he swung into the lot, then sat there, blocking the entrance, until someone blared a horn. Jeremy pulled into the first parking spot, checked his scrap of paper, checked the address on the motel office and shook his head.

One glance at the place—and one whiff of the smell coming through the open car windows—and I understood his hesitation. The motel was a dump—the lowest, cheapest form of accommodation possible, the type usually rented by the hour or by the month. No werewolf in his right mind could sleep in a place that smelled like this.

After triple-checking the address, a look of sadness mixed with apprehension washed over Jeremy's face, a look that said the situation was worse than he'd expected, and maybe worse than he was prepared to handle.

"Come on," he said, opening his door. When I made a face, he added, "Breathe through your mouth until you get used to it."

*   *   *

Jeremy knocked on a room door. After some rustling from within, the curtain cracked open, then fell shut, and the door opened. Staying almost hidden behind the door, a young man ushered us inside, then closed and locked it. It was Peter Myers, who'd left the Pack a while ago. I took one whiff of him and knew something was very wrong. There was an unnatural chemical stink to his sweat that brought back flashes of my nights prowling the alleys in Baton Rouge. Peter stepped from behind the door. A dull sheen of grease coated his long red hair, a short beard covered his cheeks and chin, and his shirt and jeans were dotted with brownish-red splotches—dried blood.

"Thank God you're—" Peter saw me and stopped. "You brought the boy?"

Jeremy hefted his suitcase onto the bed and opened it. "Antonio's out of town on business. There's no one else I could ask. Not without answering too many questions."

"Oh." Peter's gaze shot to me, then back to Jeremy. "I'm sorry. I didn't think—"

"Clayton will be fine." He handed Peter a folded set of trousers and a shirt. "Get that clothing off first, give it to me, take a shower and put these on. Then tell me what happened."

Jeremy stuffed Peter's bloodied clothing into a plastic bag and carried it out to the car. It took him a few minutes to return—he had to find a hiding place until he could burn them.

When Peter finished showering and dressing, he took a seat in the chair by the television. Jeremy and I sat on the end of the bed.

It may seem to reflect poorly on Jeremy's parental judgment

that he'd let me listen in on what was certain to be a discussion unsuitable for a young boy, but that's how things were done in the werewolf world. When it came to the violent facts of our lives, the Pack never covered our ears or sent us to the next room. These were things we had to know, and postponing such knowledge wouldn't be protecting us—it would be the worst kind of recklessness.

You couldn't let a Pack son grow up believing werewolf life was all rabbit hunts and pleasant runs through the forest, or the first time he met a mutt would be the last. So too with Peter's story; there was a lesson here to be learned for any young were-wolf.

"I know what you're thinking," Peter said, looking down at his hands as he worried a hangnail. "You're thinking that Dominic was right, that I wasn't mature enough to handle it." He looked up, meeting Jeremy's eyes. "But it wasn't like that. I didn't walk away from the Pack and forget everything. I remembered the things you and I used to talk about, how to keep better control, how to make it easier. I Changed twice a week. I hunted. I never had more than one drink at a sitting. I was more careful than I'd ever been in the Pack because I knew I had to be. One screw-up and Dominic would have me killed."

Jeremy didn't argue. It was true. The only thing more danger-ous to Pack safety than a renegade mutt was a renegade mutt who used to be a Pack wolf.

"I tried. I tried so damned hard!" Peter ripped off the hangnail, winced with the pain and stared down at the blood. "I saw it coming. That's what makes me so mad. I saw it coming, but I kept telling myself I could handle it."

He wiped his bloodied thumb on his pants. "When I started the tour, it was me and three other guys doing the A/V work. Last year, one guy quit. They said they'd hire a replacement, but they didn't. Then this summer, they fired another guy, and didn't even bother promising a replacement. So it was two of us doing the work of four. Concert days, we'd be up at dawn, work all day setting up, work through the show, get maybe two hours sleep and be right back at it. Once I was so beat, I screwed up the sound levels, and I knew if I did it again, I'd be out of a job. The other guy I work with was taking stuff to keep him awake."

"Drugs?"

Peter nodded. "For most guys here, it's like drinking coffee. Everyone does it. I told myself I'd be careful. I took a little, and it worked. I could stay up during a concert run, then crash on the tour bus afterward. I watched for other effects, but there weren't any. So when things got busier, I took some more.

"Then when I started having trouble sleeping, I took something for that. On my days off, when I got down, feeling lonely, thinking maybe I shouldn't have left the Pack, I'd take something to make me feel better. Pretty soon I was—" He swallowed. "I was taking a lot. And noticing problems—mood swings and trouble Changing…"

"And then two nights ago…?"

Peter blinked, as if surprised Jeremy knew. "There was this party, with the crew. I took some dope, no more than usual, but it made me edgy. I—I haven't Changed in a few weeks. I tried, but I couldn't, so I gave up. I was feeling real restless, so I thought maybe if I—" He glanced at me. "I thought some, uh, company might help. So I went back to this girl's room, and we were—" Another glance at me. "—together, but it only made me worse. Things got rough and she didn't like that, so she tried to leave, but I—I, uh…wasn't done. When she tried to get dressed, I didn't think, I just reacted. I threw her and she hit her head." He inhaled sharply. "I didn't think I threw her that hard, but…"

Jeremy brushed back his bangs. "Okay, we can handle this. I'll help you, but on one condition—"

"There's more," Peter said. His gaze darted away from Jeremy's. "I—she—" He stopped and swallowed. "She had a roommate. I was…" Another swallow, harder. "I was cleaning up the room when the other girl came in. I—I killed her."

Peter lurched to his feet and walked to the window. He pulled back the curtain, then quickly shut it. Jeremy said nothing, just sat there, his eyes downcast, hiding his reaction.

A few years ago, Jeremy could not have hidden his reaction. I'm not sure he would have tried. What Peter had done—knowingly killing a second human to cover up an accidental death—would have been an unforgivable lapse. He might have stayed to help him, but would have done no more, unable to understand, much less forgive. But while I knew he was horrified, his own killing of a human, though for far better cause, had leached some gray into his black-and-white view of the world. So he hid his reaction and waited for Peter to go on.

After a moment, Peter shuddered, then turned around. "The first girl—I can't say that wasn't my fault because it was, because I let myself get into that situation, but I didn't mean to kill her. With the other one, I knew what I was doing. She walked in, she saw the body, she saw me and I couldn't think of anything else to do."

"Where did you bury them?" Jeremy asked, his voice low.

"I—I didn't. I left them there."

Jeremy's head shot up. "You left—?"

"I panicked. I took off and checked into the first motel I found, and I was going to take a shower, clear my head and plan stuff, but then I just crashed. When I woke up, it was yesterday evening, and I didn't know if I should go back, so I called you—"

"Okay," Jeremy said, lifting a hand to cut him off. "We'll see what we can do. If it's too late, we'll have to deal with that. But back to my condition. There's one thing you have to agree to if you want my help."

"Anything."

Jeremy's condition seemed simple enough: Peter had to rejoin the Pack. What Peter had done was wrong, but rather than turning his back on him, as he might have done before, Jeremy could see the circumstances, see the man and see room for mercy. But only if Peter returned to the rules and support system that kept mistakes like this from happening.

The problem, as they both knew, was that if Dominic found out what had happened here, Peter was a dead man, no matter how vehemently he might promise to reform. For this, there were no second chances.

Peter could argue that the whole Pack suspected Malcolm killed the occasional human for sport, and remained not only alive, but a Pack brother in good standing. But Malcolm was a Danvers, and an integral part of the Pack—someone Dominic could rely on to keep the mutts in check and solve other unsavory "problems." Peter was a nobody, a kid who hadn't been with the Pack long enough to prove his worth. Peter had defied Dominic by taking this job, and proceeded to prove Dominic's fears well founded, so his execution would stand as a lesson to the rest of the Pack youth.

The trick, then, would be to clean up Peter's mess so well that no one would ever know it had happened. Even with that, getting him back into the Pack would require serious negotiating, but Jeremy had played go-between before, and he was ready to do it again.

Peter trusted Jeremy enough to agree. They would use the next few hours to prepare, then they would return to the murder scene after dark and—if it hadn't been discovered—clean it up.

As tempting as it would be to flee town afterward, it was too dangerous. Peter couldn't remember who, if anyone, at the party had seen him leave with the girl, so he couldn't disappear at the same time she did. He'd have to return to work and, if all seemed fine, give his notice and work out his two weeks. Jeremy and I would stay in Los Angeles with him for the first week, to help him through any complications that arose. Then Peter would hole up at Stonehaven with us while Jeremy negotiated his return to the Pack. A solid, straightforward plan...and one that was about to hit a very big, very determined obstacle.

Every adult member of the Pack knew how to dispose of a body. Normally, though, the task involved a dead mutt and took place in a forest. Even a mutt knows that if he wins the battle, he'll have a body to get rid of, so he won't pick a fight in a public setting.

Cleaning up a murder scene in an apartment was more difficult, but Jeremy knew more than the average person knew—or *should* know—about crime scenes. Body disposal was taught to werewolves approaching their first Change, and since these lessons were now Jeremy's responsibility in the Pack, he'd done what he always did—learned everything he could about the subject.

He also had hands-on experience. That lab tech may have been the first human he'd ever killed but, thanks to his father, it wasn't the first human body he'd disposed of.

All this did not, however, mean that he was an expert in the matter. He made mistakes that day, including returning to the murder scene without first making sure the crime hadn't been reported. For all we knew, someone had found the bodies, and the police were staking out the apartment, hoping the killer might return.

Luck was with us that night, though. The girls lived in a run-down tenement, the kind of place where no one would pay much attention to a scream or a thump in the upstairs apartment. And they didn't lead the kind of lives where an employer or friend or family member would start worrying if they didn't show up for a couple of days.

The apartment was exactly as Peter had left it. Or so I assume. I never saw it. The educational portion of this trip ended well before I got a look inside that room. Jeremy set me up in an alley next to the building, where I was to stand watch. This was probably just an excuse to keep me out of the apartment, but I played my role to the hilt, keeping my eyes, ears and nose on alert.

Jeremy and Peter presumably cleaned the room as best they could. Then they brought the wrapped bodies down to the car, which was parked in the back alley, loaded them up and we left.

After we buried the bodies—okay, after *Jeremy* and *Peter* buried them while I played lookout—we had one more job to do: burn Peter's bloodied clothing. Jeremy knew not to dispose of it anywhere near the bodies, so we headed out of the city. First we dropped Peter off at a nature preserve Jeremy had found on the map. Before we found a motel for the night, Peter had to Change. No matter how difficult it might be with the drugs still in his system, Jeremy insisted on it.

While Peter went for his run, Jeremy and I disposed of Peter's clothing a few miles away. As we did, Jeremy talked the situation over with me, making sure I understood what had happened and why.

Neither death was excusable. Even the second, ending a threat, while seemingly acceptable under Pack Law, was not, because Peter had caused the danger himself, like Malcolm bringing that young woman to the house, then killing her.

Jeremy explained his decision and why he'd made it—that he didn't condone what Peter had done, but he'd made a mistake and should be given a second chance. While at the time I was too young to really understand, it made sense to me.

As for the rest, Jeremy no longer worried that I might be traumatized by death, nor seemed surprised when I wasn't. At first I'm sure he wondered whether this was a cause for concern, maybe a sign that I lacked a conscience. By now, though, we'd been through enough for him to understand the truth. I couldn't grieve for those two dead girls any more than I could ever grieve for any person, human or werewolf, that I hadn't known.

That didn't mean that I couldn't understand the tragedy of their passing. Every death should have a purpose. If it doesn't, then it is tragedy, and anyone who commits such an act has violated a basic law of nature. The only excuse for killing an animal is for food. The only excuse for killing a human is protection of self or Pack. Even if I could stand there, stone-faced, as Peter and Jeremy disposed of two bodies, that didn't mean my brain wasn't processing the tragedy of it, and that I wasn't storing this lesson away in my memory. What I'd seen that day shouldn't have happened and I'd make sure I never let myself get into a similar situation.

Once we'd burned the clothing, we returned for Peter. Jeremy parked a quarter-mile from the nature preserve. Then we climbed the fence and headed into the woods. Jeremy followed Peter's trail to a pile of clothing haphazardly shoved under a tree. He inhaled deeply, sampling the wind. I did the same, and couldn't pick up a fresh scent, meaning Peter was still running.

"Can we go, too?" I asked as Jeremy pushed Peter's clothing farther under the bush.

"I suppose so," he said. "Just remember—"

"Hide my clothing better than that. Yeah, I know. Can I go find him as soon as I'm done? Or do I have to wait for you?"

Jeremy chuckled. "Since when have you ever had to wait for me?"

Jeremy was right. Even at Stonehaven, where I could gain a few minutes by tossing my clothing wherever it landed, I could never Change faster than him. No one in the Pack could, though, so that was some consolation.

When I finished, Jeremy was lying outside my thicket, head on his paws, eyes closed, as if he'd been waiting so long he'd fallen asleep. I pounced, but he rolled out of the way easily, sprang up and pinned me by the neck before I even had time to think of my next move. I sighed, breath billowing out in the cold air. He gave a low tremor of a growl that I'd learned to interpret as the wolf version of his chuckle.

He released my neck and turned, as if to run, presenting me with his flank. I shouldn't have fallen for it. Only the most incompetent wolf would turn from his opponent like that. I was young, though, young and hopeful.

When Jeremy turned, I scrambled up and dove at his flank. At the last second, he dropped to the ground and I flew over his back and pitched muzzle-first into the ground. While I lay there, sulking with a noseful of dirt, he prodded my hindquarters and gave a soft growl, telling me the game was over. We had to go find Peter.

When I got to my feet, Jeremy jerked his head up, then right. Communication in wolf form is never easy, but we've learned to supplement the basic growls, yips and snorts with enough motions to get across a more complicated message. Jeremy was telling me that the game wasn't really over; it had just changed form. Since there was no rush to find Peter, we could make a tracking sport of it. One of us would go left, the other right, neither following the trail Peter had left. We'd see who could find him first. I answered by tearing off.

After about a hundred feet, I set to work. Tracking by secondary clues is much harder than following a trail. You have to use all your senses: listening for twigs crackling underfoot, sniffing for a scent on the breeze, looking for movement in the shadows. Being overanxious to beat Jeremy, I took off after the first noise I heard and startled a couple of field mice. That was embarrassing. I forced myself to take a sixty-second breather, then I set out again.

I found a path and padded along it, nose and ears twitching for some sign of Peter. I'd gone about fifty yards when there came a noise so loud that I dove for cover, fearing gunfire.

When my heart stopped thudding, I realized something was crashing through the undergrowth. Had Peter frightened a buck? A stray dog? Whatever it was, it was large, and it was running full out, not caring how much noise it made.

I crept from my hiding spot and moved a few cautious steps down the path. The wind shifted then, bringing a scent that made my eyes widen in shock. Jeremy?

No, Jeremy would never crash through the forest like a panicked deer. I snorted, clearing my nose to sniff again. Then I caught Peter's scent... and that of another werewolf, one who definitely shouldn't be out here.

A yip rang out—the high-pitched yelp of a surprised wolf. I

didn't recognize the voice, so I knew it was Peter. A growl followed, one I *did* recognize.

I shot forward, running as fast as I could. I veered off the path to take the shortest route. Twigs whipped my face. One caught my left eye, the sudden sting forcing it closed. I narrowed the other eye and kept running.

I made it to the clearing first. There, inside, was a wolf with dark red fur—Peter—lying on his back. Looming over him was a massive black wolf.

Peter twisted and bucked, hind legs kicking, but Malcolm had him pinned. Malcolm growled, lowered his face to Peter's and looked him square in the eye. Peter struggled wildly and managed to claw Malcolm in the belly.

With a roar, Malcolm grabbed Peter by the neck ruff and dashed him headfirst into a boulder. Peter went limp. Malcolm stepped over Peter's prone body and pulled his head back for the throat slash that would end Peter's life. Then the bushes behind him parted and Jeremy leapt through.

Player

Jeremy sprang at Malcolm and hit him in the flank, knocking him to the ground. Malcolm's surprise lasted about a millisecond. Then he jumped to his feet and charged.

Jeremy tried to feint, but the momentum of his spring left him off-balance and Malcolm hit him square in the rib cage. Jeremy skidded sideways to the ground. Malcolm lunged for a throat hold, but Jeremy managed to scuttle backward fast enough to get out of his way.

As Malcolm swung around again, Jeremy leapt to his feet and dove out of his path. Jeremy barely had time to recover before Malcolm twisted around and rushed him. This time, when Jeremy tried to evade, Malcolm was ready. He swerved in mid-lunge and caught Jeremy by the hind leg, throwing him down.

As much as I wanted to believe otherwise, I knew Jeremy was no match for his father. Malcolm was a werewolf in his prime, having the experience of age yet none of its disabilities. The only wolf in the Pack who could beat him was Dominic, and even that was being called into question as age slowed Dominic's reflexes.

Mutts came to Stonehaven for one reason: to challenge the best. That "best" was not, and never would be, Jeremy.

I waited out the first few minutes, hoping I was wrong, and afraid of getting in Jeremy's way. Jeremy recovered from the first throw-down and managed to slice open Malcolm's foreleg, but that was the only hit he scored. Within five minutes, Jeremy was bleeding from his hind leg and his left ear, and the froth around his mouth was tinged with pink.

I knew then that no amount of luck was going to get Jeremy through this. So I leapt in, snarling, and threw myself on Malcolm's back.

For a full-grown wolf, this is a good offensive move, pitching your weight onto your opponent and bringing him down. For a pup, it was like dropping a terrier onto a bullmastiff. I executed my leap perfectly and landed square on his back, fangs finding purchase in the loose skin behind his neck. And all Malcolm did was huff in surprise, then fling me off.

When I got back to my feet, I changed tactics. If I couldn't be formidable, at least I could be annoying. While the two wolves fought, I darted around Malcolm's legs and tail, nipping and tripping him. It distracted him enough to prevent a quick victory, but not enough to let Jeremy win.

Finally, Malcolm tired of snarling and snapping at me. With one full-on charge, he knocked Jeremy flying into the undergrowth. Then he turned on me.

I should have run. But running would mean leaving Jeremy behind, and I'd never do that. I pulled myself up to my full height, braced my forelegs, lowered my head and snarled. Malcolm stood there, watching me, head slightly tilted, an unreadable expression in his eyes. Then he lumbered over, lowered his head until we were muzzle to muzzle and growled. I growled back.

Malcolm met my eyes and I swear he smiled. Then Jeremy hit him from behind, knocking him away from me, and the fight began again.

Any hope we had of besting Malcolm faded fast. Jeremy was hurt, and getting worse by the minute. I was only wearing myself out. Soon Malcolm had Jeremy pinned by the neck.

I went wild, attacking his head with every ounce of strength I had left. He just pinned Jeremy with his forepaws and threw me off. By the time I recovered, he had Jeremy by the throat again.

Jeremy's eyes were closed. When I saw that, everything in me went cold. Then I saw that Jeremy's chest continued to rise and fall. Malcolm loosened his grip and lifted his head. The fur around Jeremy's neck was wet, but with saliva, not blood. Malcolm hadn't bitten Jeremy, only choked him until he lost consciousness. Malcolm backed off then, gaze fixed on Jeremy.

Had he realized, in that last moment, that he couldn't kill his son? Yes. But only because, if he did, he would lose everything. Edward Danvers's will not only gave Jeremy Stonehaven and all its assets, but stipulated that on Jeremy's death—no matter how he died—the estate would go to charity. And, perhaps even worse, a letter would be delivered to Dominic or his successor, detailing crimes that would guarantee Malcolm's execution. Should Jeremy not die but be permanently incapacitated, the same provisions took effect. So Malcolm was trapped. His life and his livelihood depended on the continued good health of his son.

After a long, regret-filled stare at Jeremy, Malcolm turned to me.

I raced forward, swerved past him and wheeled, positioning myself over Jeremy's head. When he stepped toward me, I lowered my head and growled. He took another step. I snapped at his foreleg, teeth clicking hard when he pulled back. For a moment, he just looked at me. Then he turned to his original quarry: Peter, who was still unconscious.

I waited until he was far enough from Jeremy that I could be sure he wasn't trying to divert my attention. Then I sprang over top of Peter and growled. Malcolm stopped short, eyes widening. This, I suppose, he hadn't expected. Again, he stepped toward his prey. Again, I warned him off, forelegs braced, fur on end, making me look, oh, at least a good five pounds heavier.

I drew back my lips and snarled. He stopped and tilted his head, gaze locking with mine. I could feel the depth of that gaze as he studied me. He feinted left. I blocked him. He darted forward. I snapped, this time in an awkward swipe at his throat. He pulled back and, again, I saw a smile in his eyes.

Several more times he tried to get around me. I know now that he'd been toying with me, testing my willingness to protect Peter. At the time, though, I truly believed I was the only thing standing between a Pack brother and certain death, and I put everything I had into countering Malcolm's moves.

Once I even managed to snag his foreleg. When that happened, he pulled back, as if in shock. He looked down at the small wound, then at me, and I saw something in his gaze that made my stomach turn: admiration.

I lunged at him, snarling. He grabbed me by the throat and pinned me to the ground. For a minute, he held me there, not clamping down, just holding me, like a wolf with a misbehaving pup.

While holding me, he glanced at Peter. Resolution flickered in his eyes, as if he'd decided something. Then he backed off me, huffed once, billowing steam from his nostrils, and loped into the forest.

*   *   *

I kept watch over Jeremy and Peter until they awoke. Jeremy was first. About ten minutes after Malcolm left, he started twitching and moaning as if struggling to wake up. Then he shot to his feet and looked around, lips pulled back in a snarl. When he saw me, he relaxed. Jeremy circled the clearing once, sniffing the air, but Malcolm was long gone. Peter stirred then and, after a few prods from Jeremy, opened his eyes. He looked around dazedly, then his lids drooped.

When Jeremy prodded him again, he snapped at him. Jeremy snarled back and jostled Peter until he got to his feet. Peter shook himself, then blinked, as if suddenly remembering what had happened.

Jeremy herded us back to where I'd left my clothing. We took turns Changing while the other two stood guard.

Once we'd all finished, Jeremy assessed injuries, beginning with me. I had only bumps and scrapes from being thrown around by Malcolm.

"I'm sorry," Jeremy said softly as he fingered a rising bruise on my wrist, making sure the bone wasn't broken. "I shouldn't have brought you along."

"I'm okay."

A wry quarter-smile and a pat on the back. "I see that. But it shouldn't have happened. I should have guessed what he was up to back at the house."

"And what *was* he up to?" Peter said. "Besides trying to kill me."

Jeremy motioned for Peter to sit on a rock and began checking his head injury. "That, I'm afraid, was his only goal. To kill you."

"Why?" I asked.

Jeremy looked at me, as if trying to decide whether this was information I needed to have just yet. "What Peter did—killing a human after leaving the Pack—is grounds for execution."

"I know," I said. "If Dominic found out, he'd order someone to kill Peter." I paused. "And that's Malcolm's job, isn't it?"

"Oh, it's not a job," Peter muttered. "It's a pleasure."

"So Dominic found out about Peter, didn't he? He sent Malcolm after him."

"Shit," Peter said, staring at me. "How old is this kid again?"

Jeremy shook his head. "Dominic didn't send Malcolm. Ordering a Pack member—or a former Pack member—to be killed isn't, well, it isn't easy for an Alpha. It would be simpler for all concerned if that Pack member died before the Alpha had to deliver the order. Dominic would . . . appreciate that."

"Oh, I get it now," Peter said. "Malcolm kills me. *Then* he tells Dominic, probably saying I 'resisted arrest' or some shit like that. Saves Dominic from ordering an execution. So Malcolm earns himself a pat on the head from the Alpha for solving an ugly problem."

"I believe he hopes to earn more than a pat on the head. He may win Dominic's gratitude, but I think he's more interested in making a point to the rest of the Pack, proving that he can take care of problems like this swiftly and efficiently."

"Why?" I asked.

"Don't tell me he's angling to make Alpha," Peter said.

"He's been angling for years," Jeremy said. "Now he's campaigning."

Jeremy's own wounds were much worse than ours. Besides bruises around his neck, he had a gaping wound down his leg and he winced each time he bent over or straightened, probably from bruised ribs. The leg would require stitches, but for now he wrapped it with strips from his shirt. Then shrugged on his jacket, brushed off our concern and headed back to the car.

As we walked, Jeremy kept looking from side to side and discreetly sniffing the air as he searched for signs of Malcolm. He had us stick to the middle of the deserted dirt road, as far from the shadows of the embankments as possible.

Jeremy moved slowly, and although part of that was caution, it was also necessity, as his injured leg kept giving way. As we rounded the corner to where he'd parked, his foot caught on a root. He tripped and instinctively threw his weight onto his injured leg for balance. His knee buckled and he inhaled sharply.

"Physician, heal thyself," called a voice in the trees.

I caught Jeremy's arm to brace him, but he only patted my shoulder, slipped from my grasp and pulled himself up straight. When I peered into the darkness, I could make out Malcolm, perched on the trunk of our rental car.

"Leg giving you some trouble?" he said. "That's funny. *I* feel fine."

To prove it, he leapt off the car and sauntered over. Peter hung back, but Jeremy kept moving forward. When he skirted Malcolm, their eyes met and Malcolm laughed.

"Was that a glare, boy? An actual glare? Well, that's a start. Of course, a real man would take a swing at me, but that would be too much to hope for, wouldn't it?"

Jeremy put a hand between my shoulder blades and steered me toward the car.

"Not even going to ask what I want?" Malcolm said.

"We know what you want," Peter said, struggling to throw some bravado into his voice. "Me. But you're too late. You caught me off guard once. It won't happen again."

"Of course it will. You're a child. I could take you down any time. Could have done it back there if I'd wanted. Bet you're wondering why I didn't, aren't you?"

"I know why you didn't," Jeremy said as he unlocked the car.

"You could justify killing Peter quickly, and argue self-defense, but once Clayton and I became involved, things got more complicated. Kill him under those circumstances, and the Pack will wonder why you carried out his punishment yourself, instead of bringing him in. So now you're falling back on plan B—demanding that I turn him over so you can bring him to Dominic."

"You think you're clever, don't you?"

"No, but you asked what I thought, so I told you. Clayton? Peter? In the car, please."

"He's not going—" Malcolm began.

Jeremy turned to his father. "I called Dominic this afternoon. He knows I'm with Peter, and that I want to negotiate his return to the Pack. If you bring Peter in and tell Dominic what he did, then he has to order Peter's death. Given the choice between negotiating a pardon and killing a former Pack member, which do you think he'd prefer?"

"You're bluffing," Malcolm said. "You haven't called him."

Malcolm searched his son's face for some sign that he was lying, but Jeremy's shuttered expression gave nothing away.

Malcolm rolled his shoulders and leaned against the car. "You know you're being played, don't you?"

"By Peter? No, I told him to call—"

"I don't mean Peter. I'm not a fool, boy. I know why you're doing all this. You think it'll help you weasel in closer to Dominic, prove what a good Alpha you'd make."

"I—"

"You think you're being clever, proving yourself to Dominic, taking over his duties. But the truth is, you're being played and you don't even know it. Sure, Dominic might name you as his choice. In the end, though, that doesn't mean piss-all and we both know it. Even *he* knows it. So why is he going through all this trouble, making the Pack think he wants you to succeed him? Because it buys him time. No one seriously considers you Alpha material, so no one's going to push for Dominic to step down. He looks like he's doing his job, planning for the future, but the truth is, he's just securing his place for another ten years."

"No one's playing me," Jeremy said softly.

Malcolm threw back his head and laughed. "Oh, but you're a fool. A fool twice in one night, too. That must be a record. You know, I could have killed your boy out there. You led him right to me, and then you couldn't even protect him."

Jeremy flinched. He tried to cover the reaction, but couldn't.

Malcolm smiled. "Piss-poor guardian you are. Hell, he protects you better than you protect him."

Jeremy saw me still standing beside him and waved me into the car.

"He's not moving until you're safe in that car," Malcolm said. "You should have seen him when I had you down—a regular little ball of rage, all fangs and fury. He's got it. Whatever you lack, boy, he's got in spades. You know that?"

Jeremy met his father's gaze. "Yes, I do." He rumpled my hair, a rare show of affection, and nudged me toward the car. "I'm getting in now, Clay. Go on."

"I want to train him," Malcolm said.

Jeremy stopped, hand on the door, and slowly turned to his father. "You want...?"

"You heard me. I want to train the boy. Teach him how to fight."

Jeremy stood there, struggling to make sense of this request. Was he joking? I almost hoped not. As much as I loathed Malcolm, I saw the benefit in what he was offering.

Jeremy and Antonio had taught me a lot, but after that night, I knew it wasn't enough. If I wanted to protect Jeremy against Malcolm, there was only one person who could teach me how to do it: Malcolm himself.

As for why he was offering, even at that age I knew he had to have an ulterior motive, probably to turn me against Jeremy, but that would never—*could* never—happen.

"Let him train me," I said.

Jeremy blinked and, for a split second, I was afraid I'd made a horrible mistake, that even considering Malcolm's offer would make Jeremy doubt my allegiance. But after that first blink of surprise, he gave a slow nod.

"Let me take Peter back to Dominic," Jeremy said. "What happened here—all of it—is never mentioned again. In return, I'll allow you to train Clayton. But only under my supervision."

"Fine by me," Malcolm said. "Who knows, you might even learn something." He looked down at me. "I'll see you back at Stonehaven then, Clay. Make sure you rest up. We have a lot of work ahead of us, unlearning all those bad habits."

He smiled, clapped me on the back, then strolled off into the night.

Angst

Malcolm kept his end of the bargain and we kept ours. Jeremy negotiated Peter's return to the Pack. Dominic never found out what happened in Los Angeles, and if he ever suspected anything, he pretended otherwise. As Jeremy had said, given the choice between reuniting a young werewolf with the Pack or executing him, Dominic would pick the former any day.

So Malcolm taught me to fight. I still took the majority of my lessons from Jeremy and Antonio because they were around more often, but when Malcolm was at Stonehaven, he trained me every afternoon, from lunch until dinner. His motivation? Well, that wasn't immediately apparent. Malcolm didn't use the lessons as an opportunity to mock Jeremy; although Jeremy was always present, Malcolm acted as if he wasn't there. Nor did Malcolm use them to woo me from Jeremy's side in any overt way. He was a harsh taskmaster and I often left my lessons exhausted and covered in bruises, but every bruise was earned in combat, and he never treated me in any way that could ever be interpreted as abusive.

One person who was never happy with the arrangement was Antonio. I'm sure he was put out by the insinuation that his teachings were less than perfect, but there was more to it than that. When Antonio was a teenager, Malcolm had made him the same offer: to train him. Antonio had flat-out refused. When Antonio found out that Jeremy had agreed to let Malcolm train me, he hit the roof. Argued like I'd never heard him argue before, then stomped out the door, left Stonehaven and didn't return for nearly a month.

When he did return, he barreled in, found us in the study and lit into Jeremy as if he'd only just left.

"I can't believe you'd do that. After everything that son of a bitch has done to you, I cannot believe you'd let him near Clayton."

Jeremy laid down his book and looked up calmly. "I'm always there."

"And that makes it okay? Goddamn it, Jeremy, *you're* his son. Not me. Not Clayton. If he can't accept you, that's his problem."

"So you think I'm offering up Clay as a substitute?"

"Hell, no. Never. You want Clay to learn how to fight. I get that. But I can teach him and you can teach him, and he doesn't need some psycho—"

"Malcolm is the best fighter we have, and that's what I want for Clay. To learn from the best so he can be the best, because the better he can fight, the less he'll have to."

"What?"

"You heard me. The better he can fight, the less he'll have to."

"What the hell is that supposed to mean?"

"Exactly what it says. If you want to stay for dinner, there's stew on the stove. Clay? Can you set the table, please?" He glanced at Antonio. "I managed to stash a few bottles of wine in the basement storage room, where Malcolm wouldn't find them. It's a beef stew, so red would be best, if you'd like to grab a bottle."

Antonio threw up his hands and stomped off to the basement.

* * *

So Malcolm continued to train me, and seemed happy enough just to have someplace to direct his energy when he was at Stonehaven. As the first year passed, his behavior toward Jeremy changed, too. Not that he treated him any better. Instead he began to extend his attitude toward Jeremy on the training grounds into our daily lives. He ignored him. Now and then, he couldn't resist tossing off a barb or an insult, but as time passed, he no longer seemed to take the pleasure in it that he once had and preferred to carry on as if Jeremy wasn't there, which suited us all just fine.

I started high school at thirteen. As concerned as Jeremy was about my social maturity, I think he was more concerned about me getting bored if I didn't find school challenging enough, so he applied to have me start a year early at a private school outside Syracuse.

At first, the school balked. They didn't like to advance anyone that way, particularly someone who'd been homeschooled. But, as Jeremy argued, having been born in January, I was only a few weeks younger than some other kids who would be starting ninth grade that fall.

Still, they hemmed and hawed, and they put me through a battery of tests. Then they gave me an IQ test. When they didn't believe the results of the first one, they administered a second. Then they declared I was indeed ready for high school.

It wasn't nearly the hell I'd expected. Yes, I'd rather have stayed home with Jeremy, but this gave me the opportunity to further study human behavior and develop my public face. I even made a few friends—not the "come on over after school and we'll listen to my 45s" kind of friends, but classmates I could eat lunch with or team up with for joint projects.

These friends invariably came from the fringes of teenage society, the kids who were too smart, too overweight, too homely or just too odd to fit in. With these outsiders, I could feel some kinship, even if they weren't werewolves.

Gregory died when I was fourteen. Since his injury, he'd never regained his full physical strength and had always been more prone to illness than most werewolves. One night he went to bed and didn't wake up. Outside his family, Jeremy was the only one who seemed to grieve his passing.

The next landmark of my life came at fifteen, when I killed my first mutt. In the Pack, one's first kill is considered a rite of passage, something to be celebrated with a night of drinking and carousing. I was too young for either drinking or the Pack's version of "carousing," which involved women. It didn't matter because I told no one that I'd passed this landmark, not even Nick.

I kept it to myself because I didn't consider it an event worthy of commemoration. I wasn't proud of what I'd done. Nor was I ashamed of it. The need to kill trespassing mutts was an unavoidable fact of my life, and I accepted it as such, with no emotion either way.

It happened in late spring. Antonio and Nick had come up for the weekend. Nick and I were now old enough to stay home alone, so Antonio and Jeremy had gone to Syracuse for some drinking and "carousing," and we didn't expect them back before the wee hours.

Nick and I spent the evening hanging out, talking—mostly

him talking, mostly about girls. He'd snuck over a few copies of *Playboy*, and we went through those. I didn't really get it, but I played along with his enthusiasm.

When it came to sex, I was a late bloomer. I'd begun filling out and putting on some muscle, helped by the weight set that Jeremy had bought for my fourteenth birthday. I'd also shot up a few inches. In the past year or so, I'd begun showing the first signs that, while I might never be as tall as Jeremy or as muscular as Antonio, I wouldn't be the runt of the litter forever.

In other areas of puberty, though, I lagged behind. My voice only cracked when I lost my temper and shouted loudly enough to strain my vocal cords, and the only excess hair I had came when I Changed. Sex and desire were things I understood only as hypothetical concepts. So, although I felt no physical reaction on seeing the *Playboy* centerfolds, I seconded Nick's opinion that they were "hot" and tried very hard to keep my attention off the articles and on the pictorials.

After eating everything that Jeremy left out for us and sampling his brandy, we headed up to my room. I waited until Nick drifted off, then took my flashlight and sat in the corner to read. With Jeremy gone, I was the man of the house, and I didn't feel right falling asleep. Anything could happen. And that night, something did.

When the clock downstairs struck midnight, a wolf's howl echoed the last few gongs. I leapt up, dropping my book and flashlight, and opened my window. The howl came again, from deep in our back woods. I knew that it was a mutt, not because I didn't recognize the voice, but because it was a howl of challenge, the call of a wolf who has ventured onto another's territory and dares him to do anything about it.

I knew I had to act fast. Jeremy and Antonio would be home any moment now. If they heard the howl, our weekend would be ruined. Antonio would insist on handling it, Jeremy would insist on defending his own territory, and any way that it ended, no one would be happy. Better for me to take care of it.

Two things told me I was relatively safe taking on this challenge alone. First, the wolf's cry held a quaver that said he was getting on in years. Second, coming at midnight and howling in the woods rather than appearing at our front door meant he wasn't all that sure he wanted anyone to answer his challenge. This was an old wolf making his last stand, maybe ill or otherwise close to death, hoping to die doing something he'd never dared do in life—take on a Pack wolf.

So I leapt out the window, raced into the forest and Changed. Then I tracked him and killed him. It was, as I'd suspected, not a difficult task, and not one that requires any further detail. I killed him, I buried his body and I went back to bed.

That winter, I killed my second mutt. This time, the mutt presented himself at our door, so I couldn't intercede before Jeremy found out. As usual, Jeremy gave him until midnight to leave town. The mutt only laughed and said he'd be in the back forest, ready whenever Jeremy got up the nerve to take him on. I knew he wouldn't leave. And I knew Jeremy would give him until midnight. So, on pretense of working out, I went down to the basement, then climbed out a window. I Changed, lured the mutt away from the place he'd promised to meet Jeremy, and killed him. This time wasn't nearly as easy as the last, but I managed it. I stashed his body far from the assigned meeting place, and downwind so Jeremy wouldn't find it, then hurried back to the house. Late that night, after Jeremy had decided the mutt had fled, I returned and buried the corpse.

Two mutts within six months was unusual. A third one showed

up just a few months after the second. This one, fortunately, did take Jeremy's advice and left town. But that still meant three mutts in a year. Something was wrong. Yet because Jeremy knew nothing of the first one, he thought we'd only had two mutts in just over a year, both of whom had left without a fight, so he saw no cause for alarm.

When I hit sixteen, puberty finally kicked in, bringing with it a problem far more complicated than the killing of trespassing mutts. I began to feel the first tugs of sexual desire, and while that's probably confusing for any kid, my situation only made it ten times worse.

With no females of my own species, my body fixed those desires on the nearest approximation it could find—human girls. And that might have been fine, had my wolf brain not jumped in with demands of its own. On the matter of sex, the wolf in me was clear: I needed to find not a casual sexual partner, but a life partner, a mate.

I would accept a human mate, since it seemed I had little choice in the matter, but it had to be someone I wanted to spend my life with. Yet there were few humans I could envision spending an entire *weekend* with. So here I was stuck. I looked around and saw no potential life partner, and the wolf in me would accept nothing less.

That September was one of the worst times of my teen years.

I always arrived at school early so I could run twenty laps around the track, wear off excess energy before beginning my day. That was my only chance to get some physical activity in before I went home and worked out. I didn't take gym class. We were supposed to, but Jeremy had managed to convince the school that my time was better spent where my obvious assets lay—in academics.

With the help of a sympathetic teacher, who agreed that I needed to be challenged academically, I was already on the fast track to college, skipping any "extra" classes like gym or art so I could graduate early.

That morning, the football field was flooded, so the team had to move its before-school practice to the track field. I ignored them, but the disinterest wasn't mutual. After a few minutes, I noticed the football coach watching me more than he was watching his team. When I headed to the stands to grab my towel, he came over.

"What's your name, son?" he asked.

I wiped the towel over my face. "Clayton."

"You're a student here, aren't you? I know I've seen you around."

I shrugged and kept drying off.

"You took those hurdles pretty good. You on the track team?"

I shook my head, grabbed a clean shirt from my bag and peeled off my sweat-sodden one. The coach's gaze slid over my upper body.

"How much are you lifting?" he asked.

Another shrug, and I yanked on my shirt.

"Not very talkative, are you, son?"

I hefted my bag. "I gotta go."

He stepped in my path. I tensed, but pushed back. He was a teacher, and I knew I had to respect him, but it was something that I'd been having more and more difficulty faking.

"I want you to try out for the team," he said.

I swung my bag into my other hand. "What team?"

Someone laughed. I turned to see a half-dozen members of

the football team behind me, shifting into a semicircle, as if blocking my escape route. Whether they knew what they were doing wasn't clear—humans are notoriously ignorant of their body language—but that didn't keep me from interpreting it as a trap. The hairs on my neck rose.

"The football team, son," the coach said. "I want you to try out for the football team."

I knew I should take the high road, like Jeremy would, quietly demur with an excuse and a thank-you. But, as I said, I was finding this increasingly hard to do. I thought of a polite excuse, but instead what came out was: "Not interested."

A rumble rose from the boys behind me. Even the coach stiffened, his good humor sliding away.

"Not interested?" he said. "This is the *football* team, boy, not the goddamned chess club. If we want you on the team, you join. It's a little something called school spirit."

I said nothing, but my sneer answered for me.

The coach's face went bright red. "Get to the office. Now."

I wound up with a week's detention for being disrespectful to a teacher.

If that wasn't bad enough, the coach started cornering me in the halls. If I tried out, he said, there was a good chance I could make running back, maybe even quarterback, and didn't every sixteen-year-old boy want to be quarterback? Another student overheard and ran off to inform the current running back and quarterback, neither of whom was too pleased with the prospect. So then I had *them* harassing me. Finally, I snapped. As hard as Jeremy might teach me to turn the other cheek, there was a limit to how long I could do it.

The next time they challenged me to a skirmish match, I

accepted. Fortunately, no bones were broken. The wounds to the quarterback's ego were another matter, though, and instead of getting him off my back, I'd only pissed him off more. I knew I couldn't fight them—that football skirmish had been pushing it enough—so I was stuck swallowing their insults and accepting their shoves, and getting more miserable with each passing day. Soon even my school friends were avoiding me, for fear of catching the fallout.

From there, it only got worse. On Thursday, while racing home to make sure Jeremy didn't find out about my detention, I got a speeding ticket.

Jeremy had bought me a car for my sixteenth birthday, so I wouldn't have to endure the bus any longer, and this was my third ticket so far. If you worked it out—the number of times I sped versus the number of tickets I received—I was doing pretty good. But Jeremy didn't see it that way. Nor did he understand my view of traffic laws.

I understood why speed limits existed, but I saw no reason why they should apply to me. I was an excellent driver. With my enhanced senses and reflexes, I could drive eighty miles an hour and still avoid hitting a squirrel. I made my own money—transcribing notes for Jeremy's growing translation business—and I paid for my tickets, so what was the big deal? Threatening to take away my car was wrong. Wrong and unfair.

That ticket only added fuel to a fire that had been blazing all month. The source of that fire? College. Having condensed my studies, I was due to graduate next June, which meant I was supposed to head off to college in a year. I had no problem with going to college. I *wanted* to go. I enjoyed learning and I knew that I needed a good education if I wanted a career that I could pursue from home, like Jeremy did.

Now, Jeremy had *not* gone to college. He'd wanted to, and expected to, but then his grandfather died and he'd had to start working to pay the bills. So naturally he wanted me to go. The problem came with the question of where. The school had already hinted to Jeremy that I could get a scholarship pretty much anywhere I wanted. So what did he do? Started gathering information on colleges, to decide where I *should* want to go.

I knew damned well where I was going: Syracuse University. Jeremy shot down that idea as if it was the most ridiculous thing he'd ever heard. I'd already decided my major—my early studies of human society had led me to a high school anthropology course, and I'd decided that was what I wanted to pursue.

As Jeremy pointed out, Syracuse did not have a top-notch anthropology program. So I had to go elsewhere. Well, I wasn't. I just wasn't. I was staying home and going to Syracuse University. Move away to school? Wasn't happening.

On Friday, battered down by my hellish week, I returned to Stonehaven, seeking solace, and found Jeremy filling out a form to request more information from the University of Chicago. I hit the roof. Broke a chair and a couple of plates. Said a few things I shouldn't have. Then I stormed out the back door and stayed in the woods until midnight, which I figured was long enough to make my point.

When I walked into the house, I passed the study, saw Jeremy in there and kept going. He followed me.

"Your bag is by the front door. Check it and make sure I haven't left anything out."

My heart jammed into my throat. "Bag?"

"You're spending the weekend with Dominic. I have business in New York."

I scowled. "What business?"

"Nothing important," he said. "Check your bag and we'll leave."

He headed back into the study. I resisted the urge to follow. What business could he have in New York? He never took meetings in person, never needed to.

He was sending me away. Taking a break from me, just like he did with Malcolm. I suspected that was the reason behind his sudden vigor to find an out-of-state college for me: to rid himself of a boy who'd turned from a devoted child into a troublesome teen.

And what if he did have business in New York? What kind of business? Why wouldn't he discuss it with me?

There'd been a lot of that lately, closed-door phone conversations that ended the moment I walked in. He didn't trust me. He still thought of me as a child. Well, he treated me like a child, didn't he? Deciding where I should go to school, threatening to take away my car, arranging my weekends for me. It was wrong. Wrong and unfair.

Without checking my bag, I grabbed it and stormed off to the truck.

Misunderstood

I couldn't believe Nick had done this to me.

It was Saturday night. A special Saturday night planned by Nick to lift me out of my black mood, because that's the kind of friend he was. Thoughtful, considerate, generous . . . the best friend a guy could want.

I scowled into the night, took a swig of my beer and dumped the rest over the side of the deck.

It had been a great plan, one that made me regret every thoughtless thing I'd ever done to him. We'd start with a movie. He knew I liked movies, and there was nothing better to get my mind off my problems than a good action-packed thriller.

After the show, we'd go out for pizza. Then we'd go somewhere else and have more pizza. Later we'd head back to the house, and Nick would try Changing.

In the last few months Nick had begun showing the first signs of impending werewolf-hood—increased hunger, heightened senses and greater strength. We'd been trying to rush the process along with practice sessions, where we'd go into the woods and I'd coach him. So far, it hadn't worked—and everyone in the Pack swore it never would—but we kept trying.

Right after dinner, we left the estate. Like me, Nick had his own car. That's common for Pack boys—not because we need wheels to head out into the country for an urgent Change or to make a speedy getaway, but just because every teenage boy wants a car, and the Pack spoiled us, knowing our lives would be difficult enough later.

When Nick realized we were too early for the movie, he decided to stop off at a friend's place. His friend's parents were gone for the weekend, so the guy was having a party.

There are few things in life I hate more than parties. If you want to scare me with visions of hell, just tell me it's eternity squeezed into a small room full of people drinking, shouting, sweating and playing music loud enough to shatter eardrums. But Nick had planned an entire evening for me; the least I could do was give him the first half-hour of it.

So I went to the party without complaint. Then Nick found out they had a beer keg and that a girl he'd been pursuing for the last month was there... without her boyfriend.

Two and a half hours later, I was standing on the back porch, alone, glowering into the dark yard, and wondering where my life had gone so horribly wrong.

When the patio door slid open behind me, I hoped it was Nick. One sniff of perfume, though, and I knew better. Without turning, I sent off another hope: that the girl behind me had come out for a cigarette or some fresh air, not because she'd seen me through the window and decided I looked lonely. Since I'd been out here, two other girls had come out, trying to cheer me up, and only making my evening more unbearable.

I kept my gaze fixed on the yard and slumped forward against the railing, leaving my back to her.

"Nice night," she said.

I nodded.

She moved up beside me. "You're Nick's friend, aren't you?"

I made a noise in my throat. Had she been a wolf, she'd have interpreted it for what it was: a polite "leave me alone."

"Hmmm?" she said, billowing perfume as she leaned around me. "I didn't catch that."

I shrugged and moved away.

"Hey, I asked you a question," she said.

"Yeah, I'm with Nick."

I headed down the steps to the yard.

"Hey!" she called after me. "I'm talking to you."

I kept walking. She hurried after me and caught my hand. When I shook her off, she only grinned, as if it was a challenge.

"Do you have a name, Nick's friend?"

"Yeah. Not Interested."

She blinked, eyes snapping with outrage. "Excuse me?"

"Never mind. Just go back inside, okay?"

"Is that an order?"

"Just go—"

"Hey!" someone shouted from the porch.

I looked up to see a tall, muscular boy bearing down on us. One glance at his scowl, and I knew he was the girl's boyfriend. My evening was complete.

I turned to walk away. The boy grabbed my shoulder and whipped me around. I shrugged him off and struggled not to return his glare of challenge.

"What do you think you're doing with my girl?" he demanded, bringing his face down to mine.

I met his eyes. "Nothing."

"Bullshit," the girl said. "I came out here for a smoke, and he grabbed me. Tried to cop a feel."

I snorted. "Not likely."

"What the hell is that supposed to mean?" the boy snapped.

The look I turned on the girl answered for me. The boy grabbed for me again, but I knocked his hands aside before they could touch me.

"Oooh, tough guy," the boy said. "You asking for something, tough guy?"

"Yeah, I'm asking for you to leave me alone, take your girl-friend and go back inside."

"Ah'm askin' fah ya...?" The boy screwed up his face, exaggerating and mangling my drawl. "Is that English? What rock did you crawl from under, talking like that? Who brought you here?"

"Nick," the girl piped up. "Nick Sorrentino."

"Well, then, I think I should talk to ol' Nicky—"

"Leave Nick out of this," I said.

"You gonna make me?"

When I said nothing, he grabbed me by the shirtfront. I swept my arms up fast, knocking his hands off me. He stumbled back, then caught his balance and charged. I didn't budge, just whipped out my hands, slammed them into his shoulders and sent him flying backward to the ground. Before he could get up, I stepped over him.

"Whoa!" a familiar voice yelled. "Whoa! Hold on!"

I looked up to see Nick running off the porch, pushing past the small group of gathered onlookers. He waved me off the guy. I slowly backed away, then strode to the rear of the yard.

I waited, with my back to everyone, while Nick sorted it out. When I heard him walk over, I turned, expecting an apology for the way he'd abandoned me. Instead, his eyes blazed with fury.

"What the hell is the matter with you?" he hissed, bathing me in beer fumes. "I bring you to a party and you pull this shit? In front of my friends?"

"I didn't pull anything. That girl came out here—"

"And you blew her off, right? Couldn't be nice about it. It's a girl, Clay. Any normal guy—oh, wait, but you're not a normal guy, are you? You don't even try to be normal, that's the problem."

One of the partygoers on the deck shouted an insult in an exaggerated drawl. Nick winced and waited for the laughter to die down.

"See?" he said. "See? You gotta be different. Can't even bother talking normally. There's no reason why you keep that stupid accent—oh, wait, there is a reason. Because you don't want to sound like everyone else. You like being different, being an asshole, acting like you're too good for everyone. Well, let me tell you something, Clay—"

I brushed past him and headed for the front gate.

"Hey!" Nick shouted. "I'm not done!"

When I didn't stop, he jogged after me.

"You walk out that door, and you're walking home. I'm not coming after you."

I pushed open the gate and strode through.

I had money for a cab, but no idea how to summon one from a residential neighborhood. I assumed that if I called the operator, they could put me in touch with a local cab company, but first I had to find a pay phone. So I wandered up and down the streets, telling myself I was looking for a phone, but I'm sure I could have walked right past one and not noticed. What did it matter? Where would I go? Nobody wanted me around. I could probably wander the streets all night and no one would even notice I was gone.

An hour passed. When a horn blasted behind me, I jumped, expecting Nick and ready to blast him back, or maybe ignore him and keep walking. But it wasn't Nick. It was, however, a familiar car, driven by someone with a familiar face.

"Now my week really is complete," I muttered under my breath, and walked faster.

The car revved up beside me. I thought of taking off across the lawns, but that would be fleeing, and this was one person I refused to give that satisfaction. So I stopped and waited for him to roll down the passenger window.

"What?" I said.

Malcolm laughed. "There's a greeting to warm the heart."

"Go away."

"That one's even better." He leaned out the window. "Not even going to ask what I'm doing here?"

"No."

I did wonder, but given what I knew of Malcolm, if he'd said his pet demon told him where to find me, I wouldn't have doubted it. As I'd discover later, the answer was far more ordinary. Dominic had summoned him to the estate to discuss a mutt problem and, shortly after he'd arrived, Nick had called, wondering whether anyone had heard from me. Malcolm found out where the party was, made an excuse to leave and came looking for me.

"Having a rough time lately, I hear," Malcolm said. "Want to talk about it?"

"With you?" I snorted. "No."

"I don't see anyone else offering."

That arrow hit its mark. I strode away. Malcolm kept pace beside me with the car, leaning into the passenger seat so he could talk.

"Let's see if I can guess what the problem is," he said. "No one understands you."

I kept walking.

"Now, I might not be the person you'd choose to talk to about it, but I might be the best person there is. *I* understand you."

"No, you don't."

"Ah, you'd be surprised. I know you've killed two mutts at Stonehaven. Bet I'm the only one who knows that."

How did he . . . ? Again, pet demons whispering in his ear was a damned fine explanation, but I quickly thought of a simpler one.

"You found the bodies," I said.

"Found where you buried them. You have to work on your technique, Clay. It might fool Jeremy, but it won't fool me."

"And now you're going to tell him."

"Nah, I wouldn't tattle on you. You're a good kid. If you want to kill mutts for Jeremy, all the power to you. When I found that first one, I thought, 'Well, the mutt was pretty old, it wasn't a tough kill.' But then I found the second, and I was proud of you. Damned proud of you."

"I don't want—"

"I know, you don't want my admiration, but you have it. You've earned it. Now, in case you haven't noticed, we're having a problem with these mutts at Stonehaven, and I think maybe you and I should talk about it."

I hesitated.

"Do you know why they're coming around?" he asked.

I shrugged as if I didn't care.

"Well, I know why, and I think you should, too," he said. "Climb on in and we'll go someplace where we can talk."

The mutt problem *had* been weighing on my mind. This wasn't the person I wanted to discuss it with, but right now, Malcolm was right—no one else was offering. So I opened the car door.

Problem

I wasn't worried about Malcolm driving me to a dark alley and breaking my neck. Not that I could outfight him; I couldn't—not yet. But I'd lived with him long enough to understand how he operated.

If Malcolm wanted me dead, he'd have ended my life that night outside Los Angeles. Training me for a few years, lowering my defenses and then killing me might seem like a clever plan, but Malcolm could never pull it off. He was a creature of impulse, of brawn and might, not without the cunning to conceive of a long-term plan, but lacking the patience to see it to the end.

Malcolm drove to a town on the other side of the Sorrentinos' country estate, and pulled into a parking lot.

"Here?" I said.

He shrugged. "Near here. A little place I go when things get crowded at Dominic's. Come on."

He led me to an unmarked door wedged between a dry cleaner and a convenience store. I stepped inside and found myself nose to chest with a massive bald man. When he saw Malcolm, he backed out of my face.

"Hey, Mal. Been a long time." He looked down at me. "Who's the kid?"

Malcolm put a hand on my shoulder. "This is Clayton. My boy."

"You got a son? You never told me you got a son."

"You never asked. Mind if I take him inside? Don't worry, he'll stick to root beer."

"Yeah, sure, take him in. Buy him a real beer if he wants it. No one's gonna care."

Malcolm led me into a small, dark bar, where the only music came from the clink of glasses and the occasional laugh. He steered me to a table at the back.

"You want a beer?" he asked as I sat down. "Smells like you've had one already, might as well make it two."

I shook my head.

"Soda?"

I shrugged.

He went to the bar and returned with two mugs, one cola and the other beer. A red-haired woman in a faded tank top and frayed miniskirt slid over from another table.

"Malcolm," she said, and kissed his cheek. "You didn't call me."

"Do I ever?"

Her lips curved in a pout, then she saw me in the shadows.

"My son," Malcolm said. "Clayton."

"Oooh," she squealed, the sound grating down my spine. "What a cutie. He must take after his momma."

"Ha-ha," Malcolm said. "I don't mean to be rude, Deedee—well, yes I do. Clear out. I'm spending time with my boy. He's had a rough day."

"I could make it better for him." Her gaze slid over me. "End it with a bang."

I tugged my jacket tighter around me.

Malcolm shook his head. "Another time, Deedee. Clear out. Now."

She pouted and flounced away.

Malcolm sipped his beer. "So, what'd it feel like, killing your first mutt?"

I shrugged.

He leaned forward and his eyes glittered. "Don't give me that. It felt good, didn't it? Taking a life. Made you feel powerful."

I looked at him, and tried to figure out what he meant.

"Not comfortable with it yet?" he said. "I understand that. Can't be easy when *he* tells you it's wrong. But it isn't wrong. You feel that, don't you? Taking a life isn't a crime, it's an act of power."

I needed information from him, so it seemed best to play along. I nodded and hoped that was enough.

He clapped me on the shoulder. "See? I do understand."

"About the mutts," I said. "Something's happening, isn't it? That's why there's more of them coming around."

"You don't know why? You're a bright boy, Clayton. If you think about it, I'm sure you'll realize you already know the answer. Why are more mutts coming to Stonehaven?"

Stonehaven. Of course. With my own problems, I'd overlooked the obvious clue to solving this one. The mutts were coming only to Stonehaven. No one else in the Pack had reported an increase.

"You're sending them," I said. "You're testing me."

Malcolm's laugh startled the patrons at the next table. "Not bad, not bad at all. Wrong, but a good guess. I wouldn't do that to you, Clay. You're still too green to be facing mutts without backup. If I wanted to test you, I'd take you to the mutts, not send them to you. They're coming on their own. Think about it. Who lives at Stonehaven?"

I frowned. "We do. So? We've always lived—"

"Wait. Who lives there? You, Jeremy and me. Now most mutts don't know about you, so they're obviously coming to see Jeremy or me. Nothing new there but, as you said, something has changed. Something that makes them want to challenge us in particular."

I hesitated, then looked up sharply. "You're both potential Alphas. The mutts know that, don't they? That you want to be Alpha and Dominic seems to be backing Jeremy."

Malcolm nodded. "Good boy. Now why would they—?"

"Why would they want to challenge a potential Alpha?" I cut in, my brain racing ahead to fill in the blanks. "Because it's as close to an Alpha as they can get. They can't challenge Dominic. Even if they won, the Pack would hunt them down. But they could challenge an Alpha candidate. That'd be the next best thing, wouldn't it?"

"And an opportunity that doesn't come around more than once or twice in a mutt's life. If this stretches on much longer, we'll have every mutt on the continent getting up the nerve to try his luck."

I slumped into my seat. With Dominic showing no signs of giving up his position, this waiting game could continue for years. Years of having mutts on our doorstep, trespassing on our territory, threatening Jeremy.

"There is a way to stop it," Malcolm said. "If Jeremy tells Dominic he doesn't want to be Alpha, he'd be out of the race. The mutts would hear about that, and they'd stop coming after him. Now, they'd still want to take a shot at me, but most of them know I don't spend much time at home. So Stonehaven would be safe again. Jeremy would be safe again."

Malcolm really needed to work on his finesse. Play on my fears for Jeremy, and hope I could use my influence with Jeremy to persuade him to drop out of the Alpha race? Like I *had* any influence with Jeremy. He wasn't even going to let me influence where I went to college.

I said none of this to Malcolm. Instead, I nodded and he settled into his chair, smiling, pleased with his success. In a way, he had succeeded. I now realized that Jeremy was in danger, and would continue to be in danger as long as he was an Alpha candidate.

So how would I deal with that? By removing the source of the danger.

To do that, I didn't need to persuade him not to challenge Malcolm for Alpha. As angry as I was at Jeremy, I still knew he'd make a good Alpha. What I had to do was stop the mutts from coming. But how?

I told Malcolm I wanted to meet up with Nick so I didn't return to the house with him and worry Jeremy. The truth was, I wanted to get out of his company as quickly as possible, and I wanted time by myself to work on this problem.

Malcolm dropped me off where he'd picked me up. I started heading back toward the party. Once he'd driven out of sight, I resumed my aimless wandering. I'd figure out how to get to the estate later. For now, I needed to think.

How could I get mutts to stop coming to Stonehaven?

As I walked, I remembered Jeremy's "riddle" to Antonio, his explanation for why he was letting Malcolm train me. If I was a good enough fighter, I wouldn't need to fight. Not a riddle, but a logical fact, one that only now made sense. When you reached the top of your game, fewer and fewer people cared to take you on. Yes, mutts came to Stonehaven looking for a fight with Malcolm, the Pack's top fighter. Yet mutts did the same to other Pack wolves, picking the one they thought was in their league.

On average, fewer mutts came to Malcolm than to Antonio or

Wally Santos, who were the next best fighters in the Pack. Most mutts aren't suicidal—they challenge the best Pack wolf whom they think they have a shot at beating, and Malcolm was more than most cared to handle.

When a less experienced Pack wolf, like Stephen Santos, traveled, he always had to be careful. Technically mutts weren't supposed to hold territory, but Dominic didn't like to bother with mutts any more than necessary, so many settled in cities and defended them against all comers. If Stephen passed through a city that a mutt considered *his* territory, Stephen was in for a fight. When Malcolm came to town, though, all but the stupidest mutts decided it was time for a vacation.

What I had to do was make sure mutts knew that to challenge Jeremy, they had to get through me first. If I was a formidable enough fighter, few would care to bother.

Great plan. Only one problem. Such a reputation took years, maybe decades, to build. I didn't have that much time. I needed to stop these mutts before the campaign for Alpha gained momentum. To do that, I had to cheat my way to a reputation.

Instead of fighting dozens of battles, I needed to do something that would fly through the rumor mill and make every mutt in the country decide he didn't want to tangle with me. How? I had no idea.

I heard someone shout, but was too engrossed in my thoughts to look. When footsteps sounded behind me, I wheeled.

"Whoa!" Nick said, backpedaling. "I thought you heard me call you."

I shook my head and continued walking. He jogged beside me.

"Okay, you're mad," he said. "I don't blame you. I was a total jerk."

It took a moment for me to remember what he was talking

about. When I did, I brushed it off with a muttered "it's okay" and returned to my thoughts.

"I had too much to drink, and then Becky's boyfriend showed up and she took off with him, and then I walked out to the back-yard, saw you standing over Mike, and I lost it. I know you hate parties. I didn't mean to be there that long and I'm sorry."

Another mumbled "it's okay."

"I've been driving around for hours looking for you. It's too late to catch a show, but we could get pizza. Do you want pizza?"

I shook my head, still walking.

Nick exhaled loudly. "Shit, you really are mad. Okay, okay, well, at least come back to the car with me. Please?"

I stopped and blinked, returning to reality.

"Yeah, sure," I said. "Let's go."

I started for the car.

"You sure you don't want pizza?" Nick said, hurrying up be-side me. "There's this great—"

"Pizza's fine. I'm just trying to work out a problem."

"Oh, well, okay, then. Maybe I can help."

I shook my head. "Not your kind of problem." I paused. "But thanks . . . for offering."

"So we're square?"

"No. You owe me pizza, a movie and your first Change. Then we'll be square."

He grinned. "The first tonight, the second tomorrow and the third soon. Real soon, I hope."

I didn't come up with a plan that night. Or that weekend. Or that month. This was a problem that required serious deliberation, and that would take time.

Circumstances

My life swung out of its rough patch soon after that weekend. Jeremy shelved the college debate, which gave me time to cool down and see that I'd overreacted, jumping to the conclusion that he was getting rid of me. Old fears die hard, I suppose.

In trying to send me off to college he only wanted what he always wanted for me: the best. In this case, that meant the best education possible. I still had no intention of leaving Stonehaven next year, but if I wanted to stay, I needed to stop shouting and throwing things, and come up with a logical argument.

So I set to work researching the matter and within a few weeks developed a line of attack—verbal, nonconfrontational attack. After earning my undergrad degree, I wanted to go to graduate school. My goal was a career in anthropology research, and I needed a Ph.D. for that.

At that level, though, no one really cared where you'd taken your undergrad courses. It was the advanced degrees that counted. Since I had no intention of spending seven years living away from Jeremy and the Pack, it made sense for me to reserve the "good" schools for my grad degrees. As well, that would give me a few years to get accustomed to college life before I ventured out on my own.

When I was ready, I argued my case to Jeremy. He listened, asked questions and then agreed to think about it for a few days. Then he came back with a decision. As long as I promised to go to a top-tier school for my graduate degrees, I could attend undergrad classes in Syracuse.

Nick had his first Change at the end of October. Although Jeremy and I had prepared him as best we could, it wasn't easy. Yet if it was any less wondrous than he expected, he never let on, never complained.

In the past few years, the question of Alpha succession had gone from back-room rumblings to heated debate, and I'm sure that whenever Dominic walked into a room and heard conversation stop, he knew exactly what was being discussed.

Dominic had now turned over all youth training to Jeremy. He'd also put him in charge of the Legacy—the Pack history book. This latter chore I'm sure he was glad to hand off, and no one else was clamoring for the job, but it still sent a clear message. These were Alpha duties, and everyone took that to mean that any day now, Dominic would officially endorse Jeremy as his choice of successor.

That did not necessarily mean Jeremy would be the next Alpha. An Alpha will back a Pack brother as his choice, but the actual process of ascension was more democratic. Everyone in the Pack endorsed a candidate, and the one with the most power behind him won.

Right now, Jeremy had only Antonio squarely in his corner.

Although Jorge, Nick and I also supported him, we were still considered junior members, so our votes carried little weight.

For now, it didn't matter. Dominic wasn't going anywhere. When Malcolm "accidentally" swiped the first bite of meat after a Pack deer hunt, Dominic trounced him. The battle was closer than Dominic might have liked, but he won, proving he still deserved to be Alpha.

I eventually hit on a plan to stop mutts from coming to Stonehaven. It wasn't a simple scheme. It required planning— lots of planning, and lots of research on subjects that weren't readily available in the local library.

By the time I felt ready to carry out my plan, it was spring. The next problem, though, was that I needed a specific and uncommon set of circumstances. I didn't want a mutt who was too young and inexperienced, or too old and feeble . . . or too bright.

The next two mutts who showed up at Stonehaven didn't fit my needs, so I killed them quickly, disposed of the bodies and continued to wait. Winter came. Another mutt came. That time, Jeremy met him first, and had to deal with it himself. I decided then that I couldn't wait for my set of circumstances to occur naturally. I needed to create them.

September came and college began. It took time for me to adjust. Change is never easy for me, and something like this, being inundated with new faces, new schedules, new expectations, threw me off balance, making me edgy and moody.

Two weeks into the semester, a teacher scheduled me for a 5:30 p.m. conference, which totally screwed up my routine. By the time I drove back from Syracuse, it was after seven. I'd meant to grab a sandwich at the cafeteria, but was so eager to get home that I forgot.

I arrived at Stonehaven starving. I parked and bolted for the door, certain dinner would be waiting for me. Instead I found Jeremy engrossed in a new painting. The frozen shepherd's pie he'd put into the oven was still frozen because he'd been so distracted by his work that he'd forgotten to turn it on.

I blew up. Accused him of being thoughtless and insensitive to my needs. A shitty thing to say—and laughably untrue—but I was hungry.

I stormed to the kitchen, grabbed the makings of a sandwich, then decided it was too much work to assemble one and wolfed down the components separately. When my stomach was full, I knew I'd been out of line with Jeremy. I also knew that, given my recent mood swings, if I tried to say I was sorry, I was liable to turn the apology into another fight. So I fixed Jeremy a sandwich and dropped it off outside his studio door with a note saying I'd gone for a walk.

Once outside, I debated working off some energy with a run, but was too edgy to Change, so I wandered the forest, mentally working through an essay I needed to write. I was in the midst of composing my thesis statement when a movement in the trees ahead made me stop short. It was almost nine now, and dark. Though I had good night vision, with no moon overhead to help, I could only make out the shape of a tall, dark-haired man.

As proof of my distracted sense of mind, I never thought to sneak in for a sniff and a closer look. I assumed it was Jeremy and strode forward. When I stepped onto the path, the man wheeled. It wasn't Jeremy.

"Shit!" he said, jumping as he saw me. "What the hell—?" He stopped, nostrils flaring, then blinked as he realized I wasn't some neighborhood teen trespassing in Stonehaven's woods. He squinted in the darkness. "Shit. You're Malcolm's kid, aren't you?"

"No," I said. "Jeremy's in the house, and he's not coming out so don't bother—"

"Not Jeremy. The other one. The boy. The one Malcolm's been bragging about. So his phantom foster son isn't a phantom after all, huh? I figured it was bullshit, since no one's ever seen you."

"They see me. They just don't live to tell about it."

The mutt rolled his eyes. "Yeah, good one," he said, but a flicker of uncertainty in his eyes said he wasn't completely sure I was bluffing.

I sized up the mutt. Jeremy's age, decent physical condition. Yeah, he'd do. Now I just needed to persuade him to help me set up the circumstances I required.

"You know Nick Sorrentino?" I asked, circling the mutt, making him turn to watch me.

A snort. "What is this? Small talk? I came here to fight, in case you didn't figure that out, kiddo."

"Nick Sorrentino," I repeated. "Do you know who he is?"

"Sure. Antonio's kid."

"He's a friend of mine."

"Bully for you."

I stopped circling and leaned against a tree, arms crossed. The mutt visibly relaxed.

"Nick's got this problem," I said. "Maybe you can help me solve it."

"What do I look like? Dear Abby? I can't solve—"

"Yeah, I think you can. See, here's Nick's problem. He's been a full werewolf for nearly a year, but he's never fought a mutt. Never even been close to a fight. Antonio and Dominic won't let him."

The mutt sniffed. "Coddling the boy, like they do with Jorge. Figures."

"Well, that's where I'm hoping you can help. Nick wants a fight, and I want to give him one. Chance to fight the Alpha's grandson? A sweet deal for any mutt."

"You want me to fight him instead of you? Uh-uh. Even if he's a Sorrentino, he's a pup with no notches on his belt. I'm beyond that. But Malcolm's protégé?" He grinned. "Now that might be a challenge worth winning."

"It is. And I'm not trying to take it from you. Here's the deal. You want a shot at me, bring a friend for Nick. You do have friends, don't you?"

"Yeah, but—"

"I'm sure one of those friends isn't as experienced as you. He'd be happy for the chance to fight Nick. And he'd owe you one for setting it up."

The mutt paused, then peered at me. "You wouldn't be trying to get out of a fight, would—"

I pounced and knocked him to the ground, then jammed my forearm against his throat. "Do I look like I'm trying to blow off a fight?"

The mutt gasped. I eased back, but stayed on his chest.

"You're good," he wheezed.

For a moment, I wondered whether I'd miscalculated and scared him off, but then his eyes gleamed with the prospect of the bragging rights he'd earn by beating me. After all, I was just a kid. A decent fighter for my age, but an inexperienced, cocky pup nonetheless.

"Okay, sure," he said. "I know a couple of guys. Let's set something up."

So we did.

Legend

"A small fight?" Nick said, trailing down the path after me. "Just a small one."

"Yeah, sure, we'll just tell them 'hey, Nick wants a fight, but just a small one, so stop before you kill him, please.'"

"You know what I mean."

"No, I don't," I said. I stopped to readjust my knapsack, then hoisted the hockey bag again.

"I can carry that," Nick said, reaching for the hockey bag.

I grunted a negative and swung it out of his reach. He didn't need to see what was in there. It certainly wasn't hockey equipment. This just happened to be the biggest bag I could find at the sporting goods store, and the one that would look least suspicious if someone saw me hauling it around in November.

"There's no such thing as a small fight," I said. "There are short fights and there are long fights, and either way you can get killed and that's not on the agenda for today. Telling them you want a fight was a ruse." I caught his look of confusion. "An excuse."

"But I *do* want a fight."

"You'll get your chance soon enough. No need to go looking for one."

He swerved past me to open the door on the old wooden hunting cabin. I nodded my thanks and walked inside. It was empty, and had been for months, being off-season. Dozens of these cabins dotted the countryside around here. I'd scouted the area last month and found two possibilities. Both were at least a mile from the nearest house, meaning I'd have plenty of time to work, and clean up after, without fear of interruption.

"Do you want to go over it again?" I asked.

Nick shook his head.

"Okay, then go on outside and let me set up."

"I could help—"

"No," I said, and shoved him toward the door.

I'd arranged to meet the mutt and his friend at noon, a half-mile from the cabin. Convenient, but not too close.

The next step was difficult. Mentally difficult. I had to cheat. No matter how senselessly violent werewolf fights may seem, they came with set rules of behavior, what human fighters might call "gentleman's rules." You couldn't sneak up from behind. You couldn't take three friends to fight one guy. You couldn't use weapons. It had to be a fair, one-on-one, fist fight. But breaking the rules was the only way to guarantee that my plan would succeed.

Nick and I broke the first one by jumping the mutts on their way to the fight. We slipped downwind, knocked them down, then gagged and tied them. Every part of me cringed at the injustice of this, but I only had to remind myself of the alternative—a lifetime of battling trespassing mutts—and even my wolf brain agreed that this was for the best. Territory had to be protected and, even if this wasn't the way a wolf would protect it, it was acceptable under the circumstances.

After we tied them up, I gave them each a half-dose of the sedative I'd swiped from Jeremy's medical supplies. It was enough to make them too groggy to struggle, but not too groggy to walk to the cabin.

Once there, Nick took the mutt he'd been supposed to fight— the newcomer—and tied him to a tree. I double-checked the knots, and gave him more sedative, to put him to sleep. Then I took my mutt—the one who'd first come to challenge Jeremy— into the cabin.

I never took the gag from his mouth, and never said a word to him. There was nothing to say. He'd trespassed on our property, and he knew that the penalty for that might be death. The death he was about to receive, though, was a punishment far in excess of the crime.

Again, while I knew what had to be done, I also understood the unfairness of it. All I could do, then, was to make sure he'd suffer no more than he would have if we'd fought. So when we were in the cabin, I gave him the rest of the sedative dose, plus another half-shot. He was unconscious within minutes. Then I hoisted him onto the plastic-covered table, double-checked the room, making sure all the plastic sheeting was still in place, and set to work.

It took two hours. A couple of times, I thought I wouldn't be able to finish. No, I wasn't overcome by horror or disgust at the reality of what I'd decided to do. I understand that from a human point of view, maybe I should have been, but that wasn't a problem. This was a job that needed to be done, and because I knew the mutt felt nothing, it was no different than working with a corpse. To me, he was already dead.

The problem was that I had to keep him alive, and that was a feat that required more medical skill than I possessed. As part of my research, I'd studied field guides for war medicine, so I had some idea how to cauterize the wounds I was inflicting and keep him from bleeding out, but it wasn't easy.

Finally, the job was done. I pulled off the raincoat I'd donned, so the blood spatter wouldn't spook Nick, then headed outside.

By now, the other mutt was awake and struggling.

"That really did take a long time," Nick said. "What the hell were you doing in there?"

"You remember the plan, right? I'm taking him inside and you're waiting out here."

"Sure, but wouldn't it be easier—"

"No."

"It'd be safer if there were two of us—"

I grabbed Nick's arm and pulled him aside, out of earshot of the other mutt. "You're not going inside, Nick. Not going in or looking in. You promised."

"Shit, what did you—?"

"I'm trying to protect our territory. That's all you need to know."

He glanced at the cabin, then at me. "Yeah. Okay."

I took a knife from my pocket and advanced on the other mutt. His eyes widened at the sight of the knife, but I only cut the ropes holding him to the tree. Then I dragged him to his feet and shoved him toward the cabin.

He looked around, as if considering making a break for it, but could barely walk, let alone run. At the door, I glanced back once, to make sure Nick was staying outside, then went in and locked the door behind us.

*   *   *

I waited until the mutt finished emptying his stomach. The smell of vomit almost dowsed the stink of blood. Almost.

"You sick son of a bitch," he whispered, still doubled over. "How could you—?"

He puked again. I waited until the retching stopped.

"He came on my territory," I said quietly. "From now on, any mutt who comes on my territory is going to end up like this. If you want to be the last mutt to walk away alive, then there's something I need you to do for me."

He shot upright. "I am not doing anything—"

I grabbed his hand, and forced it over the heart of the mutt on the table. The other mutt's eyes went round and he jerked back.

"He's alive? He's still alive? You kept him—?"

The mutt swung at me, lost his balance on the blood-slicked plastic sheeting and skidded to the floor. I left him there, grabbed an axe from the pile of tools, then finished the job on the unconscious mutt.

"There," I said, turning to the one on the floor. "He's dead. I just wanted to show you that I *could* keep him alive. Think about that. I could do this to you, and let you live."

He lunged for my legs, but I grabbed the back of his shirt and swung him to his feet, then shoved him against the wall and held him there until his struggles stopped.

"The price for your life is this: you need to pass on what you've seen. When you leave here, you're taking the first plane out of New York State. You're flying back to your friends and telling them what happened, every detail of it. You'll warn them that if they come here, this is what they can expect. Then, once you've told them, you'll find another mutt and tell him, and another, and tell him. If you don't—"

"You'll come after me," the mutt said between clenched teeth.

His eyes blazed hate, but no amount of revulsion could cover the raw fear behind it.

"Yes, I'll come after you, but not just if you don't pass along the message. If anyone shows up here again, then I'll know you haven't done your job and I'll come after you."

"What?" he yelped. "I can't tell every last goddamned mutt in the world and even if I could, what's to say they'll listen to me?"

"If you tell the story right, they'll listen, and they'll do your job for you by passing it on."

"But what if they don't believe me? Shit, what person in their right mind could believe that someone would—?" His gaze swept the room, and he swallowed. "They won't believe me."

"Yes, they will." I dropped him, strode across the room and grabbed a handful of Polaroid shots. "If they don't, show them these."

"You took pictures? Jesus Christ! You're—you're—"

"Someone you don't ever want to meet again," I said.

I shoved the pictures into his pocket and pushed him out the door.

And so the legend began. The mutt took my photos and took my tale and spread them as far as he could. The story snowballed, as all such stories do, and over the years I've heard dozens of versions of it, each more outrageous than the last. Yet I never deny any of them. What I did was bad enough. If they think I'm capable of doing worse, why say otherwise? Sure, they think I'm the worst kind of depraved monster, but if it keeps them off our territory, that's all that matters.

According to the legend, that day was the last day any mutt ever set foot near Stonehaven. Is that true? Of course not. The story didn't spread fast enough to warn off every mutt. Even when it did, a couple who *had* heard the tale couldn't resist taking a shot at this "wolf-monster." Yet none of those mutts ever returned, so even if their friends knew they'd come and that my victim hadn't really been the last mutt to trespass at Stonehaven, they didn't let this inconsistency get in the way of a good story.

The news of what I'd done eventually spread to the Pack. As for Jeremy, while I'm sure he heard about it within a year or so, he never mentioned it to me. I don't think he knew how to handle it. He couldn't endorse my methods, but the whole Pack benefited from the results, so how could he complain? Take me aside and say "that was a very, very bad thing you did, Clay. I know why you did it, and I think it might have been the right thing to do, but please don't ever do it again"?

At thirty-one, Jeremy was still coming to terms with the ugly side of leadership—the thought that he might need to commit or sanction acts of violence to reduce the violence in our lives. As he'd said, the better we could fight, the less we'd have to. In killing the mutt so horribly, I'd tested his theory in a way I'm sure he'd never anticipated but, in the end, he saw that it did work. One act of extreme violence bought us two decades of peace at Stonehaven. No one could argue about that.

Changes

Jeremy turned thirty-two that spring. For his birthday, I decided to get him some special art supplies. In the past few years, he'd been devoting more time to his painting and I wanted to show him that even if I couldn't really share his enthusiasm, I fully supported it.

The problem was that I had no idea what "special art supplies" were, or what type Jeremy needed. So I called his mentor in New York. That was tough for me, phoning a human stranger and asking for help, but I was determined to get the best present possible, regardless of the monetary or psychological cost.

Jeremy's mentor was an artist whose career had been sidelined by arthritis, so he'd opened a gallery in New York City. Jeremy had met him five years ago, presumably while browsing or admiring in his gallery. They'd struck up a conversation and he'd been advising Jeremy ever since.

I knew Jeremy's mentor's name, but had never met the man; Jeremy kept that part of his life separate. Yet the moment I called and introduced myself, the man knew who I was. He promised to put together a bundle of supplies and mail them, and I could send him a check when I received them.

"It must be pretty exciting around there these days," he said after we'd arranged everything.

"Ummm, yeah," I said. "I guess so."

He chuckled. "I don't know how Jeremy stays so calm. When I first—" Another chuckle. "But you don't want to hear an old man reminisce. I'm just so happy for him. It's wonderful to see. It'll make things so much easier for the two of you. Young people can always use extra money."

He promised to get my supplies into the mail that week, then signed off.

Extra money? What was that about? Financially, things *had* been going much better for us lately. When I'd been younger, Jeremy had spent many a late night hunched over a calculator, juggling the bills. These days, he turned down work. We certainly weren't wealthy, but we were comfortable.

Maybe he'd been referring to the investments. Once Jeremy had begun earning extra money, he'd done the financially cautious thing and invested the extra. Some of it went into conservative stuff like bonds, but at least half had gone into the stock market, under Antonio's direction.

A few years back, Antonio had taken over the new technology sector of the family business, just as Dominic had been ready to abandon microtechnology as an unprofitable fad. Although Antonio knew nothing about computers, he had an instinctive grasp of trends and business needs, and had turned a department on the verge of extinction into a thriving part of the company.

Antonio had also invested his own money in the technology sector, and persuaded Jeremy to do the same. Just this summer, a dividend check had bought us a two-week trip to Vermont. From what Jeremy's mentor said, maybe another was on the way, and another trip in the works. I could live with that.

*   *   *

Jeremy's birthday came and went. No dividend check or special trip was mentioned, but he loved my gift, so that was enough. The next month, classes gave way to exams, bringing with it the prospect of four whole months to call my own.

After my last exam, I bolted for the parking lot...and found my car missing.

I stood in the lot and looked around. My pass was for this lot, and I was certain I'd parked right there, in my usual spot in the far row. But now I stood in front of the spot I could swear had been mine and scowled at a black Mustang convertible. A beautiful car, and any other time, I'd have lingered to appreciate it, but right now I just wanted to go home, and this was, unfortunately, not my car.

Had someone stolen mine? Yeah, as if anyone would want a fifteen-year-old Chevy that needed a swift kick to get started on cold mornings. Had it been towed? Shit, I *had* paid all my tickets, hadn't I?

A sharp tinkle of metal on asphalt cut short my thoughts. Following the sound, I looked to see a set of keys between my feet. I frowned down at them.

"Well, pick them up," said a voice behind me. "I'd have aimed for your hand, but I didn't want to startle you."

I turned to see Jeremy leaning against his truck. He waved at the keys. I scooped them up, still frowning.

"What are you doing here?" I said. "Did something happen to my car?"

"No, it's right there. Where you left it."

I turned to the Mustang, looked down at the keys in my hand, then back at the car. Jeremy burst into a rare laugh.

"I thought you might like that," he said. "Any speeding tickets you earn with it are still yours, though."

I looked from the car to Jeremy, and back again. "But how—where—?"

"I came into an unexpected bit of money and thought you deserved something new. Well, it's not new, but *newer,* and hopefully nicer."

"Shit, yeah," I said, still staring. "Thanks. Thanks a lot."

"You're welcome."

I jangled the keys in my hand, itching to try them. But I needed to be sure this was okay, that Jeremy hadn't gone into hock because I'd been bitching and moaning about my car.

"The stocks?" I said, tearing my gaze from the car.

He shook his head. "A long-term investment of another kind. I sold my first painting. Two paintings, actually. One this winter and another last month."

"Sold—? When—? I didn't even know you had any up for sale."

Jeremy brushed his bangs from his face. "I wasn't ready to admit to it. Not until something sold. Remember when we were looking for schools—or, I should say, when *I* was looking for schools? Your teachers thought you'd get a full scholarship, but when I saw the tuition prices, I was still worried. I didn't want a lack of money to hold you back. Don had been pestering me to put a few paintings in his gallery. Eventually I agreed to give it a shot."

"So they sold?"

A tiny smile. "For far more than they were worth. And since you took care of your tuition with your scholarship, I thought it only fitting that I use the money on you."

"You didn't need to—"

"No, but I wanted to. Now get in and let's go home."

I grinned. "Race you."

He shook his head and walked back to his truck.

And so our lives underwent another slow change. Over the next couple of years, Jeremy sold more paintings. He still kept up his translation business, in case the art didn't work out, but he retained only his best clients.

Malcolm continued to train me. I'd learned all the tricks he had to impart, but kept up the lessons for practice. That seemed to make him happy—or as happy as Malcolm was capable of being.

I always knew that part of his reason for training me was political. He saw in me a potentially valuable ally for his fight to become Alpha, and hoped that we'd somehow bond over these sessions and he'd woo me away from Jeremy. I came to tolerate Malcolm, but would never forget what he'd done to Jeremy, and never trust him not to do it again if things didn't go his way.

Being out in the world so much, Malcolm had been the first in the Pack to hear what I'd done to that mutt. Was he angry that I'd found another way to stop trespassing mutts, one that didn't help his cause? If he was, he never gave any sign of it.

Instead, it seemed to give him something new to brag about, that his pupil had proven not only a vicious killer but a clever strategist. Although my original plan had only been to keep mutts away from Stonehaven, after hearing what I'd done, most mutts decided they'd better not take the chance of trespassing on any Pack wolf's turf, just in case they'd misunderstood my message. By the time I was twenty, our sanctuary extended throughout Pack territory.

As for the Alpha race, it was more of an Alpha crawl. Dominic had moved Jeremy into the role of advisor, and consulted him on every matter of Pack policy. This seemed a monumental step. An Alpha traditionally acted alone or, if he consulted anyone, he did it on the side, so no one knew.

Yet it was all for show. Dominic might seek Jeremy's advice, but didn't feel obligated to follow it, or even seriously consider it.

As Malcolm had said years ago, Dominic was playing a game, slowly moving Jeremy into a leadership role, while holding fast to the reins of power. Jeremy knew this. He'd always known it. But he allowed it to happen because it put him into a position he might never have attained otherwise—that of a serious Alpha contender.

I finished my undergrad degree, and true to my word, went away to university for my graduate program. I went no farther than Columbia but, despite Dominic's offer to come live with them, I stayed in residence, which satisfied Jeremy's desire to have me experience life in the human world.

The Pack changed little during those three years. Cliff Ward died. The summer before I went to Columbia, he was killed in a mutt fight. I mourned his passing even less than I had Gregory's. He'd been a nonplayer, a sycophant of Malcolm's with no power or position in the Pack.

I knew I shouldn't feel that way. Deep down, I wanted to see all my Pack brothers as just that—*brothers*. But the longer Dominic held power, the deeper the schism became between those who supported Jeremy and those who favored Malcolm, and I couldn't help seeing Malcolm's allies as future threats to Jeremy, which made them potential enemies.

That fall, just after I'd started at Columbia, Dominic called a Pack meeting. It was just a regular Meet, and by now everyone knew better than to expect him to announce that he was stepping down. Still, there was always hope. On Saturday afternoon, though, we held the meeting portion of the weekend, and he didn't say a word about succession. In fact, he said very little of anything, just snapped a few instructions to Jeremy, then left him to lead the meeting while he stormed off to nurse a headache.

After the meeting, Nick raided the kitchen, and brought all the lunch leftovers into the sunroom, where Joey and I were basking in the heat of the September sun. As we ate, I talked about my newly discovered area of academic passion: anthropomorphic religion.

"—then, if you move to Nubia, you have the god Arensnuphis, who's depicted both as a lion and as a man wearing—"

Nick yawned. "Is anyone else ready for a nap? I don't know why, but suddenly, I'm just so tired."

I lobbed a pillow at him. "Hey, this is important stuff. If you'd gone to college, you—"

"Could be just as boring as you? Thanks, but no thanks."

I grabbed an empty plate.

Joey caught my hand. "Stick to pillows. Dominic's in a bad enough mood as it is. As for lion gods, as long as you find it interesting, Clay, that's all that matters. So, are we going out tonight?"

"Hunt," I said.

"Bar," Nick said at the same time.

Joey sighed. "Someone give me a quarter and we'll flip for it."

"Uh-uh," I said. "He can go to a bar and pick up girls anytime. Hell, he does it every night of the week—"

"Every night?" Nick said. "I don't need to pick up girls *any* night of the week. Just open my book and dial a number...if they don't call me first."

"Good, then you don't need to do it tonight," I said. "I'm here, and I want to hunt."

When he started to complain, I skewered him with a look. He closed his mouth.

"Hunt," I said to Joey. Then I glanced over at Nick. "And if we have time, we'll go to a bar afterward for a drink or two. Without girls."

Nick rolled his eyes. "Something is seriously wrong with you, buddy."

"What's wrong with who?" Malcolm strolled into the sunroom, the Santoses in tow. "You better not be talking about my boy." He clapped me on the back. "Nothing wrong with him. Nothing at all."

"Nothing a lobotomy couldn't fix," Daniel muttered.

"Hey, you guys hear that?" I said to Nick and Joey. "Sounds like a pup yipping."

"Danny-boy," Nick said. "When you going to grow up into a wolf? Still waiting for that first Change, aren't you?"

"Nah, he had that last year," I said. "Not that anyone's noticed. Still couldn't take on a mutt with two broken legs. I hear that's what happens. Guy doesn't Change until he's twenty, he never quite catches up."

Joey shot us both looks, trying to hush us. He was always telling us we should be nicer to Daniel, that if we tried, we could win him over. I didn't see the point. I tossed Joey the "you worry too much" look I'd perfected from Antonio.

"Don't listen to him," Raymond murmured to his son. "You're just fine."

"Sure he is," I said. "And any day he wants to prove it, I'm ready. I can always use a few seconds of diversion."

Nick laughed. When Malcolm joined in, Daniel reddened.

"At least I'm not some psycho who chops up—" Daniel began.

Raymond caught his son's arm to shush him, but Malcolm advanced on Daniel, looming over him.

"No, you're not, are you?" Malcolm said. "You've never even fought a mutt. Never needed to. You know why that is? Why a pup like you can run in peace, without worrying about some mutt tearing you to shreds?"

Daniel muttered something.

"Speak up!" Malcolm barked.

Raymond laid a hand on Malcolm's arm. "He knows, Mal. We're all … grateful." He choked on the word, but pressed on. "Clayton did us a big favor."

"Yeah," Stephen said. "Big favor. Now we have to go find the mutts. Even then, most of them run the other way—"

"But it's a small price to pay for being safe on our property," Raymond said. "Come on, boys. Malcolm wanted to talk to Clayton. Let's leave him alone."

"Hold on," Malcolm said. "I was going to ask Clay if he wanted to hunt tonight. A full Pack hunt."

"Sure," I said. "Did Dominic say—?"

"No, he did not," growled a voice from the doorway. Dominic strode in, followed by Antonio and Jeremy. "Since when are you allowed to set up Pack hunts, Malcolm? Getting a bit ahead of yourself, aren't you?"

Malcolm shrugged. "Sorry, Dom. I just thought since you weren't feeling well—"

"I feel fine," Dominic said, then winced, belying his words. He spun on Jeremy. "What did you tell them?"

"The truth," Jeremy said calmly. "That you have a headache, which you do."

"I don't have a headache. I *never* get headaches."

"Which is why, as I suggested, you should let me call Dr. Patterson and—"

"You'll call no one," Dominic snarled. "And there will be no Pack hunts tonight. In fact, you won't be here tonight. None of you. This Meet is adjourned. Go home."

He stalked out the door.

*   *   *

No one went home. We were accustomed to Dominic's moods, and knew that if we did take off, he'd summon us back the next day and blast us for leaving early. After his outburst, he retreated to his room, and the Meet progressed as usual.

There wasn't a Pack hunt that night. Even Malcolm knew better than to press his luck that far. Jeremy advised that Nick, Joey and I should skip our minihunt. With the mood Dominic was in, he might even see that as a breach of authority. So we went out drinking instead.

When we returned to the Sorrentino estate a little louder and more boisterous than we'd left, Jeremy met us in the garage and warned us to tone it down. Dominic's headache was worse. Jeremy was obviously worried, but Dominic only brushed off his suggestion to visit the doctor and popped some aspirin.

So we bustled off to bed. I slept in Nick's room, and Joey slept in one of the guest rooms with his father. Nick and I stayed up for a while, talking, but drifted off shortly before two.

At three-thirty, I awoke to Jeremy shaking me. One look at his face, and I leapt up.

"What's—?" I began.

"Dominic," he said, handing me my clothing from the floor. "He passed out and I can't wake him. We need to get him to the doctor, fast. Are you okay to drive?"

"Sure," I said, and grabbed the clothes.

Challenge

I drove Dominic to the hospital so fast that if I'd been pulled over, I'm sure I would have lost my license.

He'd had a stroke. Things like this are less common among werewolves—maybe because of our different physiology and maybe because of our more active lifestyle—but sometimes it doesn't matter how healthy you are, Mother Nature decides your time is up. And so it was for Dominic.

For the next three days we kept vigil at his bed in the private clinic. I wanted to stay, but Jeremy insisted there was nothing I could do and I shouldn't miss school. I did, however, skip classes that weren't absolutely necessary so I could zip across town to the clinic.

On Tuesday morning, Dominic died, having never regained consciousness. I didn't learn of it until I arrived late that afternoon and found Nick and Jorge beside an empty bed.

Antonio made the arrangements for Dominic's funeral. Or, he did his best, but Jeremy ended up quietly taking over. This is one part of Western death rituals I've never understood, that a person has just died and, within hours, those closest to him must sit in some stranger's office and decide what kind of coffin or flowers they want. As for the service itself, it was small, as are all Pack funerals. Afterward, we retreated to the Sorrentino estate to grieve.

We'd been back for less than an hour, all gathered in the living room. Each of us was lost in our own thoughts—each except Malcolm, who knew exactly where he was heading and wasn't waiting another minute to get there.

"We need an Alpha," he said. "Word gets out that Dominic died without a successor and we're in trouble. Every mutt in the country will think something's wrong with the Pack."

"We just put my father in the ground," Antonio said, lifting his head from his hands. "You can wait another goddamned—"

"No," Jorge said softly. "He's right. We need to get this over with."

"I don't mean any offense to your father, Tonio," Malcolm said. "If it seems that way, then I apologize. I'm just thinking of the Pack. We can get this over with quickly and painlessly, then let everyone get back to mourning a great Alpha. We all know how this works. I'm putting my name forward. If anyone cares to challenge me, we'll step outside right now and settle this."

"Challenge you to what?" I said. "A duel? You gonna pick swords or pistols?"

Jeremy's lips curved as he recognized his own words from so long ago.

"A fight, Clayton," Malcolm said. "To the death. That's how it works when an Alpha dies before the Pack chooses an official successor. Now, the only people here who might have a shot at winning that challenge are you and Antonio. Tonio doesn't want it. You'd make a damned fine Alpha...in ten or fifteen years. If that's what you want, I'll pick you as my successor and I'll make sure you win. That's a promise."

Jeremy cleared his throat. Malcolm turned on him before he could get a word out.

"Don't embarrass yourself, Jeremy. Just keep your damned mouth shut for once."

"No, I don't believe I can," Jeremy said. "You said that this is how we choose an Alpha when the previous one dies without a successor, but I must point out that you are mistaken."

"Bullshit. Go grab the Legacy. The last time an Alpha died without a successor—"

"—was in 1912," Jeremy said. "And they did indeed choose the next Alpha with a battle. However, there is nothing in the Law to say that's how it *must* be done. If you read the Legacy entry, it quite clearly states that a battle was how both candidates decided to handle the matter. I am putting forward myself as a challenger but, unless I agree to a fight, which I will not, then the matter must be handled in the same way all Pack successions are handled, by a vote."

"He's right," Jorge said. "Do you want to check the Legacy?"

"Never mind," Malcolm said. "He wants a vote, let's give him a vote. All in favor of me—"

"That's not how it's done," Jeremy said. "We both need to deliver our platforms, let the Pack know our plans for the future—"

"If we don't decide this fast, we won't have a future. The mutts will see to that. Everyone here knows you and they know me, and they both know what kind of leader we'd make."

"If that's what you want, that's fine by me," Jeremy said. "We'll vote. But, as the Law says, if any Pack member feels he isn't ready to make a decision, he has two days to consider the options."

With that, a decade of Alpha campaigning came to a sudden end. The vote was open, as all Pack votes are. As the former

Alpha's closest relative, Antonio led the vote, by casting his vote for Jeremy. Then he turned to Jorge.

"Jeremy," Jorge said.

Next to Stephen. "Malcolm."

"Malcolm," Andrew seconded, before being asked.

"Malcolm," his father said.

Antonio looked at Peter. "Jeremy."

On to Ross Werner. Ross cracked his knuckles then, gaze still on his hands, said, "I'm not ready."

"Oh for God's sake," Malcolm snarled. "Just pick—"

"He gets his forty-eight hours," Jeremy said. Then, to Antonio. "Should we continue? Or leave it there?"

"We'll keep going," Antonio said. "Anyone else wants time to think, just say so." He turned to me. "Clay? Do I need to ask?"

"No."

"Jeremy, then. Joey? You're next."

Joey's lips started to form Jeremy's name, but an elbow jab from his father cut him short.

"We'll take the forty-eight hours," Dennis said. "Both of us."

On to Nick. "Jeremy."

Daniel. "Malcolm."

Finally, Wally Santos. "Malcolm."

There it was. Five votes for Jeremy, five for Malcolm and three abstaining for forty-eight hours.

As far as I was concerned, Jeremy had won. Joey had been ready to name Jeremy, and would do so. His father, Dennis, liked Jeremy, and supported him, though he'd usually been too conscious of the balance of Pack power to do so openly. He'd vote for Jeremy over Malcolm though.

Ross had always been a fence-sitter, the type of guy who never wanted to offend anyone. We could sway him our way, but even if he picked Malcolm, the final result would be seven to six in Jeremy's favor. All we had to do was wait two days.

After the meeting, Joey and Dennis retreated to the guest house. Although the one-bedroom cabin was for guests, during a Meet everyone liked to stick together, so we all slept in the main house. The guest one was used for humans and, occasionally, for Pack members whom Dominic chose to punish.

When Dennis asked Antonio for the guest house key, we all knew that it meant they wanted a place to talk without being overheard. That was fine. We sent them off and Jeremy forbade Nick or me from trying to "visit" Joey and sway his father. This was a choice they had to make on their own.

The day passed, and Dennis and Joey stayed in the guest house. This was taking longer than I expected, and I began to worry that maybe instead of Joey persuading his father to support Jeremy, Dennis was working to persuade Joey to change *his* vote. While I was certain neither Dennis nor Joey wanted to see Malcolm as Alpha, I knew that Dennis feared him, and fear can be a powerful motivator.

When night fell and they still didn't return, I told Nick to cover for me, and slipped into the backyard. The guest house was in the far corner of the estate, in the wooded portion, accessible by either road or a very long path. I took the path. That way, I could tell myself I was just going for a walk and not disobeying Jeremy.

I'd gone no more than a quarter of the distance when a dark figure appeared on the path ahead. I slowed and sniffed the air. It was Joey.

"I figured your patience would be running thin," he said with a twist of a smile. "Actually, I thought it would have run out hours ago."

"Are you done, then?" I asked as I approached. "You've made up your mind?"

"Uh, yes, that's what I wanted to talk to you about."

He dropped his gaze as he spoke and I froze, certain I knew what was coming.

"Don't say it," I said. "If you tell me you're voting for Malcolm—"

"No. I can't. *We* can't. Jeremy's the right choice. We both know that. The problem is..."

He let the sentence drop off and scuffed the ground with his shoe, gaze fixed on the clods of dirt that flew up.

"The problem is..." I prompted.

"The problem is that we can't vote for Malcolm, and we don't dare vote against him."

"What the hell is that supposed to mean?"

He met my gaze. "You know what it means. He's already been out here twice—"

"What?"

"He knows very well which way we want to vote, Clay, and he's not going to let that happen. My dad and I are the weak links. Neither of us can stand up to Malcolm in a fight."

I slammed my fist into the nearest tree. "Goddamn him! And goddamn you, Joey, for not coming to me. I'll protect you. You know that."

"For today, maybe. For tomorrow, maybe. But not for the rest of my life. We vote against him and he'll take his revenge. He's already said as much. So we're leaving."

"Leaving?"

"Leaving the Pack. Tonight. I wanted to tell you—"

"Tell me what? That you're running away? That you're—"

"Don't say it, Clay," Joey said, pulling himself up straight and meeting my gaze. "I know what you think, that this is the act of a coward. It's not. It's the act of someone who doesn't care to become a martyr, no matter how much he may believe in the cause. Jeremy will win. I'm sure he will. He's smart enough to outwit Malcolm. He'll be the next Alpha, and he doesn't need our votes—or our deaths—to ensure that."

"So then you'll come back. After he's Alpha."

"I—I don't know." Joey rubbed his hand over his mouth. "It's not the same for us, Clay. We aren't Danverses or Santoses or Sorrentinos. Even in Jeremy's Pack, I'm not sure how much that would change."

"It would," I said. "Hell, I'm not a Danvers. Not really. Nobody gives a shit."

"Because you're special. Look, I didn't wait out here for two hours to argue with you. I wanted to say good-bye. I know this *will* be good-bye." Another twist of a smile. "A mutt can't be buddies with the Alpha's son, can he?"

"Joey, don't. Please—"

"We've leaving the country. Probably heading up to Canada. Dad's been to the west coast there and he thinks it would be a good place for us. Lots of room to roam. No mutts, as far as we know. Plus we wouldn't have to worry about accidentally bumping into one of you guys and forcing you to fight—"

"Shit, Joey, no one would ever—"

"But it's a consideration, right? Let's just leave it at that."

"Come back with me. We'll talk to Jeremy. He'll work this out—"

"Clay, no. Please. Let's just shake hands—"

"And let one of my friends leave the Pack and become a mutt? No way. No goddamned way!"

I spun and whammed my fist into a tree so hard it shook. When I turned back again, Joey was gone. I stood there, breathing hard, heart pounding. Then I hit the tree again, slammed my hand into it over and over, until I heard a bone crack.

Only then, when I felt real pain, did my brain clear. I raked my hand through my hair and concentrated on breathing until I could think again.

I wanted to go after Joey, to say a proper good-bye, but I knew that the moment I caught up with him, I'd start arguing again, desperate to find some way to persuade him to stay. Although I could try my best to protect Joey and Dennis, I shouldn't ask them to entrust their lives to a secondhand bodyguard.

I looked down the path.

"Good-bye," I said, then turned and headed back to the house.

When I told Jeremy what the Stillwells had decided, the news didn't seem to surprise him. He promised that when this was over we'd try to find them and bring them back into the Pack. Until then, we had to let them do what they thought was best.

The next morning, we awoke to find Ross's bedroom empty. Everything down to his toothbrush was gone. Jeremy tracked his trail to his car, which was also missing. There was no other scent mixed with his, no sign that he'd done anything other than emulated the Stillwells and decided this wasn't a fight he was prepared to join.

With that, the race for Alpha came to a grinding halt. The vote remained split evenly, and both sides knew that wouldn't change. Who of the remaining ten would switch? One of the Santoses, who despised Jeremy as much as Malcolm did? One of the Sorrentinos, all three of whom had been Jeremy's friends from childhood? Peter, who owed Jeremy his life and nearly died at the hands of Malcolm? Me? Never. The only three who might have been swayed were now gone. So we were deadlocked, and nothing in the Legacy or the Law gave us any ideas on how to break the stalemate.

Stalemate

We spent six months locked in that stalemate, neither side willing—or even able—to budge. Contrary to Malcolm's dire predictions, hordes of mutts did not descend when they heard the Pack was leaderless. They did, however, pace at the edge of our territory, like scavengers who weren't sure their prey was dead yet.

At first, Malcolm was content to bare his teeth now and then, and hope Peter or Jorge would cave, but we circled our wagons fast enough that everyone felt safe. But that only meant that Malcolm had to do more than threaten—he had to consider eliminating one of us. By the new year, we didn't so much as dare collect the mail without backup.

I managed to make it through the fall term but when it ended, I told Jeremy I wasn't going back until this problem was resolved. He argued, of course, but he understood where my priorities lay. I couldn't concentrate on school knowing my absence put everyone in danger. So I told the university I was having problems at home and arranged to resume my studies the next year.

In April, Malcolm launched his first strike. All six of us were at Stonehaven, and we'd decided to blow off some steam with a deer hunt. Once we found a deer, we split into pairs. Jeremy and Antonio had looped around in front of the stag. Nick and I chased it from the left side while Jorge and Peter took the right flank position. Then the four of us would drive it to where Jeremy and Antonio were waiting.

I was running ahead of Nick. I shouldn't have been—I should have stayed at his side—but he'd stumbled in an animal hole and, once I'd checked to make sure he was okay, I'd dashed ahead, eager to catch up before the stag realized its left flank was unprotected. After a few bounds, I could hear Nick racing up behind me. A shot cracked. Then a yelp. I wheeled to see Nick fly sideways. As I raced back to him, the smell of blood and gunpowder hit me, and I knew he'd been shot.

The next half-hour is a blur. As Peter ran to get Jeremy, I stayed over Nick, frantically licking at the blood pouring from his shoulder. When Jeremy arrived, he was in human form. I dimly recall him struggling to pull me off Nick, then Antonio arriving. I stayed as close as they would allow until I heard the words "he'll be okay." Then I slid into the nearest thicket and Changed.

When I peeked out, Peter was hurrying to Jeremy with his medical kit. I stayed hidden as I listened to them. Once I knew that Nick would survive, I crept back to my clothes. I dressed, raced to the house, grabbed my keys and took off.

Malcolm was in Syracuse, where he'd been since this all started. He'd told us exactly where he was staying, as if daring us to try something.

I should have known he'd go after Nick. He was the weakest link, being the newest werewolf, with little fight experience outside our practice sessions. Yet all this time, we'd focused on protecting Peter and Jorge, because no one, including myself, seriously thought he would harm Nick.

Malcolm liked Nick. I suppose it's naive to think that someone as ambitious and ruthless as Malcolm wouldn't kill a person he liked, but to us it made more sense that he'd go after Peter or Jorge, whom he barely tolerated. Yet it was more than that. We thought Nick was safe because he was Antonio's son and my best friend, and Antonio and I were Malcolm's favorites, no matter how little we wanted the honor.

Despite this, I never doubted that Malcolm had shot Nick. Hunters hadn't set foot on Stonehaven's property in well over a generation. The Danverses had always made it clear that they didn't want them and, since they were otherwise good neighbors, local hunters obeyed the No Trespassing signs and warned visitors to do the same.

To have a hunter come on the property, after all those years, and just happen to shoot Nick was coincidental beyond belief. Malcolm had known we were all at Stonehaven, and would likely take advantage of the full moon for a group run.

At Malcolm's hotel, I stormed down the hall to his room and pounded on the door. Daniel opened it. I shoved him aside and strode into the room, where I found Malcolm, Stephen and Andrew sitting around the television.

"Clay?" Malcolm said, pushing to his feet. "What's—?"

"Get outside," I said.

"What?"

"You heard me. You want a challenge. You've got it. Get outside now."

"Challenge? What—?"

"Did you really think you could get away with it? You'd shoot Nick and I'd just chalk it up to a tragic hunting accident?"

"Nick's been shot? Is he okay?"

I could see the lie behind Malcolm's fake shock, and I wanted to cross that room, grab him and beat him until he confessed.

But, if I did, Stephen, Andrew and Daniel would be on me in a second.

Instead I marched to the front closet, yanked it open and grabbed Stephen's shoes. Of everyone in Malcolm's camp, he was the only one who owned a rifle and could use it, having friends who were hunters. I checked the bottoms, then walked back and shoved the shoes under Malcolm's nose.

"Smell that mud?" I said. "Stonehaven's mud, still wet."

Malcolm's eyes went wide. "Stephen? Did you shoot—?"

"Don't pull that," I snapped. "Stephen's too stupid to think of it, let alone carry it out."

"You little—"

Stephen flew at me. I nailed him in the gut and he toppled backward. Daniel jumped from his spot by the wall. I met his glare.

"Try it," I said. "Go on. Show me you've grown a pair, Danny."

Daniel didn't move. Stephen got to his feet and charged. I feinted out of the way and was turning to strike when someone grabbed my hand.

I roared and wheeled to see Antonio holding me. I stopped short, but he used my momentum to yank me off balance, and threw me out the door into the hall.

"This isn't over," I heard him say to Malcolm.

The door slammed and Antonio turned on me. "Either we continue this out here or you go downstairs to the car quietly."

"But he—"

Antonio loomed over me, eyes blazing. "Where are Wally and Raymond?"

"What? I—they're not here."

"But who is, Clayton? Who is here?"

"I—I don't—"

"You're here and I'm here. The two people most likely to come after Malcolm if he hurt Nick. And where is Jeremy?"

I scrambled to my feet. "Oh shit!"

Antonio grabbed my arm. "He's okay. He's down in the car with the others. Fortunately, only one of us is as hotheaded as Malcolm hoped. Think before you act next time, Clay. If you're going to protect Jeremy, he needs to be your first priority at all times. No one else can matter. Let me look after everyone else, including Nick."

"I'm sorry," I said, rubbing my face. "I didn't think—"

"Well, that was your first mistake." He thumped me on the back. "Now, come on."

I nodded and followed him down to the car.

The next night, when Nick felt well enough to join us, Jeremy convened a meeting. The subject? How to break the stalemate. Knowing this impasse put us in danger was one thing, but seeing Nick nearly killed, on our own property, surrounded by all of us, finally brought home the urgency of the situation. Jeremy knew we had to act. Since he wasn't Alpha yet, he didn't need to make all the decisions alone. He could solicit advice.

"I'll fight Malcolm," I said as I plunked onto the sofa beside Nick. "Set it up and I'll take him out."

"Presuming you do 'take him out,' then what?" Jeremy asked.

"Well, then I give you—" I thought about what I was saying. "Er, I—uh, sorry."

"I appreciate the offer," Jeremy said softly. "But I wouldn't expect anyone to respect an Alpha who had his title won for him by another. The answer to our problem, I believe, is obvious. Malcolm clearly wants a fight, and I doubt he'll settle for anything less. If that's my only option then I'll have to—"

"No way," Antonio said.

"I know I'm not on his level," Jeremy said. "But perhaps under the right circumstances, with a good strategy, I could outwit him. Strength isn't everything."

"If Malcolm gets you in the ring, he'll fight like he's never fought before. He's been waiting for this his whole life. He'll kill you."

"Maybe that's a chance I have to take."

"It's not a chance, it's a certainty. Then the only thing you'll have accomplished is to break the Pack in half, because none of us would stick around if Malcolm becomes Alpha. The only two he'd *let* stick around are me and Clay, and if he kills you, nothing in the world would make us follow him. We'd rather be mutts."

Jeremy was silent for a moment. Then he gave a slow nod. "Maybe, then, *that's* the only solution. To break the Pack in half."

"Two Packs?" I said.

Jeremy nodded.

"It might be the only way," Jorge said.

"How would that work?" Peter asked.

"I have no idea," Jeremy said. "So let's talk about it."

By morning we'd come up with a proposal. We'd split the Pack in two, each with an Alpha. Jeremy's side would retain New York State as its territory, and Malcolm would take Pennsylvania, where the Santoses lived.

That would mean Malcolm would give up Stonehaven as his home, but Jeremy would compensate him for that with a generous monthly stipend. In time we hoped to persuade the others to move their territory farther west or south, and put more distance between us.

Antonio and Peter took the proposal to Malcolm. He turned them down flat. Wouldn't even negotiate terms. He sent back a message to Jeremy saying that the only way the Pack was splitting was if we all left the country and started a new Pack in Canada or Mexico…after Jeremy deeded Stonehaven to him. Jeremy didn't dignify that with an answer.

Over the next few days, Antonio and I held some private meetings to discuss taking matters into our own hands. Antonio wanted to kill Wally or Raymond, and thus swing the vote in our favor. I didn't see the point of such political wrangling. If you want to kill a beast, and make sure it's really dead, you don't sever a leg and hope it bleeds out—you lop off the head. Kill Malcolm and our problems would be over.

While not opposed to the general theory, Antonio knew Jeremy would figure out who had killed Malcolm and, whatever the history between them, Malcolm was still his father. To have him killed by someone Jeremy had raised would be too much. I thought Malcolm had long since lost any paternal rights, but I wasn't sure enough about the situation to test it. Not just yet.

So we reverted to discussing Antonio's plan. The trick, though, was to kill Wally or Raymond without it being obvious that we'd done so. Otherwise, we reduced Jeremy to Malcolm's level, because everyone would assume *he'd* ordered the death.

Midweek, Antonio had to return to New York for an unavoidable business meeting, and we agreed to think the problem through and come up with some ideas before he returned on the weekend. Jorge, Peter and Nick went back to New York with Antonio. Normally, Peter would have stayed with us, but after the attack on Nick, we decided he was better off with the Sorrentinos. That way I could devote my full protective attention to Jeremy.

Dinner Thursday night started like any other. Our meals were still made by the same woman who'd been cooking for us since I'd first arrived at Stonehaven. I could cook, and had been doing so on weekends, but even now that I was home full time, Jeremy knew Pearl needed the income, so we still had our meals delivered on weekdays.

That night it was her specialty: shepherd's pie. While Jeremy dished it up, I threw together a salad in the kitchen. I walked into the dining room to see him leaning over the steaming pan, spatula only partway through the first cut.

"Sniff this," he said.

The scent of hot beef and potato wafted up. My stomach rumbled.

"Smells great. Now hurry up and scoop it out or I'll take the whole dish."

I reached for the casserole, but Jeremy pulled it back.

"I'm serious. Something smells off."

"The meat?" I said, leaning in for a closer sniff. "Seems fine to me. Doesn't matter anyway." Our stomachs, like a wolf's, were strong enough to withstand meat that was undercooked or past its best-before date.

Jeremy waved me away from the food, forked up a mouthful and sampled it. Then he made a face and discreetly spat it into a napkin. I scooped up a fingerful and ate it. It tasted fine, but if Jeremy thought our food had been tampered with, I wasn't going to argue. He was entitled to a little paranoia these days.

Jeremy started for the door, paused, came back and took the casserole with him.

"Hey, if you think there's something wrong with it, I'm not going to eat it," I called after him.

After one last look in the direction of my vanished dinner, I tucked into the salad. A few minutes later, Jeremy returned.

"I called John," he said. John was Pearl's son, who'd taken over delivering our meals when his father died a few years ago. "He says he didn't see Pearl this afternoon. When he got to the house, the cooler was inside the front door, so he took it and left."

I laid down my fork. "And he didn't think that was strange?"

Jeremy shook his head. "These days, Pearl often naps in the afternoon. Even I knew that."

"Does Malcolm?"

As Jeremy pulled something from his pocket, he gave a half-shrug that I interpreted as "probably." He laid the shepherd's pie in front of me again.

"Close your eyes," he said.

I did. He instructed me to sniff and I again smelled the meal. Then he held something else in front of my nose and I inhaled a vaguely familiar odor—one that I'd also faintly smelled on our dinner.

"Yeah, that's it," I said, opening my eyes. "What is—?" I knew the answer before I even saw the bottle in Jeremy's hand. "Sedative. The stuff from your medical bag. Is any missing?"

He shook his head.

"But Malcolm's seen it before, plenty of times. We all have. If he knew the name, he'd know what to get, and he'd know it works on werewolves." I looked at the casserole. "So he dumped enough in there to kill us."

"No, we'd smell that much easily. This is just enough to knock us out."

I pushed my chair back and stood. "Well, I'm not waiting around to see what he planned to do next."

Jeremy laid a hand on my shoulder. "I think we should do exactly that. Malcolm expects us to be asleep early tonight. Let's give him what he wants, and see what he does with it."

Endgame

Three hours later, when I heard the garage doorknob turn, I was sprawled out on the sofa in the study, the most likely place for me to crash before bedtime. Sure enough, footsteps headed straight for me. I counted three sets and, almost the moment I'd finished counting, I identified them: Wally and his two oldest nephews, Stephen and Andrew.

Disappointment zinged through me as I realized Malcolm wasn't among our uninvited guests, but I wasn't surprised. As much as he might like a showdown with his son, he wasn't stupid enough to take that risk. This way, if things went bad, he could claim that the Santoses had acted on their own.

I held myself still as they came into the room. I was lying on my back, with my arm slung up to hide my face. As they walked into the room, I struggled to keep from tensing. We had to let them make the first move, or Malcolm would claim he'd only sent them to retrieve his shaving kit or something equally ridiculous.

"Out like a light," Andrew said, leaning over me.

"Probably because he scarfed down most of dinner himself," Stephen said.

"Let's just hope he left enough for Jeremy," Andrew said.

Stephen snorted. "Like it matters. Even if Jeremy's wide awake, I could take him with one hand tied behind my back."

"Maybe so," Wally said. "But you're not going to try it. Andy, I want you to stay here, make sure Clayton doesn't wake up."

"Let's skip that step," Stephen said, moving close enough that I could feel the heat of his body. "How about we stage a little 'accident'? *'Damn, Mal, I know you wanted Clay left alive, and we really tried, but he woke up and we just had to—'*"

"Don't even think about it," Wally said. "Even if he stirs, we're following orders, tying him up and leaving him alive. You don't want to test Malcolm on this."

"Goddamn it!" Stephen snarled. "He hates Malcolm. We're the ones who—"

"It's not fair, I know," Wally said softly. "When all this is over, we'll take care of Clayton, and things will change. Now, Andy, as I was saying, you stay here. If he moves, come and get me. Got it?"

"Got it."

The moment Wally and Stephen left, my heart started pounding, urging me to take care of Andrew and go protect Jeremy. Yet I knew it would take them awhile to find Jeremy . . . if they found him at all.

Jeremy had crisscrossed the house, from top to bottom, laying enough trails that they'd eventually get frustrated and give up trying to track him. Then they'd check the obvious spots he might have passed out—his bedroom, his studio, the bathroom—but he wasn't in any of those. It would be awhile before they suspected Jeremy wasn't asleep at all.

I forced myself to count off five minutes before I peeked. By that time, Andrew had retreated to Jeremy's armchair. He sat there, staring at me, unblinking, as if I could wake up and pounce in the millisecond it took him to blink. The stink of fear wafted from him. That was why Wally had left him behind, because if I did wake up, Andrew would make damned sure he called for help instead of trying to take me on by himself.

After another couple of minutes, Andrew began to relax and his gaze wandered to the bookshelf. Two more minutes passed. Then he eased up from the chair, gave me one last look and turned toward the bookshelf.

I sprang the moment his back was to me. My hand was around his mouth before he realized I'd left the sofa. I could have killed him then. But of the three Santos boys, Andrew had given me the least reason to hate him. I didn't like him, but he wasn't enough of a threat to warrant killing. So I wrapped my free hand around his throat and squeezed until he passed out. Then I lowered him to the floor and crept from the room.

As soon as I walked into the rear hallway, Jeremy slid through the back door. He motioned me to silence, cocked his head and listened. Footsteps sounded above. Jeremy waved me closer and I whispered what had happened so far—that Andrew was unconscious in the study, and Wally and Stephen were searching.

"Time to let them find me," Jeremy murmured.

Of all the parts of Jeremy's plan, I hated this one the most. But Jeremy insisted we play this to the end, that we had to know, beyond a doubt, what they had in mind.

Jeremy pointed to the kitchen. When I hesitated, he met my gaze and jabbed his finger toward the room. I muttered under my breath, but obeyed.

I slipped into the kitchen, half opened the pantry door and stood behind it. In the hallway something crashed and the footsteps above stopped.

"Clay?" Jeremy called, his voice weak, as if sedated. "Clayton?"

A softer bang as he knocked into the hall stand. Overhead the footsteps resumed, quieter now, heading for the staircase. Jeremy's unnaturally heavy footfalls thudded toward the kitchen, interspersed with the odd thump as he stumbled into a wall. By the time he threw open the kitchen door, Wally and Stephen were on the stairs, moving fast now.

"Clayton?" Jeremy called into the kitchen. "Damn it, where are—?" The squeak of his shoes as he turned. A soft intake of breath. "Wally? Stephen? What are you—?"

A thump. I dove from my hiding spot as Wally pounced on Jeremy. Not seeing me, Stephen raced across the room to join his uncle. I slammed into him and we sailed into the far wall. Stephen's eyes went wide.

"Surprised?" I said. "You wanted to fight me, you got it."

He swung, but in his haste didn't aim, and I didn't even need to duck to avoid it. I grabbed his arm, ripped it backward and heard the bone snap. Stephen howled. I put my face to his.

"What? Can't fight *me* with one arm? What about Jeremy? Care to test that boast now?"

He drove his good hand into my stomach. The air whooshed from me and I stumbled back, but when he brought his hand up again, I grabbed it and threw him over onto his back. I took his left forearm between my hands, met his wild eyes and broke the bone. While he screamed, I leaned down and whispered in his ear.

"I could stop here," I said. "You're not fighting anyone with two busted arms so, really, I should just stop. But I'm not going to. And you know why? Because you wouldn't stop if it was me lying there. Sooner or later, it's gonna come down to this, and I'm not taking the chance that you'll go after Jeremy again in the meantime."

He opened his mouth, but I grabbed him by the neck and snapped it before he could say anything. Then I tossed his body to the floor and raced across the kitchen to where Jeremy and

Wally were fighting behind the table. Jeremy had Wally in a headlock, but before he could tighten his grip, Wally managed to kick Jeremy in the stomach and wriggle free. I jumped in and grabbed Wally by the back of the shirt.

Jeremy met my gaze and, very slowly, shook his head. It took every ounce of will, but I forced myself to let go of Wally and step back. Jeremy sprang at him and they went down fighting.

That was the longest five minutes of my life. I knew Wally was at least as good a fighter as Jeremy, yet I also knew that Jeremy had to do this himself. So I welded my feet to the floor and I watched. Finally Jeremy got Wally back in that headlock and, with a sharp thrust on Wally's chin, he ended it.

Jeremy struggled to his feet and wiped his sleeve across the blood streaming from his split lip. His left eye was fast swelling shut.

"You okay?" he asked.

I managed a laugh. "Yeah, *I'm* fine. Let me grab some ice for that lip. Looks like you might need some stitches for it, too." I looked him over. "Anything else?"

He shook his head. Silly question. He could have a dozen broken bones and he still wouldn't admit to any injury I couldn't see.

He stared down at Wally and Stephen and, for a moment, looked as if he might be sick.

"It should never have come to this," he said. "I don't know where—" He paused, eyes closing. "We're Pack. We don't kill—" Another glance at the bodies and a long, slow shake of his head as his eyes filled with a quiet grief.

"Yeah, it shouldn't have happened," I said as I took a bag of frozen peas from the freezer. "But you can fix that now."

"Hmmm?"

I shot a pointed look at Wally and Stephen. "Three to five. You won."

Jeremy took the peas and shook his head. "Not like that. I won't take power by killing off the other side."

"But—"

"I have an idea," he said. "One that I hope will settle this for good. You said Andrew's alive?"

"I just knocked him out."

"Good, then. I'll call Antonio, see if he can get back here sooner than tomorrow night."

Nine o'clock Friday morning. We met at Stonehaven. When Malcolm arrived, Antonio ushered him into the living room with Raymond and Daniel. Seeing Andrew alive, Raymond's eyes lit up, but any remaining hope for his brother and eldest son died as Jeremy explained what had happened.

When Raymond heard the news, he walked quietly to the sofa and sat down. Daniel flew at me, as if it was my fault Wally and Stephen had tried to kill Jeremy. Antonio intercepted Daniel, then led him to a chair and signaled for Peter to guard him. Throughout it all, Malcolm just stood there, expressionless. Then he shook his head.

"I don't know how this happened," he said. "I knew they were getting restless, but I didn't think they'd try this."

Andrew's head shot up, and he opened his mouth, but a look from his father cut him short.

"So you had nothing to do with this," Jeremy said.

Malcolm's mouth tightened. "Are you calling me a liar, boy?"

"Yes, I am. I've been to Pearl's house. I found her body. You did a good job of making it look like a heart attack, but your scent was everywhere."

"That's because I went by there a couple of days ago—"

"Clay?" Jeremy cut in. "Tell us what you heard."

I related what Wally and Stephen had said in the study when they'd thought I'd been asleep. Malcolm rubbed a hand across his mouth and I could tell he was thinking fast.

"Clayton may have misinterpreted what he heard," Malcolm said carefully. "I knew Stephen was looking for an excuse to kill him and I'd forbidden it, but that was months ago—a general rule, not related to any specific circumstances."

"Bullshit!" I said, wheeling on Malcolm. "I didn't mishear—"

Jeremy raised his hand. "It's not important. If Malcolm says they acted alone, then we have to take his word for it. However, that leaves us with a problem." He turned to look at Andrew. "Conspiring to kill a Pack brother is a capital offense."

Andrew paled. "No, I—"

At a glare from Malcolm, Andrew closed his mouth.

Jeremy continued. "If Andrew acted on orders from someone he considered to be in an Alpha position, then he can't be held responsible. However, if he acted on his own, or along with his uncle and brother, the punishment is death. That's the Law."

Raymond glanced up. His gaze went first to his son, then to Malcolm, and a look passed between them. Raymond turned to his son and gave a small nod, telling him everything would be okay.

"Are you Alpha?" Malcolm asked quietly.

"No," Jeremy said.

"Then you can't make that decision, can you?"

"It's not a decision," Jeremy said. "I will abide by the Law. If Andrew acted on your command, he lives. If not, he dies. The only person who can 'decide' anything is you. Tell us what happened and, if necessary, the punishment will be carried out."

"By you?" Malcolm said, walking over to stand behind Andrew. "That is the Law, you know. He tried to kill you, therefore it's your right—and duty—to kill him yourself." He met Jeremy's gaze. "Can you do that... *Son?*"

Jeremy looked into Malcolm's eyes. "The question isn't how far I'll go, but how far you will... *Father.*"

They locked gazes for a moment. Then Malcolm snarled, reached up... and broke Andrew's neck.

"That's how far I'll go," he said as Andrew's body fell to the floor.

The room went silent. Jeremy paled, as shocked as the rest of us. I glanced over at Raymond. He stared at his son's body, face contorting with pain. Then he glanced up at Malcolm and, for a second, rage replaced the grief. Malcolm tensed. Then Raymond dropped his gaze, got to his feet, put his arm around Daniel and led him from the room.

A few moments later, the front door clicked shut behind them. Malcolm launched himself at Jeremy, face twisted in a snarl. I lunged into his path, and threw him against the wall. He recovered and shot back. I braced myself, but he veered past, heading for Jeremy again. I grabbed Malcolm by the shoulders. He twisted and knocked my feet out from under me, but I kept my hold and we both went down.

Once down, and fighting, it should have been a fair match. Yet instead of trying to incapacitate me, Malcolm just kept trying to throw me off, his attention still fixed on Jeremy. Within minutes, I had him pinned, my forearm jammed against his throat.

As I pressed down, he barely struggled and, for a moment, I thought this was what he wanted—a wolf's death. But then he met my eyes and, as his widened in disbelief, I realized he hadn't struggled because he hadn't really thought I'd kill him. But when he looked into my face, he saw his mistake.

Whatever bond he thought we shared only went one way. And when he saw that, a look passed over his face, something akin to grief.

"Clayton," Jeremy said sharply. "Let him up."

I stopped pressing down on Malcolm's windpipe and looked up at Jeremy. "We can't trust him, Jer. You know we can't."

"Let him up and he'll leave. There's nothing here for him." When I hesitated, he added a soft "Please."

As much as I longed to finish what I'd begun, Jeremy was right. With the Santoses gone, the fight for Alpha was over. Jeremy had won. To begin his reign by condoning the death of his defeated opponent would taint his Alphahood forever.

I grabbed Malcolm by the arm and yanked him to his feet. As I did, I leaned over him and whispered in his ear, too low for Jeremy to hear.

"I'll be waiting for an excuse," I said. "Remember that."

Without waiting for a response or a reaction, I twisted him around, grabbed him by the shoulders and escorted him to the door. Then, with Jeremy behind me, we stood and watched Malcolm leave.

He didn't look back.

As we'd feared, the fight for Alpha had indeed split the Pack in two. Only we six were left. A few months later, Ross Werner returned, and Jeremy accepted him back without comment. When another year passed with no word from Dennis and Joey, Jeremy sent me and Nick to search for them, but it was hopeless. As Joey had said, there was plenty of room to lose yourself in out there, and he and his father had done just that. Years later, we'd hear that they'd settled in Alaska. Jeremy eventually resumed contact with Dennis, but they never returned.

Under Jeremy, the Pack reinvented itself, a slow but steady process. We paid more attention to mutts, keeping them off our territory while at the same time watching them, and acting if they did anything to call attention to themselves and werewolves in general. In this, I became Jeremy's enforcer, along with Antonio. Before the next decade ended, Antonio would bow out of this job, and I'd have a new partner—one that would turn the Pack upside-down yet again, fill the void in my life...and nearly end it, on multiple occasions.

And then there was Malcolm...

There was no tidy ending to the story of Malcolm's life. No great final comeuppance. Instead, I think it ended that night when he lost the Alpha race, and lost it to the son he'd spent decades scorning and mocking.

Sometimes I think there was something Malcolm wanted more than Alphahood. A son. Not satisfied with the one he had, he tried to find that bond elsewhere and always in the wrong place. Maybe some would see tragedy there. All I see is the bastard who made Jeremy's life hell.

Whatever Malcolm got, he deserved. I just wish I'd been the one to take him out of our lives permanently. But I wasn't. Like I said, no tidy endings.

We never saw Malcolm again. We expected him to call for his things, but he never did. Over the next year we heard rumors that he'd been sighted here and there, tracking down the mutts with the best reputations and challenging them. Antonio thought that was his way of doing the "honorable" thing—suicide by mutt.

Eventually, he met one he couldn't beat. By the time the story got to us, it was six months old. Antonio went in search of the mutt who'd killed Malcolm to confirm it. Before Antonio caught up with him, Malcolm's killer became a victim of his own success—his victory having brought him a slew of challenges, including one ambitious mutt who didn't play by the rules, and had killed him.

For a few years after that, we waited, half expecting to return from a run one night and find Malcolm alive and well, stretched out on the sofa, beer in one hand, sandwich in the other. We never did clear out Malcolm's room. Just shut the door and left it. Everything else of his in the house, though, we slowly threw out. Soon there was no sign that Malcolm had ever lived at Stonehaven. For me, that exorcised him from our lives.

For Jeremy, it wasn't that easy. His father's ghost haunted Stonehaven. But Jeremy would never consider moving. He'd argue it was the perfect location for werewolves, isolated and forested, and now that he had the money to keep it up, there was no reason to consider leaving. Besides, if we left, we'd only endanger the humans who moved in, should any mutts decide to come calling. The truth, I suspected, was more what Antonio would have said. Jeremy was stubborn. This was his home and, alive or dead, Malcolm wasn't chasing him from it.

Still, every so often, Jeremy would redecorate, as if that could banish Malcolm's memory. Jeremy might have beaten his father. He might be Alpha. And he might be a damned fine Alpha, probably the best the Pack ever had. But he was different. His father hammered that lesson in and Jeremy couldn't get over it. I think he always felt he lacked something, that he wasn't a real werewolf.

Or maybe, as we began to suspect years later when the werewolves rejoined the larger supernatural world, there wasn't anything missing from Jeremy, but rather, something added.

Kitsunegari
2007

Someone was watching me.

But as I stood at the window of our hotel room, I knew that was impossible. We were fifteen stories above the dark street, and five stories above the surrounding buildings. No one could possibly look in.

I was in New York with Jaime for a few days. A work visit for her—she had a few shows lined up. In our two years together, we'd learned to take our visits where we could. My Pack Alpha duties kept me close to home; her touring kept her on the road. As difficult as that could be, it suited us. Separate responsibilities, separate lives, intersecting as often as we could manage, gorging on each other's company, then diverging, happy, sated... and exhausted, to make do with daily phone calls until the next opportunity for a "stolen weekend" arose.

I turned from the window and looked over at her, curled up in bed, asleep. Seeing her, I smiled, in spite of my unease. A sharp shake of my head and I looked away, scanning the room, inhaling deeply. Clearly no one else here. Yet I couldn't shake that feeling of being watched.

I gazed out into the night, trying to empty my mind and focus, find the origin of this disquiet. It wouldn't come, and the feeling of being watched just hung there, vague and amorphous.

I'd woken from a nightmare. I didn't remember what it was about, only that I'd bolted up, anxiety a band around my chest, pulling tighter with every breath. I'd hurried into the bathroom and called Elena.

As I heard her sleepy voice, I knew my first instinct had been wrong—nothing was amiss at home. Still I kept her on the phone while she checked Clay and the twins. I didn't need to ask her to. I had only to say I had a bad feeling and she was scrambling into the nursery, Clay's footsteps thudding as he stumbled after her, calling "what's wrong?"

But the children were fine, and I made light of it, as I always did, joking about too much wine with dinner, and apologizing for waking them.

Then I'd hung up, still left with a prickle at the back of my neck—the one that said someone was watching. So I'd moved to the window to look. But no one was there. No one could be.

"Jeremy?"

Before I could turn, warm hands slid around my waist. A warm body pressed against my back. Warm breath tickled my bare shoulder.

"You sense something, don't you?" Jaime whispered.

I didn't answer. Werewolves are supposed to deal in facts and tangible truths. We trust what we can hear, see, smell, touch and taste. We have no patience for "bad feelings" and "odd prickles."

Jaime knew better. She also knew that saying "yes, I had a strange feeling" was still too big a step for me. It was enough to simply not answer instead of brushing it off, as I would with any-one else.

"Is someone down there?" she asked.

"I don't know."

"Another werewolf?"

"I don't think so. I just…" I raked my hair back with a sigh and scanned the light-dotted streets below, searching for what I knew couldn't be seen.

She moved up beside me. "You should go out and look around."

I shook my head and pulled the drapes.

"That's not going to fix the problem," she said.

"It's nothing. Just a feeling. Meaningless."

She slid between me and the window, gaze lifting to mine, locking on. "Your feelings are never—"

I cut her off with a kiss, lifted her off the floor and pushed her back against the drapes. A deep kiss, like touching wood, grounding myself and letting all those vague sensations and odd prickles flit away.

It took her a moment, but she finally recovered enough to pull back. "You should check it out. I'm serious, and I won't be distracted—"

"Yes, you will." I scooped her up and carried her to bed.

"You'll take a look in the morning," Jaime murmured, curled up against my chest later.

"Yes, ma'am."

"I mean it." She stifled a yawn. "I'll go with you."

"All right."

"You sensed something and it bothered you. You shouldn't just brush…"

The sentence fell to mumbling as she drifted off. I closed my eyes, hoping to join her, but after a few minutes, the languor of sex wore off and that prickling of nerves returned, as insistent as a swarm of mosquitoes.

I pulled Jaime closer and buried my nose in her hair, trying again to ground myself with her scent. But it wasn't working twice.

Wisps of the dream returned. A glimpse of dark sky and darker forest. The pound of running feet and labored breathing. The musky stink of... The scent eluded me before I could process it, but I knew where I'd smelled it before—in old nightmares I hadn't had since my first Change.

As a child, I had the dreams almost weekly, waking up shaking and sweating, hands clamped over my mouth so my gasps wouldn't wake my father, always certain he'd still hear my heart pounding or that the very smell of my fear would bring him.

The twins rarely have nightmares, but when they do, it only takes a whimper to bring us running to their bedside, waking them, holding them, comforting them and dispelling their fears. That's not why my father would have come. Malcolm guzzled fear the way a drunkard gulps cheap wine.

When I was twelve, Antonio and I had been camping out behind the cabin the Pack had rented for our summer vacation. As we talked around the campfire, he'd asked whether I'd started the dreams yet—the ones of running through the forest.

The relief I felt at that moment was indescribable. All those years I'd hidden those dreams even from him, my best friend. I'd been certain they were just another of my peculiarities, something to set me apart from my Pack brothers. To discover that they were normal, that we finally shared a common trait? Indescribable.

"So all werewolves have them?" I had asked.

Antonio reached into the marshmallow bag, frowning, then shaking the empty bag.

"Don't look at me," I said. "I only had two."

"I'll go inside and grab—"

I tossed him a bag of hot dogs I'd grabbed earlier.

He grinned. "Thanks. Don't suppose you snatched a couple of beers, too?"

I answered with a look. "About the dreams, they're normal?"

He looked over at me sharply. "What did Malcolm try to tell you?"

"Nothing,"

"That bastard. He said they weren't normal, didn't he?"

"I didn't tell Malcolm anything."

"Good," he grunted. "My dad says all werewolves get them before their first Change. We dream of running as wolves, chasing, hunting. Normal werewolf stuff."

Normal werewolf stuff.

Only I didn't dream of chasing and hunting. In my dreams, I was the one being chased. The one being hunted.

The next morning, Jaime insisted I patrol the neighborhood, searching for any trace of werewolves or other threats. I resisted, but when I gave in, pretended to be humoring her, I was happy for the excuse.

We walked two blocks and I smelled only humans. The hair on my neck never prickled with that sensation of being watched. A perfectly normal, relaxing walk, unmarred by even a stray twinge of anxiety.

The rest of the day did not go as well. The feeling did return, surging and subsiding, as if someone—something—was sporadically watching me. Keeping an eye on me. Looking for a chance to ...

A chance to what?

I had no idea, but I couldn't shake that feeling—the same one I'd had all those years ago, waking from the nightmares.

The feeling of being hunted.

*   *   *

Jaime had a show that night. And, as always, I went to it with her.

As much as Jaime loves what she does for a living, it also embarrasses her. She'll suggest I relax at the hotel. I insist on attending. She balks. I persist. She grumbles and relents, secretly as relieved and pleased as I was when she "forced" me on patrol that morning. Jaime may not be much more comfortable with her career choice than I am with my premonitions, but we both appreciate the chance to share that part of ourselves, to have one person who accepts and never judges.

I settled into my seat as the lights in the theater dimmed and twinkling, starlike ones appeared overhead. I had to shift my chair to see the darkened runway below. We were in an old playhouse and I had one of the box seats—the sort that look very prestigious and often have the worst sight lines in the house.

As Jaime's introductory voiceover began, I caught the movement of a dark form against the blackness below and smiled. The lights gradually rose as she walked, seeming to tread on air, an ethereal figure in a pale green dress, pinned-up red hair spilling over her back.

I'd seen her tread that runway dozens of times, but I still couldn't pull my gaze away. That ever-latent werewolf in me watched her with great satisfaction and, yes, proprietary satisfaction. She was mine. My lover, my partner, my mate—something I never expected to find, something I'd never realized I wanted. That other part of me watched with more bemusement, perhaps even a touch of surreal disbelief. This beautiful, eminently desirable woman was mine? Had chosen me? Had pursued me... and on catching me, hadn't decided she'd made a horrible mistake? Jaime likes to talk about karma, joking that I'm her reward for good deeds. If there is such a thing, I suspect it's the other way around, that I'm the one being rewarded.

The potential investor sharing the box seat with me shifted closer for a better look, blocking my view.

"She's something, isn't she?" he said.

Jaime might joke that at forty-six, she still looked good...as long as they kept the house lights low, but even under the brightest floods, she was stunning. That was the first thing I noticed about her when we met six years ago. I regret to say it was the only thing I noticed. I wasn't starstruck by her beauty; it was simply a passing reflection. We'd been brought into a tense situation to discuss strategy. Jaime was there. They introduced us. I noticed she was a strikingly attractive woman—a dispassionate artist's eye assessment. Then I'd moved on to the situation at hand.

When Jaime joined the interracial council as the new necromancer delegate, I thought little about it. The Pack was my priority. To me, the council was like one of those annoying yet necessary committees a politician must join to represent his constituency. Whenever possible, I delegated my delegate duties to Elena.

If I did notice Jaime in those early meetings, it was only to reflect that she seemed quieter than I expected from someone who made her living on stage and screen, and when she did speak, she struck me as surprisingly inarticulate, given her career choice. Also, for a woman who cut such a poised and graceful figure onstage, she seemed oddly clumsy in person. I eventually learned there was a reason for these oddly jarring impressions...one that had to do with me.

"Yup, she's really something," the investor said again.

He'd pulled his chair up to the box ledge and leaned over it, watching Jaime as she moved through the audience below us. I considered pulling him back before his drool stained her silk dress. Or that was my excuse. As he ogled her, my wolf side narrowed its eyes and grumbled, prodding me to do something, assert my rights. But the other side only sat back, quietly gauging the threat potential and keeping my instincts in check.

"Those are great tits," he chortled. "Do you think she's had work done?"

"No, I'm quite certain she hasn't," I said, words clipped and cool.

He leaned out farther. "And that ass. She has an amazing ass." He glanced back at me. "That's the first thing I thought when I met Jaime Vegas. How much I'd like to—"

My look stopped him in midsentence. He flinched, but recovered quickly, being the type of man not given to flinching.

He shifted in his seat, then cleared his throat before announcing, "I'm investing in her production company."

I nodded.

"Quite a lot of money," the man said. "A significant investment." He caught my gaze. "I think she's going to be very grateful."

I met his gaze with my best Alpha look. "How grateful?"

His mouth opened. Closed. He squirmed. He looked out over the audience. Tried to relax in his seat. Then he cleared his throat again. "So, um, your connection to the show is...?"

"Jaime."

"You know her?"

"We've been together for two years."

"Together..."

"Yes."

I'll give the man credit—he did try to sit it out after that. He managed two minutes, during which he looked everywhere except at Jaime. Then he mumbled something about a prior engagement, and fled.

He'd been gone about five minutes when I heard someone coming—the creak of a foot on the step, the whisper of the curtains. More than that, I *felt* someone coming—that sixth-sense awareness that warns me I'm being approached from behind.

I waited for the rush of air as the curtain was pulled back. When it didn't come, I turned. The curtain was rippling as if someone had brushed past. But I couldn't see any feet under it and, when I inhaled, I smelled only the investor's cloying cologne.

I rose. At that moment, Jaime glanced up, her face lighting when she saw me. She started to smile, then stopped herself, features rearranging into a look of concern as she crouched beside an elderly woman hoping for contact with her deceased husband.

I hesitated. Jaime snuck another peek my way. I tugged my shirt, as if I'd been standing to adjust it, then sat back down.

For a moment, I disconnected from the surrounding noise, focusing on the space around me, listening and smelling and, yes, sensing. Nothing. If anyone had been there, he was gone.

I turned my attention to Jaime as she communicated with the spirit of the dead husband. As for whether he was really present, I doubted it. Jaime prefers to work without employing her necromancy skills. This is the part of her job that makes her uncomfortable, but it's necessary.

This woman wanted the reassurance that her husband had happily passed over so she could get on with her own life. What if he hadn't passed on? If he was caught in limbo? Or if his message to her was less than the missive of love she needed? She'd come to Jaime's show for comfort, not truth.

Jaime finished with the woman and passed into a section of the auditorium where she couldn't see me. I slipped behind the curtain, searching for some reassurance of my own—a scent that confirmed someone had indeed come up those stairs. But there was none.

Jaime's show ended shortly after that. I was heading backstage when a scent wafted past and I stopped short, every hair on my body rising, arms pimpling with goose bumps. When I tried to isolate the odor, though, it vanished, and I couldn't even remember what it had been, so faint it had only teased some deep memory.

Even after it was gone, that sense of unease lingered, slithering down my spine and settling in the pit of my stomach. When a draft tickled my neck, I spun to see the curtains fluttering, and caught a glimpse of a young woman, small and slight, with straight black hair falling past her shoulders.

I strode forward and yanked the curtain open. Beyond it was an empty hall. At both ends was an exit, each too far for her to have traveled in those few seconds.

"The dressing rooms are this way."

I turned as Jaime's assistant, Tara, walked up behind me. She motioned that she'd show me the way. I gave one last glance and sniff, then let the curtains fall and fell into step beside the young woman.

"Good show, wasn't it?" she said.

"Very good."

"Jaime's always at her best when you're here. There's that extra spark, you know?" Tara clutched her clipboard to her chest. "I was thinking, next month she has a show in Mexico City. It's her first south of the border, and she's really hoping to break into a more international market. Maybe we could fly you in."

"Ahem." Jaime marched toward us and mock-glared at Tara. "Jeremy is my guest, not my mascot."

She shooed her away. Before Tara left, she mouthed to me "we'll talk."

"I think I'd make a good mascot," I said. "I wouldn't need to dress in one of those awful costumes. I come with my own."

She laughed and looped her arm through mine as we walked.

It took awhile to get to the dressing room. Every few steps crew members stopped to congratulate Jaime on the show or get her word on some postshow matter. Finally we got there, and then the best part of the evening began: the postshow show.

Overheated from hours under the stage lights, Jaime barely gets the door closed before she starts shedding clothing in an artless striptease. She paces and keeps up a steady stream of excited chatter as one garment after another falls to the floor, her skin beneath shimmering with sweat, the musky smell of her scent wafting through the room. It's like Changing back after a run— that rush of activity followed by a sudden stop, left sweaty and exhilarated, adrenaline still pumping, brain still buzzing, every nerve aching for a final jolt of release . . . which I'm happy to provide the moment that last piece of clothing hits the floor.

That night, I'd barely settled in to enjoy the show when someone knocked.

"It's Tara," a voice called.

I resisted the urge to snarl at the door and settled for giving it a stern glare that made Jaime laugh.

"Give me ten minutes," she called back.

"Twenty," I murmured.

She grinned. "Make it twenty."

"Can't," Tara said. "We've got a PR emergency."

Jaime looked from me to the door. I knew she had to attend to this, and if pushed on the point, I'd insist she do so. And I knew there was always tomorrow night, and many postshow nights to come. But that didn't keep me from stifling a sigh as she called Tara in.

"We've got a woman outside who bought a fake ticket from a scalper after driving all day to see the show."

"Reimburse her for it and—"

"She wants you to contact her dearly departed someone-or-other and she's not leaving until you do. She's set up a shrine out front."

"Shit. Okay. Find her a hotel on our tab and I'll call her in the morning—"

"There are reporters."

Jaime looked at her.

"With cameras," Tara said.

Jaime glanced over at me.

"Go," I said.

"It might take awhile. Impromptu summoning followed by impromptu interview..."

"Followed by impromptu celebration. While you're busy, I'll slip out and find us something better than water to toast with."

"Presuming I pull this off."

I kissed her. "You will."

I was going to find a bottle of champagne for Jaime ... right after I checked that passage where the young woman had seemed to vanish. I needed to get that mystery out of the way, so I could relax and enjoy the rest of my weekend.

It took me a few minutes to find the passage. My sense of direction is excellent, but I had to take a roundabout route, veering onto a new path every time I scented one of the crew members, who would—like Tara—be quick to escort the boss's boyfriend back on track.

I finally reached the bottom of the box seat stairs and slipped into the curtained corridor. I inhaled, but smelled only dust. The hall was obviously used very little, with locked doors at either end.

Then I pulled the curtain back and saw that the other end opened into another room. That explained the girl's disappearance, and I was tempted to leave it at that, but couldn't shake that lingering unease. I'd rest easier when I got a good whiff of her scent to catalogue in my memory.

I stepped into a long, narrow dark room. A deep breath brought only the stink of more dust. I felt my way along, past what seemed to be stacks of chairs and tables. From the other side, I could see faint light shining under a door. As I headed toward it, the back of my neck prickled again and I slowed.

A breeze drifted past, bringing with it...Forest? I inhaled again. Yes, the scent was faint, but it definitely smelled like a forest, earthy and rich. Entangled with that scent was the one that had eluded me earlier—a musky, animal-like smell that made the back of my throat tighten. The scent from my dreams.

My fingers instinctively glided across my thigh. I clenched my fist. My fingers still twitched. It was a nervous tic I'd had since childhood. When I got anxious, my fingers started tracing out shapes. Runes. Symbols embedded deep in my brain.

Small running feet scampered across the room and I tensed, my nose jerking up, inhaling, that latent werewolf instinct kicking in. I mentally followed the sound. Too large to be a mouse. Too heavy for a rat. Too quick for a raccoon. A cat? The size seemed right, but the claws scraping on the floor suggested otherwise. A final staccato *click-click*. Then silence.

I inhaled again. The forest smell had evaporated, leaving only dust and dirt, the stink tickling my nostrils. Then a shadow moved a dozen feet ahead. A large shadow. I tensed.

A creak, and a rectangle of light as the distant door swung open. A figure moved into the rectangle. A black-haired woman, like the one I'd seen before. She glanced back, and with that flash of her face came a jolt of recognition. Then she was gone.

I hurried across the room and yanked open the door. The ripe smell of garbage hit on a blast of cool night air. Bright overhead lights blinded me as I stepped out.

As I peered down the empty alley, that face flashed in my memory. Zoe Takano. I didn't know her well, but the jolt of recognition told me I hadn't been mistaken. Zoe's face and her figure—fine-boned with shoulder-length straight black hair—matched the woman I'd seen. That would also explain why I couldn't pick up her scent. Vampires didn't have one.

As for why Zoe would be in New York and following me, I could only hazard a guess, but it was a reasonable one. Zoe was a thief; therefore she likely traveled on business. While vampires and werewolves are not the mortal enemies portrayed in popular culture, we are wary of one another, as all predators are. Zoe was warier than most, being disinclined to confrontation.

If Zoe sensed a werewolf in New York during a visit, she'd want to take a closer look and assure herself he wasn't a threat. Likewise, if my extrasensory perception picked up a vampire in the vicinity, it might interpret that as a threat and sound the alarm.

I caught a flicker of movement in a dark laneway running along the theater.

"Zoe?"

Soft-soled shoes whispered across the asphalt. That must have been what I'd heard earlier and mistaken for an animal—the scuffle and scrape of Zoe in her cat-burglar footwear.

I walked a half-dozen steps to where the open delivery area narrowed into a lane, bracketed by towering buildings.

"Zoe? It's Jeremy Danvers. Elena's..." It was a relationship hard to categorize in human terms, so I said simply, "father-in-law."

I could still hear the whisper of her shoes, but even when I squinted, I could make out only a dark form hurrying toward the distant street.

I glanced at the theater door. Jaime wouldn't be much longer. I'd ascertained the nature of the threat and acknowledged it was no threat at all. I could go back inside. Yet I'd rather get this matter settled than have a vampire stalking me all weekend. And I had promised Jaime a bottle of champagne. An excuse, then, for following Zoe a little farther.

I entered the lane. It was at least ten feet wide, but the walls on either side seemed to loom more with each step, closing in, enveloping me in shadow until even the bright street lights at the end grew dim.

Before I could blink, the darkness lifted...and I was on a wooded path leading through a forest. The buildings had become densely packed, towering trees. The stink of exhaust gave way to rich, damp forest. The honk of horns and squeal of tires became the hoot of an owl and the scream of its prey. Even the asphalt underfoot softened to packed earth.

I stopped and looked around. Whatever my mixed bag of psychic quirks, hallucinations were not among them. Nor teleportation. Yet I was clearly in a forest at twilight. Every sense confirmed it.

I walked to the trees. I could feel the bark, and yet when I tried to reach between two trunks, my hand stopped, as if hitting the building wall instead. I smiled. A vision then, overlaying reality. Interesting.

That "other" part of me wanted to linger, to explore, to discover, get to the bottom of this mystery, but the werewolf was already growing impatient. *Petty magics,* it sniffed. *A simple illusion. You've figured that out, so get moving. Ignore it. You have a job to do.*

I ran my fingers down the tree, closing my eyes and imagining the wall, and when I did, I felt not bark but brick. I opened my eyes and concentrated on seeing that wall. The tree flickered, like a projected image, wavering, the wall coming clear behind it.

Great. You can break the illusion. Even after all these years that inner voice carried the snap of my father's bark and the twist of his sarcasm. *Now stop daydreaming and move. She's getting away.*

True, but my interest in Zoe Takano was fading fast. Here was a far more intriguing mystery.

As I touched the wall, my other fingers twitched against my leg. I automatically clenched my fist, then stopped myself. I lifted my hand to the wall and let it trace a shape floating half formed in my brain. When the figure was complete, the last shimmering overlay of the trees dissipated and I was staring at brick.

At a snort, I glanced down the path—now a lane again—to see an old homeless man sitting at the end, watching me and shaking his head. I shoved my hand into my pocket and started walking. I made it three steps before the forest scene reappeared.

My fingers started moving again, twitching in my pocket, but I held them still and took a closer look at the illusion, examining it for cracks. And they were there—the slight scent of exhaust, the faint outline of buildings against the twilight sky, the "branch" underfoot that my shoe passed right through.

Was I creating this illusion? I *would* much prefer a forest path to a city alley. And while I didn't always feel like a true werewolf, there were parts of that self that I embraced—the love of wild places, the joy of the run, the wonder of changing form.

But why would I suddenly start conjuring fantasy visions for myself? Far more likely that someone was doing it for me. Zoe? Vampires had no such powers. Visions were the realm of the magical races. The more I studied this illusionary forest, the more convinced I was that I hadn't actually seen Zoe. If a pursuer wanted to set me at ease, what better way than to cloak himself in a visage that was friendly and familiar?

At the blast of a car horn, the forest vision popped like a soap bubble, and I found myself teetering on the curb, about to step into traffic.

As I backed up, a voice behind me said, "You okay, son?"

It was the homeless man, still watching me. I hesitated. Being called "son" at my age is always enough to throw me—even more when I looked at this gray-haired "old man" and realized he was probably younger than me.

"Daydreaming?" he said.

"Yes, I suppose so." I walked over. "Did a young woman come this way? Out of that lane a couple of minutes ago?"

He nodded. "Pretty girl. Asian. Real pretty."

Zoe was attractive enough, but the heartfelt emphasis he put on the words gave me pause. I pulled a twenty from my pocket and, as I handed it to him, described Zoe.

"Mmm, maybe," he said. "But her hair was longer. A lot longer. And she was real tiny. At first I thought it was a child."

Zoe was small, but not that small.

The man said she'd headed into the next alley. I thanked him and stepped away. I checked my watch. Jaime would be done soon and wondering where I was, and as tempting as this mystery was, there was an equally strong temptation pulling me back to that dressing room . . .

I shook off the impulse. The temptations that waited in the dressing room *would* wait, however much I'd like to turn my attention back to them. This was a potential threat and therefore had to take precedence.

I headed in the direction the old man had indicated and turned my focus back to that. I'd been right, then—it wasn't Zoe, but an illusion, and one only I saw. Magical suggestibility—a spell that induces the subject to pluck a similar, familiar image from his memory and transpose it over the caster. A glamour spell could make one mistake a person for someone he *expected* to see. This must work on a similar principle.

As for why it was being used on me, I could only suppose that this caster wanted me to follow her into that alley, and while the "other" side of me insisted that following strange spellcasters into an alley could never turn out well, the werewolf—and moreover, the werewolf Alpha—couldn't walk away. Be prepared and be cautious, but never ignore a threat. Investigate and neutralize.

I strode toward that presumed alley, three store lengths away. The second shop was a convenience store and the beer sign in the window made me think of Jaime again. I scanned inside, quite certain champagne wouldn't be part of their inventory. When I slowed, though, I noticed a slight figure step out onto the sidewalk farther down.

Zoe stayed there, on the sidewalk, watching me. My fingers started moving and I let them, and when they finished, the Zoe image wavered and shrunk until the woman was the one the homeless man had seen—still Japanese, about the same age, but smaller, with hair to her waist. She had an undeniable beauty that I registered dispassionately, much the same way I'd done when I first met Jaime.

Her lips curved, then parted, mouthing "Jeremy." I stepped

forward. She took a slow step back, still smiling, then turned and sprang away, feet barely seeming to touch the ground. This was body language the wolf understood, language I'd seen many times before, Elena and Clay playing "come catch me" as wolves. When I caught a glimpse of her in the windowed storefront, I swore I *did* see an animal scampering away, tail flicking, teasing. A red tail with a white tip. A fox.

I stopped short, heart ramming against my chest, fingers tracing madly, that anxiety from earlier slamming back tenfold. Every fiber in me screamed to get away. Run as fast as I could.

I glanced at the window again and saw my reflection, not as a human, but a huge, black wolf. A wolf running from a fox? Never.

I pivoted. She'd stopped again, walking slowly backward, enticing me to follow. Her reflection was faint now, but I could still see a fox, tail swishing. Her lips moved, my name on them again. Then she darted between the buildings.

When I reached the same spot, I found myself at the entrance of a very long, very dark alley. I bit back a chuckle. Cliché, but I supposed luring your opponent into a sun-bathed field of wildflowers just didn't have the same impact.

From the alley mouth, I could see her figure, cloaked in shadow at the end, the pale orb of her face turned my way, her teeth glittering as she smiled. One delicate hand lifted and waved me closer. I strode toward her.

"Who are you?" I demanded.

Consternation flashed as she realized the illusion had failed.

I repeated the question.

"I am for you," she said.

"Foryu?" I stopped a few feet from her. "Is that your name?"

She gave a girlish laugh. Her dark eyes lifted to mine. Then her long fingers moved to the top button of her knee-length coat and with one deft move, it fell open. Through the gap, I could see her body. Naked.

"I am for you," she said.

"I believe you have the wrong person."

She stepped toward me, the coat sliding open as she moved, her pale body shimmering beneath it.

"No, I do not have the wrong person," she said. "I am for you. Jeremy Malcolm Edward Danvers. Alpha of the American were-wolves. Last of the Kogitsune."

"Kogitsune?"

She stepped forward, shrugging the coat down to her shoulders. I didn't pull back and glance away, which would imply I was tempted. Instead, I looked at what she obviously wanted me to look at. She was lithe and perfectly shaped, with small, high breasts, a taut stomach and gently swelling hips. Beautiful. Too beautiful, really. If I painted her, I'd look like an amateur trying to capture idealized female beauty, and instead depicting a perfectly flawless and perfectly dull figure.

And while I must admit that having a beautiful, naked stranger offer herself to me in an alley was not unappreciated, it was like offering a juicy hamburger to a man already sated by prime steak. The desired response was not forthcoming.

She put her arms around my neck and lifted up. Her coat spread wider, naked body moving toward mine.

"You said Kogitsune," I said. "What is that?"

More consternation. She pressed her body against mine. Her lips moved to my ear.

"I will tell you everything you want to know, Jeremy Danvers. First let me..."

She whispered her suggestion, something about entwining limbs and heights of ecstasy. It reminded me of passages Jaime would read me from her romance novels—passages that made sex sound very pretty and very flowery, and were about as arousing as reading Emily Dickinson. Then she'd reinterpret and reimagine the scenes, in far earthier language, and that always worked wonders.

So as the young woman promised to take me on a guided tour of her lush hills and deep valleys, I resisted the urge to laugh—which again would certainly be the wrong response.

Instead, I politely heard her out, then took her by the shoulders and moved her away so I could better make eye contact.

"While I appreciate the—" I began.

She shrugged her coat off, letting it pool at her feet. I paused to admire. I might not be as moved by the sight as she hoped, but I was still male.

"No," I said, my gaze returning to her eyes. "All I want is answers."

She lowered herself onto her coat, one knee raised, her legs spread, giving me a clear view of the offer at hand.

Her eyes lifted to mine. "Please."

I was about to ask what she wanted, but I supposed the answer was rather obvious... at least, the answer she'd give. As for what she *really* wanted—while there was some latent teenage boy fantasy that insisted having a beautiful stranger strip and offer herself to you in an alley was perfectly normal, even at sixteen I would have known she had an ulterior motive... though I probably wouldn't have cared.

"What are you?" I asked instead.

She smiled and rose to her feet so gracefully that she seemed to slither up like a cobra rising from a vase. Some deep-rooted instinct told me the analogy was an apt one.

Her lips parted, small white teeth showing. "What do you want me to be, Jeremy Danvers?"

"Someone who answers my questions."

She slid closer, until her breasts brushed my shirt. "Later. First, tell me what you most desire."

"I just did. To have my questions answered. Starting with what you are, and moving onto why you're following me. If we can't manage that, then what I'll most desire to do—and what I will do—is leave."

A spark of anger in her eyes made my fingers move against my legs. She caught my hand and squeezed it. I pulled it away.

"What am I doing?" I asked.

She smiled and slid her hand up my chest. "It's what you're *not* doing that is the problem."

I removed her hand and traced a shape in the air. Her fingers shot forward, as if to grab mine, but she stopped herself and fixed a smile in place. She moved closer still, lifting onto her tiptoes, breasts rubbing against my chest until her nipples hardened.

"You know what I'm doing, don't you?" I said. "The runes. The symbols."

She opened the top button on my shirt. Her tongue flicked out, strangely cool against my skin. I stepped back and fastened the button.

"If you won't answer my questions, then it's time for me to leave."

She grabbed my wrist. Her grip was unnaturally strong, but I peeled her fingers off.

"Don't go," she said.

"I am," I said.

"Yes," said a voice behind me. "He is."

From behind me, Jaime's hands slid around my waist. She lifted up to kiss the back of my neck, then looked over my shoulder at the young woman.

"He's just not that into you, is he?" Jaime added.

The young woman's lips curled and a hiss escaped, one that set the hairs on my neck prickling. As Jaime moved up beside me, the young woman's gaze traveled over her.

"You're not worthy," the young woman said.

"Probably not," Jaime said. "But I am very, very lucky."

As we walked away, I kept my senses on alert, ready for a rear attack, but all stayed still behind us. I didn't look back.

Jaime didn't speak until we were on the sidewalk, then she let that possessive arm drop from my waist. I glanced over, gauging her mood. When she took my hand, I relaxed.

"I can't even let you out of my sight for ten minutes before naked girls are throwing themselves at you in alleys."

"I'd heard New Yorkers were getting friendlier . . ."

A laugh, ragged around the edges. "So are you going to tell me what that was about? A fan trying to entice you into a private portrait session?"

"Yes, that happens all the time. Art groupies. It's worse than being a rock star." I spotted the theater marquee and headed for it. "No, that young woman was far more interested in my other occupation. As the werewolf Alpha."

"She's a supernatural?" A soft rush of air whistled through Jaime's teeth. Relief. She could deal with that better than with random humans throwing themselves at me.

"Some kind of magical race. She wanted something from me."

Jaime snorted. "You think?"

"Sex was merely the enticement."

"Were you . . . ?" Her voice drifted off.

"Enticed?" I glanced at her. "I think you already saw the answer. How long were you watching?"

Her cheeks flamed as bright as her hair as she stammered de-
nials. Then, after a few steps in silence, she said, "I was there a
few minutes. It's not that I don't trust you..."

"But you've been burned before."

There had been many men in Jaime's life, but as large and di-
verse as that cast might be, they'd shared one thing in common:
none of them had treated her well. Not entirely their fault. Jaime
admits that even when she told herself she wanted a stable relationship, she chose men who couldn't provide it. And then I'm
sure she showed them only that most superficial side of herself—the vivacious, party-loving celebrity. Those who were un-
faithful probably assumed she was doing the same, and never
realized how much they'd hurt her.

Jaime knew she didn't need to worry about that with me. She
was the only woman in my life and I intended to keep it that way
for as long as she'd have me. I'd never been one to ogle or flirt
even before she came along, so I gave her no reason to feel
threatened. Still, she did, and it was something I suspected we'd
only overcome with time, when she realized I wasn't going anywhere.

I explained what had happened.

"Foxes?" she said. "At the risk of sounding like a total airhead,
is there any chance it was...a werefox? I know there's no record
of such a thing, but..."

"But that doesn't mean one couldn't exist. In this case, though,
I suspect a simpler answer. It's an illusion, presumably one she
thought, like the Zoe disguise, would intrigue me. As a werewolf,
perhaps I'd find a fox..."

"Foxy?"

I laughed. "Or simply a nonthreatening smaller predator that
should be investigated. As for what kind of demon or spellcaster
she was..."

"My money's on succubus."

I pulled open the theater door. "Is there such a thing?"

She waved at the security guard. "With my luck, yes. I spend four years chasing the guy of my dreams, finally get him, and now I have to compete with a gorgeous, twenty-year-old super-natural sex fiend."

"I was terribly conflicted, as you could see." I opened her dressing room door.

"Hmm." She passed me into the room and started plucking the pins from her hair. "I know it's childish of me to feel threatened..." She shook out her hair, pins clinking to the floor. "I shouldn't feel the need to prove myself." She slid the straps of her dress off her shoulders. "The need to reclaim my..."

"Territory?"

She unzipped the back of her dress. "That's not the way I'd put it. I've never been very good at fighting for what's mine. Not with men anyway. I'm better focusing on *keeping* what's mine."

"And how do you plan to do that?"

She let the dress slide to the floor. "I have my ways."

Jaime had nothing to worry about, but I knew she still would. When it came to her job, she was a fighter. With men, though, she fell prey to that self-doubt planted by her mother and nurtured by careless lovers. Fighting to keep a man was as alien to her as fighting to win one, as I knew from experience.

The first time I truly noticed Jaime was at a council meeting—one she *didn't* actually attend, having called to say something had come up. I'd ducked out early, leaving Elena to debate some petrifyingly dull matter of interracial politics. Earlier, I'd seen an interesting play on light a block away—the sun shining through the trees at an angle that cast an eerie glow over a playground and I wanted to get a better look, see if I could mentally capture it for a painting.

When I arrived, though, the sun had moved enough to spoil the effect. But I did find something else of interest—Jaime, sitting on a bench, staring into nothing. She was terribly embarrassed at being caught skipping the meeting, and confessed she'd had a difficult week, arrived here and realized she couldn't face the council. I suspected there was more to it than that. I didn't push, though, just invited her to join me for a cold drink so we could play hooky together.

Over that drink, she mentioned that her mother had called as she'd been heading to the meeting. She made nothing of it at the time, but as I later came to know her better, I could reflect back and see this as the real reason she hadn't been able to walk into that meeting room.

Jaime had spent her life on stage—first in beauty pageants and later as a spiritualist, with her mother exploiting her necromancy talents. Before long, she'd been the sole income provider, yet her mother never let Jaime forget what a saint she was to put up with the "burden" of her daughter's powers. Even now, Jaime paid all the bills at her mother's lavish retirement home and still had to field regular calls of complaint.

Nothing Jaime could do for her mother was ever enough, and no matter what she did with her life, it was never good enough. I knew what that felt like. I'd spent thirty years living with a father who despised me because I was different. And I'd still been a teenager when I'd had to start working to pay his keep, bound by my grandfather's will, which gave me our estate and its assets... and all the financial obligations that came with them.

So, as different as Jaime and I appeared, in this we eventually found common ground and friendship. As she became more to me than "that attractive necromancer," I began to realize that she was neither clumsy nor inarticulate…except around me. Perhaps I'm thick about such things, but it took me a long time to understand why Jaime was attracted to me. Or as she later put it, she had a horribly embarrassing third-grade crush. At first, I presumed that once she got to know me, the attraction would wane. Yet it hadn't been long before I'd begun to hope that it didn't.

I needed to know what kind of supernatural I was dealing with. So back at the hotel, I called Robert Vasic. While his stepson, Adam, was officially the council's new research consultant, it was sometimes better to call Robert—particularly on a Saturday night. He was still up, watching a late movie with his wife, Talia.

I told him about the encounter.

"A young woman cornered you in an alley, undressed and tried to seduce you? Don't you hate it when that happens?" He chuckled. "Now, you do realize that I'm no longer a priest. I can't hear confession."

"I'm not Catholic."

"Well, in that case, tell me everything."

I did.

"So this very attractive young woman offered to fulfill your every desire, and you want to know if I've ever heard of such a supernatural? If I had, it would be one of the rare times I would close my books to do field research. Such an intriguing phenomenon would require careful investigation."

The line hissed. His wife, Talia, came on as Robert laughed in the background.

"I think I'd better handle this one, before you give him a heart attack," she said. "Go take a cold shower, old man." They bantered for a minute, then Talia said, "Okay, let's see what you've got."

We discussed it, clarifying the details.

"Not ringing any bells," she mused. "I'm going to guess it's a demidemon because they often take female form. Nix are known for tempting humans, but they appeal to preexisting hidden desires." She paused. "Is everything okay with you and Jaime?"

"Everything's fine. If it's a Nix, her hidden desire radar has short-circuited. I was thinking succubus myself."

"Actually…"

"There's no such thing, is there?"

"It's just a blanket term for any demon or demidemon who seduces humans. Which really doesn't narrow it down at all. Let me talk to Robert. We'll do some digging."

I woke to the ringing of the bedside phone. I glanced over at Jaime, who was usually quick to answer, but her side of the bed was empty. The bathroom door was closed with the light on inside.

I answered. It was Robert.

"I think I have an answer for you," he said. "A fox maiden."

"Fox…?"

"It's a form of demidemon. A shape-shifter who can manifest in both human and fox form. It's indigenous to Japan. It's primary power is vision-casting. They can reshape reality for humans… or at least reshape the appearance of it."

"Like turning an alley into a forest path. That certainly seems to fit, as does the fox form and the Asian origins."

"But here's where it gets interesting. According to legend, the fox maiden is a demon of hearth and home. In myth, it mates with human men to raise a family."

"And you think that's what it was trying to do?"

"That's the *human* legend, which usually contains only grains of truth. What interests me are the fox maiden's supposed powers, in relation to its family. It's said to be fiercely protective of them, telepathically linked to them and able to sense danger they face. It's also supposed to be able to communicate with them in dreams." He paused. "Sound familiar?"

All powers I possessed. And yet...

"I know," Robert said before I could. "You have all the *alleged* powers, but the only *known* power—projecting visions—you lack."

"Along with shape-shifting into a fox." I glanced at the bathroom door. Still shut and no sound within. I half listened to Robert as I sat up to look around. On Jaime's pillow was a note, saying her morning interview had been bumped up and she'd call me when she was finished.

"...only inherit some of the demon's powers, which would explain it," Robert was saying.

"So you're theorizing that my mother was one of these fox maidens. I thought demidemons didn't sire or bear children."

"Which is one major problem with the theory. The other being the runes you draw. They're clearly protective in nature, which fits with fox maiden legend, but I can find no mention of anything like them."

"She didn't like me drawing them."

"Hmmm?"

I told him about the young woman trying to stop me from tracing a rune.

"Well, that's interesting. There must be a connection. Talia and I will keep looking. Will you be around today or busy with Jaime?"

We talked for another couple of minutes. The phone rang again as soon as I hung up. It was Tara, saying she was sending a car by in a half-hour to pick Jaime up for the interview.

"Which interview?"

"The only one she has this morning. At eleven."

I glanced at the note and quickly signed off.

*   *   *

If this "fox maiden" could shape-shift into Zoe Takano, then it wasn't a stretch to believe she could have taken on Tara's voice and lured Jaime out of the hotel. As for why, I'm sure it wasn't to apologize for trying to seduce me.

I pulled on clothing and was still buttoning my shirt in the elevator, to the raised eyebrows of a couple heading down. Going out in public, unshaven, unshowered, still dressing, ignoring all disapproving glances... how many times had I reproached Clay for doing the same thing?

For the next twenty minutes, though, that's who I seemed to be channeling: Clay. I shouldered my way through the tourists at the door. I ignored all stares when I dropped to one knee on the sidewalk, hoping to catch Jaime's scent, not even bothering with the pretense of tying my shoe. I even beat an older couple to the first cab, then impatiently snapped directions to the driver.

For that brief period, I understood how Clay saw the world. Inconsequential—save for my corner of it and those who resided there. I would never shove a stranger out of my way, but under the circumstances, I had no problem pushing past them and earning a glare. When my family was in danger, the wolf took over. Or maybe, given what Robert had said, it wasn't so much the wolf as the fox.

I'd long suspected that my mother had been another supernatural race. Jaime had urged me to investigate. She knew that, deep down, I wanted to solve this mystery. But old fears and insecurities held me back—too many years of my father's scorn and disgust at having a son who was "different," who would never be the fighter he was. Too many years of knowing I wasn't a true werewolf and desperately wanting to be.

What I wanted now, though, was to find Jaime. So for once,

I didn't give into my self-doubts, waffle and analyze the gut feeling that told me how to find her. I trusted it and let it lead the way.

It took me to a warehouse, partially renovated into some sort of studio. Jaime would have entered it without question for an interview. Inside, though, it was empty, as if closed.

I looked around, sniffing and sensing. Then I found her using a more mundane sense.

"Look, this isn't going to work out, girls." Jaime's faint voice floated from deep within the warehouse. "I know you'd love to scratch my eyes out—or worse—but as long as I'm wearing this, it seems you aren't coming close enough to try. And considering it's a permanent fashion accessory, I'd say you're shit outta luck."

The tattoo.

When we'd first started dating, Jaime had asked me to sketch a rune for her, like the ones I gave to Clay, Elena and the twins, sometimes openly, more often secreted away on scraps of paper, fulfilling an overwhelming compulsion.

Jaime had been convinced that the rune had led me to her when she'd been kidnapped, and had kept her safe. She'd insisted on having it tattooed on her ankle. I'd protested. Secretly, though, I'd been relieved when it was done.

I followed her voice and found her in the farthest part of the warehouse, a semidark section that hadn't been renovated. Backed into a corner, she sat cross-legged, displaying her ankle tattoo.

In front of her, three foxes paced, stopping now and then to snarl. Jaime only laughed and waggled her foot, sending them skittering back.

Though she appeared relaxed, I could sense her anxiety. When she saw me, she let out an audible sigh of relief.

"The cavalry has arrived," she said. "Which is exactly what you were hoping for, isn't it, girls?"

As she stood, I caught a whiff of blood. Her calves were streaked with it, and dotted with puncture wounds.

"I'm okay," she said, following my gaze. "Your rune is keeping them at bay, but they can't resist getting in the occasional nip, which is why I haven't made a run for it."

I walked between Jaime and the foxes. They let me, and let me wave her to the door, watching only to see if I'd follow. She stayed at the door. I didn't urge her to leave. I knew she wouldn't.

"Change forms so I can talk to you," I said.

They did, becoming three women so similar that I wasn't sure which, if any, was the one from the night before.

"Fox maidens," I said.

"Kitsune," the one on the right corrected, her chin lifting.

Kitsune. Japanese wasn't one of the languages I was fluent in, but I knew enough to recognize this as the word for fox. As she said it, I remembered the word the other one had used last night. Kogitsune. Little fox or fox cub.

The middle one reached for the top button on her dress. When she undid it, I lifted a hand to stop her.

"That didn't work last night and nothing has changed since then."

"No?"

The ones on each end moved forward, boxing me in. They undid their top buttons.

"Now there are three of us," the middle one said. She flashed her teeth. "Would you like to start with one ... or all?"

I could have sworn I heard a growl from the doorway and looked over to see Jaime glowering.

"One or three, it doesn't change my answer, which is still no."

"Perhaps four then? Five?" Another flash of her teeth. "I believe you'll find we are very accommodating."

"I'm sure you are," Jaime muttered too low for anyone else to catch.

"If you want me to stay, leave your clothing on," I said.

The right one curled her lip, and I was sure she was about to tell me I was staying whether I wanted to or not, but the middle one—the leader apparently—silenced her with a look.

"What is Kogitsune?" I asked.

"You are Kogitsune."

"A half-demon."

The right one's lip curled again. "Nothing so common. You are Kogitsune."

"It is a race of our blood," the leader said. "It can be passed through the line, unlike half-demons, whose blood ends with the first generation."

"And we are not demons," the left one said. "We are gods."

"Demigods?" I said.

All three pursed their lips, not caring for the distinction. There were no "gods." One could argue, as Robert did, that there were no demigods either, that it was simply a separate branch of what we called demidemons. But arguing that theological theory *with* a self-described demigod was never wise.

"Gods require devotees," the leader said. "That is how we gain our strength."

"And that is what I am, then? A member of a supernatural race of disciples, like Druids?"

"You are better than any mere Druid. We shared our blood with your kind. We chose a dying race, those who derived their magic from symbols."

Runes . . .

"We saved them by sharing our blood, making them stronger, giving them new powers, a subset of our own. In return, we asked only for their devotion."

"So is that what you want from me? Worship? And how am I supposed to . . ." I stopped, realizing I had a good idea of the answer.

"From your women, we exact a life of service. Your men—" She smiled. "They are our intimate companions and our partners in reproduction."

"Stud service?" Jaime said from across the room.

The Kitsune pretended not to hear her. "Through the Kogitsune, we discovered a way to reproduce our own kind, rare among gods and demons alike. When we are impregnated by Kogitsune men, we bear Kitsune daughters, which allowed our small race to grow and take our rightful place in the pantheon of power."

"But to track me down, after all these years... I'm sure there are younger, more willing men who would be quite happy to..." I trailed off as I remembered what the Kitsune had called me last night. Last of the Kogitsune.

"That's the problem," Jaime said. "Their stud service has dried up."

"The Kogitsune betrayed us," the one on the right spat. "They took our gifts, then turned on us, using their petty magics to—"

The middle one shushed her.

"Using their magics against you," I said, looking at the rune on Jaime's ankle. "They found a way to infuse their runes with the power to protect them against more than mere human threats. They used them to escape servitude to you."

"Servitude?" The right one's eyes blazed. "It was an honor to serve us. They—"

Again, the leader quieted her and said, calmly, "They no longer wished to be our disciples. When we argued the matter, they decided the only alternative was to stop reproducing and allow their own race to die out. But there were those who didn't want that. They ran to foreign lands and bore their children there, trying to mask them from us by breeding with inferior races."

Like werewolves...

"They hid you best of all. But now, we've found you." That teeth-baring blast of a smile. "And we are very pleased with what we have found. The American Alpha will make a fitting father for the next generation of Kitsune."

"What about the sons of the Alpha?"

"Your son is not Kogitsune," the right one said. "He is only a werewolf, and a bitten one at that."

"Not Clayton. My natural son."

"You have no natural son," the left one said, but slowly, as if hoping I'd correct her.

"I do. At least one. I was…less cautious in my youth than I should have been. I only learned of him five years ago, through happenstance. He was already twenty-two, and had gone through years of Changes. He'd realized what he was and was coping very well, so I decided there was no need to enter his life and, for his sake, I'd be better staying out of it. He was safer as a lone werewolf than the son of the Alpha."

"So he is…" The middle one's lips moved, as if calculating. "Twenty-seven?"

I nodded. "Prime breeding age for a werewolf. Like most, he has no regular lover and, at that age, werewolves feel the need to mate very strongly. They are very restless and very… energetic."

All three Kitsune smiled.

"I know he might not be Alpha, but I already have a lover, a family, a Pack and responsibilities that I won't give up without a fight. It would be easier to take the willing and younger Kogitsune."

"And the one who doesn't know the runes to keep you away," Jaime added.

"Do you know where we can find this son?" the middle one asked.

"His name is Brent. He moves around unfortunately—he's in construction—but he seems to stick to Florida and Georgia."

I could tell they didn't care for the imprecision of that answer.

"If you found me, I'm sure you can find him," I added.

It took some negotiating, but they clearly found this an attractive alternative and, finally, released me.

"Nice bluff," Jaime said as we got into a cab. "Ever consider acting?"

"Who said I was acting? I might very well have a son."

She gave me a look. When I arched a brow, she started counting off fingers.

"One, I might not have known you that long, but I'm sure you were never young enough to be so careless. You were born checking the road both ways. Two, whatever danger this kid would face as your son, it doesn't compare to what he'd face as a mutt. And you'd be the last person to argue that any wolf is better off outside the Pack. Three, Brent in construction? Like the guy you were sitting next to last night, Brent Delaney of Delaney Construction?"

She settled into her seat, shaking her head.

"You forgot number four. If I had a son, I'd have told you."

She wouldn't have the confidence to say that herself, but when I did, she nodded, obviously pleased.

"They'll be back, you know," she said after a moment.

"Well, considering how long it took them to find me, I'm hoping it'll be awhile, at least long enough for me to research this Kogitsune race and develop a plan of attack."

"And in the meantime, I need to worry about…"

"Dozens of nubile young women out there, eager to fulfill my every sexual fantasy?"

She glared. "Are you trying to bring out my competitive edge? Or make me decide I don't have a hope in hell of competing?"

"Ah, sorry. Let me rephrase that. Several reasonably attractive but probably very inexperienced young women…"

"Much better." She crossed her leg onto her lap and touched the ankle tattoo. "But this wards them off. Would it work for you?"

"I would presume so."

She took out her cell and hit speed-dial. "Tara, it's me. Yes, I know and I'm on my way to the interview now. In the meantime, could you find me a good local tattoo parlor? And set up an appointment?"

She listened, then slanted a look my way. "As soon as possible."